P9-DEI-331

brenda novak

Christmas in Silver Springs

mira

mira

ISBN-13: 978-0-7783-0812-6

Christmas in Silver Springs

Copyright © 2019 by Brenda Novak, Inc.

Printed in U.S.A.

To Sharon Sergeant, a woman who spent one of the few precious days she had left in this world, after a protracted battle with cancer, riding in a car for an entire day on her birthday to come meet me at a book signing. I choke up whenever I remember helping her to stand so that we could embrace and will never forget her beautiful smile. She was lovely and cheerful and wonderful to the very end, and she left behind a good man, a beautiful daughter, who was just entering college, and two younger boys. May you rest in peace, Sharon. I imagine you, when you're not watching over your family, happily reading in heaven.

Christmas in Silver Springs

1

Tobias Richardson couldn't help noticing the petite blonde sitting at the old-fashioned counter of the diner—and not just because she was pretty. He was sure he'd never seen her before. With a population of seven thousand, Silver Springs wasn't small enough that he'd recognize *everybody*, especially because he'd only been living here for five months. The town seemed to have gotten a lot smaller since the weather turned, though. It didn't snow in this part of California, but it was the rainy season and the region was experiencing colder than normal temperatures. Tourists weren't interested in visiting when it was chill and damp, and the same went for the many residents of LA, ninety minutes to the southeast, who had vacation homes here. This month, and probably for the next two or three, he guessed Silver Springs would be limited to the locals.

He blew on his hands, trying to warm them while waiting for the coffee he'd ordered when he first sat down. He'd managed to squeeze in a hike after work.

He didn't care that it was dark and wet by the time he was on his way back. He had a headlight to guide him to the trailhead and was willing to put up with the rain. But he was chilled to the bone. After such an arduous hike, he was starving, too, and craving a hot shower.

Again, he glanced toward the counter. He didn't want the woman to catch him staring, but something about her—besides her looks—drew his attention.

She didn't seem happy…

"Here you go." Willow Sanhurst, the barely eighteen-year-old girl who worked evenings at the Eatery, stepped between him and the woman who intrigued him, smiled broadly and put his cup on the table with a flourish. "Warming up yet?"

"Starting to."

"I can't believe you've been out hiking. It's December!"

"Little bit of rain never hurt anybody."

He'd traded out his muddy hiking books for a pair of clean shoes before coming into the restaurant. Other than that, he was only a little damp, so he wasn't sure why she was making such a big deal of it.

"You must *really* like the outdoors."

"I do," he said.

"So do I."

He got the impression he was supposed to follow that up with an invitation to go hiking with him sometime, but he didn't.

Even though they'd already discussed his hike when he'd sat down and she'd brought him water, and the diner was full of people waiting for a chance to order, she didn't move away as most waitresses would.

Before bringing the coffee to his lips, he looked up to see if there was something she needed.

As soon as their eyes met, she blushed a deep red, wiped her hands on her ruffled white apron and mumbled some remark about being careful not to burn himself—that the coffee was hot—before hurrying away.

Damn it. She had a crush on him. She'd clearly wanted to say something but hadn't been able to gather the nerve, and that made him distinctly uncomfortable. After being released from prison in July he was committed to making better choices, to building a productive life. He couldn't have some high school girl staring at him with the longing he saw shining in her eyes. If she started seriously pursuing him, he was afraid he'd end up in a bad situation just because he was so damn lonely.

With a sigh, he took a tentative sip of his coffee. This was his favorite place to eat—the comfort food and Norman Rockwell vibe reminded him of the wholesome existence he'd always secretly admired. But he'd have to quit coming here. He wouldn't allow himself to be tempted. His brother, Maddox, said over and over that his first year out of prison would be the hardest, and although Tobias acted as though he was doing fine, that he had his life under control, his journey was not as sure-footed as he let on. Sometimes, especially late at night, he felt as though he'd been cast adrift on a vast ocean and might never find safe harbor. And that sense of being so small and insignificant made him crave the substances that had gotten him into trouble in the first place.

Willow kept looking over at him, obviously hoping

to catch his eye. While he poured a dash of cream into his coffee, he considered canceling his meal. He could eat somewhere else—grab something to go and head home to shower. But just as he was about to slide out of the booth, his phone dinged with a text from Maddox, asking if he'd like to come over for dinner.

Already ate. Enjoy your night. See you at work tomorrow, he wrote back.

He knew his brother worried about him, was trying to help him adjust to life outside prison and didn't want him to backslide and become like their mother. But Maddox had recently married the girl he'd loved since high school. He deserved to be alone with Jada, his new wife, who was now pregnant, and Maya, their daughter. The last thing Tobias wanted to do was get in the way of their relationship—*again*. It was because of him they hadn't gotten together the first time around, and that had cost Maddox the first twelve years of Maya's life.

As he slid his phone in his coat pocket, he saw that it was too late to cancel his food. Willow was once again coming toward him, this time carrying a plate.

"You texting your girlfriend?" she asked, flirting with him as she put down his meat loaf and mashed potatoes.

He allowed himself another glance at the blonde sitting at the counter. Her meal had come, too, and yet she held her fork, turning it over and over in one hand, staring at her food without taking a bite.

"Did you hear me?" Willow asked.

Putting his napkin in his lap, he picked up his fork. "I'm sorry. What'd you say?"

She looked over her shoulder in the direction *he'd*

been looking and lowered her voice. "I see you've noticed Harper."

"Harper?" he repeated.

"Yeah, Harper Devlin—Axel Devlin's wife. She's been in here before."

"Who's Axel Devlin?"

"Are you kidding me? He's the lead singer of Pulse. They're, like…the biggest band on the planet!"

He'd heard of Pulse, was familiar with their music and liked it. He'd also heard the name of the band's lead singer many times. He'd just never dreamed Willow could be referring to *that* Axel Devlin—although there was no good reason why she couldn't be. A lot of celebrities came to artsy, spiritually focused Silver Springs. Quite a few, especially movie people, retired here. And he often interacted with Hudson King, a professional football player, at New Horizons Boys Ranch, where he worked doing grounds and building maintenance. Hudson did a lot to help the troubled teens who attended the boarding school—both the boys' side and the recently built girls' school on the same property. He'd donated the money to buy an ice-skating rink both sides could use. "Do they live in the area?"

"No. She and her two kids are staying with her sister for the holidays. I overheard her talking to the owner."

"She looks a little…" When he let his words trail off, Willow jumped in to finish the sentence.

"Depressed?"

"I was going to say 'lost.'"

"Probably is. I watched an interview with Axel a few months ago. He said they were splitting up. Maybe that's why."

It was none of his business, but Tobias couldn't help asking, "Did he give a reason?"

She seemed to like that they'd found something to talk about that wasn't so strained and awkward for her. "Blamed it on the travel. He has to be gone too much. Yada, yada. What else is he going to say? That he's cheating with a different girl every night?" she added with a laugh.

Tobias felt bad for Harper. It couldn't be easy to be married to a rock star. She wasn't that old, likely hadn't been prepared for that kind of life. If Tobias remembered correctly, Axel was from a small town in Idaho, and he and his band had become famous almost overnight. Now he was sitting on top of the world.

But where did that leave her?

"You said they have kids?" he asked.

"Yeah. Two little girls. I don't remember their ages—maybe eight and six? Something like that."

So Harper had married Axel *before* he'd become a big success, and they'd started a family. That indicated she'd married for love. "Where are the kids?"

"With her sister, I guess." Willow lowered her voice. "It would suck to be her, right? I mean, she has to see his name and his face *everywhere*, can't escape the constant reminder."

Now that he wasn't paying as much attention to Willow's hopeful smiles and nervousness when she was around him, Tobias could see others in the restaurant nudging their companions and pointing to Harper. Apparently a lot of people knew who she was—or word was spreading fast.

Poor thing. He understood what it was like to be the talk of the town. He'd been only seventeen when he'd been prosecuted as an adult and jailed for thirteen years. Returning to Silver Springs after his release this past summer had been like being put under a microscope. Suffering privately was one thing. Suffering publicly was something else entirely. That took what she was going through to a whole new level.

"Shouldn't be too hard for her to find someone else." He said it as though he wasn't particularly invested, but Harper had caught *his* eye, hadn't she?

"Are you kidding me?" Willow responded again. "How will anyone else ever compare?"

She had a point. It would be tough for a regular guy to match Axel, financially and otherwise. "True."

"*You're* not interested in her, are you?" Willow looked slightly crestfallen.

Apparently he hadn't been as careful to hide his feelings as he'd thought. But he was an ex-con, making a modest wage working for a correctional school. He'd never known his father, and his mother was a meth addict, constantly in and out of rehab. He knew when he was out of his league. "No."

"Good." A relieved smile curved her lips. "Because I've been watching you for a while and…well…I hope there's someone *else* in this restaurant you might be interested in." She finished in a rush, couldn't quite look at him and then hurried away—only to return with a slip of paper that had her number on it when she brought the check.

Harper shoved her garlic mashed potatoes from one side of her plate to the other as she listened to the hum of voices in the diner. Although surrounded by people, she'd never felt so alone.

"I've got a number five," the cook barked out for the waitresses.

Harper checked the menu, which she'd left open at her elbow so she'd have something to look at. It was difficult to go out in public right now. After the documentary she did with Axel last year, trying to remove the stigma of depression and using a therapist when necessary, people often recognized her, so she had little privacy.

A number five was a chicken breast with lemon-dill sauce, steamed vegetables and a gluten-free corn muffin. She'd ordered a number seven—peppercorn steak, garlic mashed potatoes and green beans, which had sounded good at first, but the only thing she'd been able to make herself eat was part of the dinner roll. She doubted it was gluten-free. Axel had made a big deal about staying away from gluten, but *he* was allergic to it, not her. And although she thought it was probably wise to avoid it, she didn't care about her diet right now. She didn't care about much of anything since her marriage had unraveled. It'd been all she could do just to hold herself together for the sake of her kids, and now Christmas would be here in only three weeks. It would be her and the girls' first Christmas without Axel. He was touring Europe and wouldn't be back until after the first of the year, since his last big concert was scheduled for New Year's Eve.

Now that everything had changed between them, they wouldn't have spent the holidays as they had in the past, anyway.

He might've asked to take the girls, however.

She could only imagine how lonely she would have

felt with them gone, and yet…she sort of wished he had taken them. She didn't feel capable of holding up her end, of putting on a brave face and telling their children that everything was going to be okay when it felt as though the ground had given way beneath her feet. She had no interest in decorating, putting up a tree or buying presents, which was why her sister had insisted she come for an extended visit, even if it meant having the girls transfer schools for a couple of months. Piper and Everly were at a church Christmas party tonight with their cousins—twin girls who were older than Everly by four years. But Harper needed to be ready to face them with a smile when they came home.

Her phone vibrated in her pocket, but she didn't bother to get it out. No doubt it was her sister. They'd had an argument before Harper stormed out of the house. Karoline had grown angry when Harper told her how little she was getting for child support. According to her sister, she was letting Axel off far too easy.

He *was* making a fortune, but Harper didn't want to fight. She was still in love with him. As soon as he'd made it clear that he didn't want to be married to her anymore, that he was no longer willing to try to work through their differences, she'd settled for the first figure his lawyer had thrown out. Otherwise, she was afraid the media would start to claim they were going through a "bitter" divorce. As she'd told Karoline, she'd make it on her own *somehow*, even though she hadn't worked in an official capacity since the first three years of her marriage, when Axel was trying so hard to get a start in show business and he'd needed her to cover their basic living expenses.

Maybe she *was* a fool to be so accommodating. But she couldn't imagine Axel would consider keeping the family together if she turned into a bitch. Besides, she didn't even know who he was anymore, he'd changed so much. She couldn't decide what she had a right to demand. Had she let Axel down? Or had *he* let her down? He'd always suffered from anxiety and depression. Maybe she hadn't done enough to help him—

"Is everything okay?"

She forced herself to look up. The waitress working the counter had paused in front of her, obviously wondering if there was something wrong with the food.

"Fine," Harper mumbled. She hadn't really come to eat. She just needed some time alone, couldn't face going back to her sister's quite yet. As nice as it was of Karoline to provide a refuge during this difficult month, being with her only sibling wasn't much easier than being alone, because now she had to constantly explain and justify her actions. And with her emotions zinging all over the place, she wasn't being consistent, *couldn't* be consistent. Most of the time, she wasn't even making a whole lot of sense.

Elvis's "Blue Christmas" came on the sound system as the waitress moved on to her other customers.

Harper took a sip of her coffee and braved a quick glance around. Although she liked this restaurant, she didn't feel she belonged in Silver Springs. Why wasn't she in Denver, where she and Axel had lived after their college days at Boise State?

Because as much as she and Axel had once believed that they'd be the exception to the rule, that nothing could come between them, they'd been wrong. Slowly but surely, Axel had lost all perspective and started car-ing more about his work than he did his family. Fame had destroyed their relationship like so many celebrities' before them.

With a sigh, she took the bill the waitress had put near her plate and paid at the register. She owed her sister more respect than to make her worry. She had to go back and face Karoline whether she wanted to or not.

Harper hadn't put on makeup for weeks, hadn't done anything with her hair, either, other than to pile it in a messy bun on her head, so it didn't bother her that it was raining. She was cold, though; couldn't seem to get warm. Tightening her oversize coat—a castoff of Axel's from the good old days when they were first married—she pushed out of the warm café into the bad weather.

Putting her head down, she stared at her feet, bracing against the gusts of wind that whipped at her hair and clothes while stepping over two or three puddles to reach the Range Rover Axel had let her keep when they split. If she got desperate, she supposed she could sell it. It had cost a pretty penny.

She was opening the driver's door when she noticed a tall, lanky man with longish dark hair crossing the lot toward her.

"Don't be frightened," he said, lifting one hand in a gesture intended to show he wasn't being aggressive. "I just… I saw you inside and…"

Prepared to rebuff him, she set her jaw. She was *not* in the mood to be hit on. But when she met his eyes, something about his expression told her that wasn't what this was about. Taking a long-stemmed white rose from inside his coat, he stepped forward to give it to her.

"Hang in there. It'll get easier," he said. Then he walked off before she could even ask for his name.

2

"Thought I heard the garage door," Karoline said, coming into the kitchen.

Harper glanced over her shoulder at her older sister, who was wearing jeans, sheepskin-lined slippers and a maroon V-neck sweater with pearl earrings. Karoline was always well put together. Her house was immaculate. Her kids were well behaved. And her husband was a podiatrist who was not only intelligent and well-spoken but kind. Karoline managed life better than anyone Harper had ever met, which was intimidating, especially now that *her* life was in shambles. "Sorry about what happened earlier," she mumbled.

Her sister sat on a bar stool at the island. "It's okay. I'm sorry, too. After you left, Terrance told me I should've let it go."

"He overheard us?" Harper's brother-in-law had been watching TV in the other room and hadn't participated in the argument. He didn't care for large displays of emotion, so she could see why he'd stay out of it.

"Yeah. He thinks I'm right. I *know* I'm right. But he also thinks you're not ready to hear it."

"Then he's right, too."

Karoline propped her chin up with one fist. "Look, I understand that you're going through hell, and I don't mean to make it worse. I just don't want to see Axel get the best of you. He has you on the ropes right now and yet you're still trying to play nice. Since I don't love him the way you do, I have a different perspective, and I was trying to use that perspective to put you in a better position."

"I know. You've done a lot for me, and I'm grateful." She reached into the cupboard above her sister's double ovens, retrieving a small vase.

"Where did you get that?" Karoline asked when Harper filled the vase with water and put the rose she'd been given inside it.

"Some man gave it to me."

"Some man..."

"Yes."

"*What* man?"

"I don't know. He didn't tell me his name."

Karoline scowled, obviously suspicious. "Where did you meet him?"

"I didn't meet him. Not really. He came up to me in the parking lot as I was leaving the Eatery and handed me this."

"Was he selling them? Or looking for some type of donation?"

Harper balked at telling her sister what the stranger had said. She was embarrassed to admit she'd been so transparent, and she didn't want to cheapen the gesture by having Karoline claim he must've had some ulterior motive, as she'd first assumed. "No."

"Roses aren't exactly in bloom this time of year. Where'd he get it?"

"You can buy a rose anytime."

"So he bought it."

"Yes. From the grocery store across the street."

"How do you know?"

"I saw the price tag, okay? It was still wrapped around the stem."

"He spent money to buy you a rose and he doesn't even know you?"

"It was only seven dollars, Karol. Relax. He was just being nice."

When her sister didn't respond right away, Harper used the opportunity to change the subject. "What time will the girls be ready to come home?"

"Terrance left to pick them up right before you arrived."

"Oh. I could've done it. You should've called me."

"I tried."

Harper winced at her tone. "I couldn't really talk in the restaurant," she said. She could've texted Karoline but, fortunately, her sister didn't point that out.

"No worries."

Harper set the rose in the middle of the granite-topped island. Her sister had done a lot of decorating, but none of it could top the natural beauty of that one perfect flower. It reminded her that she needed to return to the basics and keep life simple, which, for her, meant continuing to put one foot in front of the other no matter how painful the situation.

It'll get easier...

"Why would you ever wear *that*?" Karoline asked, grimacing at Harper's coat as Harper took it off.

"It's warm."

Her sister rolled her eyes. "I don't care how warm it is. Get rid of it. Get rid of everything of his."

"Don't say that."

"He's not coming back, Harper. The divorce will be final this week. If he regrets what he did, he would've said so by now, would've tried to save his family."

"He's been pretty distracted."

"Yeah—by sleeping with other women."

Harper bristled. "We don't *know* he's been sleeping with other women."

"He's a thirty-two-year-old rock star who hasn't had time for his wife in ages. I think it's safe to assume."

"If he has, it's because so many women, *beautiful* women, throw themselves at him. How would you or I deal with the same kind of attention? The same kind of worship? It's possible we wouldn't do any better."

Her sister shook her head. "You're too understanding, Harper. One of a kind."

"If that's true, what happened to my marriage?"

"Axel happened. But he's stupid to throw you away. He's going to wind up with nothing in the end."

"He won't wind up with *nothing*. Even if his career suddenly tanks, he'll have what he's already achieved. Besides, he's always been charismatic. He could easily find someone else even if he wasn't famous." That was one of her biggest issues with the divorce. These days, she felt so inherently replaceable, as if there was nothing special about her, nothing worth hanging on to—ironic, given that in the beginning he'd made her feel as though she was the only person who could ever fulfill him.

Be careful what you wish for. She remembered her

mother telling her that while Harper was working so hard to help Axel make it in the music biz.

She should've listened. Her mother, a superior court judge in Idaho, where the family had been raised, was always right. Her father, who was in commercial real estate, agreed that it was never wise to disregard her advice.

"You mean we won't have the pleasure of even that much revenge?" Karoline asked.

"Probably not," Harper admitted.

"That sucks."

The door opened and the girls spilled into the house, laughing and talking about the party and how the Santa who'd shown up was someone they'd recognized, under that red suit, as one of their teachers from school. As she'd been doing for almost eight months, Harper pretended to be interested in regular life and tried to contribute to the conversation, but she was infinitely relieved when the kids were in bed and she could once again lay down the burden of putting on a good show.

The night wasn't over, though. Once Harper was finally alone, Karoline knocked and poked her head into the room. "You okay?"

Harper forced one more smile. "Yeah, of course."

"About that man who gave you the rose…"

Piper and Everly hadn't noticed the flower on the island. At least, they hadn't mentioned it. Maybe they assumed Terrance had given it to Karoline. It wasn't elaborate enough to have come from their father, who used to send her vast arrays of flowers to try to placate her whenever he broke another promise. "What about him?"

"How old was he?"

"Around my age."

"What'd he look like?"

She rolled her eyes. "He was just some guy, Karo-line."

"You don't know what he looked like?"

"Of course I do, but…" Reining in her irritation, she let her breath go. "Okay, he was maybe six foot three with dark hair and really unusual, light-colored eyes."

"How light?"

"I don't know!" She'd been pretty defensive at the time, hadn't been evaluating his looks.

"Seriously?"

"It was tough to see in the parking lot! The lights there aren't very bright, but his eyes seemed to be a…a pale green, I guess. With thick eyelashes," she added.

"So he was handsome."

She remembered his bold jaw and the dark stubble covering it, the high cheekbones, the shape of his mouth, which was quite sensual even from a strictly objective point of view. "Yeah. Why?"

"I'm wondering if I know him…"

"You're making a big deal out of nothing. It was just a sweet gesture, one that cheered me up when I needed it. It's not as though anything will ever come of it."

"I wish something *would* come of it," Karoline grumbled. "That's exactly what you need—and what Axel deserves."

"Being angry with Axel isn't going to change anything."

"It helps. Trust me. You should try it."

The door closed and Harper slumped back on the bed. But after the house had gone quiet and she knew everyone was asleep, she couldn't resist pulling out her laptop to watch the YouTube video of her soon-to-be *ex*-husband's latest concert.

He looked amazing.

His performance *was* amazing.

He didn't seem to be hurting at all.

When Tobias arrived at the sixteen-acre tangerine orchard where he lived, there was a strange car in the driveway. He tried to pull around it to his usual spot near the small house he was renting behind the 1920s farmhouse closer to the road. But the old beat-up Chevy Impala was parked such that there wasn't enough room on either side.

With a sigh, he shoved his gearshift into Park. He'd have to go to the door and ask the driver to move it. He couldn't leave his truck out on the road. Someone coming around the bend might not see it, especially in the rain. And it wouldn't do any good to leave it where it was, tucked behind the Impala. The driver would just have to knock on *his* door and ask him to move it later.

On the other hand, it had been a big step for his landlord to start dating again. Uriah had been married for fifty years before he lost his wife, and the old guy still wasn't comfortable with moving on. So Tobias didn't want to interrupt if he could avoid it…

He checked his watch. Uriah's lady friends typically didn't come over, except to bring him a meal or a piece of pie or something. If one ever did, she didn't stay long. Uriah was nothing if not old-fashioned. He picked up whomever he asked out, took her on an official date and then drove her home.

Besides, he'd been a farmer all his life. He was in

bed by ten and up at the crack of dawn, and it was almost ten now.

If Tobias just waited for a few minutes, whoever it was would probably leave.

But then, she might not. And he was dying to get in the shower.

"Better get it over with," he muttered and climbed out, ducking his head against the wind and the rain.

Before he even reached the stoop, he could hear voices coming from inside the house. Uriah was getting on in years and losing his hearing, so he spoke loudly. Tobias spent a lot of time with him eating dinner, playing chess, restoring an old Buick in the detached garage or helping out with chores around the property, so he was used to the volume of his voice. But it was surprising to him that both voices were male.

Apparently, whoever was driving the Impala *wasn't* one of the women Uriah was dating.

Tobias turned to take a closer look at the car blocking his way. The license plate was so dirty and the weather so bad that he hadn't noticed when he first drove up, but it had Maryland plates.

Who did Uriah know from Maryland?

And then it hit him. This wasn't Carl, was it?

Tobias had never met Uriah's only child, but he'd heard enough about him to be leery. The two had been estranged for years. Uriah rarely mentioned him, but from what Tobias had heard from Aiyana Turner, who owned the school where Tobias worked and knew just about everyone in Silver Springs, Carl hadn't even come to his mother's funeral fifteen months ago.

What was he doing here now?

Tobias took the porch steps in one leap and banged on the door. He expected Uriah to answer. But the door opened almost immediately and the face looking out at him was much younger—around forty.

The resemblance between father and son was striking, eradicating any doubt Tobias had left as to the identity of Uriah's guest. While Uriah was tall and thin and wore his salt-and-pepper hair in a military-style flattop, Carl wore his long, and it didn't look as though he'd washed it recently. He didn't resemble his father in stature or bearing, but the narrow bridge of his nose, the long shape of his face and the flat slash of a mouth were very similar to Uriah's, although those features were somehow more attractive in the older man.

"Who are *you*?" Carl asked.

Before Tobias could answer, Uriah managed to get out of the recliner, which gave him a bit more trouble than usual since he was trying to do it in a hurry, and came to the door himself. "Carl! Is that any way to greet a person?"

"What?" Carl said, instantly defensive. "Did I say something wrong? Do I owe this guy something?"

Uriah scowled. "That's enough."

Tobias had met a lot of men in prison. Those who acted like Carl were seldom *good* news. They often tried to pick on everyone else, but Tobias wasn't the type of person to let them get away with it. Carl was Uriah's son, however, and Tobias respected his landlord—who had become his friend—so he maintained a pleasant expression. "Sorry to bother you," he said. "I was just hoping you could move your car."

Carl's eyebrows jerked together. "What for?"

"So he can get through," Uriah explained. "He lives

in the back house. I was about to tell you I rented it out."

"This guy lives on the property? In *my* house?"

Tobias felt his back and shoulder muscles tense. It'd been a long time since he'd taken such an instant dislike to someone. But Uriah seemed determined to defuse the situation, although Tobias could tell he was embarrassed by his son's behavior.

"Carl, this is Tobias Richardson," he said, speaking with almost exaggerated calm. "He's lived here for four or five months. Helps out around the place, in addition to working at New Horizons. I've come to rely on him a great deal."

Even Tobias could feel Uriah's desire for Carl to behave, but he was willing to bet that if Carl *did* behave, it wouldn't be for long.

"Why's he wearing tights?" Carl asked, looking him up and down.

Tobias gritted his teeth. "They're not *tights*. They're for hiking or jogging."

Carl ignored him. "So *this* is the son you never had?" he said to his father.

"I didn't say that," Uriah protested.

From what I've heard, it wouldn't take much to be a better son than you. Those words rose to the tip of Tobias's tongue. But he held back. "I'm just the renter," he said as though he and Uriah weren't as close as they'd become. "And if you're not going anywhere, I'll leave my truck where it is." He started to walk away. He didn't want any part of Carl. If Uriah was excited to have his son home, if he thought they might be able to patch things up, Tobias wasn't going to get in the way. He understood how much that relationship had to mean to the old guy. The fact that Uriah never talked about Carl served as the biggest indicator. His inability to get along with his own son had created a deep wound, one he tried to keep hidden. But, other than Maddox, Uriah was the best man Tobias had ever known. As far as Tobias was concerned, Carl didn't deserve a father like him.

"Wait," Carl said. "I don't want to be blocked in."

Keeping his fingers outstretched so they didn't automatically curl into fists, Tobias waited while Carl went in search of his keys.

Uriah stood at the door with him, but he didn't say anything. Tobias could only imagine what he had to be feeling. Hope? The desire to make everything all right, at last, mixed with the knowledge that, even now, he probably couldn't? Aiyana had told Tobias that Carl was moody at best. Through the years, he'd often lost his temper and started kicking the furniture or throwing things. Uriah had tried to help him a number of times. It wasn't until Uriah came home one day to find Carl so enraged he was choking his mother that he made his son leave and told him never to come back.

Now that Shirley was gone and her safety wasn't a concern, Tobias couldn't see Uriah turning Carl away even if he crossed the line, and that worried Tobias.

But maybe he was jumping to conclusions. Maybe Carl was only home for the holidays.

He pulled up the collar of his coat to cut the wind as Carl strode past him and, after exchanging a look with Uriah, followed a complaining Carl down the steps. "It's cold out here!" he muttered as though Tobias was purposely putting him out.

Once Carl moved his Impala to the side, he waved

Tobias past, obviously impatient to get back into the warmth of the house.

Tobias stared at him for a few seconds and knew in that moment they would never be friends.

When Carl simply glared back at him, he drove past the Impala to park in his customary spot.

Behind him, Carl didn't say anything as he got out and trudged inside, so Tobias didn't say anything, either. "Prick," he muttered and went into his own house, where he turned on the TV and tried to forget about Axel Devlin's wife, who'd looked so sad in the diner, and the fact that vulnerable, seventy-six-year-old Uriah had someone who was potentially dangerous staying with him.

Tobias was still having difficulty relaxing an hour later when he received a text from his ex-girlfriend. Tonya Sparks, the sister of his last cellmate, had managed to give him enough hope to be able to endure his final year in prison, but things had fallen apart between them almost as soon as he was released.

I'm having a Christmas party on the 21st at 7:00 p.m. here at my place. I was hoping you'd come.

They spent some time together here and there, but Tobias knew they weren't good for each other. Tonya partied a lot and didn't have any direction in her life. She reminded him too much of his mother. He was better off staying away from her.

He'd been trying to, but it wasn't easy since Maddox had gotten married. Tobias hadn't been out of prison long enough to have made many friends. Sometimes he hung out with two of Aiyana's sons—Elijah and

Gavin, who also worked at the school—but they were married with kids and couldn't do a whole lot after hours. If he wasn't out hiking or mountain biking, he usually spent his evenings with Uriah. But until Carl went back to Maryland, if he even planned to, Tobias had a feeling that was about to change.

What the hell. He had to steer clear of his mother. She was using again, and he couldn't risk getting caught up in that. He had to stay away from the eighteen-year-old at the diner who'd given him her number. He had to avoid being a nuisance to Maddox so that Maddox could enjoy his new wife and the daughter he never knew he had until last summer. And now he had to give Uriah some space so that he could potentially rebuild his relationship with his troubled son.

But a man had to have *some* friends, didn't he?

Yeah. I'll be there, he wrote.

3

Axel called the following morning after Harper had rolled out of bed and brushed her teeth. She hated herself for being so excited when she saw his face come up on her screen. But he was and always had been the love of her life. She'd never dreamed she'd have to live without him, so she'd never prepared herself for the possibility, which was probably why the divorce had devastated her so much.

Wasn't it during the documentary that he'd told the world she was the best person he'd ever known? That was only twelve months ago! How had everything fallen apart since then? What'd happened to always remembering what was important in life, as they'd promised each other right from the start?

He'd lost sight of it, after all.

Or was it *her* fault? He claimed she wasn't being supportive enough. That she didn't understand how much good he could do in his career, and he had a point. He threw a benefit concert for St. Jude Hospital every summer and raised at least a million dollars with each one. To command that kind of audience, he had to keep writing, performing and promoting his music. She felt selfish for craving more of his attention. But during the long days and nights when she took care of their children alone, they drifted further and further apart.

Promising herself she wouldn't argue with him no matter what he said, she quietly slipped back into her bedroom and closed the door so there was no chance of Karoline overhearing and then critiquing her side of the conversation. Everyone else was in the kitchen having pancakes for breakfast, which Terrance made every Saturday morning, and she wanted as much privacy as she could get.

"Hello?" She put some lift into her voice—which took considerable effort.

"Harper? How are you?"

Not good. She felt as though she'd been in a terrible car accident and was still stumbling around the scene, shocked by all the wreckage and unable to think clearly. But he didn't want to hear her complaints. As he'd become more and more popular, *she'd* become less and less important to him. And the less important she became, the more she'd tried to get them back to where they once were—and the more that aggravated him. It was a terrible cycle. Revealing her pain and neediness, her complete and utter uncertainty on how to proceed from here, only chased him further away.

"Great," she lied. "And you?"

"Exhausted." He sighed audibly. "This tour is really kicking my ass."

"You put a lot into every show," she said, and that was true. She admired his work ethic, the huge amount of energy he gave his fans. He was a phenomenal performer. "How are the girls?"

They missed their daddy. She almost said so. They wanted him back as much as she did. But, again, she refrained. He'd interpret that as criticism, and he wouldn't call if all he got was a guilt trip. "Having a great time with their cousins," she said instead.

"That's good. Do they like their new school?"

It was an adjustment, just like everything else they were going through. Harper hated that she'd made them move, but she'd had no choice. Without the support of her sister, she was afraid she'd melt down entirely. "For the most part. When will you be back in the States?"

"Looks like it won't be until mid-January."

"Does that mean you added a new show or…"

"No, I have to do some promotional stuff for the label while I'm across the pond."

"Right. Promotional stuff is important."

There was a brief pause during which she cursed herself for sounding so mechanical and insincere and knew he'd picked up on it when he asked, "Are you being sarcastic?"

She cleared her throat. "No, not at all. It's just… with Christmas coming up in a couple of weeks… I don't know, I guess I'm thinking of how much Piper and Everly are hoping you'll be back sooner than you planned, not later."

"I wish I could, but it doesn't make sense to keep flying back and forth. The travel is killing me. You know how anxious I get on a plane. I had to take a Xanax just to make it over here."

It was difficult to feel any empathy. She was too numb—and when the numbness receded, which occasionally it did, she was hit with such agonizing pain she was grateful when the numbness returned. "I'll tell them that…that you'll be back as soon as you can."

"I appreciate it. Listen, I'm transferring some money into your account. Can you get them Christmas presents from me?"

She stared at her reflection in the mirror above the dresser—the dark circles under her eyes, the haggard, almost-gaunt look that was beginning to creep into her face. "What would you like me to get them?"

"Whatever they're asking for."

He didn't even know what they wanted, didn't seem to particularly care. "Okay…"

"Oh, and my mother would like to see the girls. She just asked me when you'd be back in Colorado."

So he'd called his mother first? Harper knew his mother wasn't thrilled about the divorce, either, but maybe she was a better actor. "I don't know yet."

"Well, can you give her a call? Let her talk to the girls for a few minutes, at least? I don't think she expected you to be gone for quite so long."

"Of course," she managed to say.

Karoline knocked on her door. "Harper? What's taking you so long? We're almost finished eating."

"Be right there!" she called out. Then she told Axel, "I have to go." She wasn't sure she could tolerate much more of the conversation. She felt like a dam holding back an entire reservoir of feeling—a dam that had little cracks and fissures that were threatening the entire structure. If she wasn't careful, she'd break into a million tiny pieces, releasing a flood of hurt, anger and recrimination.

Even so, she thought of Piper and Everly before

she let him go. She knew how disappointed they'd be if he called and they didn't have a chance to talk to him. "Or...if you've got a minute, I'll go get the girls."

"Not now," he said. "I'll have to call later. I'm late for a meeting with our social media coordinator."

Biting back what immediately came to her lips—that surely his social media coordinator wasn't more important than his children—she managed a "No problem." This wasn't the man she'd married, she told herself. That man had always put his family first. This was some preoccupied stranger who didn't seem to know them very well, let alone care.

Karoline knocked again, then opened the door. "Harper?"

Harper said a quick goodbye and disconnected before turning to face her sister. "Sorry. I got held up. I'm ready now."

Karoline frowned as she studied her. "That was him, wasn't it?"

She hesitated but ultimately nodded.

"What'd he have to say?"

"He's sending money so I can get the girls some Christmas presents."

"From him?"

"Yeah."

"How thoughtful of him," she said.

Harper tried to ignore the heavy sarcasm. Her conversation with Axel had stung badly enough. "We'd better go eat."

Karoline caught her arm as Harper tried to pass her. "I'm considering taking the girls to LA."

"*Your* girls?"

"Yours, too."

"For…"

"A Disneyland trip."

"When?"

"Today."

"But…it's a two-hour drive to Orange County! They'll miss half the day by the time we can get there."

"We won't be going to Disneyland until tomorrow. Actually, we might even wait until Monday. It'll be less crowded then."

"So why do you want to leave today?"

"Why not? It was June the last time we took a family vacation."

"Oh. You plan to stay. For how long?"

"Five or six days. Maybe a week. We could also go to the San Diego Zoo, the La Brea Tar Pits, shopping on Rodeo Drive. There's so much to do."

"Then we'd better get packed."

Her sister gave her a pointed look. "*You'll* need to pack only if you want to go with us."

Harper blinked at her. "What do you mean?"

"Terrance is off work for the holidays, so this is a good time for us," her sister said. "We're willing to take Everly and Piper without you—to give you a chance to recover. I feel like you could use that."

The prospect of being alone, of having even a few days without the heavy responsibility of trying to pretend she was okay for the sake of her children, was tempting. "Are you sure that would be okay?" she asked tentatively.

Her sister seemed resolute. "Positive. We'd like them to build some good memories that include Aunt Karoline and Uncle Terrance and their cousins."

Somehow Axel could be gone for weeks, miss

birthdays and holidays, and feel no guilt. But Harper couldn't miss a few days at Disneyland without feeling as though she was letting her children down. "Shouldn't *I* be part of those memories?"

"*You* should pull yourself together while they're happily engaged with us."

The lump that rose in Harper's throat made it difficult to speak. "I'm trying. You know that, don't you?"

"I do," she said softly. "And you'll figure it out, I promise."

Hoping and praying her sister was right, she nodded as though she believed it was true, even though she wasn't entirely convinced. So what if she wasn't bleeding on the outside? She'd never felt so deeply wounded.

"When is Axel coming back, by the way?" Karoline asked.

"Not for several weeks."

"Piper is under the impression he plans to surprise her for Christmas. You've heard her talk about that, right? That's what she's asking Santa Claus for. She's mentioned it to me several times."

Briefly closing her eyes, Harper imagined the disappointment her daughters would suffer and wished there was some way to avoid it—or at least help them understand. "I'll have a talk with her and Everly and... and try to let them down easy."

"Okay, but wait until we get back. Let's not ruin the trip."

Harper folded her arms as if that might hold her together. "Thank you, Karol. Thanks for everything."

"That's what sisters are for," Karoline said. But even as Harper followed her out to breakfast, she wondered if one week alone would make much of a difference.

It'd been eight months since Axel had first told her he wanted out of their marriage, and it hadn't gotten any easier.

Tobias was afraid he was in for a long weekend. The weather wasn't good enough that he felt like hiking again or biking, either, so he'd spent the morning cleaning his house, and had gotten caught up on laundry and other chores. But now he couldn't decide what to do next. He would've liked to spend the afternoon working on the Buick with Uriah. They were almost ready to put it up for sale. They'd be splitting the profits, and he was excited about that. But he didn't want to stick around if Carl was going to be there. The brown Impala was still parked in the drive, over far enough that Tobias could get past it. He decided to take the opportunity to leave so Uriah could focus on his son— and so he didn't have to run into Carl himself.

As he climbed into his truck, he considered going to Maddox's house. He really enjoyed spending time with Maya, his niece. She was always trying to come up with a new type of cookie to sell at Sugar Mama, the cookie shop Jada's mother owned in town, and used him as one of her taste testers. But he worried he spent too much time at his brother's place as it was and didn't want Jada to think of him as a pain in the ass. Didn't want to do anything to harm the close relationship he and Maddox finally had the chance to rebuild.

Besides, he never knew whether her brother, Atticus, would be there. Atticus treated him well enough. Since he also worked at New Horizons, they saw each other occasionally on campus and were thrown together whenever Jada and Maddox hosted some kind of event, like the party they threw when they announced the sex of the baby they were having in May.

But those were difficult times for Tobias. He hated having to face Atticus knowing *he* was the one who'd put him in that wheelchair. That terrible night seemed like a lifetime ago and yet he couldn't escape it.

Instead of going to Maddox's, he drove to The Daily Grind, a quaint redbrick coffee shop with black-and-gold lettering on the windows and comfortable leather chairs. Since Silver Springs didn't allow chain stores within the city limits, there wasn't a Starbucks in town or a McDonald's or any other fast-food joint. There were only mom-and-pop establishments, and of the coffee shops, The Daily Grind was by far the most popular. It was always filled with hipsters typing away on laptops, and this afternoon was no exception.

Tobias figured he'd grab a cup of coffee and hang out for a bit, then go over to the school. He already spent a lot of time at New Horizons, often staying late to help out with football practice, teach the fundamentals of basketball to any students who were hanging around the courts—he'd gotten pretty good at the sport in prison—practice skating with the kids at the new ice rink or tutor those who were taking auto shop. He'd been put away before he could finish high school, so he didn't have a traditional college education, but he'd taken advantage of whatever classes were offered in prison, and they'd made a decent mechanic out of him. He could fix almost any kind of vehicle and hoped to own his own repair shop one day.

After Tobias placed his order, someone stood up to leave, enabling him to snag a seat at a small corner table near a window that had a Christmas wreath hanging in the middle of it. The guy who'd just walked out had left his newspaper behind, which was lucky. Tobias wanted to check out the sports page and hadn't thought to buy a paper on his way over, but before he could even turn to that section, he heard the barista call out a name that made him look up.

"Harper!"

He'd only ever heard of one Harper.

A quick glance at the faces around the counter confirmed it *was* Harper Devlin, the woman he'd noticed at the Eatery last night.

What were the chances that he'd run into her again, especially so soon?

She didn't hear the barista. At least, she didn't react when he called her name. Standing to one side, away from the line that snaked out the door, she stared off into space, obviously a million miles away.

That was when Tobias realized there was a song by Pulse playing on the sound system. He could hear Axel Devlin singing, "I will always love you." Had he written those lyrics for her?

"Harper?" the barista called again.

Still no reaction. She was completely lost in thought.

Dropping the newspaper, Tobias got up and claimed her drink for her. But even as he approached, she didn't seem to see or hear him.

"Hey, you okay?" He gave her arm a slight nudge as he held out her coffee.

Startled, she glanced up and, as her eyes finally focused, he noticed the shimmer of unshed tears—which she immediately blinked away. "You," she said, recognizing him.

She took her drink, and he slipped his hands in the

pockets of his sweatshirt. "Yes, me. But don't worry, I'm not following you. When I heard the barista call your name, I looked up and there you were."

She didn't so much as smile. "Thanks."

"Are you okay? Because I think you could use a minute to sit down and relax, and I just happen to have a table." He motioned to where he'd left the paper.

She seemed as lost or bewildered as she'd been last night. "Do you know my sister or my brother-in-law?"

"I've only been in town for five months, so I doubt it. What are their names?"

"Karoline and Terrance Mathewson. He's a podiatrist. She's a housewife who gets involved in about every good cause that comes along—even helped out with the tree-lighting ceremony downtown a week ago. They have two twelve-year-old daughters, identical twins—Amanda and Miranda."

"They sound like stellar citizens, so I'm sorry to say no, I've never heard of them."

She narrowed her eyes. "You have no frame of reference where I'm concerned. I'm a *total* stranger to you."

"Last night the waitress told me you were Axel Devlin's wife. I guess that's a frame of reference."

Glancing away from him in the crowded coffee shop, she took a sip of her drink. "Is that why you bought me the rose? Because you thought I was married to someone famous and that makes me more desirable?"

She wasn't wearing makeup. She had on a pair of yoga pants and a parka with ear warmers and looked as though she'd just rolled out of bed. But he couldn't see how fancier clothes or makeup could make her any more appealing. He loved her golden, dewy-looking skin and the cornflower blue of her eyes. He could all too easily identify with the pain he saw in them.

Actually, that was what drew him more than anything else.

"Your connection to Axel had no bearing on it whatsoever," he said. "I just thought you were beautiful, and it seemed as though you could use the encouragement."

Tucking the fine strands of blond hair falling from her ponytail behind her ears, she stepped back. "I'm sorry. I'm—I'm not open to a relationship."

The compliment had spooked her, as he'd known it might. But he was only being honest. "That's good."

She seemed taken aback. "It is?"

"Yes—because I'm the *last* guy you should ever get with even if you were."

Her mouth fell open. "Why's that?"

"Never mind. Now that you have your drink, I'll leave you alone."

She caught him by the sleeve as he turned away. "You're going?"

"Isn't that what you want me to do?"

She bit her bottom lip. "I don't know. You're... confusing. I don't think I've ever met anyone like you."

He couldn't imagine she'd associated with many ex-cons. No doubt she'd be horrified if he were to tell her he'd spent more than 40 percent of his life behind bars. Chances were she wouldn't even be willing to talk to him.

He'd met other women like that, who thought he must be the devil incarnate, especially here in Silver Springs, where so many people knew Jada's family and how he'd hurt them. Some women were drawn to the "danger" of associating with a "bad boy" like him but, sadly, those who *were* drawn to him were often like Tonya—a mess themselves.

"That's probably a safe assumption," he said with a grin.

She seemed further confused by his response and the fact that he not only accepted her words, he agreed with them. "Let me get this straight. What, exactly, are you offering me?"

He gestured at the table. "A seat."

"That's all?"

"What more do you want?"

"I don't know. I don't know *anything* right now. I feel like I've just been put through a meat grinder."

He'd never experienced heartbreak on the level she seemed to be experiencing it—not the romantic kind. But pain was pain, and he was certainly acquainted with that. "Well…I'm a good listener, if you need to talk."

She kept her gaze fastened to his as she took another sip of her drink. "A man who looks as good as you do is never quite *that* harmless."

He heard the barista call his name above their conversation and those of everyone else in the shop. His coffee was ready. "How long will you be in town?" he asked.

"Not long. Just a few weeks."

"How much damage could knowing me do in such a short time?"

"I'm already a wreck. I doubt knowing you could do *any* more damage," she admitted.

"Then what do you have to lose?" He held out his hand. "Can I see your phone?"

She pulled her cell from her purse and, somewhat

skeptically, let him take it, watching as he added his name and number to her contacts. "I'll leave you alone for today. You can have my table. But if you need a friend while you're here, you've got someone to call," he said and picked up his drink before walking out.

4

At least now she knew his name. Harper slid her phone back in her purse and carried her drink over to the window so she could watch Tobias Richardson leave. She thought he might glance back at her. Oddly enough, she sort of wanted him to. There was something intriguing about him. She'd noticed that despite what she was going through, which meant it was obvious. At least to her.

But he didn't look back. He took a sip of his coffee as he strode purposefully toward the parking lot and disappeared from view.

With a sigh, she turned to take the table he'd vacated, only to find that someone else had beaten her to it. A young girl wearing a beanie similar to the one he'd been wearing was just pushing his newspaper out of the way and setting up her laptop.

"Are *you* Axel Devlin's wife?"

The voice came from right behind her. Harper cringed inside as she turned to see who'd asked that question. Fame had its benefits. Since Axel's music had taken off, they hadn't had to worry about how they'd cover the basics. That had come as a relief. It had been lean in the early years, when she'd been struggling to support them, especially because their first child had come so fast. But the loss of privacy was difficult, especially for an introvert like her.

Anyway, for the past several months, this question was the one she'd dreaded most. She didn't know how to answer it. Or, rather, she was *reluctant* to answer it. At first it was because she'd hoped Axel would change his mind and stop the proceedings, that it would never go this far. And now that their divorce was almost a done deal, she was embarrassed to have failed. She didn't want to call herself his *ex*-wife. Considering how hard she'd tried to be the best mother and spouse she could, she'd never thought she'd be *anyone's* ex.

Somehow, she managed a smile and hoped it didn't appear as wobbly as it felt. "Yes." She had two more days before "yes" would be a lie, so she was going with it. "Someone's waiting for me. I'm afraid I have to go," she mumbled and cut through the crowd before the young woman who'd engaged her could say anything more.

Keeping her head down so that no one else could catch her eye, she hurried toward the safety of her Range Rover, and then on to the privacy of her sister's empty house. There, she wouldn't have to worry about prying questions, curious stares or the pitying smiles of those who'd already heard about the demise of her marriage. She could be *completely* alone.

But now that her sister's family and her own children were gone, she wasn't sure being alone felt any better, which was why she'd gone to the coffee shop in the first place.

* * *

You busy tonight? If not, can you come by the store? I
want you to try my new cookies. I think I'm really onto
something with this one.

Tobias smiled as he read that text from Maya. He'd
just pulled into his driveway and parked in front of his
house after spending the afternoon skating with quite
a few of the students at New Horizons. Although he
hadn't had much experience with ice-skating when he
was a kid—someone who'd grown up in sunny LA,
and as poor as he'd been, didn't have much opportunity
to get on the ice—he'd been a natural on rollerblades
and that skill had easily transferred over. He'd gotten
good enough that he wished he'd had the chance to play
hockey, or any other organized sport, when he was a
kid. Prison had taken such a huge chunk of his life.

But he couldn't feel sorry for himself. It was because
of him that Atticus hadn't had the chance to play sports,
either. Atticus couldn't ice-skate or do anything else
that required the use of his legs even *now*. Which was
the only reason Tobias wasn't already backing up to
go try those cookies at Sugar Mama. He was leery of
going anywhere near the cookie shop. He never knew
when he might run into Susan—Maya's grandmother
and Jada's mother—who owned the store. Susan hated
him so much she gave new meaning to the saying "If
looks could kill." One night back in August, she came
over to his house and physically attacked him. He deserved that and more—honestly, he didn't blame her
for her hurt and anger—but that didn't mean he was
going to put himself in a situation where she might go
off on him again.

While he was staring at his phone, trying to decide whether to take the risk for Maya's sake, Uriah knocked on his window.

Tobias jumped. He hadn't seen the old man coming. "Hey, what's up?" he asked after rolling down his window.

"Would you like to come in and have some dinner? Hazel Saunders brought over a delicious taco casserole an hour ago, and I've got it warming in the oven."

Tobias wasn't one to miss a home-cooked meal. After having a mother who rarely bothered to feed them, and then eating prison grub for thirteen years, there wasn't anything he enjoyed more. He was hungry, too. But when he saw movement from the corner of his eye, he realized Carl was standing in the shadows, looking on, and hesitated.

Uriah was just being nice, trying to include him. Tobias didn't want him acting out of obligation, though—not when he had the opportunity to enjoy a meal with his son after being estranged for so many years. Rebuilding that relationship took precedence over all else.

"I'd love to, but I've already got other plans," he said. "Maya's invented another cookie. She wants me to rush right over and give it a try."

Uriah's craggy face registered a hint of understanding, as though he knew Tobias was trying to make himself scarce. "You sure you won't have a quick bite before you go? There's plenty…"

"No, I'll grab something in town. Do you need groceries or anything else while I'm out?"

The orchard where they lived wasn't more than ten minutes from the store. It wasn't a big deal to make a supply run. But, as a matter of convenience, they often did this kind of favor for each other. "Gallon of milk would be good, if you happen to remember."

"You got it," Tobias said and pretended not to see Carl scowling at him from Uriah's porch as he backed down the drive.

After scouting out the alley behind Sugar Mama to be sure Susan's car wasn't there, Tobias parked down the street from the store, so that no one would see his truck directly in front of it. He was just getting out when he heard his phone ping. He'd gotten another text.

He assumed it was from Maya, that she was wondering if he was coming or not since he'd never replied to her first message. But when he dug his phone from his pocket, he could see that it was from a number he didn't recognize.

I shouldn't call him, right?

Call who? he wondered. Since there was no introduction, no preface to that one sentence, Tobias at first assumed it was a wrong number. He almost wrote back to say as much, but then he remembered giving his number to Harper Devlin this morning.

This couldn't be her, could it?

Who's 'him'? he texted back so he wouldn't have to ask, "Who's *this*?"

Axel.

He stiffened. Sure enough, it was Harper. She'd reached out to him. Instead of heading to the store, he leaned against his truck while he responded. You realize that by texting me, you've given me your number.

Yes, but you don't know where I'm staying. Anyway, you said you weren't dangerous.

Define *dangerous*.

Any kind of threat to my well-being.

Then I'm not dangerous.

There was a long pause before she wrote: Under what kind of definition would you be dangerous?

He chose not to answer that question. If he just wanted to be her friend, to provide a shoulder she could cry on, she didn't need to know he was a felon. You should definitely NOT call Axel.

No question? Your answer is an unequivocal no?

It's an unequivocal no. That's why I put the emphasis on *not*. ;-)

Explain to me why. I think that's what I need to hear.

You had to ask me, didn't you? That means you're fighting the urge, and if you're fighting the urge it's because you know better.

I just miss him so much...

Go spend some time with your kids and quit thinking about him. He'll either come back or he won't. Leave that up to him.

I'm pretty sure he's not coming back. The divorce will be final in two days. And he doesn't act like he cares at all.

Then it's his loss, Harper. Keep putting one foot in front of the other. You'll eventually recover and be just fine without him.

It doesn't feel like that's possible. Anyway, I can't spend time with my kids right now. They're in LA with my sister and her family.

Until when?

Next weekend.

So you're alone?

For the entire week.

You could get yourself into a lot of trouble in that much time. Why didn't you go with them?

I thought I wanted to be alone. I thought I needed some time to think. So did my sister.

But it's not helping?

This is only Day 1, and already I'm going crazy, teetering on the brink of caving and begging him to come back.

Tell me you're not drinking.

What does that have to do with anything?

If you're drinking, you will cave.

I'm not drinking. Although…I'm considering it. It would be a relief to climb inside a bottle. I don't want to feel this way anymore.

Then consider this: the only thing worse than breaking down and calling him when you know you shouldn't would be drunk calling him. And when you sober up? You'll just have to face what you did while you were drunk.

You're right. So…how do I stop myself?

He stared at her text for several seconds while considering his response. Get your mind on something else.

That's impossible. Have you ever been through a divorce?

No. Never been married.

Why not?

Because he'd been a kid when he went into prison, and he'd only been out for five months. Just haven't found the right girl, I guess.

What about your folks? Did they stay together?

They never got together.

Who raised you?

My mother. Sort of. I'm not sure you could call it "raising." My brother and I more or less raised ourselves.

And your father? He wasn't in the picture?

I don't even remember him.

I see. I'm sorry.

Don't be. This isn't about me.

You're the one who said to get my mind on something else. ;-)

I'm the distraction?

You did tell me you were a good listener.

That's true. How am I doing so far?

I haven't called Axel yet. I count that as a success. What do you do for a living?

I work at New Horizons. Maintenance, repair and grounds, he added so she wouldn't think he had some lofty job or the kind of education his brother, who'd recently become the principal of the new girls' side of the school, did. While he had no plans to give her the dirtier details of his life, he also wasn't out to make her think she'd found someone she might be interested in.

New Horizons is that correctional school not too far outside town, right? The one for troubled kids?

Did he tell her *he'd* been one of those kids? That he'd wound up in a much worse place than a correctional school?

No. This wasn't about him. This was about her—about helping her get through this rough patch in her life. *He* could be anyone. Most are good kids who are just a little turned around at the moment.

He happened to glance up while waiting to see if she'd continue the conversation and froze. Atticus was rolling down the sidewalk toward him.

"Shoot," he muttered under his breath. He often wondered if it was as hard for Atticus to see him as it was for him to see Atticus. If it was, Jada's brother never gave any indication.

Shoving his phone back in his pocket, Tobias pushed away from the truck. "Hey, man. You're looking good."

"Gotta please the ladies," Atticus joked as they exchanged their usual hand slap, fist bump, half hug.

"You got your eye on someone special these days?"

"No. Too hard to narrow it down," he joked.

"The women of Silver Springs had better watch out." Tobias laughed, but this subject made him even more uncomfortable than simply encountering Atticus in his wheelchair. He didn't know if he'd robbed Atticus of a sex life when he'd robbed him of the ability to walk—and absolutely cringed at the thought that maybe he had.

If only he could take back what he'd done that night…

But he couldn't. He had to live with it. And that was the greatest punishment there was, far worse than prison. "Did you just leave the store?"

"Yeah. Maya texted me. Wanted me to come down and try her new cookie."

"Well? What's the verdict?"

"This one's pretty damn good."

"Must be if your mother's letting her sell it in the store."

"Yeah. It's been selling so well my mom's thinking about offering it through the holidays, and Maya earns fifty cents toward her college fund for every cookie sold."

"That's pretty cool of Susan."

"She's not *all* bad," he said wryly.

Atticus knew how Susan felt about Tobias. Most of the town did. Susan would barely speak to Jada since her daughter had married Maddox. She blamed Maddox almost as much as she blamed Tobias for what had happened to Atticus, since it was Maddox who'd taken Jada and Atticus to the party that fateful night.

"She's not bad at all," Tobias said. "I know that."

"Sure you do," he teased. "Anyway, it was Maya's idea to add ice-cream cookies to the menu last summer, and the store's been doing much better since then. I think my mom feels she owes Maya a little something."

"I'm glad business is picking up," Tobias said and meant it. Since nothing could compensate the Brookses for what they'd lost, he couldn't wish enough good things to happen for Jada and her family.

Tobias looked down the street, checking to see if

anyone was standing near the entrance to the store. "Susan doesn't happen to be in there right now, does she?" he asked, lowering his voice.

Atticus clearly found the question funny. "No, the coast is clear."

Tobias wiped his forehead as though he was wiping away sweat. "Good to know, man. Thanks."

"No problem." Atticus started to wheel himself away but turned back before Tobias could get too far. "Hey, I'm going to the Blue Suede Shoe. You should come down afterward. We'll have a drink and play a quick game of darts."

"You're on. I'll see you there," he said and headed to the store.

As he drew closer, he thought of Harper and the conversation he'd abandoned, but he didn't pull out his phone. He wanted to get in and out of Sugar Mama while Susan was gone.

"I hear there's a new cookie in this place that's pretty darn good," he called out as he strode through the door.

Maya appeared to be running the store by herself. She did that for brief periods of time, if her grandmother or Pamela Kent—the woman who helped Susan with the store—had to run an errand. But Tobias knew Maya wouldn't be alone for long, not at only thirteen, so he didn't plan on staying more than a few minutes.

"Uncle Tobias!" She hurried out from behind the counter to give him a big hug.

"Atticus says your cookies are selling like crazy, Squirt."

"Well, not like *crazy*. But they're doing pretty good. It didn't hurt that Daddy bought three dozen to take to the faculty meeting at school yesterday," she added with an impish grin.

Tobias had watched how quickly and effortlessly Maya and Maddox had grown close and wondered how Susan felt about having the son-in-law she didn't approve of turn out to be such a good father. "Word will spread. Soon it'll be the bestselling cookie in the store."

"I don't want that," she said, tempering her excitement. "That might make Grandma feel bad." She hurried back around the counter. "But here, taste one." She took the lid off the tray of samples and held it out.

He selected a small piece of a chocolate-chip cookie that had an abundance of gooey slices of various candy bars on top, some with caramel and peanuts and others with toffee.

"I call it the Outrageous," she said as he chewed and swallowed.

"Wow. It's *delicious*."

Her expression grew earnest. "Really? You like it? You're not just saying that to be nice?"

He gave her a wry grin. "When have I ever been nice?"

"You're *always* nice. You might look tough with all those muscles, but…"

"I'm not?" he said with a laugh.

"You're tough but nice, too!"

"Well, don't tell anyone. I can't have you spreading rumors like that."

She rolled her eyes. "I can't believe everyone can't see it."

Her grandmother didn't think he had one single redeeming quality. And because of what he'd done, he tended to believe Susan over others. He knew he always would. "How many of these incredible cookies do you have left?" he asked.

"In this batch? Only twelve." She motioned to the tray behind the glass. "But I'll bake more in the morning."

"Well, I shouldn't take them all. Then you won't have any to sell for the rest of the day, and we need to have as many people try them as possible. So…give me six."

Her face lit up. "Are you sure? You like them that much?"

He would've bought that many even if they tasted like dirt, but fortunately, he did like them. "You've got a winner without question. And I bet they taste even better as an ice-cream sandwich."

"They do! Should I make you one?"

"Not right now." He didn't want to take the time. "Atticus is waiting for me down at the Blue Suede Shoe. He's looking to beat me at darts again."

She laughed because Atticus beat everyone at darts. "Just don't put as much money on it as you did last time," she advised sagely.

"Come on. Have some faith in me," he said, but he knew that if he ever started to win he'd purposely lose.

She rang him up but didn't hand him the bag. "Before you go, there's something I've been meaning to tell you. But I don't want it to make you feel bad," she added.

Tobias had just dug his keys from his pocket. "What's wrong? This doesn't have anything to do with your grandmother, does it?" He was afraid Susan had told Maya he wasn't allowed in the store, or she wouldn't be allowed to help in the store if she continued to associate with him.

"No, it's nothing to do with Grandma. It's about Uncle Atticus."

She knew how Atticus had lost the use of his legs, so the way she was approaching this subject made him uneasy. "What about him?"

She nibbled nervously on her bottom lip. "It's one of those things that maybe I shouldn't talk about, but I want to fix, so I think it might be good to tell you. You know what I mean?"

"No. I'm completely lost here. Can you help me out by explaining a little more clearly what's going on?"

She blew out a sigh. "Will you promise you won't feel like you *have* to do it? Because it's just an idea…"

"I'm open to all your ideas, and I'll take it as well as I can. How's that?"

"Actually…maybe I shouldn't say anything." She shifted from foot to foot, wringing her hands. "My mom told me not to."

"Maya, there's obviously something troubling you. Tell me what it is."

"It's nothing *big*. It's just… Well, Atticus saw this video, and I could tell it got him really excited, because he kept watching it over and over. And…you're so big and strong. And you go all the time."

"It's not getting any clearer," he said. "*Where* do I go all the time?"

"Hiking!"

"That's what the video was about?"

"Yes. It was of a man carrying his friend, who was like Atticus, on his back when he went hiking."

"Because…"

"Because the disabled guy wanted to go but he

couldn't walk!" she said with some exasperation, as if that should have been obvious.

Finally catching on to where she was going with this, Tobias felt his pulse speed up. "An able-bodied man carried a disabled man because it was the only way he could experience it, too."

"Yeah. And I thought…" She gave him a sheepish look.

"You thought I could do that for Atticus."

She nodded. "For his birthday this summer. I bet he'd love to see Yosemite. Mom and Dad took me there for my birthday, and I told him how beautiful it was, and I showed him pictures and stuff, but he didn't get to be there with us and see it like I did, because there are so many places he couldn't go."

Tobias wasn't sure how to respond. It wasn't as though he was *unwilling* to do something like that. He would do anything to give Atticus a fuller life. But was he physically capable of carrying another man *while hiking Yosemite*? Most of the hikes in the park weren't easy even without that much weight on his back.

"How did he carry the other man?" he asked. "I mean, other than being strong. What'd he put him in? Some kind of backpack contraption?"

"That's what it looked like. Sort of like those things parents use to carry children on their backs."

Children were small, probably not more than fifty to seventy-five pounds. Atticus wasn't large as men went, but he had to be close to a hundred and fifty pounds.

Still, he'd once read that military personnel carried as much as a hundred and thirty pounds of gear into battle. If he planned well and took frequent rests it *could* be possible…

"We'd have to find one that would be comfortable," he said, thinking aloud. "And I'd have to train. A lot. Put on a heavier and heavier pack until I build up my stamina."

"I bet you could do it," she said, her face flushed with excitement.

Tobias felt it would be wise to temper that excitement. "Even if I could, I'm not convinced he'd be willing to try it, Maya. It's one thing to experience a hike and another to feel so dependent. Atticus is good at taking care of himself. He might have a problem with letting another man haul him around. Especially me."

"No, he likes you," she said somberly. "A lot. I bet he'd be grateful."

Was that true? Was it something Atticus would truly want and enjoy?

If so, Tobias would like to give it to him. But he'd have to test it first. Make sure he was capable before he made the offer. Even if he felt confident he could do it, he had no idea how to suggest it to Atticus. *Hey, I'd like to take you on one of the greatest hikes of all time—and you'd want to go with me, right? After all, I'm only the guy who shot you.*

That should go over well, especially with Susan if she caught wind of it. And what if he fell and hurt Atticus again?

That frightened Tobias more than any other part...

"What do you think?" Maya asked, her eyes round and hopeful.

"I think you have a heart of gold, little girl. But don't mention this to anyone else, okay? Let me mull it over for a while first."

She nodded right away. "Okay."

"Promise?"

"I promise," she said, crossing her heart.

"Good." He took the cookies and got out of the store as soon as possible—but not because he was afraid Susan would show up. At that point, he wasn't even thinking about Susan. He didn't want his niece to know how deeply her suggestion had affected him. Just imagining himself carrying Atticus up a mountain like Half Dome—showing him what Tobias considered to be one of the most beautiful places on earth, especially on Atticus's birthday—brought a huge lump to his throat.

He knew it would be more about the spiritual journey than the physical one.

5

I have cookies.

It had been a while since Tobias had responded. Harper had asked him where he'd grown up and had never gotten an answer, so she'd thought he'd lost interest in the conversation. She wouldn't have blamed him if he had. In her current situation, she wasn't very entertaining. She was, however, grateful to have someone new in her life who was willing to offer a bit of encouragement and advice—without pressing her for all the dirty details of her divorce. Before her sister had left for LA, Karoline had told her to be careful of the guy who'd given her the flower, that if he popped up again he might turn out to be a reporter looking for the inside scoop. But Tobias hadn't even asked her why she and Axel had split up. He didn't seem particularly interested in Axel, which was shocking. *Everyone* was interested in Axel. Harper was so used to taking a back seat to her famous husband that it felt great to have someone seek *her* friendship.

The kind you eat? she wrote, trying to understand this random text from him.

Yup. Fresh baked. Chocolate chip topped with candy bars.

Feeling slightly better to have heard from him again, she sniffed as she curled her bare feet underneath her on the couch, where she'd been letting herself cry while watching old movies. Since the kids weren't here, she had no reason to hold back, figuring she'd better get it all out while they were gone. Tempting...

They may not be healthy, but they won't impair your judgment. :) You haven't broken down and called Axel, have you?

She dashed a hand across her cheeks before responding. Not yet.

Good. Make him come to you.

She smiled despite her tears. It was comments like this that made her trust Tobias, to a degree. So is a cookie my reward?

If you'll tell me where you're staying, I can bring it to you. Or you could come to my place. My landlord and his son are on the property, so you don't have to worry about being alone with a stranger.

She thought of the security system her sister had recently purchased for the house. Karoline and Terrance could see anyone who came to their door via an app on their smartphones. She couldn't let Tobias come over, not unless she wanted her sister and brother-in-law to know he was there. Where do you live?

Honey Hollow Tangerine Orchard—about ten minutes outside town.

Are you there now?

I am. Come over whenever you'd like.

Should she do it?

Why not? If she didn't, she'd just continue to mope and think about the disaster her marriage had become. Hanging out with a new friend had to be better than wallowing in self-pity.

Are you hungry? I could bring a pizza or Chinese takeout, she wrote.

Chinese sounds good.

She asked what kind of Chinese food he liked and ordered it before going to wash her face and change her clothes. She was almost ready to leave when her phone rang. For the first time in ages, she wasn't hoping and praying it was Axel.

She considered that a small victory right there.

It wasn't Axel, anyway; it was her sister.

"Are you okay?" Karoline asked as soon as she answered.

"I'm fine. You guys having fun?"

"We got a hotel with an indoor pool. We're about to head down and enjoy the water."

"Sounds great." Harper considered telling her sister

that she was going to have dinner with the guy who'd given her the rose but decided not to. It was no big deal—so why mention it? "I think I'll do some Christmas shopping while you're gone."

"That's a good idea. Remember, just because changes are difficult in the beginning doesn't mean they won't turn out to be the best thing in the end. As much as you love Axel, if he can't love you back enough to focus on you and fulfill you, what have you really got? I watched you try to keep him steady and happy for so long. I bet one day you'll be relieved that his mood swings are no longer your problem."

"It wasn't like that in the beginning," Harper said.

"He's *always* been sensitive, temperamental and high-strung."

"As well as larger-than-life, ultra-creative, dynamic and just plain fun."

"I'm not saying he's *all* bad. Until he broke your heart, I liked him a lot. But look at how he made you feel when you were around him—as though his happiness was somehow your responsibility. As far as I'm concerned, he sucked up all the sunlight and left you to try to flourish with what was left."

"He didn't *intend* to do that," Harper argued.

"Doesn't matter. That was the reality."

She drew a deep breath. "Maybe that's true, to a point."

"It is. One day you'll see it, too."

"I hope so. Anyway, give the girls my love."

"I will."

Once they disconnected, Harper stared at herself in the mirror. "Is she right?" she asked her troubled reflection. "Will you be better-off without him?"

Although it was tough to see that now, she had to admit Axel hadn't made her feel very good about herself during the past few years. He blamed her for everything that disappointed or annoyed him. She'd ascribed the difficulties they'd faced to the stress of his career and his high-strung temperament. Challenges were to be expected. But it was more than that. He pointed out the negatives in *any* situation—and in her.

Trying to fulfill someone like that was exhausting, because there were negatives in *every* situation. She could never compensate for them all, could never be perfect enough.

Maybe, once her heart healed, she *would* be happier on her own.

Tobias Richardson had the door cracked open when she arrived, and she could hear music coming from inside.

OneRepublic. Thank God it wasn't anything by Pulse.

"Hello?" Harper knocked on the doorframe so she wouldn't inadvertently push the door open before he was ready. She'd already seen an older gentleman, who she figured must be his landlord. Not entirely sure where to go, she'd pulled onto the property and stopped, and he'd come outside. But before he could actually approach her car, she'd noticed the smaller house behind his and realized that had to be where Tobias lived. After all, Tobias had texted her, It's the second house. So she'd just waved to let the old man know she was fine, and he did the same as she rolled by.

"Hello?" she said again when Tobias didn't answer.

She'd knocked timidly the first time, so it was possible he hadn't heard her.

She glanced at what she guessed was his truck—an older Ford parked to one side. Her car was behind his, and for a brief second, she was tempted to get back into it. Visiting him at his house suddenly seemed more intimate than she'd imagined, especially when he finally appeared and she could see that he'd just stepped out of the shower. He'd pulled on a pair of faded jeans, but he was toweling off his hair and hadn't yet put on a shirt.

Axel was so thin he was downright skinny, his entire chest and arms were covered in tattoos and he wore his hair long. He looked like what he was—the quintessential rocker. Tobias, on the other hand, didn't look like that at all. He had long hair, too, and a couple of tattoos, but he was quite a bit taller than Axel, had broader shoulders and a more athletic build.

"Come in." He gestured at the table as an invitation to put down the food. "I'll be with you in a sec. Just need to grab a shirt."

As he disappeared into the bedroom, she breathed a sigh of relief that he would soon be fully clothed. She'd certainly seen other shirtless men in her life. It shouldn't have made her feel awkward. But her new friend was particularly attractive, and that somehow changed things.

"Something wrong?" he asked when he returned to find her still standing in the entryway, holding the food.

She cleared her throat. She was already here; it would be stupid to leave, especially because she could tell he hadn't thought twice about letting her in before finding a shirt. Even what he'd chosen to wear—an old T-shirt and jeans—suggested he wasn't *trying* to impress her.

"No, nothing," she said and put the food on the table.

"Can I get you a drink? A beer or…" He checked his fridge. "A beer?"

She laughed. "A beer would be perfect."

"Great. I happen to have plenty."

As he got out the beer and pulled the food containers and chopsticks from the sack, she walked around his living room. He didn't have many furnishings, nothing beyond the basics. His most prized possessions seemed to be a mountain bike and a fancy backpack he had stashed in one corner. "You mountain bike?"

He looked up. "Whenever I get the chance."

"You hike, too, I see."

"I do."

Returning to the table, she watched as he got two plates from the cupboard. "You told me you've only lived here for five months. What first brought you to the area? Your job?"

"No, my brother's here."

In one of his texts, he'd indicated that he and his brother had basically raised themselves. "How old is he?"

"Maddox? Not quite a year older."

"And you two are close?"

"Always have been." After opening the food boxes, he held up the chopsticks. "Should we use forks instead?"

"I could show you how to use the chopsticks, if you'd like to give them a try."

He considered her for a second. "Okay. Why not?" he said with a shrug.

She broke apart a set of chopsticks and positioned them in her right hand, showing him how easy it was to manipulate them if he held them correctly. "Now you try."

He seemed to handle them okay, but he put a couple of forks on the table just in case.

"Where did you grow up?" she asked after they'd both sat down and he'd waited for her to dish up some honey-walnut shrimp, pork fried rice, chow mein and cashew chicken.

"LA," he replied as he got his own food. "You?"

"Boise."

"Axel went to school at Boise State, if I remember right. Is that where you met him?"

"Yeah. He's from Denver, but his brother, Rowen, played football for Boise State, so he wanted to go to school there. They roomed together Rowen's senior year."

"Is that when he started Pulse—while he was in college? Or did he know his bandmates before that?"

"He grew up with one of them. The other two he met at Boise State. That's when they started playing in earnest." She didn't mention it, but she also sang. That was how she'd first met Axel—at a Battle of the Bands event in Boise. She'd been a backup singer for a competing band, a band she'd thought was good. But when she'd watched Pulse perform, she'd known they were better. And the panel of judges had agreed. Pulse had won the contest.

Tobias managed to bring some rice to his mouth

using his chopsticks, which was impressive, given that rice was one of the hardest foods to eat that way.

"Nice job," she said.

He grinned. "Thanks. Now that I've learned how, I'm going to eat everything with chopsticks, even soup. Why wash silverware?"

She rolled her eyes. "Bachelors…"

He showed off by taking another bite with his chopsticks. But when he used them to flip one of the shrimp into the air and catch it in his mouth, she grew suspicious. "Wait a second…you can't be *that* good already."

"Okay, so maybe I've done this before," he said with a wink.

"Why did you pretend you hadn't?"

He spread his arms in an apparent attempt to make himself look more innocent. "I didn't want to put any pressure on you, in case *you* didn't know how."

"I'm better with chopsticks than you are!" she said.

He arched his eyebrows. "Prove it."

"Fine." She used hers to flip a shrimp in the air but it fell onto the table since she couldn't quite catch it with her mouth. "Dang!"

"You've almost got it," he said. "Here, I'll toss you one so all you have to do is concentrate on catching it. That might be where you're weak."

When she missed for the second time, he tsked as he shook his head. "*Not* as good as me, I'm afraid."

She pretended outrage. "Try it one more time." She opened her mouth, but instead of tossing the shrimp, he stuck it right inside. "There you go. But I'll expect to see some improvement the next time we have dinner together."

"Who said there'll be a next time?" she asked.

He didn't seem worried. He just flipped another shrimp into his mouth. "There will be a next time. No one else has my skill with chopsticks." He leaned forward, chewing as though it tasted much better eating it the way he was. "And I'm the only friend you've got here. Right?"

She glowered at him. "I could make other friends. Easily. I'm a likable person."

"You're on the rebound. It'll be *much* safer if you hang out with me."

The twinkle in his eyes told her he was joking again, but she was curious to hear his rationale. "Because…"

"Because I'm probably the only guy in town who wouldn't take you to bed even if you begged me to."

"You don't want to sleep with me?" she said, somewhat shocked that he'd be bold enough to state that right up front. She was also a little curious. He'd told her she was beautiful. Didn't that mean he found her sexually attractive, too?

"I wouldn't say that," he said.

A picture of his bare chest flashed through her mind, and she felt something she hadn't felt in a long time—a zing of sexual awareness. "You're saying you wouldn't even if you wanted to."

He didn't answer. He took a drink of his beer and changed the subject. "It's crazy how successful Axel's been. What was it like to be part of all that?"

She wanted an answer to her own question, but she knew it was best to let it go. She was still in love with Axel, wasn't interested in other men—even men as attractive as her new friend. "You mean when he hit the big time? A lot of work."

He moved his chopsticks in a circular motion as if to state, *Yeah, yeah. That's what they all say.*

"Other than that," he managed when he'd swallowed.

Everyone imagined fame and fortune as the be-all and end-all, that life would be easy from then on. But it was more like those stories she'd read about people who won the lottery. They weren't always happier afterward. As a matter of fact, she'd been happier before Pulse had become so popular. "Exciting. Exhilarating." She drew a deep breath. "And challenging, because it introduces entirely new pressures."

"Like…"

"It's difficult to explain, but it's *so* hard not to get lost in it."

"I don't think I'd like it," he said simply.

Didn't most people want to be rich and famous—or at least believe they did? "Why not?"

"The lack of freedom," he replied without hesitation.

"What do you mean? More money equals more freedom, doesn't it?"

His chewing slowed. "I wouldn't mind being rich. But famous? I would feel like my life was no longer my own. So if the two have to go together, I'd say no to both. Freedom is what matters most to me. I'd rather be poor than lose that."

She quit eating as she considered his answer. "Things *definitely* got a little out of control. I never felt I could ask my husband to stay home and watch the girls so I could run to the store. His time was suddenly too valuable, you know? He'd get upset when I complained and would tell me I could hire someone if I needed help, but it wasn't the same. I didn't want to be surrounded by hired assistants. I just wanted to have a normal family life." She stabbed her chopsticks into her chow mein several times without picking up any food. "I also wanted another baby, but he wasn't interested. He said it was hard enough feeling guilty about not being able to do things with the kids we did have."

"His focus changed."

"No question. And the weird part is…I can't even blame him. He's extremely talented. He *should* be making music. But it wasn't fun to feel like excess baggage he'd rather dump."

"So you left him?"

"No, the divorce was his idea. As imperfect as it was, I was willing to tolerate the situation for the sake of my marriage and my girls."

"Well, this might not be what you want to hear, but have you ever considered that maybe he did you a favor?"

"My sister's tried to tell me that. Just tonight, as a matter of fact."

"It could be like open-heart surgery. Doesn't feel good. Isn't anything you'd ask for if you could avoid it. But if you need the operation, it could save your life."

She smiled. "It's hard to have that kind of perspective now, but…we'll see."

"Well, in case you're still tempted to call him, I have something planned to keep you busy."

"What's that?"

"We're going ice-skating."

She shook her head. "Oh, no, we're not. I'd rather not be out in public. People would take one look at us and assume we're on a date."

"You won't be out in public. It'll be just the two of us."

"How can you arrange that?" she asked skeptically.

"I have my own rink."

She narrowed her eyes. "Where? It's not cold enough in this part of the state."

"It's an indoor rink, and it's not actually mine. It's at the school where I work. But I have the keys to all the facilities, and I have permission to use them whenever I want."

"Okay. But we still have one problem left."

"And that is…"

"I don't know how to skate."

"No worries. I'll teach you." He got up, scooped his keys off the counter and lifted them for her to see. "You interested? It's nearly Christmas, after all. Isn't ice-skating something people like to do at Christmastime?"

She didn't care much about Christmas this year, simply hadn't caught the spirit. But when she thought of what the rest of her night would be like if she *didn't* go with him, she stood up and started putting away the food. "Why not?"

6

It'd been a long time since Tobias had felt the "magic" of Christmas. His mother had never had a lot of money, but when she wasn't spending everything she did have on drugs or alcohol, she'd tried to make the holidays special. As a kid, he'd loved December. Some years, it was the only time he got new clothes, which he always needed because he grew so fast.

Once he went to prison, however, December became the hardest month of the year. The days were shorter and the nights longer, the weather was cold and dreary, and not being able to spend Christmas with Maddox and his mother had made him feel as though his sentence would last forever. Inmates were served a better meal on the twenty-fifth—ham, corn, a Jell-O salad, a dinner roll and scalloped potatoes, with a piece of pie for dessert—but it was still cafeteria food, which was never good to begin with. And there were no gifts, nothing like that.

Actually, there *were* gifts—just not the kind he cared to remember. His first year behind bars, he'd come back from the mess hall to find a bag of candy on his bed. As inconsequential as that might sound to someone on the outside, he'd been barely more than a kid at the time and in prison everything was bartered like money, even candy. Problem was, he couldn't accept it. His cellmate warned him that doing so would commit him to the guy who'd left it. He'd returned it right away and, about a week later, he'd been cornered and severely beaten.

He'd had to fight *a lot* until he established himself as someone who wouldn't tolerate being victimized. He was never sexually assaulted, as he'd feared he would be for the first few years, but rebuffing the men who made advances had nearly cost him a kidney once.

He tried not to dwell on those times. If he did think of the Christmases he'd spent in the belly of the beast, he focused on the extra money his brother always put on his books. That made January more tolerable since he could buy a few extras from the commissary.

Still, for thirteen years, he'd dreaded Christmas. So ice-skating with Harper while Pentatonix sang "Mary, Did You Know?" on the sound system was like something out of a movie for him. He doubted she'd be here with him if she knew what he'd done and that he'd only gotten out of prison five months ago, but he pushed that out of his mind. He wasn't going to ruin this one night. He was going to forget that terrible incident at the party and what had happened to him and Atticus as a result and pretend to be what she thought he was—just a normal guy teaching her how to ice-skate.

"You're doing great," he said as he bent to retie the laces that had come loose on her right skate.

"What are you talking about?" She rested her hands on his shoulders so she wouldn't fall. "You've literally been holding me up. I never realized ice-skating was so hard. Hockey players and figure skaters make it look almost effortless."

"It takes some getting used to, that's all."

"If I fall, I'm afraid I'm going to pull you down with me."

"I won't let you fall." Harper's cheeks were rosy and her breath misted slightly in the air as he stood and took her hands again. "Are you warm enough to keep going?" he asked.

Her gaze flew to his face. "Don't tell me you're tired already."

"Just making sure you aren't freezing to death."

"No, I'm enjoying this. I feel—I feel happy, almost like a kid again."

"Then we'll keep going." He smiled and felt his chest tighten a little when she smiled back at him. How had Axel Devlin ever let her go? Tobias couldn't imagine *any* man doing that, but he was glad he'd brought her to the rink. They'd been laughing and talking since they'd gotten here. She couldn't have had much time to worry about her divorce.

"You're going to owe me some hot chocolate after this," she said, blowing rings into the air while he guided her carefully across the ice.

He gave her a challenging look. "I thought you didn't want to go out in public with me."

"I don't. But hot chocolate isn't hard to make. Can't we do it at your place?"

Surprised that she planned to go back to his house, he shrugged. "Sure. Why not? We'll have to stop by the store first, though. I don't keep hot chocolate on hand."

"You've probably never had anyone else ask for it."

"Can't say I have. But now that I know you like it, I'll have some in the cupboard while you're in town."

She wobbled and nearly fell, but he lifted her back on her skates before she could hit the ice.

"Why are you being so nice to me?" she asked, suddenly much more intense as she looked up at him.

"I know what it feels like to need a friend."

She fell silent, but she didn't look away.

"What?" he asked.

"What if…"

"Go on…"

"What if I don't go back to my sister's this week?"

"Don't tell me you're considering tracking Axel down, wherever he's at!"

"No, I'm thinking that maybe, if you don't mind, I'll just stay with you."

When he coughed in surprise, they *both* nearly fell. That was the last thing he'd expected her to say. She'd been so careful to make sure he understood she wasn't open to a relationship. "Why would you do that?" he asked once he'd caught his balance and steadied her, too.

"Because I want to live a little. I married young and became a mother only a year later. I've carried the bulk of the responsibility for my children and everything else that wasn't strictly music related ever since. And you make me feel good. I like being around you. Do I have to have a reason beyond that?"

He brought them to a stop and gripped her shoulders instead of her hands. "Harper, you have to be careful."

"Of what?"

"It would be easy to think…" He scrambled for the right words. "To think you feel more for me than you do, I guess. That's why rebound relationships are so common after a big breakup. But what you're feeling isn't real—it's just some psychological construct that kicks in when you suddenly find yourself at loose ends after being in a close relationship. It's natural to try to avoid feeling the loss."

"It might not be *real*, but it's a relief. So am I a bad person for wanting to roll with it? I'm tired of feeling awful!"

"I understand that, but we can't hang out if it's going to get confusing for you."

"I'm not going to get confused."

"But I'm trying to help you, not make matters worse. Getting involved with me would be… Would be totally reckless."

"So? Why can't *I* be reckless for a change? Have a fling with a sexy stranger while my kids are gone? I'm sure Axel isn't denying himself for *my* sake."

Tobias had been in prison throughout most of his sexual prime. A very raw and powerful lust welled up at the possibility of sleeping with Harper for an entire week. He'd been attracted to her from the very beginning, and that attraction was only growing stronger the more time they spent together. But they couldn't cross the boundaries they'd already established. She didn't really know who he was—or what he'd done. And when their affair ended, he didn't want her to walk away and leave him as devastated as *she'd* been when she arrived in Silver Springs. He was trying hard to protect himself from anything that could throw him off course, and he had a feeling Harper could do significant damage. "We shouldn't," he insisted.

She lowered her voice. "You're saying you don't want me to stay…"

"No, that's not what I'm saying."

"Then you have a girlfriend or…or a wife you haven't told me about."

"No, there's no one else."

"Then what do we have to lose?"

He could lose everything—what small amount of control he'd gained over his life in the past five months. But he didn't have the heart to say no. He could see why she might want to change things. From what he'd learned about her so far, she'd always been the "good girl." He couldn't blame her for being tired of it. "You can stay for a few days, if you want," he relented. "But I'll sleep on the couch."

"It's not fair to put you out of your own bed," she protested. "*I'll* sleep on the couch. I just need a change of pace, to not feel bound by rules. Following them hasn't gotten me anywhere, anyway."

When he'd given her that rose and then his number, he'd never dreamed it would result in having a roommate, even for a few days. He told himself she'd come to her senses eventually. But they skated for another hour, then stopped at a grocery store for cocoa mix and went home. After they'd had hot chocolate, she still didn't change her mind. She had him follow her to her sister's house so she could get her toothbrush and a few other things. And to avoid the camera, so her sister wouldn't know she wasn't going to be home, she climbed out a back window and ran down the street a few blocks to where she'd asked him to wait in his truck.

"I can't believe I'm doing this," she said, breathless, as she climbed in.

He'd been thinking about trying, once again, to talk her out of it, but she seemed so relieved and happy he decided he could figure out a way to keep them both out of trouble.

All he had to do was make sure things didn't go too far.

Harper had never done anything this out of character. Once she'd convinced Tobias to keep his own room and he'd gone to bed, she lay awake, staring at the ceiling in his small living room and thinking about how impetuous she'd been to even suggest she spend the week with a man she barely knew.

But, strangely enough, she felt safe around Tobias, comfortable. He seemed to understand grief and how hard it was to recover from the blow she'd sustained. And when she imagined what it would be like in her sister's big house at this moment—with everyone gone and the rest of the night yawning before her—she was glad for the change of scenery and situation.

She certainly wasn't tempted to call Axel while she was here, so there was that, too.

Burrowing deeper into the comforter Tobias had taken off his bed, she breathed in the scent of his cologne and decided that, crazy as it seemed, she'd made the right decision. She felt better than she had in ages. But he was right. It would be a mistake to sleep together. She had too much responsibility to be that impulsive.

Kicking off the covers, she got up to dig her phone out of her purse and turn it to Vibrate. She didn't want the ring to wake him if her sister or her girls called early in the morning.

She was just putting her cell on the coffee table when she noticed the wallpaper on her phone and pulled it back to take a closer look. Behind the apps was a photo of her and Axel from their college days, when they were still dating. Because it had been so rainy and muddy that night, he was carrying her on his back and both of them were wet and laughing. The friend who'd snapped it had just sent it to her a few months ago, and since it represented the foundation on which she'd built her life—what she'd been trying so hard to save—she'd set it as her background picture, as if her stubborn denial could change reality.

Navigating to her photo albums, she scrolled through the photos she had saved until she came up with one of her and the girls alone—which wasn't hard to find because Axel had been gone so much the past few years—and set that as her background instead.

She couldn't help feeling a tremendous sense of loss as Axel's smiling face disappeared from her screen. He was also disappearing from her life, and he was taking a very important part of her with him.

But she had no choice—she had to let him go.

"You okay out there?" Tobias called.

He'd obviously heard her moving around.

Swallowing the lump in her throat, she locked her phone and curled back into the bedding he'd provided. "Better than I'd be anywhere else. Thank you."

Some kind of outburst yanked Tobias from a deep sleep. When he first opened his eyes, he blinked at the darkness, trying to make sense of what he'd heard. He thought it was just another nightmare. Although he'd never mentioned it to anyone, not even Maddox, occasionally he dreamed that he was back in prison and was once again forced to fight for his life. There'd been one inmate in particular who'd given him trouble for the first three years. It was that guy—Rocco Stefani—who'd come after Tobias with a shiv. By some miracle, Tobias had managed to wrench it away and turn it on *him*, and he'd done enough damage that they'd carried Rocco off to the infirmary for two weeks.

Rocco was no threat to him after that, but they were both given another three years for the incident.

"Tobias?"

The uncertainty in the female voice calling out to him suddenly reminded him of where he was. *Not* in Soledad. Prison was behind him now. He was renting a small house in an orchard outside Silver Springs—and he had rock star Axel Devlin's soon-to-be ex-wife sleeping on his couch.

He heard the sound that had awakened him again—loud screaming and cursing. It was Uriah and Carl.

"Son of a bitch!" he yelled and jumped out of bed.

"What is it?" Harper asked, her voice filled with fear. "What's going on?"

"Stay here and lock the door after I leave. Sounds like my landlord's having a fight with his prick of a son." He shoved his legs into the jeans he'd taken off only a few hours ago but didn't bother to fasten them before he ran, barefoot, to the front house.

The light was on, but he couldn't hear any more screaming. It was a miracle he'd heard it the first time. It wasn't as if this was summer. Since the weather had turned cold, he'd been forced to sleep with his windows closed. Uriah and Carl must've been screaming outside at some point.

"Uriah?" he called, flinging open the back door and hurrying into the kitchen without even knocking.

There was no answer. He heard a door slam, so he started toward the living room, but Uriah suddenly blocked his path, hands lifted as though he wanted Tobias to remain calm. "It's okay, Tobias. Everything's okay."

Tobias tried to look around the old man to find Carl. "What's happening? What's going on?"

"Nothing that… Nothing I can't handle," he said, but his face was white as a sheet, and Tobias could see blood trickling down from the corner of his mouth.

"Did he *hit* you?" he asked, immediately enraged.

"No, I tripped and fell into the doorframe."

"But it was because of him, right?"

Uriah's gnarled hand was shaking as he wiped the blood from his mouth. "He has…emotional issues. He's not normal."

"That's what I'm worried about." Tobias tried to get through to the living room, but Uriah caught him by the arm.

"Please, let's not make it worse."

"Make *what* worse?"

Outside, Tobias heard an engine rumble to life. He slipped away from Uriah so he could get to the front door, but by the time he reached the porch, Carl was backing down the driveway like a maniac. He nearly got into an accident with another vehicle as he pulled onto the highway.

"Where's he going?" Tobias asked.

Carl's tires squealed and then his headlights swung into the road.

With a sigh, Uriah sank into his recliner and shook his head. "I don't know. I'm just glad he's gone."

"Do you want me to go after him? Bring his ass back here to take responsibility for whatever he's done?"

Uriah covered his eyes with one hand and didn't answer.

"Uriah?"

"No. It won't do any good. Nothing ever changes. He's been like this since he was a boy."

Tobias had so much adrenaline pouring through him he wanted to chase Carl down. "What set him off?"

"He's got an old friend who lives in town. Derrick Jessup. Derrick was a terrible influence. He was trouble then, and he's trouble now. Still lives at home. Rarely has a job. Anyway, before we went to bed, Derrick called and wanted Carl to meet him at a bar. Carl asked for money, and I wouldn't give it to him."

"And then…"

"And then I caught him going through my wallet while I was sleeping and tried to stop him." His bushy eyebrows drew together in a show of his typical stubbornness. "I won't allow him to steal from me."

"So he hit you?"

"No. He started yelling and screaming and throwing things. I was trying to get him to stop when I tripped."

"Did he at least help you up?"

"When he saw the blood, he just took off."

Tobias walked out onto the porch, listening to find out if Carl had doubled back. When all remained quiet, he came back in, closed the door and locked it. "Did he take his stuff? Is he gone for good?"

"His stuff is still here."

"Which means he's probably coming back. Can I gather it up and leave it on the porch for him?"

"He doesn't have anywhere else to go, Tobias. He's lost another job, been evicted from his apartment."

"But it isn't safe to have him here. He isn't stable. Who knows what he might do."

"He's my *son*," Uriah said simply.

Tobias wanted to argue that it didn't matter. Carl shouldn't be allowed back in the house.

But this wasn't his house, and it wasn't his call.

Biting his tongue so he wouldn't say too much and make this night even more difficult for his landlord, he stalked into the kitchen and got a bag of ice, which he wrapped in a towel and brought to Uriah. "Here, put this on your face."

Uriah didn't respond.

Tobias squatted across from him. "Uriah…"

His eyes finally met Tobias's. "I'm getting too old for this."

Tobias wanted to agree, but he knew how torn Uriah had to be. He and Maddox felt the same about their mother. They should've cut her out of their lives long ago. But family was family, so they kept trying to get her to change and improve.

He gripped Uriah's forearm by way of encouragement. "You going to be okay?"

"I think so."

"Will you call me when he comes back?"

He finally accepted the ice pack. "What for?"

"I'd like to have a talk with him, get a few things straight."

A bit of Uriah's sense of humor resurfaced as he

managed a wry smile. "You mean you'd like to threaten him."

Tobias grinned as he stood. "Damn right. He needs to know there'll be hell to pay if he ever causes you to get hurt again."

Uriah sobered. "What makes some people do what they do?"

Tobias shook his head. "I wish I could tell you."

"Tobias?" a female voice called.

Harper. He'd left the kitchen door standing open when he'd run inside, and she'd come through it.

"In here!"

She appeared in the doorway to the living room, wearing the sweats she'd put on to sleep. "Is everything okay?" she asked, her forehead creased in concern.

He rested his hands on his hips as he looked between her and his landlord. "For now," he said.

7

Although they'd returned to the house, and Tobias had gone back into his bedroom, Harper had been sleeping in fits and starts. Almost every time she closed her eyes, she'd hear Tobias tossing and turning or getting up to go to the bathroom and would wake up, too. Those were such small noises—noises that normally wouldn't bother her—but she was too aware of him to drift off for any length of time. And now, although he'd moved quietly, she could sense that he was in the same room she was.

"What time is it?" she asked, covering a yawn.

Tobias turned from where he'd been standing at the kitchen window, keeping watch on the drive. "Nearly four."

Two hours since the fight between Carl and Uriah. Somehow it seemed longer. "Is something wrong?"

"No."

"Then why can't you sleep?"

Instead of an explanation, she received an apology. "Sorry if I'm keeping you up. You should go into my bedroom and close the door. If I get tired again, I'll take the couch."

"I'm fine here." Pushing up onto one elbow, she rested her head on her palm. "Are you okay?"

He turned back to the window. "Yeah. I'm just... restless."

"You're worried about Uriah."

"I'm pissed off," he stated more forcefully.

She studied what she could see of him via the moonlight streaming in through the window—the mussed hair, the faded jeans, the bare back. "At his son?"

"Yes. That dude is *such* a douchebag. There's no telling what he might do."

As she'd guessed, Tobias was worried. But that wasn't how he interpreted what he was feeling, and the fact that he could get it wrong made her smile. Maybe he *was* mad, but it was primarily because he was worried. "Has Carl come back?"

"I can't see that far down the drive. But I haven't spotted any headlights. Or heard an engine. So probably not yet." He pinched his own shoulder as if he was trying to relieve some tension. "He will, though."

That was why he couldn't sleep. He was waiting for Carl to return. "How do you know? Because he left his stuff?"

"Not only that. He needs Uriah too badly to leave, doesn't have any way to support himself."

"He could get a job, couldn't he?"

"Even if he could, there's no way he'd be able to keep it."

"So...what are you going to do when he shows up?" She was a little worried herself, and didn't want Tobias to get himself into trouble.

He sighed audibly. "I'm not sure it's my place to do anything. That's the problem. I don't want to stick my nose where it doesn't belong. If Uriah wants to make peace with his son, that's his choice. But I doubt Carl will ever change, so having him here won't lead to anything good."

"It's hard for a parent to give up."

When he didn't respond, she thought maybe he was thinking, *It wasn't hard for my parents.* She knew he hadn't had an easy childhood. He'd said a few things about it since they'd met, but he hadn't given many details, and he didn't bring it up now.

"You don't think there's any chance that what happened tonight will just…blow over?" she asked.

"It might," he replied. "For a while. But something else will happen later. That's the thing. Carl only cares about Carl. And now that his mother, Uriah's wife, is gone, Uriah doesn't have anyone to protect, so I don't see him taking the necessary steps to make Carl stay away."

"He'll set aside his own needs and safety to keep trying to help his son."

"Yes."

She hadn't had the chance to speak to Uriah for more than a few minutes, but she'd gotten the same impression—that Uriah was so concerned about his son he wasn't willing to send him away again. When Tobias expressed his fears, Uriah minimized them, which was partly why Tobias was feeling so helpless in his concern. "How long have you known Uriah?" she asked.

"Since I moved here five months ago."

"You seem close, even though you haven't been in town all that long."

"We've played hours and hours of chess and done

a lot of things around the orchard. You get to know someone pretty fast when you spend that much time with him."

"True." She adjusted the comforter. "Tobias?"

He seemed distracted. "What?"

"Would it be easier for you to get through the night if you took me home? It's been generous of you to offer me your friendship, but I don't want to become a nuisance."

He turned around and leaned against the counter, which meant she was once again confronted with his bare chest. "Do you *want* to go home?"

She *should* want to leave. But, strangely enough, she didn't, despite the disruption Carl had caused. "No. I like being here, with you. You make me feel... I don't know. It's hard to explain. Good, I guess. You make me feel good."

He didn't thank her or return the compliment, but he didn't need to. She could tell that he liked her, too, just by the expression on his face.

The silence stretched for so long that her heart started to thump in her chest. Was *his* pulse racing, too? She couldn't help admiring how attractive he was; she'd have to be blind not to see it.

She cleared her throat. "I think it's because you don't have any expectations," she said, elaborating just to fill the room with sound and ease the tension. "You take what comes, don't try to force anything or examine people too closely. I like that. It's...liberating for those around you, if that makes sense."

"I've learned not to expect too much," he said, but before she could question him on what, specifically, he was referring to, he added, "Go into my bedroom and get some sleep. Morning will be here before you know it."

"What will you do?" she asked.

"I'll hang out here, maybe watch some TV."

She sat up, pulling the bedding with her. "Let's watch together."

"There's no need for you to stay up."

"I've got the whole week to myself. I'm not worried about getting enough sleep. We can always take a nap later, if we want to."

He hesitated. "Are you seriously planning to stay all week?"

She shrugged. "Why not? But only if it's okay with you. I'll tell you what—I'll stay as long as you want me here."

"I doubt you'll stay *that* long," he muttered, but he walked over, turned on the TV and sat on the far end of the couch with the remote in his hand.

"Do you have Netflix or any movie channels?" she asked.

"I do. What would you like to watch?"

They agreed on a psychological thriller. Then she gathered up the bedding, slid closer to him and put the comforter around them both.

When Tobias woke up, light was streaming through the kitchen window, the only window without a blind, and the TV was off. He couldn't remember turning it off, but he figured he must have—until he grew alert enough to realize he wasn't alone. Harper hadn't gone into the bedroom after the movie ended. She was right there, snuggled up against him, her head on his shoulder.

He needed to change his position. His foot had gone to sleep. But he was reluctant to move. Her hand rested on his bare chest and her leg was slung over his.

There wasn't any other way for them to fit on the narrow couch, so he told himself not to get too excited. It probably didn't mean a whole lot. But her openness and trust were even more intoxicating than the weight of her pressing him into the cushions.

His arm tightened around her as the desire to kiss her rose inside him. He'd kissed quite a few girls when he was a kid. Since he'd had little adult supervision, and he'd seen his mother making out so many times and with so many different men, he'd become sexually aware early. But he hadn't been with many women since being released from prison. He'd decided he needed to heal first, get on his feet so he'd have something to offer a partner. And if he *ever* wanted to be liked in this place, he had to be careful. Otherwise, his actions would reflect poorly on his brother—and Aiyana Turner, since she'd been kind enough to give him a job. So there was that, too.

Besides, he'd known that getting involved too soon, or with the wrong person, could destroy his peace of mind quicker than anything else. He'd seen it happen with his mother far too many times. So after breaking things off with Tonya, he'd been with only one other woman in the past five months—a one-night stand he'd later regretted. After calling him incessantly for three weeks, the woman had shown up out of the blue, despite what he'd already told her on the phone, and wound up sobbing on his front doorstep when he had to reiterate that he wasn't interested in continuing the relationship.

Harper stirred and raised her head. As soon as she saw that he was awake, their eyes met, and when she moved her leg, he knew she could feel his erection.

He held his breath, waiting to see how she'd react. He thought she should get off him and move away in a hurry. Being so close to her, and in this particular position, he wasn't feeling much self-control.

But she didn't.

That was sort of an invitation, wasn't it?

He lowered his gaze to her lips. Surely one kiss couldn't hurt.

Halfway hoping she'd stop him, he lifted his free hand to caress her cheek. It would be so easy to get lost in her and in what he was feeling in this moment.

Gently stroking the back of her head, he touched his lips to hers—but just barely. He still wasn't convinced he should allow himself to take this liberty. Things he couldn't resist were usually things he *should* resist. They always got him into trouble. But when her eyes closed, he knew there was no point in debating with himself. If she liked this as much as he did, he'd already lost the battle.

The warmth of her mouth sent a burning sensation through him like a shot of the best whiskey. Instinctively, his fingers delved into her thick, silky hair, and she shifted until she was completely astride him.

The pressure made him grow even harder, and he deepened the kiss, letting his tongue meet and move against hers. He was tempted to peel off her sweatshirt and take this to the next level right away. His fingers itched to touch her bare skin and to bring her naked body against his.

He might've acted on the impulse. What had started

out as a somewhat tentative exploration was quickly growing into a breathless, hungry frenzy. They couldn't seem to kiss each other deeply enough to satisfy—until the doorknob rattled.

Someone was trying to come in.

Harper heard it, too. She sat up, her chest rising and falling as she struggled to catch her breath. "Are you expecting company?" she gasped.

He didn't get the chance to answer before he heard, "Tobias? Where are you? Since when did you start locking the damn door?"

"It's my brother," he whispered and they both scrambled off the couch. "Would you rather hide in the bedroom so he doesn't see you, or…"

"I guess." She hurried to gather up the bedding. "Probably best to keep rumors in town to a minimum. My sister and brother-in-law live here, after all."

He was helping Harper fill her arms with the comforter and pillows when the door swung open. Maddox used to live in the house before marrying Jada. Tobias had forgotten he still had a key.

Harper and Maddox froze when they saw each other, and Tobias winced. "It didn't occur to you that the door was locked for a reason?" he asked his brother.

Maddox blinked several times. "Sorry, I didn't expect… You've never mentioned a… I should've waited," he finished lamely and glanced back at the door, which was standing open since he'd been too shocked to bother closing it. "Should I go now? Or do I at least get an introduction?"

Tobias rubbed his forehead with three fingers. Although he didn't want Harper to suffer any backlash for being with him, he wasn't worried about that right now. He knew his brother wouldn't say anything to anyone, except maybe Jada, who'd be just as discreet. He was more concerned about the warnings his brother would voice when they were alone later. While class and station had never mattered less in their society than they did now, it was still a problem for an ex-con to want someone like Harper. "Maybe I can call you later," he said to his brother.

"Okay…" Maddox turned to go but Harper stopped him.

"No, you can stay," she said and, after setting the bedding aside, made one failed attempt to smooth down her hair before holding out her hand. "I'm Harper."

She didn't provide her last name and Tobias could easily guess why, but that didn't give her the anonymity she craved. Maddox's eyebrows slid up. "Not Harper Devlin…"

Squaring her shoulders, she lifted her chin. "Yes, as a matter of fact."

"Axel Devlin's *wife*," Maddox clarified.

"*Ex*-wife," she corrected him. "My divorce will be final tomorrow."

"That's a relief. I mean, I—I'm sorry… Divorces are rough," he finished, still obviously off center.

"Yes, they are," she agreed.

"I didn't realize you knew my brother. Or, rather, that he knew you."

"We met at the Eatery the other night."

"That's a good restaurant." He scratched his neck. "Well…welcome to Silver Springs. I hope you like the area."

"Thank you. I do. It's lovely here."

"How'd you know Axel Devlin's wife was in town?" Tobias asked.

"Are you kidding?" Maddox replied. "I'm the principal of a girls' school, remember? She's all I've heard about for the past week."

"Maddox works at the same school I do," Tobias explained to Harper.

"I work on the girls' side, and Tobias works on the girls' *and* boys' sides, but we see each other often," Maddox said, elaborating.

The way Harper folded her arms across her chest gave Tobias the impression that she was somewhat self-conscious about her appearance. "Then it's a good thing you two get along."

Maddox's gaze shifted between them. Tobias could tell he was assuming they'd slept together. Tobias was still in his jeans and Harper had on her sweats, but he was shirtless, they were both barefoot and their hair was mussed—not to mention she'd been holding the bedding when he arrived as though she was eager to stash the evidence.

Hoping to shield her, Tobias stepped between them. "I'd offer you breakfast, but…"

Fortunately, Maddox got the point. "Right. No. I've got a lot to do today, anyway. I just… I wanted to tell you something."

The now somber tone of Maddox's voice piqued Tobias's interest. He knew when his brother had something important to say. "What's that?"

"Uriah's son was picked up for a DUI last night."

Tobias wasn't surprised. The only surprise was that his brother would know about the incident before he did. "Did Uriah call you or—"

"No. He wasn't even aware of it until I told him a few minutes ago."

"What happened?"

"Carl ran a red light and nearly T-boned Atticus."

The mention of Atticus made Tobias stand taller. He remembered his conversation with Maya at the cookie store and what he planned to do for her other uncle—if Atticus *wanted* to hike Yosemite as she claimed. He'd been so distracted by Harper he hadn't thought of a way to approach Atticus about it yet, but he still wanted to. "Is Atticus okay?"

"He's fine. They didn't actually collide. But Atticus crashed into a parked car when he veered away and had to call me to come get him. He didn't want to wake his mother and upset her."

"Where is he now?"

"At home, I guess. That's where I took him. A tow came for his truck. It's not drivable at the moment but should be fixed in a week or so."

"Carl's insurance will cover it?"

"If he has coverage. Otherwise, Atticus's will kick in."

So Atticus wouldn't lose his autonomy. That also came as a relief. Since his vehicle was equipped with hand controls and a lift for his wheelchair, it wasn't as though it would be as easy to replace as a regular pickup, so he was glad it could be repaired. "What happened to Carl? Anything?"

"Not a scratch. The cops came, took him to jail and impounded his vehicle."

"And now?"

"I assume he's still in jail, since Uriah didn't know what happened until I told him."

Tobias shoved his hands in his pockets. "How'd he take the news?" He'd been trying to talk some sense into the old man last night. He thought this incident might help, but he knew it would also be disappointing for Uriah to hear.

Maddox sighed. "He took it as well as could be expected."

"I don't want Carl coming back here," Tobias said. "He doesn't treat his father right, and he can't control his temper. I'm afraid something *really* bad will happen." Something far worse than what had already happened—both to Uriah and to Atticus—last night.

"Well, if Uriah will listen to anyone, he'll listen to you. He loves you like a second son." Maddox's gaze shifted back to Harper. "I'm sorry to barge in like I did, but it was very nice meeting you."

She smiled even though Tobias could tell she was still a little uncomfortable. "No problem," she said. "You, too."

Tobias followed his brother out onto the stoop, so he was the only one who saw the incredulous look Maddox shot him—a look that said, *Holy shit! Harper Devlin?*

"I'll call you later," Tobias said.

Maddox stepped off the stoop, but Tobias called him back. "And, if you don't mind, I'll take my extra key now."

A look of chagrin came over Maddox's face as he retrieved it from his pocket. "Right. Here you go. Sorry about that."

Tobias had to smile as his brother walked down the drive. He went back in prepared to apologize for the intrusion, but Harper didn't seem upset. "Your brother is almost as handsome as you are," she said when he'd closed the door.

"Are you kidding me? He's *nowhere* near as handsome as I am!" he joked, and she laughed.

Tobias thought of the kiss Maddox had interrupted but was more relieved than he was upset. Harper wasn't in a position to start a relationship. He wasn't the right person to start one with. And she wasn't the type of woman who could just knock him off balance; she could completely *wreck* him, and he knew it. He'd been sailing along fairly nicely the past few months. He didn't want to crash and flounder on the rocks. He'd made enough mistakes in his life, and he'd paid a heavy price. "I'll make eggs and toast. Sound good?"

"Yeah, I'm hungry. Do you have any coffee?"

"I do. Starting it now."

She lifted the blind on the living room window and peered out. "The rain has cleared up."

"Great. What would you like to do today?"

She picked up her phone and tapped the screen. "I need to check in with my sister and my girls."

"And then…"

"Then I'm up for anything—anything that means I won't have time to think."

He waggled his eyebrows at her. "So it's still my job to provide a distraction?"

She studied him for a moment. "Do you mind?"

"Not at all."

"Good. Because you're proving to be quite adept at it."

He was pretty sure she was referring to what had happened on the couch. He was afraid that if they stayed at his place, they'd simply wind up in a similar situation—and might not be interrupted the next time. "Let's get out of here. Drive over to the coast."

She carried the sheets and blankets into the bedroom.

"Harper?" he called when she made no comment.

"Yes?"

He'd dragged out a frying pan, then put it on the stove and went to peer into the bedroom. "What do you think? Do you want to go over to the coast? Santa Barbara's only about forty-five minutes away."

The expression on her face was thoughtful. He got the feeling she was about to ask him about something—likely their kiss. He could tell by her reluctance.

Fortunately, she must've changed her mind at the last second. "Sure."

He breathed a sigh of relief as he returned to the kitchen. She was going to let it go. Good. Now they could pretend it never happened.

8

She'd kissed another man—for the first time in almost a decade! Harper couldn't believe it. Something she couldn't have conceived of doing just a few days ago had happened so easily and naturally. And at no point during the encounter had she considered pushing him away.

Why? How had she been able to enjoy that kind of contact with Tobias when she'd thought it would be months, or possibly years, before she could even think of touching—or being touched by—another man?

Was she trying to prove that she was desirable? Rebuild her self-esteem on the heels of the rejection she'd suffered? Get some sort of misguided revenge on Axel?

Or was she acting on even baser impulses—a craving for physical pleasure after going without sex for six months?

She didn't have any answers, but she knew she had to be careful. She couldn't get into another relationship this soon. Everly and Piper were still struggling to adjust to life without their daddy living in the house. She had to be sensitive to that, especially because something that flared up so quickly was bound to be a mistake.

Taking her phone with her, she stepped out of Tobias's house to call her girls while he cleaned up after breakfast. Since neither of her children was old enough to have a cell phone, she couldn't call them directly, so she dialed Karoline's number.

"Hey," her sister said.

"Hey," she responded.

"You're up, huh?"

"Yeah. Have been for a while."

"I didn't want to wake you, which is why you haven't heard from me, but I've been worried about you. You okay?"

Guilt bit deeply, making Harper pause. Karoline would be surprised to learn she wasn't alone—or even at home.

Should she say something about that? She didn't want Karoline to think she was abusing her compassion. But at the same time, her sister had taken the girls to give her the chance to recover, and she *was* feeling much better. She hadn't called Axel once, had barely thought of him. Did the method matter as long as it didn't hurt anyone else?

She decided to keep her mouth shut. She had only a few more days before she'd be forced to face reality again. If she spoke up, her sister might rush home to be sure she wasn't getting herself in trouble, bringing it all to an end, and she wasn't ready for this small reprieve to be over.

Axel had abandoned them to pursue his fabulous career. Surely she could have a guilt-free week while her children spent time in LA going to Disneyland and other fun places with her sister.

"Yeah," she said into the phone. "I'm doing much better."

"You are?" Surprise filled Karoline's voice. "Why do you think that's the case?"

Of course Karoline would demand specifics. "I'm... trying to look at things from a different perspective," she said.

"That's good!"

Harper seized the opportunity to change the subject. "How are the girls?"

"They're fabulous. Having a blast."

She was about to ask to speak to them when her sister lowered her voice. "Have you heard from Axel?"

"Not since you left," Harper replied. He hadn't called her—usually didn't call very often. He didn't like the guilt it created. And she was proud of the fact that she hadn't broken down and called him. For the past eight months it had been almost impossible to stop herself.

"Everly keeps asking if she can phone him," Karoline explained. "So far, I've put her off. But...should I let her do it?"

Harper had no problem with her daughters contacting their father. She *wanted* them to remain close to Axel. He'd been such an integral part of their happiness. Her only hesitation was that she was afraid they'd discover what she'd already learned: he didn't seem to care as much as he had before—about any of them. "I guess. Hopefully, he'll give them a few minutes. If not, blame the time change. That's what I've been doing."

"I think I should place the blame squarely where it belongs!"

"No, that'll just hurt the girls, Karoline."

"Then maybe I should have a talk with him first."

Harper gripped her phone more tightly. "Don't. You know how touchy he can be. If you set him off, you'll get into an argument. And maybe it'll be for nothing. Maybe he'll get his head on straight before Piper and Everly have to accept too many harsh realities."

"I get the impression he's drifting further away, Harper. Anyway, I don't believe in walking on eggshells for anyone. Just because he's more emotional than I am, or some big star these days, doesn't mean I should have to treat him any differently than I do anyone else."

Harper tucked her hair behind her ears. "I know you think I'm being too much of a pushover. You've made that clear. But I'm trying to keep things as pleasant as possible for the sake of my kids. That's important— especially now, at Christmastime."

Silence.

"Karoline?"

"Fine. I under*stand*," her sister said with some reluctance. Karoline was so eager to come to her defense. Sometimes that helped; other times it only made matters worse. "I won't get involved. I'll just let her use my phone and hope for the best."

"He might surprise you."

"I doubt it," she said dryly.

Harper had been pacing back and forth with her head down. As she came toward Tobias's truck, she spotted movement out of the corner of her eye and looked up to see Uriah, dressed in work overalls and a ball cap, walking toward her.

"Morning," he said as he passed, but he looked tired and drawn, and she felt sorry about what he was going through.

"Morning," she replied.

"Who was that?" Karoline asked.

Harper caught her breath. She'd spoken without thinking. Her sister, who believed she was home alone, was on the phone.

As Uriah disappeared into the garage, she was tempted to come clean. She was usually such a transparent person. But now that she'd waited until they were so deep in the conversation, she knew Karoline would read too much into the fact that she was with the guy who'd given her the flower. "I'm out for…for breakfast," she fudged, telling herself that her words were at least partially true; she was out and she'd just had breakfast.

Fortunately, that seemed to satisfy her sister. "Oh, that's nice," she said. "You need to get out and start circulating again. That's what I've been saying all along. Let go of the old and embrace the new."

Harper bit her bottom lip. She'd been embracing another man when she first woke up. She might've done *more* than embrace him had Maddox not interrupted when he had. Although she was glad she and Tobias hadn't gone any further, there was a part of her that figured people had one-night stands all the time. Why would it be such a big deal if they slept together?

Maybe it would've been smart to break through that barrier while she'd had the chance. She couldn't imagine being interested in anyone else; that she was interested in *him* came as a shock. Not because he wasn't appealing. She just hadn't met a man since she'd gotten together with Axel who could even remotely tempt her.

But Tobias was different. Not only was he sexy, he was also kind and easygoing and patient—all things that Axel typically was not, she noted grimly. Had Tobias not been so intent on keeping her at bay, she probably would've gone to bed with him last night.

"I'm glad you feel that way," she said to Karoline.

She'd walked back to Tobias's truck. She couldn't see Uriah anymore, but she could hear him tinkering inside the garage. And when she looked the other way, down the drive, she could see a younger man standing on Uriah's back porch.

That had to be Carl, didn't it? She could see the family resemblance. If he'd required bail to be released from custody, Uriah must've arranged it while she and Tobias were having breakfast.

She glanced at Tobias's door, which stood partway open from when she'd come outside. He wouldn't be happy when he learned Carl was back.

Carl seemed about to chase down his father. Perhaps he wanted to talk about what he'd done. With one hand raised to block the sun, he squinted while looking toward the garage. But the moment he saw her, his expression turned sour. She got the impression he didn't want her on the property—or maybe seeing her reminded him that Tobias was on the property, too, and that was what he didn't like. Either way, he dropped his hand and stomped into his father's house.

"Can I talk to the girls?" Harper asked her sister. She'd interrupted Karoline, who was going on about the shopping they'd done yesterday, but she was suddenly eager to get off the phone.

"Um, sure," her sister said.

Karoline put Everly on first, and then Piper. They both gushed about all the fun they were having. They told Harper they loved and missed her, but Harper felt reassured when she disconnected that her choice to stay behind in Silver Springs wasn't causing her children any distress.

"Everything okay?" Tobias asked.

Harper whirled around. She hadn't realized he'd come to the stoop and was looking out at her. With a nod, she slid her phone into her pocket. "Yeah. Everything's fine."

"That's good." He held the door as she came in. "Do you want a shower before we go?"

It was a practical question, not a come-on. That was what got her. He wasn't trying to entice her into his bed. After that heated kiss this morning, he'd backed off completely—and for some strange reason that only made her *more* interested in touching him, especially now that she'd been reassured that her children were safe and happy, and she didn't have to worry about them.

"Carl's been released from jail," she said, still trying to talk herself out of what was going through her mind.

Tobias frowned. "What do you think I should do? Should I go have a talk with him? Or let it go?"

The muscles in his arms and chest moved appealingly under his smooth skin as he combed his fingers through his hair. Harper knew she shouldn't be noticing such things, but she was suddenly very preoccupied with his body.

"I guess I don't have any business getting involved," he went on, oblivious to her thoughts. "But if *someone* doesn't do something…" He shook his head, visibly frustrated by the fact there was no clear answer.

"It's a tough call," she said. "Maybe wait a bit? Feel your way through it? I would guess Carl's contrite at the moment. So maybe everything will be all right for today."

He walked over and peered out the window over the sink, where he'd been keeping vigil during the night. He must not have seen anything that concerned him, though, because when he faced her again, he seemed to be of a different mind. "Yeah. Let's get out of here. I'll figure it out later."

He obviously expected her to go get ready, but she didn't. She was thinking about that kiss on the couch. His lips had been so warm and soft, and they'd molded perfectly to hers. "My kids will be back in four, five days, tops," she announced.

Confusion creased his forehead. "And that's a problem?"

"Not a problem. I'll be anxious to see them. It's just…" She gathered her nerve. "Are you sure you want to leave?"

"You don't want to go to the beach anymore?" he asked, cocking his head.

She drew a deep breath. "What *I* want is standing right here."

His Adam's apple moved as he straightened. "And you mentioned four or five days because…"

"Whatever happens, it all ends there." Filled with nervous energy, she ran her palms up and down her thighs. "I can't… I can't bring home another guy to my girls. Not this soon."

"I see. So you're saying…"

What *was* she saying? She should take advantage of this opportunity, shouldn't she? Who knew how many months or years it would be before…before someone like him came along again?

"I'm saying we might want to make better use of our time."

His jaw dropped. "Are you *propositioning* me?"

Feeling her face heat, she swallowed against a dry throat. "I guess I am."

"Well…damn," he said.

She could tell he was interested—at least, she thought so. But he also seemed stunned, and he was so slow to react she suddenly felt insecure. "What does *damn* mean?"

His caution evaporated as he moved—now quite purposefully—toward her. "It means that's an offer I can't refuse."

Now that she knew she was going to get what she'd asked for, she took a step back. "We could wait until we get home from the beach if…if you'd rather," she said, slightly overwhelmed by what she'd started.

"Are you kidding? The next four or five days will disappear quickly enough as it is."

He didn't crowd her. He stopped a few feet away and simply held out his hand.

Butterflies filled her stomach as she looked down at his big palm and long fingers. She could tell he worked with his hands. They weren't nearly as perfect as Axel's—they had a few calluses and scars—but they were very masculine, just like the rest of him.

"Harper?"

Was she really going through with this?

"It's not too late to change your mind," he said, and that was probably why she didn't.

Putting her hand in his, she gave him a tentative smile and let him draw her into the bedroom.

Tobias was doing everything he'd promised himself he wouldn't—everything he knew he shouldn't—but he wasn't going to miss out on this, not if Harper wanted the same thing. If they both understood the rules going in, it should be fine. Depending on when her kids came back, they just had the better part of a week to be together. No one could get hurt in that amount of time. Then the holidays would be upon them, so they'd both be busy. And after that?

She'd be gone.

Instead of taking her straight to bed, he pressed her up against the wall just inside his bedroom and kissed her. He wanted to let the heat between them grow slowly and naturally, to ease into their lovemaking in case she was nervous. But the second their mouths met, he could tell this wasn't going to be a slow burn. She was as hungry for this kind of contact as he was.

She parted her lips, accepting his tongue, which sent such a flood of testosterone through his blood he had to prop both arms against the wall to compensate for the sudden weakness in his knees.

"I *love* the way you kiss." She pulled the tie from his hair before tightening her arms around his neck. "Everyone should be kissed like this at least once in their lives."

He hadn't had a lot of practice with kissing in the

past thirteen years, so he was glad to hear the positive feedback. But he could tell she liked it even before she spoke up. They seemed totally compatible. There was nothing awkward about kissing or touching her. It was the most natural, perfect progression on earth, which just went to show what great chemistry could do. "How is it different from other men?"

"It's just so…focused. As if kissing me is the only thing that matters, the only thing you're thinking about."

"It *is* the only thing I'm thinking about," he admitted and kissed her again, deep and long, before framing her face with his hands. "You're *gorgeous*. You know that, don't you? The first time I saw you, sitting up at that counter…"

He let his words fade away. He'd been about to try to articulate how that moment had affected him—how she'd captured his attention from the very first. But he couldn't explain *why* that would be the case, and he didn't want to ruin it by being overly dramatic.

"What?" she prodded. "What did you think?"

He pressed his forehead to hers. "I thought you looked sad," he said, remembering.

"I *was* sad."

He toyed with her hair. "I also thought…"

Her hand trailed lightly along his jaw. "What?"

The excitement she caused when she reached his mouth and ran her thumb back and forth over his bottom lip made his heart pound. "You took my breath away. And it's like that now. I can't believe I'm with you—that I get to make love to you."

"I can't believe this is happening, either," she said.

"I never dreamed I'd want anyone else, not so soon. But you're not like other guys."

He knew why. How many other men had she slept with who'd finished growing up in prison? But he refused to think about Atticus or the past. A four-day fling didn't demand full disclosure, which came as a bit of a relief. He didn't want to tell Harper what he'd done, and hoped she'd never find out. It would change the way she looked at him. And he didn't think he could bear to see her good opinion of him destroyed.

"Axel was crazy to leave you," he said.

Her smile wobbled. "I'm just a woman. I can't compete with stardom."

He kissed her. "I'd rather have you."

"You're almost too good to be true, Tobias Richardson," she whispered against his lips.

Those words hit him hard. He *was* too good to be true. She didn't know what he'd seen and done in his life—the drugs, the violence, the loneliness, which had, at times, been so profound he'd thought he'd go mad before they released him. Touching her so intimately— as though he was just like any other man, just like she assumed he was—felt deceptive.

He started to pull away but she caught his face and rose up on tiptoe to kiss him. Then he was lost all over again, especially because he got the impression that what they were doing meant something to her—in spite of all the reasons it shouldn't.

He tried to tell himself that was simply what he wanted to believe, or it was hormones playing tricks on him. They didn't know each other well enough for this to have any real meaning. She was still in love

with her ex-husband, who happened to be a rock star—
someone he could never compete with.

But he was surprised by how sincere she seemed
to be. There was nothing mechanical about the way
she touched him, nothing that led him to believe she
was using him as a stand-in. And that turned out to be
such a powerful aphrodisiac that even though he felt
terrible for not revealing the kind of man he was, he
couldn't bring himself to pull away.

He did the opposite. He held her hands over her head
and reached for the hem of her sweatshirt.

He caught his breath as he yanked it off and tossed
it somewhere on his bedroom floor. "Oh, God," he
whispered as he looked down at her.

"Tobias?"

He forced himself to lift his gaze. "What?"

She blushed. "You're staring."

"Could any man see you without a shirt and *not*
stare?"

She laughed as she brought his hand to her breast,
and he closed his eyes, savoring the feel of her soft
flesh as it filled his palm. That was when everything
started to move much faster. Once again, she dragged
his mouth to hers. And then he couldn't think anymore,
couldn't even consider resisting.

The rest of their clothes came off, one article after
another. Somehow, he managed to get a condom from
his nightstand and roll it on. Her nails scraped down
his back, right on that delicious border between pleasure and pain, and she locked her legs around his hips,
groaning as she took him inside her.

For a moment, Tobias was afraid it would all be
over too soon. He grappled with control as they fell

onto the mattress, kissing and touching and straining to explore every inch of each other.

They rolled around for several minutes during which he kissed her neck, her breasts—anything he could reach—before she ended up on top. He loved the sight of her straddling him so much he was pretty sure it was his idea. But it might've been hers. As everything intensified, he'd lost track of who was instigating what. He just knew he'd never been this drunk on desire.

Her gaze locked with his as she began to move, very slowly, almost experimentally at first, and then with more intent.

"That's it," he said when he could tell how much she was enjoying herself. "How does it feel?"

"It's good," she replied breathlessly. "Better than good." She began to rock harder and faster.

"Let go," he said. "Don't hold back."

Her eyes slid closed. "You're perfect at this," she told him.

He put his hands on her thighs to guide and support her so she wouldn't tire too quickly—and felt his pulse go crazy when she threw her head back and began to ride him in earnest.

"You've got it," he said, mesmerized by the emotions playing out on her face.

She moaned in response, and her gasps grew in frequency and volume as she drew closer to climax.

"Yes. You're almost there." Tobias had to let go of her thighs and start clinging to the bedding. He was using every mind trick he knew not to ruin this for her—and was infinitely relieved when the sounds she made changed from what he would interpret as *so close* to *hell, yes!*

He'd made it. But he didn't have time to savor the victory. He could feel his muscles contract as his own climax rose inside him and rolled through the rest of his body—all the more powerful because he'd struggled to hold on for so long.

When it was over, she stayed where she was, staring down at him as they both caught their breath.

"Wow," she said when she was ready to speak. "That might've been the best orgasm I've ever had."

Flattered even though he wasn't sure he had a right to take all the credit, he smiled. "It's been a tough few months, so it's no wonder. You were due."

"It wasn't just that," she said. "It was you."

He reached up to pull her down beside him, but something off to the side must've caught her eye because a look of surprise came over her face—and then a look of horror.

"What is it?" he asked.

She scrambled off the bed, nearly tripping on the blankets.

"Harper?"

She didn't respond. With a desperate, strangled sound, she grabbed her phone from where it must've fallen out of the pocket of her sweats when she kicked them off and quickly tapped on the screen.

Completely confused, Tobias rose up on his elbows as she sank onto the bed. "What's happened?"

Tears rolled down her cheeks as she turned the front of her phone so that he could see her call record.

It took him a moment to realize what she was showing him, but then it became obvious. She'd just ended a call to Axel.

Feeling some of the horror she obviously felt, Tobias's chest constricted. "Don't tell me we somehow pocket-dialed Axel when we took off your pants…"

She cringed as though she couldn't bear to hear the words spoken aloud but nodded.

Tobias sat up. "Do you think he… Do you think he actually picked up?"

"Let's hope the whole thing isn't on his voice mail!" she cried.

A recording *would* be worse. "How long was the call?"

She held the phone out again, so that Tobias could check for himself. His heart sank when he saw it had lasted nearly fifteen minutes. "Oh shit. Maybe he didn't realize what was happening."

"I said it was the best orgasm I've ever had!"

Pressing a palm to his forehead, he fell back onto the pillows. "I'm sorry. Especially if I was the one who accidentally hit the call button."

"I took off my own pants. It was probably me." She dashed a hand across her cheeks. "I was a fool to think… Never mind. Will you take me home? Please?"

Tobias felt as though he'd just been kicked in the stomach. And if *he* felt that bad, she had to feel worse. He didn't want such a fabulous encounter to end this way. He was tempted to try to talk her out of leaving, to console her somehow, but he didn't feel it was fair to push her into staying any longer than she wanted to—especially because she didn't really know who he was.

"Of course," he said softly and got out of bed to dress.

9

Harper couldn't even look at Tobias. What she'd done was just more proof of how badly she was unraveling. She should've told her sister what she was up to when they talked on the phone. Karoline would've put a quick stop to it. Karoline didn't make mistakes, not like this.

While they were driving, Harper could feel Tobias glance over at her every few minutes. Although he didn't say anything, he had to be wondering if she'd lost her mind. This morning, she'd been so aggressive—and now she was so cold.

But she didn't know what she wanted. She was just looking for some way to anesthetize herself, to escape the crushing heartbreak Axel's defection had caused. He'd thrown her for such a loop she couldn't seem to recover. But now she'd involved someone else in her misery, and that wasn't fair.

"I'm sorry," she mumbled as Tobias came to a stop down the street from her sister's house so the neighbors wouldn't see her getting out of his truck.

Obviously being careful not to touch her in any suggestive way, he reached across her lap to open the door. "You don't have anything to apologize for."

A cool gust of air swept into the cab. The rain had stopped, but the wind was back. "Yes, I do. My head is…is not where it should be. With the way I've been acting, it's kind of scary that I'm the mother of two children, right?" She laughed as though she was making a joke, but he didn't so much as crack a smile. He slung one arm over the steering wheel while he studied her, and it was difficult not to think of him lying beneath her. Those memories were so fresh.

"That's not how I look at it," he said.

She'd been planning to leave it at an apology, but this took her by surprise. "How do *you* look at it?"

"I'm sure you're a fine mother. You're just going through a hard time."

"My divorce doesn't give me the excuse to behave the way I'm behaving, Tobias. I didn't mean to…to negatively impact your life. I should've left you alone. You tried to tell me."

It was noon, but they both looked as though they'd just got out of bed—because they had. As soon as she'd made it clear that she wanted to go home, they'd pulled on their clothes and he'd grabbed his keys and followed her out to his truck.

"I don't regret what we did today, Harper," he said matter-of-factly.

She drew a deep breath. "That helps. Thank you," she said and stepped out and closed the door. She couldn't bear to look at his handsome face any longer—and she definitely didn't want to think about the rest of him.

As she hurried away, she guessed he was watching her, because it wasn't until she neared her sister's yard that she heard his engine rev, indicating he was pulling away.

She stopped to watch his tailgate disappear around the corner, and then, inexplicably, started crying again. She hated the way their morning had ended. Even worse than that, her phone kept vibrating in her pocket, and she was afraid to get it out and look at it. It had to be Axel. No doubt he was mad as hell. It was one thing to sleep with another guy. She supposed, since they were essentially divorced, she had that right. But inviting Axel into the bedroom while she did? That was something else entirely.

She groaned at the memory of seeing her phone lit up on the floor of Tobias's bedroom, alerting her to the fact that she'd somehow placed a call.

"I'm *such* an idiot," she muttered as she passed the decorations in the yard and let herself in through the front door. She knew if her sister or brother-in-law checked the security system on the house, they'd find no record of her leaving in the first place. But at this point, she had bigger things to worry about.

Determined to ignore her ringing phone, she stripped off her clothes, dumped them in the hamper and went straight to the shower, where she stood under the hot spray far longer than she'd ever stayed there before. It was the only place she felt safe; she didn't want to face the outside world.

But then she started thinking about Axel and how he might react. He was so vocal, so excitable. If he couldn't get through to her, he might decide to call her sister.

"Oh, no!" she cried as soon as the idea struck her, and she got out, dried off and grabbed her phone.

It wasn't vibrating anymore. But she had missed *ten* calls from him.

Clasping a towel around her, she sank onto her bed and navigated to voice mail.

Sure enough, Axel had left a number of messages. Before calling him back, she listened to each one. She figured they might tell her how best to approach the situation.

Message #1: "Harper, are you kidding me? What the hell was that?"

Message #2: "Harper, you'd better pick up the damn phone! Who are you with?"

Message #3: "Seriously? You're not going to answer? In case you've forgotten, we still have two children together!"

Message #4: "Harper, where are our daughters while you're fucking this guy?"

That one struck a hard enough blow that she almost couldn't continue. But there were six more—and she forced herself to listen to them all. He wasn't just angry; he was *furious*. It was eight hours later in London, so she'd interrupted him while he was having dinner with his bandmates and their manager. How would she like it, he yelled in the last one, if he called and made her listen to him screwing another woman, especially while she was at a business meeting?

How was she going to explain?

There was no *good* way. She'd never even mentioned that she was dating someone—because she wasn't. And the fact that it came out of nowhere only made the whole thing worse.

The screen on her phone lit up again. Damn!

There he was. She'd wanted to take the initiative so it wouldn't look like she was avoiding him.

She let it ring. She'd call him in a few minutes, she told herself. When *she* decided. But the risk that he might involve other people made her press the answer button.

Too nervous to remain sitting, Harper stood. "Hello?"

"Harper?"

She winced. "Yes?" she said tentatively. She expected him to start yelling right away. So she was surprised when he seemed to be at a loss for words.

Curling her fingernails into her palms, she tried to think of some way to begin the conversation herself. But then he said, "Please tell me that wasn't what it sounded like."

Was there any chance she could claim otherwise? She thought back over the way she'd been moaning, and what she'd said to Tobias right after they'd finished, and knew there wasn't. She wished she could just disappear. "Would you believe me if I said yes?" she asked.

"Wow…"

She squeezed her eyes closed.

"Holy shit," he added. "It *was* real."

She gripped the towel that much tighter. "I didn't mean to call you, Axel. It was an accident. I'm sorry."

"When I told Rory what I thought I was hearing, he said you were faking it. That you were probably alone and trying to make me jealous."

Rory was the band's drummer. As she'd feared, she'd upset Axel so badly he'd started talking to other people about it. She just hoped he hadn't called any of his family—or hers. "No. Like I said, it was an accident. I wasn't trying to make you jealous."

Silence.

"Axel? I'm sorry that…that it happened."

"Is he there with you now?"

"No."

"He's gone?"

"Yes!" she clarified impatiently.

"Who was he?"

She rubbed her forehead in an effort to relieve the headache that was starting. "Just…someone I met."

"Where?"

"Here in Silver Springs."

"Already? You haven't been there very long."

"I don't know what to tell you."

"Our divorce isn't even final!"

She stiffened. "You're saying *you* haven't slept with anyone else?"

It was his turn for silence.

"That's what I thought," she said.

"So you were trying to get even."

What she'd done was so out of character he was still looking for answers. But she didn't have any to offer him. She hadn't expected to do what she'd done, and she certainly hadn't *planned* it. "No! It wasn't like that at all. It was a pocket dial. Do you think I *wanted* you to hear what…what you heard? Something that private? I'm mortified!"

"Private. Are you forgetting who you're talking to?"

No, but he hadn't been in that room with her. She hadn't even been thinking of him, which she'd considered a great thing at the time. "We're no longer together," she said, relying on that as her only defense.

"And you seem to be totally over it. From what I heard, you're having one hell of a good time."

He was wounded because of what she'd said, and she could see why it might damage his ego. He wasn't a bad lover, not by any stretch of the imagination. She couldn't pinpoint what made today with Tobias so special, but she didn't intend to talk about it. On some level, she supposed she was still stuck on the part of their conversation where he'd basically admitted that he'd been with at least one other woman—the part where he'd asked if she was getting even. When had he first been with someone else? And why? Hadn't she been enough to satisfy him? How many women had there been? Had he begun to care about someone else? Was that how she'd lost him?

She had so many questions. But would it do her any good to ask them? What did it matter? He didn't love her anymore. That was what had destroyed their marriage, nothing else.

She pinched the bridge of her nose as the conversation lapsed into another terrible, stilted silence. They were both angry and hurt. She thought *he* was ultimately to blame, but he probably thought she was.

"Where are the girls?" he asked at length.

"With Karoline at Disneyland."

"They went to Disneyland? Without you?"

"Karoline offered to take them, so…"

"So you decided to stay behind and fuck your new boyfriend."

The profanity made her feel cheap as well as stupid. Which was what he'd intended, of course. Maybe that was why she didn't bother to tell him that Tobias wasn't her boyfriend. She didn't feel Axel had the right to know. "Is there anything wrong with that?" she asked instead.

He didn't answer. Again, he seemed to be at a loss for words.

"Good luck on your tour, Axel," she said. "As soon as you transfer the money, I'll get those presents you mentioned for the girls. If you need anything else, it'd be better if you texted me. We really don't have any reason to call each other anymore."

"You're hanging up?" He sounded stunned.

"What else is there to say?" she replied and disconnected.

As she sank onto the bed, she thought she'd cry some more. She usually wound up in tears after talking to Axel, and today had been emotional all the way around.

But, strangely enough, she didn't feel the need. She was done trying to win him back. He'd taken her for granted for far too long, and the constant rejection had been torture. If she couldn't fulfill him, maybe he *should* find someone else.

Her phone gave one short buzz, indicating a text message. She was so afraid it would be from him, and that it would be ugly, she was afraid to look at it.

But it wasn't Axel. Karoline had just sent her a picture of the girls.

We're at Universal Studios having a great time. Please don't worry about anything!

As direct and no-nonsense as her sister could be, there really was no one with a better heart.

Thank you for being there for me, she wrote back. I'm done with Axel. Moving on.

For real?

Yes. It's over. I don't know what I've been hanging on to.

That's my baby sister. Forget him. You're going to be just fine on your own, Karoline texted back and added a smiley face for good measure.

Harper doubted her sister would be so happy if she knew exactly how this change of heart had finally come to pass.

After Tobias pulled into his driveway and parked, he didn't immediately get out. He sat there, staring straight ahead, seeing nothing. He felt as though he'd just survived some kind of life-altering event, which was weird. He'd slept with a woman. So what? He didn't think sex—even for a man like him who'd gone thirteen years without it—was supposed to leave him feeling shell-shocked.

But making love to Harper hadn't been like making love to Tonya or the woman he'd picked up that one night in Santa Barbara. Those encounters had been enjoyable, of course, but he hadn't been quite as vulnerable. He'd had to let down his defenses in order to get that intimate with Harper—being with her had somehow demanded it—and that had made it almost a transcendent experience.

He scrubbed a hand over his face and focused on his surroundings. He didn't know how long he'd been sitting there, but there was nothing to be gained from wasting more time. Eventually, he'd forget about this morning—forget about *her*.

But he knew it wouldn't be easy.

"She told you from the beginning it couldn't last," he berated himself as he pulled the keys from the ignition. "What more did you expect?"

He'd expected four more days. Maybe *that* was the loss he was mourning.

He figured he'd shower and go over to Maddox's house. Seeing Maddox, Jada and Maya should distract him from the funk he'd fallen into when Harper saw that she'd accidentally called her ex-husband. Jada would probably invite him to stay for dinner. Her best friend, Tiffany Martinez, might also be there. While he didn't have any romantic interest in Tiffany, who was also single, he liked her a lot. And she seemed satisfied with being his friend, so he could feel comfortable around her. She was one of the first to be kind to him when he was released from prison, and he'd always have a soft spot in his heart for her.

He had his head down as he approached the back of his house, almost didn't see Carl standing in the shadows. When he did, he came to an abrupt stop. He hadn't bothered to lock his house when he left. He hardly ever locked his house. But his mountain bike was worth quite a bit—almost as much as his truck— so he should be more vigilant in the future, especially now that Carl was around. Tobias had the sneaking suspicion Carl had been snooping through his stuff. He'd noticed that Uriah's truck was gone when he drove in, so there was no one keeping an eye on Carl. And there was something about Carl's body language that made Tobias leery.

"What are you doing back here?" Tobias asked.

A dark glower descended on Carl's face. "What do you mean? I own the place. I can go anywhere I want."

But there was no reason for him to be loitering in the little area Tobias considered his yard. There was nothing of particular interest here and nothing that could be done for the trees in the orchard or the pixie tangerines that grew on them. "Your father owns the property, not you," Tobias said. "And you *can't* go anywhere you want. I'd better not ever find you inside my house."

Carl puffed out his chest. "Who the hell do you think you are? You can't tell me what I can and can't do. You're just the renter. From what my dad told me, you're not even on a lease. That means he could kick you out at any time, as long as he gives you thirty days' notice."

Tobias clenched his jaw. "And your point is?"

"My point is you'd better find someplace else to live, because my dad built this house for *me*, and I plan on moving back in."

Although Carl tried to stalk past Tobias, Tobias stepped in front of him and lowered his voice. "You need to watch yourself while you're here."

Carl's eyes narrowed. "Or…"

"Your father's getting old and frail. You can't treat him the way you used to. It's time to quit being such a dick and grow up."

"Don't try to pretend you're better than me," he said with a sneer.

Tobias leaned down to get right in his face. "I may

not be better than you or anyone else, but if you ever hurt your father again, I'll show you just how bad I can be."

Carl flushed bright red. "How dare you!"

"It's not an empty threat," Tobias said and purposely knocked into his shoulder as he passed, causing Carl to stumble back.

When Carl called out his name, Tobias's hands automatically curled into fists as he turned. After the past hour, he was looking for a target and the darker part of him, the part that was still as angry as he'd been as a teenager, hoped Carl would be it. "You got something more to say to me?"

Uriah's son looked as though he had plenty to say, but when he saw Tobias's expression and stance, he seemed to think twice. "You'd better start packing your bags," he said but was careful to stay out of reach as he circled around Tobias and hurried toward the safety of the big farmhouse.

Tobias was just talking himself out of chasing the little bastard down when his phone went off. Too intent on watching Carl's retreating back to answer it, he ignored the first few rings. But then he heaved a sigh and pulled his phone from his pocket.

It was Maddox.

Knowing his brother would advise him not to get into it with Carl, even if it was well deserved, he hit the talk button. "'Lo?"

"Tobias, I'm sorry to bother you again, especially if Harper's still with you, but—"

"She's gone," he broke in. "You don't have to worry about her."

Maddox hesitated. "Everything okay?"

"Why wouldn't it be?" he asked as though he didn't feel like shit.

"You sound...on edge."

Tobias let the door slam as he went into his house and started looking through everything to make sure none of his stuff had been disturbed. Fortunately, his bike, his TV, his backpack and everything else he really cared about was still there. "Carl's doing whatever he can to piss me off," he muttered. "That's all."

"Don't tell me that douchebag's causing trouble again."

"Yes. No!" he quickly said, reversing his position. "It's not what you think. Uriah's fine. He's not even home. Anyway, never mind. What's going on?" It hadn't been all that long since his brother had stopped by, so why was he calling?

"It's Atticus."

The tone of Maddox's voice made Tobias uneasy. "And? What's wrong?"

"He's in the hospital."

Forgetting about Carl, Tobias quickly switched the phone to his other ear. "Why? What's happened?"

"We're not entirely sure at this point. Susan got up and went to work this morning, but she needed him to watch the store while she drove over to Santa Barbara for some supplies. When she tried calling him she couldn't get him to pick up, so she tried the neighbor, who went over to rouse him and found him unresponsive."

"Unresponsive. What does that mean? He wasn't breathing?"

"He *was* breathing, but he was unconscious."

"And now?"

"He's awake. They're running all kinds of tests to figure out what could be wrong, but I know how much you care about him, so…I wanted you to know."

"Are you going over to the hospital?"

"I'm there now. Susan, Maya and Jada are up in the room with him, so I decided not to crowd in."

He'd decided not to crowd in because his mother-in-law still blamed him for what Tobias had done thirteen years ago and wouldn't speak to him. But Maddox rarely mentioned Susan and how she treated him. He knew Tobias felt bad enough. Maddox was just eleven months older, but he'd always tried to look out for Tobias. "Will you let me know if there's an hour or so when everyone will be gone?"

"You'd like to come see him?"

"Yeah."

"Sure. I'll do what I can to get you a few minutes, but you'd better drive over to the hospital now, because if I can manage it, it'll be a very small window. You know how protective Susan is."

"I do." He also knew that if she got wind of him being there, she'd do everything she could to drive him away. "I'm going to shower. Then I'll be right over."

"I'll be here."

"Thanks." He was about to hang up when Maddox said, "Wait—you haven't told me what's going on between you and Harper Devlin."

"There's nothing going on," he said.

"It sure looked like there was."

"Looks can be deceiving. Anyway, I don't want to talk about it."

There was a slight pause. "What's wrong? Don't tell me you've already had an argument."

It was much worse than an argument, which was why Tobias preferred not to talk about it. Also, he couldn't imagine Harper would want anyone else to know, even his brother. "No argument. We're just friends, anyway."

"You're saying you didn't sleep with her?"

"Maddox, stop."

"So you *did* sleep with her."

"I've got to go…"

"*Something's* happening between you two—"

"I'm hanging up now," he said and disconnected.

10

Tobias hung out in the hospital lobby with Maddox until Jada and Maya came down. Then they all went to dinner. When they returned to the hospital, they were hoping Susan would be gone, but they could see her car in the parking lot.

"Maybe she's going to stay all night," Tobias complained.

"She can't stay *all* night," Jada said. "If she doesn't get some sleep, her lupus might flare up again. She pushes herself too hard as it is. I worry about her—despite how she feels about me." She touched his forearm. "Let me go see what's going on."

Maya decided to stay in the waiting room with them. They teased her about some of the boys she knew from New Horizons, and she joked right back, but Tobias guessed she felt the tension. She was close to her grandmother, helped out at Sugar Mama all the time, but she loved them, too, which was why she hadn't gone back up to Atticus's room when Jada did. Her grandmother hated them so much it made her defensive. No doubt Maya was staying in case Susan came down and saw them; she knew Susan would be less likely to make a scene if she was there.

When Jada returned, she looked relieved. "He's doing better," she said. "The doctors are saying he must've hit his head in the accident, because his brain is bruised. But he's going to be okay, so my mother should feel reassured enough to leave soon." She looked at Tobias. "I'm sorry it's taking so long. Would you rather go home and try again tomorrow night?"

"No, I'll wait." He didn't have anything better to do. If he went home he'd just start thinking about Harper—or maybe he'd kick Carl's ass, which would provide an outlet for the anger, frustration and concern that was roiling around inside him but certainly wouldn't improve his reputation in Silver Springs.

Maddox and Jada left around nine. They had to take Maya home; she had school in the morning. Tobias considered leaving when they did. He didn't want to confront Susan on his own, but he also refused to be that big of a coward.

He hung out for two more hours before deciding to give up. It was getting late, and he had to work in the morning. He'd just stood up to get the keys out of his pocket when he heard the ding of the elevator around the corner.

Sitting down as fast as possible, he lifted a magazine to cover his face, just in case, and, sure enough, when he peeked around the edges, he saw Susan pass by.

Fortunately, she didn't so much as glance his way. She stared straight ahead as she moved tiredly toward the exit.

"Finally," he muttered when she was gone. He was the only one left in the waiting room. He'd been afraid that even with a magazine covering his face, she'd recognize him. No doubt she would have if she'd been paying attention.

When he was sure she wasn't going to turn back, he strode over to the elevator. As much as Tobias didn't care for Susan, he had to admire the depth of her love for her son. He'd always envied the boys in school who had devoted mothers. His mother had rarely come to class, showed up at only one or two school events during his entire childhood. She couldn't even pack him or Maddox a decent lunch, he remembered as he watched the numbers light up at the top of the elevator. If she ever tried, she'd simply stuff a bunch of junk food in a bag and hand it over—not that he'd minded that when he was a kid. Taking anything from home made for a good day, since he and Maddox had almost always been on the free-lunch program.

He got off on the fourth floor. Jada had given him Atticus's room number, so he was fairly confident he'd be able to find it. What he didn't know was how he'd be received. Atticus claimed to have forgiven him, and these days he was friendly whenever they ran into each other. But this recent accident could easily have reminded him of all the things he couldn't do—because of Tobias. It was even possible that Atticus might've been able to avoid hitting anything at all last night, if only he'd had the use of his legs. Then he wouldn't be here.

"Hello?" He knocked on the doorframe, since the door stood open, but received no response, so he peeked inside.

He had the right room. Atticus was lying in the bed with his eyes closed.

Tobias looked up and down the hallway. It was well after visiting hours, but Maddox had indicated the hospital wasn't strict on that policy, not if whoever was there wasn't causing a problem.

A nurse hurried past, but she was intent on getting wherever she was going and didn't pay him any mind.

He stepped inside the room and took the chair next to the bed; he didn't say anything for quite some time, just watched Atticus breathe. If only he hadn't gone to the party that terrible night, or hadn't taken acid, or hadn't found that gun, which had belonged to the parents of the boy who was throwing the party.

But he *had* gone to the party, he *had* been tripping on acid and, when he was hallucinating and out of his mind, thinking he was seeing some kind of monster, he'd shot an eleven-year-old boy—Jada's younger brother, whom she'd brought to the party against her parents' wishes.

As a result, Atticus was now paraplegic. The knowledge of the pain he'd caused, and the permanence of the loss, continued to torment Tobias. Tobias wasn't sure he'd ever be able to forgive himself, constantly struggled with what he'd done—some days worse than others. Although Maddox advised him to let it go, the past held him like a vise, and sometimes that vise tightened to such a painful degree he thought it would crush him entirely. It was in those moments that he was tempted to take up his old self-defeating behaviors.

"Hey. What are you doing here?"

Startled that Atticus could talk and sound so normal, Tobias turned to him. He'd assumed Atticus was out for the night. "I'm…here to check on you," he said lamely.

"In the middle of the night?"

"Your mother just left."

He managed a crooked grin. "How long did you have to wait for that?"

Tobias didn't see any reason to tell him it had been most of the evening. "I didn't mind. There was no need to upset her."

In a weak and slightly uncoordinated movement, Atticus gestured at his own prone position. "This isn't your fault, you know. This accident had—" he took a deep breath as though summoning strength "—nothing to do with you."

Tobias rocked back. "I didn't say it did."

"But that's what you were thinking. I could see it on your face."

Tobias hadn't realized he was so transparent—or that Atticus had been looking at him that closely. "I'm sorry, Atticus. For what I did thirteen years ago. I'm sorry for that every single day of my life."

"I know. But not everything that happens is a consequence of that one night. You have to let it go. Otherwise, you'll just…destroy yourself."

"I can't believe you don't wish that for me."

"That isn't what I want."

It was what his mother wanted. She would love nothing more. The negative energy that radiated off Susan was partly what helped feed Tobias's self-loathing. "Could you have avoided that parked car if you'd had the use of your legs?" It was a direct question, the type Tobias typically tried to avoid with Atticus, simply because it was so awkward, but he had to ask, had to know.

"Does it matter?" Atticus responded.

"You're kidding, right?"

"No. I'm going to be fine, so let's not even go there."

"You wouldn't be fine if your neighbor hadn't—"

"Dude," he broke in. "Will you do me a favor?"

Tobias waited to see what he'd ask.

"Will you stop ripping yourself apart? What happened at that party was just…one of those things. You didn't even know what you were doing." He scowled in an obvious attempt to get through to Tobias. "Please, *let it go*. You're only making it worse. If you can't get past it, you'll pull down Maddox and Jada and Maya. Do you think I want to see them suffer?"

Resting his elbows on his knees, Tobias dropped his head into his hands. What Atticus said made sense. And it made sense when Maddox said similar things. But internalizing it, being *able* to let it go, that was the hard part. "I'm trying," he said softly.

"I mean it, Tobias. I like you. I like you a lot. If you really want to help me, quit beating yourself up."

The lump that rose in Tobias's throat made it difficult to speak. He didn't dare try for fear his voice would break. So he sat there until he could overcome his emotions. Then he said, "I'm going to hike Half Dome this summer."

Atticus's eyes had drifted shut. "Oh, yeah? I've driven through Yosemite. It might be the most gorgeous place on earth."

"I agree. It's even prettier when you get up on some of the trails."

Atticus lifted his eyelids, but they looked heavy. Tobias guessed the doctor had given him a sedative so he wouldn't move around too much. "I bet," he said.

"That's why…" Once again wrestling with his emotions, Tobias took a deep breath. "That's why I'd like to take you with me."

"Take me with you…where?" He sounded a bit more alert.

"Hiking."

His eyebrows knit in a frown. "How do you propose to do that?"

"You've already seen how—in a video online."

"I can't even imagine what you're talking about," he said, but he was mumbling, winding down like a clock running out of battery power.

"We can talk about it later," Tobias said. "I was just wondering if you'd be open to it."

"To what?" He seemed to be drifting away despite his efforts to maintain the conversation.

"Hiking in Yosemite."

"I'd love to go hiking," he managed to say.

"Then that's what we'll do. We'll figure out a way for me to carry you."

Atticus said nothing. The meds had pulled him under.

Unable to resist, Tobias squeezed his hand as he stood to leave. "Get well."

When Tobias returned home, he found a plate of brownies on his doorstep. Thinking they might be from Harper, he got excited—until he read the attached note.

I was sad that you didn't make it back to the Eatery this weekend. :(I thought you might come in to see me again. My dad's out in LA, visiting his new girlfriend. Now would be a great time to call me. Doesn't matter how late.

Willow had signed her name, with a lot of *X*'s and *O*'s, as well as her number.

"Damn. And now I have to deal with *this*," he groaned, carrying in the plate.

He was sitting at the kitchen table with a tall glass of milk, eating one brownie after another while trying to decide how to let her down easy, when he heard a knock.

Who would be out this late? It was after one. *My dad's out of town...*

"Oh, God," he whispered when his mind snapped back to that part of Willow's note. Surely it wasn't her. Surely she hadn't been waiting around for him to get home.

He thought about pretending he was already asleep, but all the lights were on.

The knock sounded again. "Tobias?"

It wasn't Willow; it was Uriah. Tobias would've breathed a sigh of relief, except that hearing from his landlord so late wasn't normal, either. Had something else happened with Carl?

Pushing the plate of brownies aside, he got up to see what was going on.

Uriah was dressed in his overalls, and he *looked* okay... "What are you doing up this time of night?" he asked as he stood back to let the old man in.

"I've been waiting for you," he said as he crossed the threshold. "I was hoping we could talk without Carl around."

Tobias scratched his head. "Would you like to sit down?"

"No, I'll only be a minute."

"Is this where you give me thirty days' notice?" If

so, why couldn't Carl hear that? It was exactly what he'd been hoping for.

"What?" Uriah said. "I'm not going to give you notice. Where'd you get that idea?"

"Carl told me to pack my bags. Said he'd be moving in."

"That kid." He shook his head with a mixture of disgust and exhaustion. "If he wants to stay, he can live up at the other house with me."

"If that's the only alternative, I think I *should* let him have this house. Maybe that much separation would make it easier for the two of you to get along. At least you wouldn't have to worry about him coming into your bedroom at night and rifling through your wallet."

Uriah waved an age-spotted hand. "I'm not going to ask you to leave. I don't want you to go. That's what I came to tell you. Having Carl here doesn't change anything as far as your housing situation goes."

"Well, I'm pretty sure Carl disagrees." Tobias thought of finding Uriah's son outside his door earlier and the uneasy feeling it had given him.

"Doesn't matter to me," Uriah said. "Even if I don't kick him out, I can't imagine he'll stick around for long. As much as I wish he could pull his life together, I'm too realistic to believe it'll happen. What are the chances he'll be able to change after all these years?"

What were the chances he even wanted to? Tobias didn't get the impression Carl felt any remorse. Didn't last night prove it?

He suspected that Uriah was harboring more hope than he was willing to acknowledge. He just didn't want to be disappointed in the end. Otherwise, he would've sent his son packing when Carl tried to steal from him last night—and then went out, got drunk and nearly killed Atticus. "So what do *you* think will happen?" Tobias asked.

"He'll realize that living here isn't like being on easy street—that I expect him to work and help grow and harvest the tangerines. And after he gets tired of butting heads with me, he'll take off again."

Tobias couldn't help being skeptical. The way Carl had been talking about the property suggested he'd come to take control of his father's assets. That meant staying long-term. "Even though he has no money, no job and no place to live."

Uriah rolled his eyes. "I know. Doesn't make a damn bit of sense. But he's never done the smart thing. Never had any self-discipline."

Tobias was tempted to explain why he thought this visit from Carl would be different. It wasn't simply a matter of Uriah biding his time until Carl took off again—the same cycle he'd grown accustomed to in the past. With his mother gone and his father getting on in years, Carl's expectations had changed. He didn't feel he had to build a life of his own or contribute to anything. He was expecting to inherit from his father, and he believed, at that point, all his problems would be over.

As far as Tobias was concerned, that was a recipe for disaster. "What about the DUI? He'll have to be around to go to court for that. And they've suspended his license, haven't they?"

"Yes, but that shouldn't take more than a few months to sort out. I'm just glad Atticus wasn't injured any worse than he was. Poor kid."

Again, Tobias was tempted to tell Uriah what he believed would be a more likely scenario when it came to Carl, but he doubted that would make any difference. Now that Carl couldn't drive, he couldn't work even if he got a job, and there was no way his father would kick him out on the street. For better or for worse, Carl would be living on the property—at least until he handled the fallout of his DUI.

"From what I've heard, DUIs aren't cheap," Tobias pointed out.

The disgust Uriah felt about the way his son lived revealed itself again in his expression. "I'll have to pay for everything, of course. No surprise there. He doesn't have two nickels to rub together. But I'm going to make him work it off."

That sounded good in theory, but Tobias guessed it would only turn into another source of conflict when Carl tried to weasel out of it.

"Even if Carl does leave fairly soon, he probably won't just drive off into the sunset," Tobias said. "You realize that. Something will set him off, make him angry enough to go. And what he does in that moment? *That's* what I'm worried about."

Uriah shoved his hands in his overalls and frowned at the wall, seemingly deep in thought.

"You don't have anything to say to that?"

His eyes focused on Tobias again. "I guess I'm just hoping that, for once, things will go a different way."

Tobias knew that Uriah's love for Carl warred with his better judgment. His response confirmed it. And decisions that were made for emotional reasons didn't respond to logic.

Telling himself he'd done all he could, Tobias

nodded. "Okay. I understand. And I'll be here if you need me."

Uriah's well-lined face lit up. "You'll put up with him, too? You won't let him chase you away?"

"I won't let him chase me away." He couldn't. If he left, there'd be no one to make sure Carl wasn't mistreating Uriah.

Uriah's beard growth rasped as he rubbed a hand over his chin. "Thank you."

Tobias picked up the plate of brownies. "Would you like one?"

Uriah took a brownie off the top. "These look good. Where'd you get them? From Harper?"

Tobias refused to say who they were from. He didn't want Uriah to think he'd done anything to entice a teenager to his house. "You didn't see who it was when she came by?"

"No. Must've come while I was gone. I had to run some errands earlier."

"What about the security cameras? You haven't checked your computer?"

"Not lately. I've had too many other things to worry about."

"They're from a waitress I met," Tobias explained, keeping his answer vague.

"You dating her, too?"

"No. And before you came over, I was sitting here trying to think of the right way to let her know it." Although he was now of a mind to wait. There was no need to wake Willow in the middle of the night just to reject her, not when he could easily do it during the day.

Finished with his brownie, Uriah dusted the crumbs

from his hands. "Those aren't too bad. I say you give her a chance. Maybe she'll bring more."

Tobias chuckled. "Sorry. Not interested. Even if I was, can you imagine what her friends and family would think if she brought home a guy like me?" He was no longer talking about Willow, but Uriah didn't need to know that.

"I'd be happy to have you marry *my* daughter if I had one," he said. "Matter of fact, I'd consider her lucky to have found such a good man."

The tension Tobias had been feeling suddenly eased. What with Harper going home the way she had, Atticus landing in the hospital and Carl causing so many problems, he hadn't realized how uptight he'd become. But, other than Maddox, it was Uriah who'd helped stabilize him after he was released from Soledad, Uriah who'd made him feel as though someone was willing to give him another chance. And his landlord was still playing that role, which was why Tobias felt so much loyalty to him.

"You're getting sentimental in your old age," he teased. Neither one of them was comfortable showing emotion, but nothing meant more to Tobias than hearing those words, especially from someone who was familiar with his history—and could forgive him for it.

11

Harper woke with a headache. She hadn't slept well. Despite being exhausted, she'd tossed and turned, replaying the time she'd spent in Tobias's bed as well as the terrible moment right after, when she'd realized she'd somehow placed a call to Axel. She cringed every time she thought of it, doubted she'd ever get completely over the embarrassment and prayed he wouldn't tell anyone besides Rory, who already knew.

For the past eight months, she'd also been watching as the day of her divorce marched inexorably closer—and now, here it was. That hit her hard but, fortunately, she was beginning to transition from hurt to anger. She'd read that was a normal part of the grieving process and was grateful for it. Without anger, she would never have the strength to pull herself together.

At least she hadn't cried since her last contact with Axel. That was an accomplishment. She hadn't called him since then or texted him, either. Living without him wasn't anything she would've chosen, but she had to stop trying to go back, had to deal with reality and start moving forward again.

After she called to check on the girls, she spent the

next three hours going through thousands of photos and videos on her phone and getting rid of any that featured Axel. She couldn't bring herself to delete them completely. That would feel like erasing more than a decade of her life. But she put them all in one file labeled Failed Ten Years and sent it to the cloud so it would no longer be on her phone. She figured that was a step in the right direction.

If she'd been home, she would've gotten up and gone through the house, too—put everything of his in the garage so he could pick it up when he returned to the States. He'd left so many of his belongings behind, even his prized set of golf clubs. She had his childhood memorabilia and yearbooks in the attic. But he was busy, didn't have time to deal with it, and she'd allowed him to leave these things behind because she simply *couldn't* believe he wasn't coming back to her.

After she finished cleaning out her albums—paring down her collection of photos and videos—she grabbed her laptop and went online to search for what a divorced person should do next.

Most websites suggested closing any joint bank accounts and opening new ones, so she got ready and went to a local branch of the bank they used, where she opened her own account for the first time since college.

The whole experience felt weird, alien, *terrible*, but she told herself it'd get easier.

When she left, she texted Axel to let him know what she'd done.

I have a new bank account. When you get a minute, could you call me for the routing numbers and account information so you can make your child support payments?

It was late in Europe. She wasn't expecting an immediate response, but she got one.

What are you doing, Harper?

She climbed into the Range Rover but sat in the parking lot to text him back. What do you mean? I just told you.

You're not even in Colorado, where we live.

She gazed at the people coming and going in the lot. Although it probably seemed like just another day to them, it was the first day of a very different life for her.

So? There's a branch of the bank we use here in Silver Springs. No need to wait until I get back.

There was no need not to, either. What's the rush?

She shook her head. She'd thought he'd be relieved that he wouldn't have to prod her to get off his coattails. Why wait, Axel? We're divorced. As of today, you're a free man.

She was angry enough to add something snarky—that she hoped he was happy after destroying their family. But she didn't want to be the kind of person who'd act that way, angry or not. Besides, he had to be happier without her, since he hadn't come back to her.

What instigated this? he asked. That guy you're seeing?

She chuckled without mirth. No. Tobias has nothing to do with it. I'm starting my life over today.

PS, she added, don't forget to change your will.

You don't want my money when I'm gone?

She considered the question. No, she didn't want his money. The only thing she'd ever been interested in was his heart. Give it to the girls. I'll make my own, she wrote back. Good luck with your next concert. Again she was tempted to add a snarky comment—*I hope you enjoy whatever groupie you take home with you this time.* But, closing her eyes and taking a deep breath, she locked her phone so she couldn't accidentally dial him again and slipped it into her purse before backing out of the parking space.

Tobias felt like the walking dead. It had been a long day at work, especially going on so little sleep. Just after lunch, the parents of one of the students on the boys' side of New Horizons had gotten out of her car without putting the transmission in Park, and it had rolled down the steep embankment of the overfill lot into the administration building.

Fortunately, no one had been hurt. The car had, however, run over the blow-up Santa that Aiyana had put out front, which Tobias found sort of funny. The part he *didn't* find funny was that it also crashed into the building hard enough to punch a hole through the wall. He'd been working all day to clear away the rubble and get as much of the building repaired as possible—

so everyone wouldn't freeze to death before he could schedule a contractor to come out and take care of it later in the week.

Tobias couldn't wait to go home, shower and fall into bed. But he walked over to the smaller administration building on the girls' side of the campus so he could visit his brother, if he hadn't gone home yet.

Apparently hearing his footsteps, Maddox looked up from the papers spread out before him as Tobias reached the open doorway. "Hey, what are you still doing here?" he asked.

"I could ask you the same." Tobias walked in and sank into one of the two vinyl chairs across from Maddox's desk, stretching his legs in front of him. "It's after five. Everyone else is gone. But knowing how hard you work, I thought I'd take a chance."

"Now that I live on campus," Maddox said, "I sometimes stay a little later. Without the drive, I can get home pretty quickly."

"I've been dealing with that crash. You heard what happened?"

"Yeah. Haven't had a chance to go look, though. Was it bad?"

"Car came right into the lobby."

"Good thing no one was sitting there at the time. Was Betty behind her reception desk?"

"Yeah, but it didn't come quite that far. Thank goodness. Scared the hell out of her, though."

"What'd the owner of the car have to say?"

"What *could* she say? She was embarrassed and apologized profusely."

Maddox started to straighten his desk in preparation for leaving. "Would you like to come over for dinner tonight?"

"No, I'd rather not put any more pressure on Jada, not with her brother in the hospital." He also didn't want to be too visible right now. It would be easy for his sister-in-law to blame him for the difficulties between her mother and her husband. "How is Atticus, by the way? Have you heard anything?"

"Jada called after lunch to say he's doing better. If they don't release him today, they'll do it tomorrow."

"Did they ever figure out if there was anything to worry about besides the bruise on his brain?"

"No, that's it. Did you get to see him last night?"

"For a few minutes."

"How'd that go?"

Tobias crossed his ankles. "He was drugged up, so I'm not sure he'll remember, but it was…good." He couldn't help wondering if Jada's brother would bring up the hiking thing again. If he didn't, Tobias doubted he'd broach the subject again. Given the fact that Tobias was the reason Atticus couldn't hike, maybe it would be too awkward. Or just too physically demanding. Tobias was a strong hiker, but he'd never attempted to carry another human being up such steep inclines.

"You didn't run into Susan, did you?" Maddox asked with some chagrin.

"No. Saw her leave, though. Fortunately, she didn't notice me as she walked out."

"I try not to complain about her, but…"

"She's still giving you a hard time?"

Maddox threw up his hands. "It's not me I care about. She can treat me any way she wants. I hate what this is doing to *Jada*. Why is she forcing her daughter to choose between us? And why is she putting her granddaughter in such a difficult spot? Maya feels defensive and wary when she shouldn't have to. Even Atticus has gotten over the past."

"You wouldn't be in this situation if it wasn't for me. None of you. I'm sorry. I think about it all the time."

Maddox waved his words away. "Don't apologize. I don't want an apology. And *stop* thinking about it. I'm just blowing off steam. Having Atticus in the hospital has brought it all to the forefront again, because it's harder for Susan and me to avoid each other."

"I wish you didn't have to avoid each other."

"It is what it is. There's nothing more you can do."

If only there *was* some way to atone. But he couldn't restore what he'd taken.

With a sigh, Tobias got to his feet. "I'd better get going."

"Wait a second." Maddox stood, too. "How're Carl and Uriah getting along?"

"Now that Carl doesn't have a license and won't be able to drive, he won't be leaving anytime soon. I know that much."

"Oh, joy. He'll be at the orchard *all* the time."

"Right. You know how that will go. He wasn't at the house twenty-four hours before the first incident."

"Shit."

"And he's starting to mess with me."

Maddox grew more alert. "In what way?"

"Lurking by my place even though there's no reason for him to be there. Making snide comments. That sort of thing."

"He's an absolute ass."

"I'd love to teach him a lesson."

An anxious look came over Maddox's face. "But you won't, right? You can't touch him, Tob."

"I know," he grumbled. "I won't."

"Great." He rubbed his temples. "So...on to more positive subjects. Tell me about Harper."

What was positive about that? As far as Tobias was concerned, that was the most sensitive subject yet. "I already told you about her. There's nothing going on there."

Maddox peered more closely at him. "Why don't I believe you?"

"I don't know. Maybe because you're not listening?"

"I saw how you reacted when you felt she was threatened by my presence. I swear you would've fought *me* for her sake."

Tobias stretched his neck. "That's an exaggeration. I was just being polite."

"Sure you were," he said with a laugh. "But I can see why. She's beautiful, isn't she?"

Tobias narrowed his eyes. "Is this a trap?"

His brother sobered. "A warning. You know how much I think of you. As far as I'm concerned, you should be able to have any woman you want."

"Except someone like Harper?" Tobias could tell by Maddox's tone where he was going with that statement.

Maddox winced but nodded. "Yeah, except someone like Harper. Trying to get her would be like...like wishing for the moon. And I don't want to see you hurt. So, please, don't set yourself up for that kind of disappointment."

"I won't." He acted as though what he felt for Harper wasn't any big deal. But after he'd said goodbye to his brother and was walking toward the parking lot, he couldn't help checking his phone to see if he'd heard from her. He was *so* tempted to text her. He wanted to know how Axel had reacted to what he'd heard—if he'd been hard on her or if it had all blown over. He also wanted to know how Harper was feeling about what they'd done—if she regretted it.

He supposed he was even wondering if she wanted to do it again. Because he knew what *he* wanted. Whether it would ultimately run him into a brick wall or not, he'd take Harper back to bed in a heartbeat.

Carl was standing outside smoking pot when Tobias arrived home. Tobias would've ignored him—he preferred not to have any interaction with Carl—but Carl was once again loitering right outside Tobias's door.

Feeling his muscles tense in aggravation as well as dislike, Tobias stepped out of his truck and shut the door a little harder than he'd intended.

"Bad day?" Carl blew the pungent smoke into the air.

Tobias had a funny feeling that Carl was being annoying on purpose. He knew that Tobias wouldn't be happy to find him here. The orchard consisted of sixteen acres! There was no need for them to cross paths so often. Carl could go behind the garage or the barn, which was even farther away from the two houses, if he wanted to have a joint without his father seeing him.

"Not too bad," Tobias replied with a shrug.

"You just come from work?"

"That's right."

"You're a lucky man," Carl said. "At least you can work."

Tobias arched an eyebrow at him. "You're saying you can't?"

"Injured my back at my last job." He smiled through the haze, giving Tobias the impression he didn't really lament the injury. "I'm on disability."

So *that* was how he'd been getting by. Public assistance also explained why Carl couldn't quite manage on his own. Disability didn't pay a great deal, not to people who weren't earning much at the time they were injured.

"Where were you working when you got hurt?" Tobias expected him to say roofing or framing or some other occupation where back injuries were common. He was *not* expecting Carl to say what he did.

"At a gas station."

"You hurt your back *at a gas station*?" Tobias didn't bother hiding his skepticism.

Carl stared at his joint for a few seconds before letting the smoke curl out through his nose. "Yup. Freak accident. Slipped while mopping the floor. My back hasn't been the same since."

Tobias was willing to bet there'd been no accident—at least not one from which Carl hadn't fully recovered. But he wasn't in the best of moods. Maybe he was painting Carl as even more of a scam artist and loser than he was.

"That's unfortunate." Tobias gestured toward his door. "Do you mind?"

Instead of stepping aside, Carl took another hit of his joint. "Look, there's no reason you and I have to be enemies."

Where was this coming from? Carl hadn't minded

becoming enemies when he'd told Tobias to find another place to live. "As long as you don't get in my way, we won't have any problems," Tobias said.

Instead of getting angry, Carl studied him dispassionately. The marijuana seemed to have mellowed his usually caustic personality. "Okay, I admit we got off on the wrong foot. But I'm not the asshole you think I am." He gestured toward the house. "Why don't we go inside and share this? Relax, have some fun, get to know each other? Hanging out with you has got to beat hanging out with my old man."

Tobias wanted to say that *he* much preferred Uriah. He wasn't going to spend time alone with Carl. He had no interest in becoming friends with someone like him. But if he could find a way to get along with Carl, living on the same property would be far more pleasant for them both. It would be easier on Uriah, too. "I don't smoke," he said.

"Aw, come on. What's a little weed between friends?"

Tobias had learned his lesson. Other than the occasional beer or glass of wine, he didn't get involved with anything that altered his state of mind. Nowadays, he only got high on exercise and nature. "I said I'm not interested."

"What the hell? What kind of prick are you?"

Tobias's phone went off, creating just enough of a diversion to harness his impulse to slug the guy.

Still, Carl must've seen the look in his eyes because he scurried out of the way, allowing Tobias to stalk into his house and slam the door without responding.

Although his phone continued to ring, Tobias needed time to rein in his temper, so he ignored it at first. Then when he tried to silence the ringer, he saw that it was Atticus.

Because he thought Atticus might need something, Tobias answered despite his reluctance to talk to anyone—let alone Jada's brother—after his most recent encounter with Carl. "'Lo?"

"Hey."

"What's going on?" Tobias asked. "How are you feeling?"

"Better."

"Good. Are they going to release you today?"

"That's what my doctor's saying."

"When? Do you need a ride home?"

"No. My mother will pick me up."

"So…" Tobias grappled for something else to say. "How long will it take to get your truck fixed?"

"Don't know yet. Shouldn't take too long, but I haven't had a chance to deal with any of that yet."

"Of course not. Is there anything I can do to help? Call the repair shop or—"

"No. I've got it."

There was an awkward silence before Atticus continued, "I was just wondering…"

Tobias could tell Atticus was having a difficult time stating the reason he'd called.

"Last night when you were here…"

"Yes…"

"Were you saying something about…about the two of us going hiking in Yosemite, or did I dream that?"

"I mentioned it. Are you interested?" Torn between hoping he'd have the opportunity to do something special for Atticus and fearing he wouldn't be capable of pulling it off even if they were both committed to it, he held his breath.

"I am, but…how would we manage, considering… Well, considering? I mean, you'd have to carry me the whole way. Do you realize how difficult that would be, even with a carrier?"

Tobias almost admitted that he was worried, too. It would take *a lot* of training on his part. Even then, there was no guarantee he'd be strong enough. But he didn't want to confess that to Atticus. "I haven't been able to find the video you mentioned—the one with the man carrying the disabled person. But…was he anywhere close to your size?"

"That's hard to say. He looked like it. I'll find it so I can show you, and you can judge for yourself."

"Okay."

"If we decide it's feasible, when would you like to go?"

"The weather should be about perfect on your birthday."

No response.

"Atticus? You still there?"

"Yeah. I'm imagining hiking Yosemite for my birthday. I'd like that," he said, his voice turning dreamy. "I think I'd like that a lot."

"So would I," Tobias said.

"Something to plan for."

"Yes."

"Okay."

Tobias stared at his phone long after he'd disconnected. He would have to forget all his concerns and start training. Carrying Atticus up Half Dome would require every bit of energy, strength, resilience and willpower he could muster.

But he was grateful to have something so challenging to concentrate on. Then maybe he'd be too tired and preoccupied to think about Harper.

12

On Tuesday, Harper drove to LA so she could go to Disneyland with her girls. Karoline had been shocked to hear that she was coming, but Harper had insisted she no longer needed time alone, that she was set on her new path and preferred not to miss out on this opportunity to build such great family memories. She was afraid she'd go back to Tobias's house if she didn't take up her responsibilities as a mother. She found herself thinking about him all the time—almost obsessively so, which shocked her. They'd only spent a couple of days together. It wasn't as if she knew him well.

Occasionally she also found herself thinking about how different this trip would be if Axel were with them. She missed having a complete family, missed the safety, security and peace of mind it afforded. She'd told him he could keep his money and she'd earn her own, but it wasn't entirely clear how she was going to do that. It'd been a number of years since she'd been part of the workforce.

Still, she didn't reach out to him. Something had changed in that bedroom with Tobias. She couldn't name what, but it had put some much-needed distance between her and her ex-husband.

Maybe it was the embarrassment she felt about what he'd heard via that pocket dial. Or maybe it was that the encounter had shown her other possibilities. The rest of her life didn't have to be nothing but doom and gloom because Axel had decided to opt out of their marriage.

Tobias had provided a glimmer of hope, she decided. He'd shown her that Axel wasn't the only desirable man in the world.

Ironically, once she stopped calling her ex-husband, he started calling her—and not just to get her banking info. It got to the point that she silenced her phone and began ignoring him. She had to. She wouldn't have any chance of maintaining her resolve and starting over if she didn't.

After three calls in a row that she sent straight to voice mail—partly because she needed emotional distance and partly because she was afraid he'd start in on what he'd heard that day—he texted her an angry message for not picking up. Really? We can't even talk anymore? What the hell is going on with you? Have you lost your mind?

Planning to deal with him later, she put her phone back in her purse, but while they were walking through Adventureland, she saw her sister answer a call and felt anxious. She hadn't told Karoline about Tobias. She was hoping Karoline wouldn't have to know.

But what if Axel, frustrated by her lack of response, had turned to calling her sister?

As Karoline moved away from them when they got in line for the *Indiana Jones* exhibit, Harper felt her stomach sink. *You'd better not be tattling on me*, she thought, but when her sister glanced back at her with a hint of surprise on her face, Harper knew what was going on.

"Damn it, Axel," she muttered to herself.

"What'd you say, Mommy?" Everly was so excited about the ride she couldn't keep from hopping and twirling.

Supremely conscious of her sister talking on the phone ten yards away, Harper pulled her coat tighter. Southern California never got too cold, but it was chilly today. "Nothing."

"Aren't you coming with us, Aunt Karoline?" Piper called out.

Karoline didn't respond. She was too deep in conversation.

Terrance answered for her, "She's not much for the rougher rides. We'll let her off the hook on this one, okay?"

When they reached the front of the line, Karoline was still on the phone but waved for them to go on without her.

Harper kept her smile firmly in place for the sake of her girls, her nieces and her brother-in-law, and pretended to enjoy herself as they loaded up and then careened around in the cart, but her stomach was in knots when she got off, and it had nothing to do with the ride.

Karoline was off the phone and waiting for them as they emerged.

"How was it?" she asked Piper, who ran ahead of them.

"It was *awesome*!" Piper turned around to face Harper as she, Everly, Terrance and the twins caught up. "Can we go again?"

"We have a FastPass for Space Mountain. Let's go there first," Terrance suggested.

As they started off, Karoline caught Harper's arm. "I have to go to the bathroom. Harper and I will meet you at the exit when you get off."

"You're not coming with us?" Everly, in particular, seemed to be enjoying the fact that Harper was acting more like herself than she had since Axel moved out.

Harper exchanged a look with Karoline. She didn't see why there had to be any big rush to explain what'd happened with Tobias, but she knew her sister. If Karoline was upset, her shock would only turn to anger if Harper put it off. "I'm betting you'll want to ride it more than once. I'll go the next time, okay, honey?"

Reluctantly, Everly let go of her hand and Harper waved as the small group rushed off.

Once they were gone, Karoline didn't even turn toward the restrooms. "What *happened* after we left LA?" she asked.

How much had Axel told her?

Hoping he'd had the decency to leave out the more embarrassing details, Harper hitched her purse higher on her shoulder. Axel wasn't all that great at keeping secrets, but he wasn't vindictive. If he'd told Karoline, it was because he was hurt, or suddenly insecure, not because he was out to get her. But still… "I learned that Axel isn't the only man in the world, I guess," she said.

Her sister studied her closely. "And how did you learn that?"

"By meeting someone I found—" she searched for the appropriate word "—interesting."

"You mean *attractive*."

She thought of Tobias, how he'd put on her skates

and kept her from falling every time she wobbled on the ice. He was big and strong and kind. She also thought of his smile—how sexy it was—and the way he kissed and did other things that were even more enjoyable. "Interesting *and* attractive."

Karoline's jaw dropped. "So you *are* dating someone else."

Was that all Axel had said—that there was now another man in the picture? "One date isn't 'dating' someone."

"It's a step in the right direction. Why didn't you tell me?"

"Because it was nothing." She held her breath, waiting to see if her sister would contradict her. If Axel had told her she'd slept with this other man, Karoline would definitely have something to say about it.

"You're not planning to see him again?"

Harper let her breath go in relief. Apparently, Axel hadn't said *too* much. "No."

"Why not?"

Because she knew where it would go if she did. "I'll be returning to Colorado with my kids, where I'll get back on my feet and continue to heal before I risk my heart again."

"He knows that?"

"Of course."

Karoline didn't respond right away. After a few seconds, she said, "That's why you won't accept Axel's calls…"

Harper raked her fingers through her hair. "It's not that I won't accept them. It's more that…that there's no reason for him to call me. He ended our marriage. And now that it's over, I need to move on. If I'm talking to him all the time that'll be much harder. If he needs something, he can always text me."

"That's what I've been trying to tell you!"

"Then you should be glad."

"I *am*. I'm just wondering who this other guy is. Don't tell me he's the one who gave you the rose…"

Harper didn't see any harm in admitting that. "As a matter of fact, he is."

"What's his name?"

"Does it matter? You won't know him. He's never heard of you or Terrance. He's only lived in Silver Springs for five months."

"Does he have any kids?"

"No. Never been married."

Karoline nodded, obviously satisfied with her answers. "Well…I'm ecstatic that you seem to be on the road to recovery."

"I *am* on the road to recovery," Harper insisted. "It'll take some time, but…I'll get there."

Her sister nudged her. "Axel is pretty freaked out," she confided with a gleeful chuckle.

Harper couldn't help being *a little* pleased. "What'd he say?"

"He asked if I knew who you were seeing. If he was a decent guy. If he'd be good for the girls. But I bet it wasn't about the girls at all. I bet it's hard for him to imagine another man taking his place."

"He didn't consider that possibility before? Didn't believe I'd ever move on?"

"You've always been so in love with him, I honestly doubt he did. The entire world is falling at his feet right now. How dare you defect?"

"I didn't defect." Harper's mind wandered to the

night he'd first said he was unsatisfied in their marriage. She'd never experienced anything quite so painful. After he'd mentioned the word *divorce*, she could hardly breathe. "He kicked me to the curb."

"Exactly. As far as I'm concerned, it serves him right that you're not waiting around, hoping to get him back."

Harper wasn't sure she'd go *that* far. She wasn't pursuing him, but she did want her family to be whole again, and, to a point, she still loved Axel. She supposed part of her always would. They'd shared ten years of their lives, had two children, belonged to each other's families. It wasn't easy to unravel all of that.

But if he didn't love her in return, and she couldn't make him happy, she wasn't going to continue to plead with him. "Who knows how I'll feel tomorrow." She shrugged. "I'm just taking it one day at a time."

"That's all you can do." Her sister slipped an arm around her and lowered her voice. "You're stronger than you know. I'm so proud of you," she said, giving her a squeeze.

Harper winced. She doubted Karoline would be proud of how she'd come to be where she was at, but she didn't see how it would help the situation to confess.

She smiled as her sister began to propel her toward Space Mountain so they could wait for their families.

Everly and Piper were just coming out of the ride, both of them laughing, when her phone vibrated with another text.

"I bet this is him," she told Karoline, but Karoline was no longer listening. She was moving forward, talking to her twins, who were telling her she just *had* to go back on the ride with them.

Harper pulled out her phone. But the text wasn't from Axel. It was from Tobias:

How are you?

Her heart began to pound. She'd been so tempted to contact him, so tempted to see him again.

Telling herself she wouldn't respond, she slid her phone back in her purse. But when everyone else was preoccupied with choosing a Disneyland sweatshirt to take home, and she stood off in a corner, waiting for Everly to try hers on, she couldn't resist taking her phone out again—just to read and reread those three words with his name attached.

After parking in his own drive, Tobias checked his phone one last time. Harper hadn't responded to his text.

He told himself not to be disappointed; after all, it was what he'd expected.

Still, he couldn't help feeling let down as he climbed out of his truck. When he closed his eyes, he could still smell her hair, feel her skin. He'd never been so into someone.

It's probably only because you can't have her. Forget you ever met her.

Trying to shrug off the melancholy that'd set in along with some more bad weather, he turned his focus to the night ahead. On his way home from work, he'd stopped and bought groceries. He didn't feel like going out, so he was planning to cook. But since he'd missed learning the basic skills most other people picked up in young adulthood, he wasn't very good in the kitchen. He could make a few things—mostly breakfast. If he did dinner, it involved a steak, a burger, some kind of fish, a burrito or a chicken salad. Or he simply opened a can of soup. Not a very extensive repertoire, but he got by. And normally, whenever he went to the trouble of making a meal, he invited Uriah to join him.

Uriah did the same for him. They were both often alone at night, so it made sense. They usually finished the evening with a game of chess. Unlike cooking, chess was something Tobias *was* very good at. Uriah couldn't beat him, but he liked to try.

Thinking it was time to give the old man another chance, Tobias left the groceries in his truck and started toward Uriah's house. They'd grown so comfortable with each other that he would often knock, open the door before Uriah could even respond and shout that dinner was at his place tonight. But before he could get that far, he considered the possibility of having to invite Carl, too, and changed his mind. If Carl was going to be there, he'd rather eat alone.

Reversing direction, he strode back to unload the groceries.

He'd already put the perishables in the fridge and formed his meat patty when he realized the onion he'd bought hadn't made it into the house.

Damn. He needed it for his burger.

It was much darker out than it had been only fifteen minutes earlier, and it was raining again, but he didn't bother to put on a jacket. He wasn't going to be out long.

Hunched against the cold, he searched his truck. Sure enough, the onion had fallen out of the bag and rolled under the seat. He'd found it and was almost back inside when he heard raised voices.

"Give me those keys! You don't have a license!"

"Oh, my God! Will you chill out? I'm just going to get a six-pack. It's right down the street."

Tobias leaned around the corner of the house to take a peek at what was going on. He could see two figures in the halo of the porch light at Uriah's house. Carl and Uriah were outside, arguing.

"Then you'll have to dust off the old bicycle in the garage and ride that in the rain, because I'm not letting you get behind the wheel," Uriah said.

Carl wrenched open the door of his vehicle despite his father's protests. "I'm almost forty years old. You have no say over what I do!"

"Are you going to force me to call the cops?" Uriah grabbed the door handle, trying to stop him. "Do you want to go back to jail? Is that what you're after? Because that's what's going to happen if you do this."

Carl yanked the door so suddenly it nearly made Uriah fall. "You'd do that, too. Wouldn't you?"

"Carl, don't make this any harder than it has to be. We can live without beer for one night," Uriah said, speaking more calmly. "I'll pick some up tomorrow."

Setting his jaw, Tobias strolled down the drive, tossing the onion between his hands to keep them busy. He wanted to throw it and break Carl's windshield, but he knew the psychologist he'd worked with at the prison would say it wasn't an "appropriate response." They'd talked a lot about appropriate responses, mostly because what was appropriate in prison—because it was inevitable or sometimes the only way to survive—wasn't appropriate out of prison. And while he'd learned to cope with living on the inside, she'd wanted him to understand that living on the outside would require a different set of skills.

"What's going on?" he asked as if he didn't already know.

Clearly agitated, Uriah gestured toward his son. "I can't let him drive. If he gets caught, he'll be in even more trouble than he is already."

"I'm *not* going to get caught!" Carl snapped. "It's a straight shot. I'll be back in less than twenty minutes. I don't know why you need to get involved. I can run my own life."

The argument could be made that he didn't do a very good job of it. Everyone pretty much agreed on that. But Tobias decided the psychologist he'd worked with at the prison would also counsel him not to say so. *That will only escalate the situation*, she'd say.

Problem was, deep down he wanted to escalate the situation, because he was dying to teach Carl a lesson. But now that Tobias was out of prison, he was choosing to use diplomacy instead of brute strength—even though, in this case, he was convinced brute strength would get the message across much faster. "There's no need for anyone to go anywhere," he said. "I just got back from the store. I've got plenty of beer."

Uriah looked relieved and hopeful that this was a solution Carl would accept. "Hear that? Tobias has beer," he repeated as if Carl couldn't hear for himself. "There's no need to go anywhere. And I can get some more tomorrow."

When Carl's gaze shifted between them, Tobias thought he was about to flip them both the bird and drive off. Carl glanced into the driver's seat of his car, but Uriah was still hanging on to his door, and Tobias was ready should anything that threatened Uriah happen. Maybe those two factors made Carl realize he should just let this one go.

"Fine," he said, now sullen. "How many cans ya got?"

"Enough," Tobias said.

Carl glared at him. He understood that Tobias had only stepped in for Uriah's sake and seemed to resent the interference. But finally he stalked into the house and slammed the door.

"Thanks," Uriah murmured. "And don't worry. This won't happen again."

"How do you know?" Now soaked and chilled to the bone, Tobias continued throwing the onion back and forth.

"Because I'm going to hide his keys."

Tobias flung his wet hair out of his face with a quick toss of his head. "And what about *your* keys?"

"I'll hide those, too."

"I don't think that's the answer. If he demands you give them to him—"

"I can manage," Uriah interrupted.

Tobias wasn't convinced. He held up the onion. "I'm making burgers, if you'd like to come eat and get away for a while."

Uriah frowned. "I'd love to. But I don't dare leave him when he's like this. For all I know, he'll burn down the house while I'm gone."

Tobias felt his eyebrows go up. "You just said you can manage."

"Yeah, well, we both know I was lying." With a sigh, he started toward the house.

Tobias caught his arm. "So what you're really saying is that you're going to take your chances."

"It's what Shirley would want me to do," he replied, his voice even softer.

Tobias shook his head. "No. I don't think she'd want you to risk yourself for his sake."

"I'm getting old, Tobias. If I could help my son get stable before I pass away, I'll consider whatever I've gone through or will go through to be worth it."

Tobias didn't think it was possible for Carl to get on an even keel. That would take too much effort on *his* part. He had to see the need and want to change, or nothing would happen.

He opened his mouth to say so—but then he closed it again. How could he be so sure Carl would fail? He didn't know what the future held. He only knew that Uriah was essentially asking him to back off and let him have this chance to try. And if anyone should be willing to offer others a second chance, it was him. Uriah, Maddox, Jada, Maya, Aiyana and Atticus had all been kind enough to give *him* a second chance, hadn't they? "Okay," he said. "I'll get the beer."

Tobias carried a six-pack over to Uriah's and put it on the kitchen counter without speaking to Carl, who sat in the living room, in Uriah's recliner, glowering at the TV. He seemed to have lost his desire to have a beer, which made Tobias suspect he'd been more interested in scoring some weed. Although marijuana was now legal in California, it was definitely something Uriah wouldn't get for him.

"Have a good night," he told Uriah.

Uriah stepped outside onto the stoop with him. "I appreciate your patience," he said.

Tobias jerked his head toward the house, to indicate Carl. "He's lucky to have you. I just wish he realized that."

To avoid getting any wetter, Tobias jogged back to his own house, where he finished cooking his burger and ate his dinner while watching TV.

Afterward, he felt at loose ends, frustrated and worried about the situation with Uriah and Carl, and he couldn't quit checking his phone, hoping that Harper would respond.

An hour or so later, he was lying on the couch, watching the news while he considered going to the Blue Suede Shoe to shoot some pool—he figured it might help get his mind on other things—when he heard a knock.

Assuming it was Uriah, and wondering if he was going to have to play referee again already, he yelled, "Come in."

The door swung open. But it wasn't Uriah who walked into his kitchen; it was Willow from the Eatery.

13

Oh, shit. Tobias had never responded to Willow's message with those brownies! He'd had a lot of other things on his mind and, hesitant to hurt her feelings, he'd put it off.

That was a bad decision because now here she was.

"Hello." He jumped to his feet.

She closed the door. "It's so cold tonight."

"Yeah. I was out earlier. It's chilly." He raked his fingers through his hair. "What's going on?"

"Didn't you get my brownies?" she asked uncertainly.

What was left of them was sitting on the counter. "Yes. Yes, I did. And they were…er…delicious." He gestured toward the plate. "As you can see, they're almost gone."

Obviously self-conscious, she hugged her coat close as she looked up at him from underneath her eyelashes. "What about the note? Did you get that, too?"

"I did, yes. And I was going to respond. But…I've been really busy." He knew that was a lame excuse, but he didn't want to hurt her feelings.

"So…are you interested? I mean… I've had a thing

for you ever since I first saw you." She blushed and glanced away.

Tobias reached out to touch her elbow, a gesture intended to soften his words. "You're a beautiful girl, Willow. Don't get me wrong. It's just that… Well, you're too young for me."

Her eyes widened. "What does age matter? I'm old enough. I'm an adult. I turned eighteen last month. I told you that at the diner, remember?"

"I remember, but—"

"You can't get in trouble for anything we do."

"That's not the only consideration. I'm *thirty*. That's twelve years' difference."

"I don't care!" She grabbed his hand and brought it inside her coat to her heart—at least, he thought that was her intent, but whatever she was wearing seemed to be low-cut, and the softness of her breast filled his hand.

Clearing his throat, he pulled away. "We're in very different stages of life. I mean, you're still in high school."

"Yes, but I'll graduate in the spring. What're a few months? After that, I could even move in here with you." She lowered her voice. "If you wanted me to. Think about having this in your bed every night." When she dropped her coat, he realized she wasn't just wearing a low-cut blouse or sweater. She was wearing red see-through lingerie with black high heels.

She looked good, but she reminded him of a little girl playing dress-up.

Picking up her coat from the floor, he tried to give it back to her. "Willow, listen. I'm not the right guy for you. Can you imagine how your parents would react if you started seeing someone so much older? And then there's my record. They won't want you getting involved with me."

"They'll get over it. *I'm* not worried about your past. You were seventeen when…when everything happened."

"True. But I've spent an eternity behind bars since then, and yet you're only a year older than I was when I went in."

She seemed stricken. "But you're all I ever dream about! I bought this outfit for you." She gestured at the skimpy underwire bra and thong. "Feeling you inside me—that's all I want for Christmas."

"Don't say that," he told her.

"Do you know how many guys at my high school would *love* to see me like this?" she fired back.

"I'm sure almost *any* guy would love to see you like this, but you're making a mistake. What you're feeling for me is…is just a crush. You don't really know me."

"What are you talking about? You've been coming to the Eatery since I started working there. I thought *I* was the reason."

He stopped her from lifting his shirt. "Willow—"

"I've been saving my virginity for you, Tobias," she whispered, standing on her toes to kiss his neck. "I want *you* to be my first."

Shit. "I'm, uh…flattered." He dropped her coat, trying to get her away from him, so he had to pick it up again. "But I can't let you make this mistake."

Her bottom lip jutted out when he settled her coat around her shoulders to cover her up. "You don't want me?"

"Sex should mean something," he explained. "That's when it's good. Don't…don't sell yourself short, okay?"

"You don't want me," she said again. Only this time it wasn't a question; it was a statement.

"I can't be with you," he explained.

She stuffed her arms back inside her coat. "You don't know anything. You don't deserve me—deserve this," she said, gesturing at her body.

"I agree," he said, relieved when she gave up and stomped toward the door.

"I can't believe you'd lead me on, only to embarrass me like this," she said before grabbing the doorknob.

He caught the door so it wouldn't hit the wall when she flung it open. "I'm sorry. But you'll find the right man one day. Just…don't be in too much of a hurry."

She didn't respond. She rushed from the house, leaving him standing there, feeling like a jerk for not heading this off by texting her the moment he read her note. Maybe then he could've avoided this.

After he gave her a small lead, he walked out to make sure she didn't pull too far into the orchard and get stuck in the mud. It wasn't easy to turn around on the long drive. That was when he saw Carl standing under the eaves of his father's house, smoking a cigarette.

"Hey, sweet thing!" he called out when he saw Willow. "Where ya going so fast? Somethin' wrong?"

Willow didn't answer him. She got in her car, revved the engine and nearly hit Carl's piece-of-crap vehicle as she hauled ass down the drive. She didn't get stuck in the mud, didn't even come into danger of it, because she didn't bother to turn around.

"Whoa! What the hell!" Carl stepped out into the rain to watch her go. Then he looked at Tobias. "What'd you do? Try to get in her pants?"

"Stay out of it," Tobias snapped and went back inside, where he tried to relax, but he was even more listless than he'd been before his encounter with Willow.

Finally, he changed his shirt, scooped his keys off the counter and headed to the Blue Suede Shoe. The flashing neon sign was only a block away when he glanced over and saw Susan sitting at the same intersection. She noticed him, too, and gave him that dirty look of hers—the one that made him feel as though he wasn't worth the air he was breathing.

It distressed Tobias that she had the power to cut him so deeply, but she had good reason to hate him, so he just looked away and let her start off first as soon as the light turned green.

This just wasn't his night, he decided. And he didn't feel a whole lot better later on, even though he beat all challengers at pool.

It didn't matter what he did.

All he could think about was Harper.

The rest of the week went by *very* slowly. Harper had always loved the Christmas season, but she was learning that it could be hell when you were suffering. All the twinkling lights, and the cheerily decorated houses and yards and rooms—even the smiling faces—somehow rubbed salt in the wound. And it took such energy to keep up with everyone else's good cheer.

Her mother often said that time took care of everything, but Pearl never added that time moved on leaden feet when you most needed it to race. Right now time felt like it was standing still.

Although almost every moment was a struggle,

Harper didn't let herself call Axel, not even when she remembered the tender times they'd shared, the past Christmases, most of which—at least in the early years—had been so idyllic. And she responded to his many attempts to contact her with a brief text here and there. She wanted to be a fair ex, but it would be far too easy to backslide if she wasn't vigilant.

She didn't let herself respond to Tobias, either. She had responsibilities, and she was going to see to those responsibilities instead of allowing herself to collapse under their weight and run into the arms of a stranger.

"Hey."

Harper jumped. She hadn't realized Karoline had come into the kitchen, hadn't heard a thing. "Hey," she responded, quickly pasting on the smile she'd been wearing the whole time they were in LA. They were home now, but with Christmas only two weeks away, they were focusing on festive activities.

"I just talked to Mom."

"What'd she say?" Harper asked. "Are she and Dad still coming out for Christmas?"

"Not anymore. Aunt Elaine had another ministroke last night."

"Is she okay?"

"She's going to be fine, but she's been having so many health problems that Mom feels they should go to her house and help with Christmas."

"It's too bad what Elaine has been going through."

"I'm sad for her, and a little disappointed for us," Karoline admitted. "But Mom and Dad said they'd come for Easter. You will, too, won't you?"

"Of course. Or you can all come to my house."

"Where are the kids?" Karoline asked.

"Stringing popcorn for a garland in the family room." Karoline had decorated the tree that stood in the front window, where all the neighbors could see it, but she'd set up a second tree for the kids.

"You're not helping them?"

"I am. I just came in to get a drink." She'd also been using the privacy of the empty kitchen to let down her guard for a moment, but she couldn't say that.

"So they're having fun?"

"A blast." Harper walked over to set her empty glass in the sink.

"I'm thinking we should make gingerbread houses this year." Karoline held out the magazine in her hands to show Harper several elaborately decorated gingerbread houses. "Look at these. Aren't they beautiful?"

Harper considered the pictures. Normally, she would've loved to make gingerbread houses. But in her current state, she didn't have the energy to take on something that required so much work and creativity. "You mean…like, one? Or more than one?"

"Each of the girls will want to make her own."

"Probably."

"We should each make one, too."

Harper laughed. "What on earth will we do with that many gingerbread houses?"

"Take pictures of them, post them on social media—and then give them away."

"To who?"

"Whoever could use some Christmas cheer! We'll take over a plate of cookies, too."

Harper slid her gaze over to the clock. It was only seven on a Friday night. But somehow, all she wanted to do was go to bed. "Are you talking about doing this *tonight*?"

"No, the girls are busy with the tree. We could do it tomorrow morning. I just need to run over and buy the candy and stuff." She got her keys from the drawer where she kept them. "Want to go with me? Terrance is here to look after the girls."

"Sure," Harper lied and dutifully went to get her coat.

Her phone rang while they were driving.

"That's probably one of the girls wondering where we are," Karoline said.

Harper was almost afraid to look at her screen. If by chance it was Tobias, she wouldn't want her sister to know. But he hadn't contacted her since asking that one question, so she figured she didn't have much to worry about. "It's Matt," she said, surprised to see his picture.

"From the band?"

"Yeah."

"What could he want?"

"I don't know." She felt a moment's panic. "I hope there's nothing wrong with Axel." She answered before Karoline could say anything else. "Hello?"

"Harper, do you have a minute?"

"Is everything okay?" she asked instead of answering.

"With…"

"The band? The tour? Axel?"

"Everything's fine. Except…"

Karoline stopped at a red light, watching Harper curiously.

"Except…" Harper prompted.

"It's Axel. He isn't the same. We can't get him to focus, and we need him to be on top of his game, you know? This is a big tour, a *huge* opportunity for us—and he's the front man."

"I don't understand," she said. "What's wrong with him?"

"You're driving him crazy, cutting him off the way you have!"

Harper stiffened at the accusation in his voice. "I haven't 'cut him off.' We're divorced."

"He's losing his mind thinking you're with this other guy."

"I'm not *with* anyone."

"You and I both know what I'm referring to."

Harper was relieved that he didn't get specific. On the one hand, what she did, especially now, was none of his business. But on the other hand... Well, Axel had involved him.

"That phone call crushed him," he went on. "He can't concentrate, doesn't want to sing. He keeps asking to return to the States, is missing his kids."

It was about time he missed his kids. Harper had begun to wonder if that was ever going to happen. "The world won't end if he cuts the tour short and comes back to see them."

"What are you talking about? He can't cut the tour short! People have bought tickets. The promoters will never work with us again."

"Then I don't know what to say. I wasn't the one who planned the tour over Christmas, and it wasn't my idea to get the divorce."

"I understand that. But...can't you talk to him? Reassure him? Figure out some way to keep him going so we can finish this thing?"

"How am I supposed to do that?" she asked.

"Just let him know you're not really with that guy you were…with."

"I've told him that!"

"Then be more convincing!"

Embarrassed that she had to talk about that night with Matt of all people, Harper began to massage her forehead. "Look, I'm not out to hurt Axel. I'm trying to recover and move on. I have to do what's best for *me* now, have to remain strong for the sake of our girls."

"Seems like a hell of a way to do it."

"What?"

"Never mind. So you won't even try?"

Squeezing her eyes closed, she continued to massage her forehead.

"Harper?" Karoline said. "What is it?"

Harper waved her off. "Fine," she said into the phone. "I'll call him. But not right now. Later. I'm at the store."

"Thanks, Harper. We really appreciate it. I'm telling you, he's not the same since…that happened."

Shame sent a prickle down Harper's spine. "I'll do what I can," she said and hit the end button.

Karoline was, of course, waiting to hear everything. "What's going on?"

"It sounds like Axel's getting homesick."

"Homesick!"

"Matt says he's missing the girls, wants me to convince him to hold out until the tour is over."

"And you're going to do that?"

"At this point, I'd rather he not come back. Maybe I'll be stronger if I have more time."

"Good point. So what are you going to do?"

"I'm going to encourage him to stay. Do you want him coming to Silver Springs for Christmas?"

"No. I want him to be willing to come, but…I guess I don't want him to actually come. That would be awkward, since we're all pretty mad at him for leaving you in the dust."

Harper didn't like the way Karoline was characterizing her, but she had enough going on, didn't need to start an argument with her all too frank sister. "Well, I don't want him to come, either. And I don't want him to take the girls to Colorado." She loved spending time with Piper and Everly, but she'd also been using them as the reason she couldn't call Tobias.

If they were gone, she had no idea what she might do.

"This is what it looks like," Atticus said.

Tobias sucked the foam from his beer as he watched the YouTube video Atticus had called up on his phone—the video of the hiker carrying a disabled friend on his back. "That might be possible."

"But it looks crazy, right?"

"It might *be* crazy." Tobias leaned back in his seat. "You need to consider the risk. If I take one wrong step, you could get hurt."

Atticus played the video again. "Wouldn't you face the same risk? I can't imagine it would feel good to fall with a hundred and fifty pounds strapped to your back. You'd hit the rocks pretty hard."

"I guess that's true." But *he* didn't matter—at least

not to most people. Those who knew his past considered him to be no good, not worth their concern. It was Atticus they'd all be worried about, except for Maddox, of course. Maddox would probably advise him not to do it.

"But you're still willing to try?"

"Sure, I'm down," Tobias said. What else could he say? Atticus was so excited about the possibility.

Jada's brother took a drink of his own beer. "How will you train for this?"

"I've always lifted. Been doing it in the weight room at the school since I left prison. But I'll bulk up to improve my strength, and I'll run to improve my stamina. I'll hike more, too, of course."

Atticus lifted his beer toward the bar window. "In *this* weather?"

"It doesn't get too bad, not around here."

A rush of cool wind whipped into the Blue Suede Shoe as the door opened and Maddox and Jada walked in. Tobias had called and invited them to come as soon as Atticus had set up this little meeting. He always felt more comfortable when they were around, felt as though fewer people were staring at him and Atticus. It made more sense that Atticus would be in a group that included his sister than alone with the man who'd cost him the use of his legs.

"Should we do some test hikes together?" Atticus asked as Tobias waved them over.

"That'd be a good idea."

"When?"

"In the spring, when the rainy season's over and I've had a chance to prepare. After the weather warms we'll have a couple of months before your birthday. That should be enough time."

"Are you thinking we should go out once a week or…"

"Yeah. Once a week would be enough—every Saturday or Sunday—so you'll have a chance to get accustomed to riding in the pack. You might not like it. I'm guessing it'll feel pretty damn unstable, since you won't have any control. You'll have to decide whether you feel comfortable relying on me."

"I trust you," he said without hesitation.

His trust actually made Tobias *more* nervous. He didn't want to disappoint him. "What about your mother? Have you told her what we're planning to do? Will she let you go?"

"I haven't told her, and I don't care if she likes it. We both know she'll try to stop me, but I'm going to do it, anyway. I'm not ten years old."

"True, but…what if she shows up on my doorstep with a few choice words about this idea?" He distinctly remembered the last time she'd paid him a visit. She'd screamed and struck and clawed at him—vented all her rage and hate.

"If that happens, tell her to mind her own business."

He shook his head. "You know I would never disrespect your mother."

"Then tell her to take it up with me."

Tobias finished his own beer. "Okay," he said as he watched Maddox and Jada, who'd been waiting at the bar, finally get a chance to order.

Atticus gazed toward them, too, but Tobias could tell he wasn't really seeing them. His eyes were glassy, and a dreamy smile stretched across his face. "This will be *so* cool. I'm going to get a GoPro so I can film it."

"The view at the top is spectacular," Tobias said. "There's no place like Yosemite."

"Have you seen that documentary—*Free Solo*?"

"I have."

"Man, that dude's cool."

"That dude's *amazing*." Tobias shifted so that Maddox could sit down. "El Capitan is a three-thousand-foot vertical rock face."

"He's the only one to ever climb it without ropes."

Jada sat across from them, next to her brother. "What are you talking about?"

"Tobias is going to take me hiking," Atticus announced.

Jada, who'd reached for the pretzels in the middle of the table, froze. "He's going to do *what*?"

"I'll show you," Atticus said.

As Atticus sat forward so he could call the video back up on his phone, Tobias wondered how Jada was going to react. She'd know her mother wouldn't like the idea. "I saw this on YouTube several months ago," Atticus explained and hit Play.

Both Maddox and Jada watched without speaking. When it was over, they exchanged a look. Then Maddox said, "You and Atticus are going to do *that*."

"Why not?" Atticus said as he put his phone away.

"Why *not*?" Jada gaped at her brother. "Are you drunk?"

"Hell, no! Your brother-in-law is as strong as an ox. If anyone can carry me, he can. Anyway, I only weigh a hundred and fifty pounds."

The waitress interrupted to see if Tobias or Atticus wanted another drink.

"I'll have another beer," Atticus told her.

Tobias waved her off.

"I guess it depends on where you're going," Maddox said slowly, as though he was being careful with his response. "Hiking around here might be okay. The hills aren't too bad."

"Hell, no," Atticus said. "We're not going around here. We're tackling Yosemite!"

Maddox blinked in surprise. "That would be quite a feat."

Atticus shrugged. "We can do it. We're going to train for it. And since I might never make it out there again, I'm going to film the whole thing."

"This is because of that movie *Free Solo*, isn't it?" Jada asked her brother. "You've been obsessed with it."

"It wasn't *my* idea." Atticus pointed at Tobias. "*He* offered."

Both Jada and Maddox turned expectantly to Tobias.

"It'll be a challenge, but it's something we'd like to do," he said. "For Atticus's birthday."

There was another long pause, during which Jada started to nibble worriedly on her bottom lip.

"Yosemite is a beautiful place," Maddox said. Tobias knew he wasn't giving his blessing to the project. He'd said something completely neutral—his way of indicating they'd discuss it later. But Tobias wasn't opposed to hearing him out. Maybe someone *should* talk some sense into them.

He and Atticus both let the conversation segue to another subject and then another… When Atticus's truck would be fixed (not for another week—a friend had brought him to the Blue Suede Shoe but then had to go to work, and Jada would drive him home). How long Carl might remain in town. (Everyone agreed the sooner he left the better.) Whether it was even safe for him to be living with his father. (Tobias didn't think so.) And Susan's health (which was in decline). They talked about Aiyana Turner, their boss, and how she and Cal Buchanan had been together for some time but hadn't yet married, and why Aiyana, even though she was obviously head over heels in love, was so resistant to taking that step.

"She's just scared," Maddox said.

"Scared of what?" Atticus asked. "He adores her."

"Scared that marriage will change things between them. I get the impression she's been burned in the past and doesn't want to give a man that much power over her life, so she keeps putting Cal off."

"You don't think she trusts him?" Tobias asked.

"She doesn't trust giving another person that much say in her life—doesn't want to be that beholden."

"So you doubt they'll ever get married," Jada said.

Maddox slid his now-empty glass away. "If something were to happen to Cal—his health began to decline or he needed her in some other way—she'd do it. They're both just so busy right now that it's easy to keep making excuses."

There was no one like Aiyana. She'd done a lot for Maddox, giving him a job. And she'd supported Tobias in the same way. Tobias hated to think where he'd be without her willingness to take a stand against his detractors and give him a second chance.

They were talking about going to Jada and Maddox's for Christmas Eve, and whether they should try to invite Susan, knowing she'd probably refuse to come, when Tobias went to the bathroom.

"You ready to get your ass kicked at darts?" Atticus joked when he returned.

Tobias grinned at him. "Might as well get it over with."

Maddox and Jada were following them over to the dartboards in the corner when Maddox touched Tobias's arm.

"What is it?" Tobias murmured, falling back as Jada and Atticus went ahead.

A slight hand gesture told him he should look at the bar, and when he did, he saw Harper.

She was still wearing her coat—had obviously just come in—and was standing with her back to him, talking to a woman who seemed about the same age, and a man who looked a few years older.

"That's her, isn't it?" Maddox said.

Tobias's heart began to race. He'd been dying to hear from Harper for the better part of a week, and yet he'd received nothing. "Yeah. That's her."

He told himself to look away, to continue on to the gaming area behind the pool tables. The place wasn't crowded, but it wasn't empty, either. Depending on how long she stayed and what she did, he thought he *might* be able to play without her ever noticing him.

But then she turned—and saw him.

14

"Something wrong?" Karoline's forehead creased as she watched Harper.

Harper tore her gaze away from Tobias. "No, nothing."

Fortunately, the bartender interrupted at that moment, so instead of pressing her, as she normally would have, Karoline turned to order.

"This is okay, isn't it?" Terrance whispered behind his wife's back. "I know Karoline had to sort of strong-arm you into coming out tonight, but it's only because she's concerned about you, wants you to get out and have some adult fun."

"So her answer is to almost *force* me?" Harper muttered.

"I choose to see her approach as…encouraging you," he said with a wink.

Living with Karoline and Terrance was teaching Harper how Terrance, such a mellow man, coped with the steamroller that was her sister. He focused on her intentions, not how she fulfilled them. And Harper had to admit Karoline's intentions were always good. That was why *she* put up with her, too.

"I know." She could've argued that her sister occasionally pushed too hard, but her mind wasn't on the conversation. It was on Tobias and his expression when he saw her. He hadn't done anything to indicate he recognized her, hadn't so much as smiled. He was letting her know he didn't expect anything, not even a greeting. But that left what felt like a heavy stone lodged in her stomach. She should've responded to his text. She felt bad that she hadn't. But she'd known that striking up any kind of conversation with him, even one in which she just assured him she was okay, would weaken her defenses.

Karoline cleared her throat in an exaggerated fashion. "Hello? The bartender's waiting. Are you two going to order a drink?"

"I'll have a Moscow mule." To her own ears, her voice sounded tinny and mechanical, but Karoline didn't seem to think anything of it. She looked at Terrance expectantly, and he said he'd have a scotch and water.

They waited for their drinks before finding a table. By then, Tobias was in the corner, playing darts with Maddox, a beautiful pregnant woman Harper didn't recognize—she guessed it had to be Maddox's wife from the way they touched—and a man in a wheelchair she'd never seen before. She had no idea who he was or how he was connected to the group and tried not to glance over there every few seconds, but it wasn't easy. The way Tobias looked in his jeans made her remember certain things she was trying to forget—like how impressive he was without them.

Fortunately, for a change, her eagle-eyed sister didn't notice her preoccupation. It was Terrance who seemed to realize that something wasn't quite right. He watched her closely as Karoline helped the waitress clear away the glasses left by two previous customers.

"So? How'd it go with Axel?" Karoline asked as the waitress finished wiping the table and they sat down.

"Has something changed with him?" Terrance asked in his typical even tone.

Harper shook her head. She didn't want to get into that. "No, nothing new."

Ice clinked against Karoline's glass as she brought it to her lips. "What are you talking about? He's been so resolute throughout the divorce. Until now."

"True." Harper had been hoping he'd have second thoughts. It had seemed far too easy for him to walk away, made her wonder if he'd ever really cared about her.

"Matt called earlier to tell Harper that Axel's freaking out, doesn't want to continue the tour," Karoline confided to Terrance.

He raised his eyebrows. "Why's he freaking out?"

His wife offered him a conspirator's smile. "Harper mentioned that she's been seeing someone else."

Terrance looked at Harper. "Who? The guy you went on a date with last weekend?"

Harper didn't like talking about that date because it wasn't the date part that had set Axel off. "Axel's just getting homesick," she said. "He's been abroad for weeks. All that travel would have to get old at some point—no matter how much success you're having."

Karoline rested her elbows on the table. "Is that what he said?"

Harper had called Axel after she and Karoline returned from the store but before they'd gotten ready to go out for a drink. He'd said he was conflicted about the divorce, but that was more than she planned to reveal.

Only a week or two ago, that would've been such welcome news. Harper had waited forever, it seemed, to hear him say those words. She would've told him to come back to her, that she still loved him.

But now? She felt more angry than excited. How could he put her through so much and then, when it was all over, act as though it might've been a mistake? She'd pleaded with him to reconsider, to think about their children, to imagine adding stepparents to their children's lives, to help her avoid having to take turns being with their children for every special occasion in the future. She couldn't believe he couldn't see how much better it would be to stay together. Their marriage hadn't been that bad.

"More or less," she said.

"Would you ever get back with him?" Terrance asked.

She didn't know the answer to that question. She supposed she'd wait and see if Axel's feelings of regret lingered. For all she knew, he'd feel differently tomorrow. It could be that he *was* just lonely or homesick or having a bout of depression, and he thought some reassurance that he hadn't lost anything he couldn't get back would make it better. "I'm not sure," she admitted.

Terrance toyed with the condensation on his glass. "You don't think you could forgive him?"

Harper found it difficult to talk about Axel while Tobias was around. The hairs on the back of her neck had been standing up ever since she'd seen him—but in a good way. It was as if she could *feel* his presence even when she wasn't looking at him, even though he was in the back of the bar ignoring her. "I could forgive him. It's just… How would I ever trust his love? I mean, how will I know he won't change his mind a second time? Decide he's done with me next year or the year after? Or in ten years? I don't want to live with the fear that he might call it quits at any moment. I don't want to go through what I've been through all over again."

Karoline's hand covered hers for a brief moment. "Those are valid points."

"People go through periods where they lose sight of what used to be important to them, though," Terrance pointed out. "Maybe he deserves a second chance."

Karoline scowled at her husband. "How reliable do you think Axel will be now that he's so famous?"

"Anyway, it's not worth discussing," Harper said. "He didn't come out and ask for a chance. He just said he misses me."

He'd also asked if she still loved him, if she'd really enjoyed sex with Tobias more than she'd enjoyed sex with him and whether she'd be willing to leave the girls with Karoline and come to Europe and finish off the tour with him. She'd said she'd always love him…to a point. She'd avoided the question about Tobias. The two men couldn't be compared in that way; they were so different. She'd told him that she hadn't meant to say anything negative about their sex life, because it *had* been good—until the end, at least, when Axel had become so distracted that he never felt present when they made love.

And she'd refused to leave the girls for Christmas.

But as far as she was concerned, that was all private—strictly between her and Axel—so she was relieved when Karoline let the conversation drift away from him and they began to talk about their trip to Disneyland and what the girls wanted for Christmas. They hadn't been able to do much shopping while they were in LA because they'd had the kids with them, so Karoline suggested they drive to Santa Barbara to finish up sometime soon.

Harper agreed and then, after they'd all had another drink, Karoline got up to dance with her husband.

The alcohol was giving Harper a buzz. She was finally relaxing, enjoying the atmosphere and the twinkle of the Christmas lights that were strung around the place. But Tobias had been on her mind since she'd seen him. Whenever Terrance and Karoline weren't watching her, she craned her neck to see if he was still in the bar. And when her sister and brother-in-law disappeared into the crowd, she looked again.

Sure enough, he was exactly where he'd been before, playing darts. She was relieved when she saw him. She didn't want him to leave. She wanted to talk to him, to try to explain why he hadn't heard from her.

But she couldn't catch his eye. He never looked her way, seemed determined not to.

Karoline and Terrance kept dancing even after the first song ended, so, hoping for a chance to apologize or at least feel better about how things had ended between them, and having drunk enough to summon the nerve, Harper walked over to Tobias and his group.

As soon as Tobias's friends glanced up at her, however, she regretted being so bold. What had she been thinking? What was she going to say? She'd interrupted their game!

"I, uh…" She wiped her palms on her new skinny jeans. "I just wanted to say…hi," she finished lamely.

Tobias didn't seem pleased that she'd made the effort; he seemed reserved, guarded. "Hi," he responded.

The man in the wheelchair looked between them. "You two know each other?"

"We bumped into each other at the Eatery once." Tobias spoke up before she could answer. She got the impression that he wanted to downplay their earlier interaction as much as possible, which was, of course, fine with her. Maybe he was even doing it for her sake. "Harper, this is Atticus Brooks. He lives here in town and works at the same school I do." He indicated the woman who was sitting on Maddox's lap. "Jada, here, is his sister."

"I can see the family resemblance." Harper held out her hand to Atticus. "Hello."

Atticus seemed a bit starstruck. "Aren't you Axel Devlin's wife?"

Harper hated being recognized. To her, it wasn't fun to be related to someone famous. She hated the curiosity it engendered, the intrusion of the press, the feeling that there were people out there who were *happy* that she and her husband had split up—or were talking about it and forming opinions even though they were complete strangers.

"*Ex*-wife," she clarified. After thinking of herself as a divorcée for almost a week, it was getting easier to make that distinction.

"And you know Maddox," Tobias said, continuing the introductions. "Jada's his wife."

"We have a teenage daughter and will be having a

new baby in the spring," Jada confided. "Our daughter is over at her best friend's."

Grateful that Maddox had been nice enough not to mention where they'd met, or to correct Tobias when he made it sound as though their contact had been far more casual than it was, Harper smiled at them both. "It's a pleasure."

Atticus offered her four darts. "Would you like to play? You could team up with Tobias while I go get a drink."

She laughed. "I doubt he'll want me on his team. I'm not very good."

"Neither is he," Atticus teased. "I just beat him. *Again.*"

"I'm better than Maddox," Tobias grumbled. "It's Jada who might give me some trouble."

"You *know* I'm not very good," Jada said at the same time her husband joked, "We should head over to the pool tables if you're going to be that cocky."

Harper could tell they were teasing each other and smiled.

"Don't worry about me," Atticus told them. "I'll find you wherever you are." He stopped wheeling himself away. "Anyone else want a drink?"

Tobias looked at Harper as though he expected her to beg off and leave—as though he was saying, *Now's your chance.*

But she wasn't ready to leave, not before she figured out if he was angry with her or just feeling awkward.

"If they have any IPAs on draft, I'll take one," she said. "If not, get me whatever they've got."

"Done," Atticus said and made his way to the bar.

Maddox gestured at the dartboard. "You can go first," he said to Harper.

She smiled tentatively at Tobias. She was hoping for some encouragement or any sign that he was glad she'd come over. But he didn't give her that sign. He wouldn't even look at her. And he moved away from her as though he wanted to avoid any accidental contact.

"Is it okay if I play with you guys?" she asked him.

He put down his glass. "Of course. But Atticus can be your partner. I'd better not start another game."

Harper froze. He was leaving?

"Where are you going?" Jada asked, obviously as surprised as she was.

Tobias wouldn't look at Jada anymore, either. "Home. With Carl at the house, who knows what might happen. I should get back."

Maddox shifted uncomfortably. "But we were just about to start a game."

"It won't take Atticus long to get the drinks."

"Tobias—" Maddox began, but Tobias talked over him by saying good-night. Then he walked out.

Tobias paced up and down the back alley of the Blue Suede Shoe. It was freezing outside and raining, but he was so numb he could hardly feel it. He was too preoccupied with trying to figure out what he should do. His first instinct was to go back inside. He hadn't been very polite to Harper. He didn't want her to think he was an asshole. But she'd caught him off guard. He hadn't been prepared to run into her, especially when he was with Atticus. He didn't want her to be anywhere near Jada's brother. Atticus's wheelchair would raise questions. It always did. People were curious to find out what'd happened to him, and if Harper asked that question, the answer would instantly destroy any positive feelings she might have toward him, even the memory of their time together before that pocket dial.

"Shit," he cursed and finally climbed into his truck. He should just leave. Why would he do anything else? He couldn't expect her to understand that he hadn't really intended to hurt anyone that night so many years ago. That he'd been only seventeen when he'd made the stupid decision to drop acid. That he didn't even know what he was doing when he pulled the trigger. No one cared about the circumstances; the results were all that mattered.

He was better-off getting out of there and never talking to her again. And she was better-off not associating with him. She could get just about any guy she wanted; why would she ever want him?

Hoping to distract himself from the emotions churning in his gut, he turned up the music until sound thumped through the entire vehicle, and drove home. He'd barely walked into the house when his brother called.

"What the hell is wrong with you?" Maddox demanded.

Tobias could hear the music from the Blue Suede Shoe in the background, even though his ears were still ringing from the classic rock tunes he'd been blasting in his truck. "I don't want to talk about it."

"Why? I know you like her. I can tell."

"What I feel doesn't matter." He tossed his keys on the counter. "It's over between us—if there was ever anything to begin with."

"That's just it. She wouldn't have made the attempt to hang out with you tonight if she didn't want to be with you. It took guts to walk across that bar and approach you."

"It didn't mean anything. She was just being nice."

"And *you* had to be rude?"

"I wasn't rude! I didn't want to be standing there when she asked why Atticus is in a wheelchair."

Silence.

"So that's it," Maddox said at length.

Tobias clenched a fist in his hair. "Yeah, that's it."

"You haven't told her."

"Of course I haven't told her! Would *you*? How do you tell someone about something like that?"

"You mean, how do you tell someone you want to think well of you."

"Of course that's what I mean."

He heard his brother take a deep breath and then release it.

"Tobias, if you're hoping this thing between you and Harper will turn into something, you're going to have to come clean eventually."

He turned on the TV and propped his feet on the coffee table. Fortunately, all had been quiet when he passed Uriah's house. He was in no mood to deal with Carl, afraid of what he might do if he was provoked. "What are you talking about? You told me not to get my hopes up, remember?"

"I know, but…I like her. So does Jada."

"How does that change anything? She's leaving after Christmas."

"Then what does it matter if she finds out?"

"I don't want her to know if she doesn't have to."

"I think you might be selling her short."

"In what way?"

"I believe she likes you more than you realize."

Tobias pressed three fingers to his forehead. "Harper's too good for me. You told me that yourself."

"No, I didn't. I said I didn't want you to get hurt. But now…"

"Believe me, you were right the first time."

"Either way, sometimes you have to take a risk."

"Maddox, she's Axel Devlin's ex-wife. *Axel Devlin*. Almost every woman in America wants to be with him. He's not only famous, he's loaded. And the worst thing he's probably ever encountered is a cold. Compare that to me. I've spent thirteen years behind bars, have had to watch my back, fight for my life, do things most men never have to. And you know how we grew up." He stared down at the various nicks and gouges that marked his hands. "Even if she could get beyond what I did, I have too many battle scars."

He heard Jada say something in the background.

"Jada says to tell you it's Christmas," Maddox said. "That means anything can happen."

"Yeah, for people like Axel."

"Maybe for you, too. Just so you know, once you walked away, Harper apologized for interrupting us, but we managed to convince her not to hurry back to her table."

"So where is she now?"

"With her sister and her sister's husband. She only played one quick game."

"With you, Jada and Atticus."

"Yes. And she never once asked how he lost the

use of his legs. To be honest, she seemed much more worried about you than she did Atticus."

"You don't have to try to mollify me. I'm not a child."

"I just want you to know how it went."

"It doesn't make any difference. Quit worrying. I'm okay. It's all okay."

"Tobias, you have a lot to offer. Don't think you don't. There's no one more loyal, more willing to protect those he loves—"

"Stop. I told you I'm fine," he said and disconnected.

With a sigh, Tobias turned the channel to *Sports-Center*, but he must've nodded off soon after he learned of the latest Clippers victory, because it was late when he opened his eyes again. For a moment he thought the television had awakened him. But then he heard a sound that let him know otherwise.

Someone was at the door.

15

Harper knew she had no business showing up at Tobias's house, but ever since he'd walked out on her at the Blue Suede Shoe, she'd felt sick inside. She'd been so caught up in her own problems she hadn't been very thoughtful when it came to him. After all, it had been her idea to sleep together in the first place, and her mistake with the phone. It wasn't as though *he'd* done anything wrong.

The night was so cold she could see her breath misting in the air while she waited for him to answer her knock. She'd passed Carl when she drove in. He was standing under the eaves of his father's house, smoking. The end of his cigarette had glowed red, and she could smell the tobacco once she got out of the car.

He'd seemed restless, bored, which made her uneasy. She'd ducked her head and hurried to Tobias's stoop without speaking to him, and he hadn't said anything to her, either. She was relieved about that. Already uncomfortable coming here so late, she hated that she now had a witness to her visit.

But who was Carl going to tell? *He* didn't know her sister or Terrance. He'd just returned to town after a long absence, and they'd moved here while he was living elsewhere.

In any case, she was dying to see Tobias again.

When he came to the door, she could hear the TV behind him, but she could tell she'd woken him up. She wasn't surprised; it was nearly two in the morning. She'd spent the past hour, ever since she and her sister and brother-in-law had come back from the bar, pacing in her bedroom, trying to talk herself out of sneaking out of their house like a teenager. She could've texted him if the only thing she was interested in was apologizing.

She wanted more than that.

"Harper." He blinked as if she was the last person he'd expected.

"Can I come in?"

He pushed the door wider, making room for her, and she shivered as she brushed past him. His house smelled like he'd just pulled a fresh load of warm laundry from the dryer.

She liked being here, she realized. She felt *good* here, had wanted to return ever since she'd left. There was no question that Tobias was a bit rough and unpolished, but she liked him, too. The tattoos. The long hair. His simple, minimalist approach to life. She supposed it didn't hurt that he was gorgeous, too.

"Are you okay?" he asked.

Suddenly a little nervous, she drew a deep breath. "Yes, everything's fine."

He rubbed a hand over his face, obviously trying to shake off the last vestiges of sleep. "Then…what's going on?"

"I'm not sure," she said. "I just…had to see you."

"You want to…talk?" he guessed.

Closing her eyes, she kneaded her forehead. "No, not really."

"So…"

She dropped her hand as she looked up at him. "You're all I can think about. It's crazy. We don't even know each other that well. And yet…"

Now he was fully awake and watching her with far more interest. "And yet?"

"I'm dying to touch you, and I'm dying to feel your hands on me."

"Then what the hell took you so long to come back?" He sounded almost angry. But she had reasons—good ones. She just didn't want to think about them right now. She only wanted to think about *him*, the way he tasted and smelled and how his body felt against hers.

"My situation. My children. The fact that I'll be leaving soon. All of it."

"None of that's changed," he pointed out.

"I know. I have nothing to say to that except, after seeing you at the bar, I couldn't stop myself from coming over here."

"I guess Axel didn't treat you too badly after the last time…"

Tobias still hadn't reached for her. Was he going to turn her away? "He's not happy about it, but I don't care."

They stared at each other.

"What is it?" she whispered, and then she felt she knew. "You don't want me anymore. I'm sorry for waking you up. I'll go."

She turned to let herself out, had already yanked open the door when she felt his hands settle on her shoulders. The warmth of his fingers seemed to travel clear through her coat.

"No," he said, his mouth at her ear. "Don't leave."

She needed to get out while she still could. She'd made a mistake coming here. It wasn't fair to get involved with him, not when she was already so lost and confused.

But she let him close the door, and she didn't resist when he turned her to face him.

He wore an intense expression as he gazed down at her, one that probably mirrored her own. She was feeling so much, far more than she thought she should.

He searched her face, seemed torn himself. But then he bent his head to kiss her.

She told herself she'd only let it go so far. One kiss. One embrace. That wasn't asking too much, was it?

But the second their mouths touched, she knew she wasn't going to leave until she'd taken everything he was willing to give her.

He tasted even better than she remembered, kissed even better, too. The softness of his lips and the warmth of his body as he leaned into her made her tingle from head to toe.

She delved into the long strands of his hair and curled them around her fingers.

Her excitement and arousal leaped to a whole new level when she heard him groan.

Arching into him, she closed her eyes as his mouth traveled down her neck and he peeled back her coat so that he could reach the sensitive skin above her blouse.

Then he straightened. "Where's your phone?" he asked.

After she dug it out of her purse, he turned it off and put it on the kitchen table before guiding her into the bedroom.

Tobias wouldn't let himself think about *anything*— not what Harper knew or didn't know about his past, not the rock star she'd been married to, that she had kids she'd most likely never want him to meet or that she'd soon be leaving Silver Springs. She was here in his arms; he had this one night. That was all he could be certain of. In case it ended here, he planned to make the most of it. Other than his brother, nothing good stayed in his life for very long. He'd learned not to expect it.

It wasn't hard to get lost in Harper. The feel of her nipples tightening against his tongue. The curve of her waist. The way she slid her legs between his. All of it put him right on the edge of climax. But he took his time with her, reveling in her trust and the eagerness of her responses—and making the most of each new sensation, each new quiver and gasp.

"You're *so* beautiful," he told her, admiring her bare body in the moonlight filtering through the blinds.

She'd turned off the light when he removed her clothes. He didn't mind that; the darkness contributed to the overall effect of disconnecting from the rest of the world and forcing time to stand still for just a little while. *This* was his Christmas present, he decided. He didn't care if he ever got anything else. But he also wanted to see her a bit more clearly, to memorize the heavy-lidded expression on her face. Nothing made him quite as hard as the way she was looking up at him right now. As though he really mattered.

She groaned and covered his hand with both of hers as he found the sensitive spot he'd been looking for. "That's good," she said on a long exhalation. "That's so crazy good."

He tilted his head to take her nipple in his mouth again, but she caught his face with both hands and brought it up so that he'd have to meet her gaze.

"You are so…"

"What?" he murmured when she didn't finish that statement.

"Fucking amazing."

When he started to laugh, she did, too. He kissed her nose. "Let's see if we can make you swear a few more times."

"Holy shit," she said, almost immediately, but they were too caught up in pleasure to laugh. Her smile faded, and she allowed herself to be carried away by what he was doing with his hand.

"Now," she whispered. "I need you inside me."

He'd been drowning in testosterone just watching her hips move with his hand, hoped he wouldn't climax as soon as he pushed inside her, so he took a few seconds to regroup while putting on a condom. Then he tried to distract himself as he rolled her beneath him by thinking of something distinctly *un*erotic.

But it was no use. She was licking his ear and whispering how much she loved it when he fucked her like this—he wasn't sure if her choice of words was a continuation of the joke or not, but they were certainly effective—and when he slowed down and touched her face in a silent plea for the help he needed to be able to last, she only made matters worse by pulling his thumb into her mouth.

The gentle sucking action combined with the softness of her breasts rubbing against his chest with every thrust and the way she locked her legs around his hips, encouraging him to move faster and take them both higher, made it impossible for him to do anything except succumb to his body's urging to do exactly that—until he cried out in release.

"Shit," he said once he'd regained his breath. "I'm sorry."

"No, it's fine," she said. "I *wanted* to see you lose it. You were trying so hard to hang on."

He scowled at her. "You knew that and didn't help me?"

Her lips curved into a devilish smile. "I wanted to see what you were like when you were completely overcome."

"Yeah, well, now you know it's not as much fun for you."

She nipped at his shoulder. "It won't be a bad thing in the end. It'll just give me a reason to stay a little longer."

"You don't have to leave right away?"

"Not unless you want me to. It won't get light for a few hours."

He smiled. He liked the idea of her staying. Somehow sleeping with her like this was even more intimate than having sex. "Then you're not going anywhere," he said and started kissing his way down her stomach.

Harper had Tobias set an alarm so they wouldn't oversleep and curled into his warmth. "I love the way you smell," she murmured as he pulled the blankets up around them. "I've never had that kind of reaction to anyone but you—you just smell *good*."

"That surprises me, since we both smell like sex," he said with a laugh.

She laughed, too, as he smoothed her hair back. "I like that smell. Don't you?"

"Absolutely." He leaned up on one elbow. "So…you cuss like a sailor—"

"Only when I'm highly aroused," she joked.

"Only when you're highly aroused," he echoed, "and you like the scent of sex. Anything else I should know about you?"

She pulled him back down with her and burrowed closer. "I think that's enough for one evening."

He assumed she'd drifted off to sleep. She wasn't moving and her breathing seemed steady. But after a few minutes, she roused herself enough to ask, "What are you doing for Christmas?"

"Depends."

"On…"

"A couple of things."

"Are you being purposely evasive?" she asked.

He chuckled. "No. I'll go to Maddox and Jada's house, if Jada's mother isn't going to be there."

"And if she is?"

"I'll stay here."

"Why's that?"

He hesitated. This was dangerous territory, which was why he'd tried to avoid getting into a conversation on the topic. "She's…difficult. Hanging around with her isn't exactly fun, especially at Christmas." That was a euphemistic explanation, but it was true— Susan *was* difficult—so he figured he could leave it at that and still feel as though he was being somewhat honest.

"But if you stay here, won't you be alone? Because Maddox will have to be with his wife and daughter, won't he?"

"He will, but I'll just buy a turkey dinner and have my mother over."

"Your mother wouldn't do a dinner herself?"

"My mother isn't the homemaker type."

"What type is she?"

His eyelids were feeling heavy. "She's the meth-addict type."

Silence. "Oh. I see. That's why you said you and Maddox had to raise yourselves."

"Sadly, she's more of a child than we ever were."

"Do you even know how to roast a turkey?" she asked.

She was lying so close to him her lips nearly brushed his when she spoke. He loved that. "I didn't say anything about *roasting* it. I said I'd *buy* a turkey dinner."

"From where?"

"I've heard the larger grocery stores sell them. Uriah mentioned it once. I'll have him over, too, if Carl's gone by then."

"So you'll have a store-bought turkey dinner with your mother and your landlord."

"Maybe." He wasn't sure why she was still talking about this.

"And then?"

"I don't know. I'll go on a hike, I guess."

"You really like being outdoors."

"I do." After being cooped up in a six-by-eight-foot cell with only one hour of yard time a day, he couldn't be outside enough. That was part of the reason he liked his job. He was never stuck behind a desk; he was always moving, always busy.

When she fell silent again, he started to drift off—until she asked, "What happened to Atticus? Why's he in a wheelchair?"

A shot of adrenaline brought Tobias back to full consciousness. His heart was pounding again, but this time it had nothing to do with being aroused. *This* was the question he'd been dreading.

"Tobias?" she said, but he didn't answer. He pretended to be asleep.

Tobias woke up to the sensation of Harper kissing his chest and neck. "Are you too tired to wake up?" she whispered.

"Too tired for *this*? Are you kidding?" he mumbled and proved it by moving her hand a little lower.

"Impressive. I guess we won't have any trouble."

"None at all."

"I just hope you don't have to get up early."

"No. But what about you? You've got children."

"They're not that little anymore, so it's not a problem if they roll out of bed before I do. Besides, my brother-in-law will be there. He always gets up and makes breakfast on Saturday. Everything will be fine, as long as they don't catch me sneaking back in. Then I might have some explaining to do."

He ran his fingertips down the length of her arm. "I don't like the idea of you driving home alone when it's so late. I'll follow you to make sure you get there safely."

"I'll be okay. There's no need to make you leave

this nice warm bed. But I could maybe delay a few more minutes…"

He grinned at her. "It's my lucky night."

16

Even after she'd made love with Tobias again, Harper had no desire to leave. She wished she could sleep in his arms and then wake up and have breakfast with him.

"How was that?" he asked, nuzzling her neck.

She knew what he was referring to. "Now you're just being cocky," she joked.

He gave her a sexy grin. "It was good, right?"

She laughed. He wanted to hear her say it. "It was good," she agreed.

He raised his head to catch her eye. "Does that mean you'll be coming back?"

She tensed. She wasn't sure she could make that commitment.

"Never mind," he said before she could come up with an answer and, pulling away from her without so much as a final peck, climbed out of bed.

"It's a possibility," she said. "There's just…a lot going on in my life."

"And you're leaving town in a couple of weeks never to return. No worries. I got the memo. Consider me notified."

Cold and strangely bereft without him against her, she squinted at the sudden brightness when he snapped on the light so they could find their clothes. "Are you upset?"

"Of course not," he said. "You don't owe me anything."

That had been the wrong question to ask. She didn't really sense that he was *upset*. It was more that his defenses had come up. From the beginning he'd been so open with her she wasn't expecting that. "I'll text you," she said.

"You don't have to," he responded. "I wasn't asking for anything. I just thought since you had a couple more weeks here we might see each other again. But there's no pressure."

He let go of the idea so quickly and easily, she got the impression he felt he should've known better than to ask.

With a sigh, she slid out of bed. "Don't bother getting dressed," she said when he picked up his boxers. "You don't have to walk me out."

"It's four thirty in the morning. I'm going to walk you out *and* I'm going to follow you home."

Oddly enough, she wanted to touch him again. Already. Put her hand on his warm chest to see if she could feel the thump of his heart. What was *that* all about? "There's no need. Really."

"I'm going to make sure you arrive safely, Harper," he said as though he couldn't be talked out of it.

She remembered seeing Carl standing in the shadows when she arrived and felt reassured that she'd have Tobias with her on the way out. She didn't like Uriah's son any more than Tobias did, didn't want to have him standing there, watching her leave. "Okay. Thank you."

"What'd you drive over?" he asked.

"Terrance's little car. With all the boxes that held the Christmas decorations out of the attic now, he can't park in the garage, so it's the easiest car to take without waking anyone."

"How'd you get the keys? Don't tell me he leaves them in the ignition."

"No. Karoline and Terrance both keep their keys in the kitchen." Their cars were too new to have an ignition like the kind he meant, anyway. All you had to do was press a button on the fob. But she didn't say that. She didn't want the disparity between their lifestyles to be an issue.

"That's convenient, at least." He started to go into the bathroom, but she stopped him.

"What's that from?" she asked, eyeing the scar she'd been able to feel as her hands roved over him in the dark last night. It was so big she thought maybe he'd had a kidney transplant or something.

He turned in surprise. "What's what from?"

"That scar on your lower back."

His expression grew shuttered as he touched the raised flesh. "Oh, that. I got it in a fight when I was younger," he said, sounding somewhat noncommittal.

She managed to find her panties, which had been kicked under the bed. "A *fight*? Must've been a bad one."

He gave her an enigmatic smile. "Not too bad," he said and closed the door.

Harper hesitated before she finished dressing. She didn't want the night to end like this, hated the physical and emotional distance that had come between them, especially after having such a wonderful time together. But one glance at the clock on her phone and she knew she had to forget everything else and get back. Terrance woke up as early as six some mornings. If she didn't want to be busted, she needed to sneak in before he was even beginning to stir.

Uriah knocked bright and early. After only three hours of sleep, Tobias was bleary-eyed when he let his landlord in.

"Rough night?" Uriah grinned the second he saw him looking so disheveled and tired.

Tobias couldn't help smiling in return, even though he wasn't happy about being rousted out of bed. "Not what I'd consider rough, no." He didn't like the fact that Harper hadn't been willing to say she'd see him again, but having her over was probably more than he should've expected anyway, given the circumstances. Most guys with his kind of background never had the chance to touch a woman like Harper, let alone make love to her several times.

Tobias motioned to a chair. "Want to sit down?"

"No, I'm only going to be a minute."

"What's up?"

He took off his cap and twisted it in his large, calloused hands. "Who came over last night?"

"Harper. The girl you met."

"Does that mean it's getting serious between you two?"

"Not at all," he replied.

Uriah scratched the back of his neck. "You're just like your brother."

"In what way?"

"Jada used to sneak over here late at night, too."

"It's hard to get away with anything these days, what with places like Home Depot selling security systems for only a few hundred bucks," Tobias joked.

"Unless something's damaged or missing, I don't pay much attention to the security feeds. Who you have over, and when, is none of my business. I was just hoping you might be able to tell me what happened to Carl."

"What happened to Carl?" Tobias repeated.

"He was at the house when I went to bed but was gone this morning. That's why I checked the security feeds—to see when he left. But the only thing I could make out was a car that didn't belong to him. It drove in, and a woman hurried to your house. Several hours later, she backed down the drive, and you followed her in your truck before returning after twenty minutes or so."

Tobias skipped over the part about Harper. "Carl knows you have a security system as well as I do. I'm guessing he purposely parked outside the range of the camera on that side of the house, so you wouldn't realize he ever left."

"That's what I think, too. He was probably planning to be back before now, so that I'd never find out. But that's part of the reason I'm worried. He's *not* back. Why would he let himself get busted?"

Because he doesn't give a shit. Tobias was tempted to say it, but he bit his tongue and tried to recall if Carl's vehicle had been parked to one side, near the rows of tangerine trees, when he followed Harper home.

He'd been so focused on her he hadn't thought to

check. "I didn't see it when I went out—or when I came back, for that matter. Unless I overlooked it. That's entirely possible. I wasn't thinking about Carl."

Uriah clicked his tongue and shook his head. "That boy just won't listen."

Tobias shoved his hands in the pockets of the soft, worn jeans he'd yanked on when he'd heard someone at his door. "Are you going to call the police?"

"If he doesn't get home soon, I'll have to," Uriah said. "I can't let him run around without a license, doing God knows what."

In that moment they both heard the sound of an engine.

Uriah stepped out onto the stoop and peered around the edge of the house.

"That him?" Tobias asked, leaning on the doorframe.

The old man cursed under his breath. "Sure is."

"Should I grab a shirt so I can be there when you talk to him?" It was too cold to go outside without one.

"No, I can handle it." With another disgusted shake of his head, Uriah stepped off the stoop and went to confront his son.

Tobias peered out his kitchen window long after he closed the door. He could hear raised voices, could see Uriah and Carl gesticulating. But finally, Uriah pivoted and stalked back into his house, and Carl opened his car door, sat in the driver's seat and lit a cigarette.

The argument seemed to be over. For now.

Tobias was curious about where Carl had gone last night, but he didn't want to get involved when tempers were hot—not if he didn't have to. Uriah would tell him later.

Once he felt somewhat reassured that he wouldn't need to intervene, he went back to bed. He'd been planning to go on a hike. That conversation with Atticus at the Blue Suede Shoe—where they'd revealed their plans to Maddox and Jada—had motivated him to start his training. But he'd have to wait until Sunday now. He was no good today.

He fell asleep almost immediately and didn't wake up until Maddox came over to watch the UCLA game. Jada and Maya were helping Susan at Sugar Mama. The cookie store was extra busy because of Christmas, so that left Tobias's brother with a free afternoon.

"What do you have there?" Tobias indicated the reusable grocery bag Maddox was carrying as he came in.

"Seven-layer dip, tortilla chips, pulled pork and rolls for sandwiches." He grinned. "I'm hoping you at least have the beer."

Tobias remembered the six-pack he'd given Uriah to mollify Carl. "I've got a couple left."

"Only a couple?"

"Should be enough."

Maddox gave him a skeptical eye. "You look like you just rolled out of bed."

Tobias scowled. "I was up late last night."

"Doing what? It was only ten thirty when you left the bar."

He didn't answer, merely started to help Maddox spread out the food—a welcome sight and something he'd have to thank his sister-in-law for making and sending.

Maddox stopped him. "Are you going to answer me?"

"I don't think so."

"Then this has to do with a woman."

Tobias shrugged him off. "Let it go."

"Don't tell me Harper came here after she left the bar…"

"Actually, she did. For a few minutes," he admitted as though it was no big deal.

"A few *minutes*? Bullshit," Maddox said and laughed. "From the look of you, she kept you up a lot longer than that."

Tobias was starving. He used a tortilla chip to scoop some of the dip into his mouth. "Maybe a *little* longer," he said with a smile.

Maddox gaped at him.

"What?"

"She stayed the night with you?"

"Not *all* of it."

"But some of it. Holy shit! I told you she really likes you."

"She's hurt and lonely and confused. It might have no meaning at all."

Maddox didn't argue. "How'd you cover for your unfriendly behavior at the bar?"

"I didn't."

"So she still doesn't know about Atticus."

Tobias was beginning to feel uncomfortable. "No. But she doesn't need to."

"You're getting in deep," his brother warned.

"She wouldn't even commit to seeing me again. It's fine."

"But there're plenty of people in town who'd recognize your name if she mentions it. She could easily hear about what happened."

"No one *she's* going to talk to knows me or anything about my past," he said, reluctant to consider the possibility. "She'll be here another two weeks, maybe three. How many people do you think she'll talk to—other than her family—in that time? When you're visiting a place, you don't go around announcing the name of the guy you slept with a few times."

Maddox pursed his lips. "Hmm. Maybe you're right," he said, but he didn't seem completely convinced that Tobias had no reason to worry.

Eager to be done with the conversation, Tobias went over to turn on the TV. "If we're not going to end up together—if that isn't even a possibility—I'd rather let her believe I'm just a regular guy, a *good* guy, instead of ruining what she feels for me by telling her about Atticus. Besides, she may not ever come back. I was shocked she came last night, never expected it."

"She didn't ask what happened to Atticus?" Maddox spoke louder to compensate for the volume of the TV, since the game had come roaring on. "You were so convinced she would."

"She *did* ask, for your information," Tobias said.

Maddox's gaze grew sharper. "And you…"

Tobias looked away. "Pretended to be asleep."

"Why not just explain to her?"

"This isn't the type of girl who would date an ex-con, Maddox."

His brother set his hands on his hips as though he'd argue, but ultimately dropped them and shrugged. "That was my concern in the first place. Anyway, you know her better than I do," he said and allowed himself to be distracted by the football game.

"Who are you going to give your gingerbread house to, Mommy?" Everly asked.

Harper blinked, pulling herself out of the well of her own thoughts. "Oh, I don't know," she said as she wiped a bit of frosting from her daughter's pug nose. "Maybe Aunt Karoline has a neighbor she'd like me to give it to."

"I'm going to keep mine," Piper announced.

"That's fine." Karoline was adding "snow" to her front yard and had, of course, made the most elaborate creation of the six of them. She'd used melted suckers to form stained-glass windows, which looked beautiful. When the girls saw what she was doing, they'd tried to copy hers, but theirs hadn't turned out quite so well. Neither had Terrance's. His was probably the worst. Karoline was forcing him to participate, since this was "family time," but his heart clearly wasn't in it.

Fortunately, Harper had known better than to attempt anything too tricky, going on so little sleep. She'd kept hers small and simple with a "thatched" roof made of Frosted Mini-Wheats, a path through the yard made of crushed Life Savers, peppermint sticks for a handrail and a cute gingerbread man stepping out of the door.

"Yours is *so* pretty, Aunt Karoline," Everly gushed.

Harper hid a smile when Karoline thanked her. Her sister was driven to be the best and do the best no matter what challenge she was taking on, so Karoline's had turned out like a cathedral, and the girls' had turned out like something occupied by the Three Little Pigs. One breath from the Big Bad Wolf and down they'd go. But they were proud of them, and that was all that mattered. Harper's was somewhere in between—more like a bungalow than a cathedral.

"I'm going to give mine to a homeless person," Everly announced. "So they get something for Christmas."

"That's very nice of you, Everly," Harper said.

Amanda and Miranda both picked friends to be the recipients of theirs, and Terrance said his wife could do whatever she wanted with his.

Harper doubted his would be leaving the house. Karoline would never want to be associated with something that sloppy. He probably could've done better if he'd been truly interested, but Harper kept seeing him try to catch a glimpse of the college playoff game on TV in the other room.

"We'll let the kids eat yours," Karoline said, and Harper nearly laughed out loud. She'd known her sister wouldn't deem it good enough to be given away.

Once that was established, the conversation came back around to who should receive Harper's.

"There are a lot of people in our church who'd like it," Karoline mused. "Do you want me to pick someone?"

Harper almost agreed. She was flattered hers had, at least, passed muster. But then she remembered Tobias talking about buying a Christmas dinner for his mother and Uriah, which sounded like a dismal way to spend the holidays, and decided—if she could do it without raising too much curiosity—she'd like to take it to him. "I think I'll give mine to the guy who handed me that rose at the Eatery," she announced as if she didn't know him a whole lot better now.

Karoline's and Terrance's heads came up. They'd seen her talking to Tobias at the bar and had questioned her when she got back to the table. She'd insisted that it meant nothing, she'd just been saying hello, and the fact that Tobias had left the group and walked out only a few minutes later certainly lent her story some credibility.

Still, she could tell that her sister and brother-in-law were curious about him.

"*What* rose?" Piper asked.

Harper took the frosting bag so she could retwist the back end. Otherwise, all the frosting they had left was going to squish into her daughter's small hands. "The one that was here on the island in a vase," she replied.

Piper frowned. "I don't remember it."

"It was before you left for Disneyland." Harper gave the decorator bag back to her. "It died, so I had to throw it out."

Miranda wrinkled her nose. "Someone gave that to you? I thought you didn't know anyone here—other than us."

Harper finished her house by sprinkling green sugar on various parts of her landscaping. "I didn't know him."

"So why did he give you a rose?" Amanda asked.

"He could tell that I was sad and wanted to cheer me up. Nice, right? And now maybe we can do something nice for him."

"Sounds good to me," Miranda said.

Once the decision had been made, Harper felt excited about stopping by Tobias's house with a plate of cookies and her gingerbread house. She wanted to see him again, and if she had everyone with her, she couldn't stay overnight, like she knew she would if she went over later.

With a far greater interest in making her house as

cute as possible, she added a tiny Christmas tree in the front yard and a few other decorations. She was eager to get her coat and set off—until Karoline insisted they would also sing Christmas carols at each stop.

"I don't want to sing," Harper said. "We won't have any accompaniment, and it's not like we've practiced or anything."

"We don't need to practice. I've got booklets with the lyrics. And you, especially, have a great voice. Caroling isn't about skill, anyway. It's about making someone smile."

This was coming from her perfectionist sister? The one time Harper knew that what they were planning wouldn't turn out to be good, her sister said it didn't matter? "It'll be hard for anyone to smile if we suck."

"We won't suck," Karoline said.

Harper considered how uncomfortable it would be to stand outside Tobias's door and sing to him with her girls, her sister, her brother-in-law and her nieces. She'd probably been too hasty when she suggested paying him a visit. But she couldn't back out now. That would only draw more attention to how she might or might not feel about him. "I don't know..."

"Don't be a scrooge, Aunt Harper!" Miranda said.

"Yeah, we want to sing. Don't we, Piper?" Everly pleaded.

"*I* want to sing," Piper dutifully replied.

Harper sighed. She was outnumbered. "Fine. Maybe one or two songs."

As soon as the girls were finished, Karoline sent them to get bundled up.

"Do *I* have to go?" Terrance asked when it was just the three of them.

Karoline arched an eyebrow at him.

"The game's on," he said by way of complaint.

"You're recording it, aren't you?"

"Yes," he said with a sigh.

"Then..." Her look grew even sharper.

"Oh, fine," he grumbled and went to get his coat.

17

Tobias showered and threw on a T-shirt and some gym shorts. With the game over and Maddox gone, he was going to New Horizons to use the weight room. He hadn't gotten out to hike this morning, but he could lift before the day was over. That was part of his training, too.

A knock sounded while he was looking for his keys.

Setting his gym bag on the kitchen table, Tobias opened the door to find a group of seven people.

One of them was Harper.

He would've said hello, but her sister—he recognized Karoline from the Blue Suede Shoe—burst into "God Rest Ye Merry, Gentlemen" and soon they were all singing, including Harper, who was holding a gingerbread house and seemed massively embarrassed.

Every time he looked at her, her gaze slid down to the concrete, but Tobias couldn't help smiling. These four girls, two women and one man, all bundled up and carrying holiday treats, looked like they'd stepped right off the front of a Christmas card. He'd never had carolers come by to sing to him, even before he went to prison.

They sang "Do You Hear What I Hear?" and "O Holy Night," before Harper called it quits by muttering something like "That's enough," and stepped forward to hand him the gingerbread house.

"This is for *me*?" he said.

"Yeah. It's just a little something I made."

"That's real candy. You can eat it." The smallest and clearly the youngest of the girls piped up. She had to be Harper's. With long blond hair and cornflower blue eyes, she was the spitting image of her mother. "But it probably won't taste that good," she confided, "'cause the frosting is sort of like glue."

"It's more for decoration," Harper explained as Tobias chuckled.

"That's why we brought you these, too." Another little girl, this one with auburn hair and freckles sprinkled across her nose, stepped up to give him a plate of cookies. "They're sugar cookies," she announced. "My *favorite*. Only, we were running out of frosting so Aunt Karoline said I could only put on a little, and we were saving our sprinkles for the houses."

"You must be Harper's oldest," he said.

Harper rested her hands on her daughter's shoulders. "Yes. This is Everly."

Tobias squatted down. He was holding the gingerbread house *and* the cookies, but he managed to hang on to both. "How old are you, Everly?"

"Eight." She pulled the smaller child, who'd spoken before, closer to her. "This is my sister, Piper. She's six."

So he was getting to meet Harper's daughters, after all. "Thanks for singing to me. And for the treats," he said as he stood.

"I don't believe we've ever met," Karoline said. "I'm Harper's sister, Karoline Mathewson."

Tobias set what they'd given him on the kitchen table so he could shake hands. Harper's worried expression told him that she'd hoped to swing by, give him the treats and move on. But Karoline was set on being properly introduced.

"Karoline, this is Tobias Richardson," she said.

Karoline held out her hand. "It's very nice to meet you." Her fingers clasped his tightly, confidently, before she released him so he could shake hands with her husband. "This is my husband, Terrance, and my twins, Amanda and Miranda, who are twelve," she added.

"It's a pleasure," Terrance said as their hands came together.

Tobias nodded. "Likewise."

"Harper tells me you've only been in the area for a short while," Karoline said.

"That's true."

"Where were you before you came here?"

Tobias felt himself tensing. He didn't want Karoline to pepper him with questions until he was forced to either reveal his past or lie about it. If he was ever going to tell Harper, this wasn't how he wanted it to come out. "I was born and raised in LA," he said, skipping the part in between.

"What brought you to Silver Springs?"

"Karoline, this isn't Twenty Questions," Harper muttered.

"My brother lives here," Tobias volunteered. "And there was a job I thought I might enjoy."

Undaunted, Karoline continued, "Harper told me you work at New Horizons."

"I do."

"What do you do there?"

"Karoline, that's enough," Harper complained but, again, Tobias felt it would be rude not to answer.

"I maintain the grounds and the equipment," he said, feeling a bit self-conscious. His job was steady and paid fairly, but it couldn't compete with the fame and fortune of being a successful rock star.

"Who's your brother?" Karoline wanted to know.

Clearly exasperated, Harper made an impatient sound and rolled her eyes.

"I'm just thinking that if his brother's been in town longer than he has, I might know him," Karoline explained to her.

"His name is Maddox," Tobias said.

"He's the principal of the girls' side of New Horizons," Harper added. "You don't know him, do you?"

"No," Karoline admitted.

"Well, there you go." Harper motioned toward the drive. "Now, we'd better keep moving. It's only going to get darker and colder."

Tobias wondered if it had been rude of him not to invite them in. He'd never had carolers, so he didn't know the protocol. In case it wasn't too late, he said, "It *is* getting cold. Would you like to come in and warm up before you go somewhere else? I could make some hot chocolate."

Thanks to Harper he had some in the cupboard. But he wished he'd cleaned his house today. If he'd known that Harper and her family would be stopping by, he would've washed the dishes he had stacked in the sink.

"No, thank you." Harper spoke quickly, trying to get ahead of her sister. "We just wanted to wish you a merry Christmas."

When their eyes met, he felt a strange sensation in the pit of his stomach. Was this goodbye? Her way of saying, *It was fun while it lasted. Here're some cookies.*

He hated how that made him feel. In prison, he'd gotten damn good at defending himself against any and every threat. As rough an environment as that was, he could navigate it. But nothing there had prepared him for how easily he could be hurt when it came to love—or whatever it was that made him want a real chance with Harper. Every time he saw her, he felt like he was standing there with his heart in his hand. "Thank you," he said. "Merry Christmas."

Harper grabbed her girls' hands and started to march off, but the younger daughter pulled away just before they could round the corner. "My mommy told us in the car that you taught her how to ice-skate," she said with a shy smile.

"I did," he said. "Would you like me to teach you?"

"*I* would!" Her older sister spoke at the same time Piper said she'd like it, too.

"Have your mother give me a call, and we'll set up a time to go to the rink before you leave town. Your cousins and aunt and uncle can come, too."

"Mom?" Everly asked. "When can we go?"

Harper didn't seem to like being put on the spot. "We'll have to see," she said vaguely.

They began to complain but she continued to lead them away.

Tobias hoped Harper really would ask him. But he was pretty sure that "we'll see" was her way of saying no.

Fortunately, Karoline didn't say anything once they got in the car. They finished caroling and dropping off treats, and then they left the kids at home with Terrance, who was eager to finally watch the game he'd recorded, so they could get some Christmas shopping done.

But Karoline hadn't forgotten about Tobias. That became apparent as soon as they were alone. "Why didn't you tell me the guy who gave you that rose was so freaking good-looking?" she asked as they pulled out of the drive.

Careful not to take the bait, Harper turned on the radio. "Tobias? He's not bad." She'd managed to pull off an indifferent tone, but had to avert her gaze to avoid giving her true opinion. Tobias *was* gorgeous. And he seemed to get better-looking every day. But his looks weren't the only reason he appealed to her. She liked almost everything about him—so far. The way he talked, the way he laughed, the way he kissed, the way he made love. He was street-smart. Savvy. Unpretentious. *Real*. He was also completely unaffected by his own good looks, humble in a way she'd never encountered.

"Not *bad*?" her sister echoed. "He's so tall. And what a body!"

Harper shot her a quelling look. "Stop."

"I may be married, but I still have eyes!" she joked. "He's about as masculine a guy as I've ever met. You should go out with him again. If having *his* attention doesn't help rebuild your self-esteem, I don't know what would."

"He hasn't asked me out again," she fudged.

"He said he'd take us all ice-skating. That's an invitation right there. Why not accept it?"

"Because I'm not ready to introduce Everly and Piper to a new love interest. It's too soon. And even if it wasn't too soon, why would I get involved with someone who lives in Silver Springs when the girls and I will be leaving in a couple of weeks?"

Karoline slowed to make the turn that would put them on the winding highway to the coast. "There's nothing holding you in Colorado, Harper."

Harper wished she'd never suggested taking that gingerbread house to Tobias. She wouldn't have if he hadn't been on her mind so much. "What are you talking about?" She put some slack in her seat belt, which suddenly seemed to be choking her. "That's where my house is. That's where the kids go to school. That's where my in-laws live, and the girls are close to their grandma and grandpa Devlin—a lot closer than they are to our mom and dad, who are so involved in their careers they don't have time for grandkids."

Karoline turned down the music. "Axel should've thought of what it would do to the relationship between his kids and his parents before he asked you for a divorce. It's not your fault that your marriage didn't work out. You were a great mother and an even better wife. So why should you be the one staying put like a dutiful daughter-in-law while he's off singing and making millions God knows where? Especially if there are places, like Silver Springs, where you might be happier?"

"You barely met Tobias!" she cried. "Now you think I should move here so I can date him?"

"I'm just saying you should keep your options open."

"And *I'm* trying not to do anything I might regret. I need to think of my kids. This past year hasn't been easy on them."

"I can't argue with you there," she relented. "But damn. You're not going to find a guy like *that* around every corner."

Harper didn't say anything.

"Although...I can't imagine he makes a lot of money," Karoline continued. "How much could someone who maintains the grounds and equipment of a correctional school earn in a month, anyway?"

"Will you stop?" Harper said. "I'm not going to evaluate him on his earning potential!"

Obviously annoyed by her reaction, Karoline fell silent, but at least she backed off and, by the time they reached Santa Barbara, seemed to have forgotten about Tobias. They talked about who would make what for Christmas dinner and whether Harper should get Axel a Christmas gift. The last time he'd called he'd mentioned that he was getting her one.

"I say no," Karoline said as she ducked into the dressing room of a cute little boutique to try on a dress for a friend's party on Saturday.

"I think you're right," Harper said. "After everything I've been through this year because of him, I'm not in the mood to shop for him. Gifts are supposed to be heartfelt, not obligatory."

Feeling released from the pressure of that decision, Harper continued to wander around the store. She was still waiting for Karoline to come out when she received two texts in rapid succession.

One was from Axel. I miss you, babe.

The other was from Tobias. Let me know if you're coming over tonight. I'll pick you up.

Harper told herself not to give in—to either man. She wasn't sure why it took knowing that she was sleeping with someone else to make Axel finally miss her, so she didn't trust his sudden turnaround. And she'd written Tobias back to let him know she wouldn't be coming, simply because it was the right thing to do. Even if it wasn't, she needed some rest. She was exhausted.

But after she went to bed, she tossed and turned for a long time, fighting the urge to change her mind.

To her credit, she didn't. She managed to go to sleep. She was proud of that the following morning. But by the time Sunday night came around, he was, once again, all she could think about. And she was no longer so proud of herself for holding out; she regretted that she'd lost valuable time she could've spent with him. It wasn't as though she had an unlimited number of days before she had to leave town.

What am I doing? she asked herself. She wished she could say Tobias was merely an escape from all her negative emotions. Someone she could get lost in. Maybe she wouldn't be so concerned if that was the extent of it. But she genuinely liked him. Possibly too much. That was the real concern, wasn't it? That she was getting in over her head—already?

Finally, after everyone else in the house was asleep,

she pulled out her phone to text him. You awake? she wrote.

She waited for several minutes and didn't get a response, so she told herself to let it go. If he was lying awake, thinking of her, he would've texted her back.

But the fact that she'd already missed last night and didn't have a long time left in Silver Springs suddenly made her desperate to take advantage of the time she did have before she had to go back to Colorado and build a new life out of the rubble of her old one.

When fifteen minutes had passed and she still hadn't heard anything, she gathered the nerve to call him.

"Did I wake you?" she asked when he answered.

"No," he said simply.

So why hadn't he texted her back? He didn't offer an explanation.

"Okay, then… What are you doing?" Did he already have company? He'd said he wasn't dating anyone, but he could've met someone since then. She had no doubt there were plenty of women who'd love to spend time with him. And it wasn't as though she had any right to expect him to give up other relationships, not when *she* was the one who kept insisting they keep expectations low.

"Just trying to go to sleep," he said. "I have to work in the morning."

"Oh. Right. Tomorrow's Monday. Of course. I'm sorry for bothering you," she said and hung up.

"Shit. Shit, shit, shit!" she muttered, squeezing her eyes closed. She shouldn't have called him. She was acting so inconsistent. He had to be wondering what the hell was going on.

Her phone vibrated in her hand.

He was calling her back.

Part of her didn't want to answer, but she knew that wouldn't be fair. She'd called him first, and *he'd* picked up. "Hello?"

"*Damn it*, Harper."

"What?" She was surprised by the frustration in his voice.

"You're giving me such conflicting signals."

She let her breath seep out in a long sigh. "I know. I'm sorry."

"So? Are you coming over or not?"

She caught her breath. "Do you want me to?"

"You know I do! I've made no secret of that."

"I'm scared of what I'm doing, Tobias. Of what *we're* doing."

"Is that a no?"

"Shit," she muttered again.

"Harper?"

Taking a deep breath, she climbed out of bed and started grabbing her clothes so she could get dressed. "It's a yes," she said. "I'll be at the corner in twenty minutes."

Harper shivered as she climbed out of her bedroom window and hurried around to the front. It was a cold night, and the Christmas lights adorning the houses on Karoline's street glowed dimly through the thick fog that had rolled in when the sun went down and the temperature dropped.

Tobias was at the corner, as promised. By the time Harper could see his taillights, she was winded—from daring to sneak out again more than the exertion of running down the block.

When she opened the passenger door, he clasped her hand and pulled her into the warmth of the cab. But she didn't give him the chance to drive off as he obviously planned. She scooted across the seat and kissed him.

"So the gingerbread house *wasn't* my consolation prize?" he whispered against her lips.

"You don't like it?"

"I like having you in my arms a lot better."

His warm lips, the stubble on his jaw, the smooth skin of his neck, the solidness of his chest—it all felt so satisfying. She loved his broad shoulders more than any other part of him "What about the cookies?" she asked.

"This is better than those, too."

"You're sounding pretty ungrateful. You know that?" she teased. "I had to brave letting my sister meet you to bring you those treats."

"I like that you did. I liked meeting your girls, too. But *nothing* beats this." His hands slipped under her coat and shirt, and he flattened his palms against her bare back as he massaged the muscles along her spine.

Resting her forehead against his, she held his face in her hands as she gazed into his eyes. "I've missed you."

He didn't respond.

"You don't have anything to say?" she said. "That's a big admission."

"I don't know whether to trust it," he admitted.

She ran her thumb over his bottom lip. "Neither do I. I keep telling myself that we just met, that I'm on the rebound. But when I'm with you—I can't describe how good it feels. And when I'm not with you, I want to be."

Still maintaining eye contact, he outlined the rim of her ear with his fingertip. "I have no defense against you," he said simply, and the way he kissed her next, with so much tenderness, made her feel as though she was spinning through space, free-falling—and loving every minute of it.

18

When the alarm went off, Tobias could feel the softness of Harper's breasts against his bare back, the weight of her arm looped around his waist and her legs tucked up under his. He hated that he had to move, because then she would, too, and once again their time together would be over. The few hours he'd had with her had gone far too fast.

"How can hours pass like minutes?" he grumbled, setting his phone on the nightstand after stopping the annoying jingle.

She leaned up and kissed his shoulder as he slumped back onto the pillow. "I wish I could stay longer."

He turned over so he could roll her beneath him for a final kiss.

"It's harder to leave you every time I come here," Harper said, tucking his hair behind one ear when he lifted his head.

"So when are you coming back?" he asked. "And this time, don't tell me you're not."

"Feeling pretty confident, are you?"

He could hear the smile in her voice and knew she was joking. "Just hoping we're making some progress."

She laughed. "Fine. I'm coming back. I think I've figured out that as long as I'm in Silver Springs, you're part of the experience."

"Now we're getting somewhere," he said with a grin. "But..."

Sobering, he rested the bulk of his weight on his elbows so he wouldn't crush her. "Seeing me doesn't mean you have to sneak out, Harper. I have more to offer than sex, you know. We could actually go someplace once in a while. You wouldn't even have to worry about Axel finding out, since he already knows about me. Let me take you to dinner or hiking or ice-skating. Even the girls want to go ice-skating."

She rolled her eyes. "Ugh. You're never satisfied."

She was still teasing him, but he was entirely serious. "What would it hurt?"

She finally sobered, too. "Nothing, I guess. It's just... I don't want to openly date anyone right now, what with my kids and—"

"Why not?" he broke in. "Dating is just dating. It's letting me buy you a meal here and there. It's going out and having a good time. It's not a commitment, nothing that will hurt your girls. As you keep reminding me, you won't be here very long, so it's not as though things could ever get serious."

She studied him in the moonlight slipping through the blinds while sliding her hands up and down his back.

He touched the tip of her nose with one finger. "Well?"

"Okay," she relented. "Where do you want to go? And when?"

"I'll take you to dinner in Santa Barbara tonight."

"Tonight?" she said with a laugh.

"There's no reason to wait. Christmas will be here in a week. You'll have to spend the twenty-fourth and twenty-fifth with your family. And you'll be leaving shortly after that. Why waste any time?"

"Now I'm really starting to get worried," she said. "Because..."

"Because I feel like I should say no, but I don't want to."

"Then don't." He held his breath while awaiting her final answer.

She pulled him in for another kiss. "Fine. Dinner tonight."

He rolled off, back onto his own side of the bed. "I'll pick you up at six. The drive will take almost an hour."

"I'll be ready."

He watched as she got up and started to dress. "Would you like to bring the girls? I could find a place they'd enjoy."

She glanced over her shoulder at him. "No. Not this time."

He backed off. There was no need to press for more than she felt comfortable with. "Okay," he said and got up to dress, too.

This time when he dropped Harper off, Tobias drove away feeling excited, hopeful. He kept telling himself not to fully embrace those emotions. He'd be stupid to assume this was going to end well, but he was also determined not to ruin *now* with what might happen *later*. If he could've stopped seeing her, he would have. He'd tried not to answer his phone tonight. He just hadn't been able to resist.

At this point, he was along for the ride.

When he was almost back, he saw a pair of taillights turn into the orchard ahead of him and knew that Carl was getting home. Evidently, Carl was continuing to ignore his father and was still driving without a license. Who could say what else he was doing. Tobias knew Uriah wouldn't be able to let Carl behave the way he was indefinitely, which meant it would all come to a head at some point. He just hoped they could get through Christmas and Harper going back to Colorado before anything happened. Tobias wanted to enjoy the next two weeks, not get into trouble for beating Carl's ass—even if Carl deserved it.

To avoid *any* type of encounter with Uriah's son, he drove ten minutes past the orchard and then doubled back to give Carl time to go inside. Tobias wasn't in any hurry to get home. He was so happy about how things had gone with Harper that he doubted he'd be able to fall back asleep, anyway.

Fortunately, when he pulled down the drive, he didn't see Carl standing in the shadows, smoking, like he so often did after Uriah went to bed. He thought the coast was clear until he reached his door. Then he heard a voice coming from behind him.

"Who's the girl?"

The hair rose on the back of Tobias's neck as he turned to find Carl leaning against the side of the garage about fifteen feet away. "None of your business," he replied.

Thank God he'd locked his door. He'd been doing that religiously the past week, ever since Carl had made him uneasy about it. He hated that Carl seemed so focused on him and what he did, had no doubt the little bastard would've gone inside the second he saw Tobias pulling out of the drive—if the house had been open.

"Why does she only come over in the middle of the night?" he asked. "She married or somethin'? You messin' around with some other man's woman?"

Tobias was tempted to march over, lift Carl by the shirtfront and threaten him within an inch of his life, tell him that if he ever said or did anything that might hurt Harper in any way, he'd be sorry. But showing he cared that much would only reveal that Carl had hit a tender spot. Tobias couldn't be that stupid.

He took his house key from his pocket. "Why do you want to know? I can't imagine you care about what I do."

"No, but the man she's married to might."

"She's not married. Sorry to disappoint you."

"Then what's with all the sneaking around?"

"I don't know what you're talking about. She has odd work hours."

"Odd work hours," he said with a chuckle. "That's a good one."

Tobias felt his muscles bunch. *Go inside. Don't let him get under your skin.*

Swinging the door wide, he was about to cross the threshold when Carl said, "Does she know about the other girl you had over not too long ago?"

Unable to resist a response, Tobias whirled around. "I didn't have that other girl over. She dropped by. There's a difference. And she won't be coming back."

"She looked upset when she left. What'd you do to her?"

"Nothing."

"So you like this one better."

"This fascination you've got with me is flattering, but I don't see why you should even notice what I do," Tobias said.

"I think you're interesting. And I'm bored."

"There's plenty of work around here, if you're bored."

He lit a cigarette. "I bet you believe almost any chick would like to ride what you got between your legs," he said and took a long drag. "But do they know what kind of man you *really* are?"

Tobias's hands curled into fists almost of their own accord. "What are you talking about?"

"Everyone thinks *I'm* such a loser," he said. "At least I've never shot anyone."

A premonition of danger, the threat Carl now posed, made Tobias's skin tighten and prickle. But, once again, he knew he couldn't let on that Carl had hit a nerve. He had to act as though he had nothing to hide. "Why don't you go to bed, Carl?" he asked and yawned as though he was tired. "That's old news."

"Wasn't old news to me," Carl retorted. "That man I crashed into? Atticus Brooks? Some bitch I met at the bar tonight told me *you're* the one who crippled him."

Tobias clenched his jaw. "Like I said, old news."

Carl pushed off from the barn. "That so? Does my father know you shot an eleven-year-old boy? Because first thing in the morning, I'm going to tell him. I bet he won't think so highly of you after *that*."

"*Everyone* knows about my past," Tobias said with a shrug and went inside. He'd been desperately trying to disarm Carl by acting cool, but he wasn't nearly as unruffled as he'd tried to appear.

There was one person who didn't know, and he didn't want her to find out.

Especially now that things were going so well.

The next day Harper was so much happier than she'd been since coming to Silver Springs that Karoline commented on it. "You seem so...*up* today. So energetic."

It was astonishing how much her frame of mind contributed to her energy level, Harper thought. Since she'd spent part of the night with Tobias, she hadn't gotten a lot of sleep, and yet she felt more like her old self than she had since she'd learned Axel wanted a divorce—maybe even before that. She didn't have to worry about the growing tension between her and Axel anymore, at least not in the same way. She didn't have to keep trying to please him so she could turn her marriage around. She didn't have to mitigate the stress *he* was feeling because of his job. She didn't have to be careful about what she said for fear she'd set him off. And she didn't have to be frustrated that he wasn't around to help with the kids or spend time with her, because she no longer expected it.

She'd been released from *all* of that—and would soon be having dinner with Tobias, which she was looking forward to. Instead of feeling hurt and abandoned, she was beginning to feel—she was afraid to even think the word for fear she'd jinx herself—*free*.

"I'm doing *much* better," she admitted. She'd put on some Christmas music and had been humming along to Bruce Springsteen's version of "Santa Claus Is Comin' to Town" when Karoline returned from the post office and walked in to find her on the floor with tape, scissors, a stack of gifts and various kinds of wrapping paper. She'd been alone in the house since breakfast an hour ago. Terrance was outside raking the leaves, and the girls were in school through Friday.

"It's like Mom says, I guess. Time heals all wounds."

Harper thought Tobias had more to do with it than time. She hadn't started to improve until she'd met him; she'd been in the very depths of despair the night he'd handed her that rose. "I guess. I'm just glad it's no longer so hard to get up in the morning."

"So it was the right thing to do to have you stay with us?" she asked.

"I think so. It's been just what I needed." Harper got up to give her sister a hug. Karoline wasn't much for displays of affection, but Harper wanted to express her gratitude. Her sister was always so strong and decisive and willing to sacrifice in order to lift those around her. Maybe, at times, she was a little *too* opinionated and frank, but she was *there*. Always in Harper's corner. Which was what mattered most. "I couldn't have a better sister," she said.

The pat Karoline gave Harper's back was awkward, but what she said was very kind. "I don't know how *any* man could leave you."

Harper smiled as she pulled away. "Guess what?"

"What?"

"I've agreed to go out with Tobias again."

Her sister's eyes widened. "You have? Where's he taking you?"

"To dinner—tonight in Santa Barbara. Is that okay? Would you mind watching the girls so I can go?"

"Of course not! When did he ask you?"

Harper couldn't quite meet her sister's eyes when she replied, "Last night."

"He texted you? Did he like the gingerbread house and cookies?"

Harper chose not to answer the first question. "He did."

"Good! Well, I'm glad we went over there, then. And I'm excited you're having dinner with him. Are you nervous at all?"

"Not really." Harper went right back to her wrapping so that her expression couldn't give too much away. "It'll be fun to get out."

"So…are we telling the girls you're going on a date with the man they met?"

Harper had been deliberating about that all morning. "I don't know. Do you think it'll bother them that I'm seeing someone other than their father?"

"I think what bothers them is seeing you unhappy. The better you are, the better they are."

"It's not as though anything or anyone could ever come between us."

"They know that, which is why I'm betting they'll be fine with it."

"It's not too selfish?"

"You're just trying to move on, Harper. That's actually the healthier way to go."

Heartened by her sister's words, Harper drew a deep breath. "True. Thanks. That gives me more confidence."

"*Now* are you willing to admit that you really like this Tobias guy?" she asked with a grin.

Harper felt her face warm. "Yeah."

"After seeing him, I can understand why you might

want to get to know him better," she said with a laugh and started to walk out of the room.

Harper thought she was gone, but then she heard her sister's voice again and realized she'd turned back at the last second. "Harper?"

"Yes?"

"Just…be careful, okay?"

"About…"

"You know the cliché about jumping from the frying pan into the fire, right?"

"Of course." Their mother used it all the time.

"Take things slow," she said and left.

Harper dropped her head in her hands. *Slow?* She'd already slept with Tobias—several times.

Tobias hadn't considered cutting his hair since he'd been released from prison. He'd kept it so short you could see his scalp all the time he'd been locked up— not because he had to but because he considered long hair to be a liability in a fight, and he never put himself at a disadvantage. He'd been jumped often enough that he was *always* ready. So being able to wear it longer— to feel safe enough to let it grow—was something he considered a luxury.

After meeting Harper's sister and brother-in-law, however, he'd been thinking about getting it cut. He knew he'd look a lot more presentable when he appeared at the door to pick her up. He wasn't a rock star, wasn't making millions like Axel, but that didn't mean he couldn't look like someone they wouldn't mind seeing her go out with.

He wasn't sure what to suggest to the barber, though. He had to go in with at least some idea of how he wanted his hair to look when he walked out, didn't he? He didn't want to pick up Harper and have her disappointed by what she saw.

As soon as he got off work—at three, since he worked enough overtime that Aiyana didn't mind letting him go early—he called Jada, thinking that if anyone could give him some good advice in the hair department, it would be her.

"Hey, how's my favorite brother-in-law?" she asked as soon as she picked up.

He had to hand it to her. She'd been nothing but kind to him, despite his past with her brother. He'd never forget the day, right before he was to be released, when he'd received a letter from her best friend, Tiffany Martinez. He'd been so nervous to open it, had expected to read the ugliest of recriminations.

But that wasn't what Tiffany had written. She'd sent him a short letter wishing him well and saying she hoped he could build a good life, and she'd included a release cheat sheet—a description of all the technological advances that'd happened while he was out of circulation to help him get up to speed—as well as some money. That was all generous enough, but the part that really got to him was where she said Jada had contributed so he'd have some cash with which to get a start on the outside.

Knowing that the sister of the boy he'd shot had been forgiving enough to do something like that had brought tears to his eyes. As much as he'd been looking forward to regaining his freedom, he'd been scared shitless at the same time. He'd essentially grown up in prison. He'd gone in as a boy and was coming out a man, and he didn't know if he'd be able to navigate the real world or if he'd been locked up for so long he'd become institutionalized.

Would he be able to function like a normal person? Find work despite his record? Lead a stable life?

Or would he fall into despair, turn to drugs and screw everything up like his mother constantly did?

There'd been so many question marks back then. A lot of fear and uncertainty, too. And since his brother had moved back to Silver Springs, and he'd had nowhere else to go, he'd had to face a lot of hatred. So he'd never been more grateful for anything than that one act of kindness, the memory of which—along with the love Jada had offered him since—had helped him hang on during even the toughest of times.

"I have a favor to ask you," he told her.

"Of course. Anything. What do you need?"

"I'm thinking about getting my hair cut."

"Okay."

"And I have no idea what I should tell the barber."

There was a slight pause. "Why are you suddenly considering a haircut?"

"I have a date tonight."

"Someone special?"

When he hesitated, she said, "Don't tell me it's Harper Devlin."

He didn't see any reason not to admit it. He didn't think their date was a secret. That was probably the most exciting part. By agreeing to go out for dinner with him, she was legitimizing their relationship as much as she could. "Yes."

"Maddox told me you were sleeping with her!"

Tobias laughed. "Wow, okay. Thank him for his discretion."

"You know he tells me everything," she said, laughing, too. "But you don't have anything to worry about. My lips are sealed."

"Thank you. So…can you help me with my hair?"

"Of course. Tell me where you're going, and I'll meet you there."

"That's just it. I don't know where to go. Where does Maddox go?"

She heaved a dramatic sigh. "It's a good thing you called me. Let me see if I can get you an appointment with his stylist."

"It isn't a place where you just walk in?"

"No, it's not. But it won't take long to see if Manny's there today and if he can squeeze you in."

"Okay. Let me know."

Five minutes later, she called back to say they were in luck. Manny would give him a cut if he could come right over to the salon.

As he left the house, Tobias saw Carl half-heartedly spraying the Pixie Tangerines on the trees of his father's orchard with water. Tobias had done the same thing for Uriah three weeks ago; it was something citrus growers did to protect their harvest before a frost. Uriah had explained that since Silver Springs pixies had a long growing season—they were on the tree for eighteen months from blossom to harvest—they had to survive the winter, and although it seemed counterintuitive, spraying them with water caused ice to form when temperatures dropped, releasing heat to the ripening fruit and keeping it from freezing on the inside.

Carl must've picked up on Tobias's movement in his peripheral vision, because he looked over, but he didn't try to say anything. Fortunately, they were too far away from each other.

Ignoring the slimy bastard, Tobias climbed into the cab of his truck. He wondered how it had gone when Carl had spilled the "secret" about his record—how Uriah had responded. Uriah knew about the past, of course. He'd known all along, so Tobias wasn't worried about how he'd react. But the fact that Uriah knew and hadn't let on to Carl might only have increased the jealousy Carl seemed to feel where he was concerned.

And jealousy was such an ugly emotion. There was no telling what it might cause Carl to do.

19

"Wow. You clean up well," Karoline said. "I really like the haircut."

Tobias had secretly hoped he wouldn't have to face Harper's sister. So, of course, she'd been the one to answer the door. But at least he was prepared. Jada had helped him pick out a new shirt, slacks and shoes. No one he'd known in prison would recognize him. He looked as much like a doctor as Terrance did. "Thank you."

She waved him past her and into the living room, which was empty even though the television was on. "Have a seat. I'll let Harper know you're here."

He'd put on some cologne. Since he typically didn't wear cologne, he hoped he'd been conservative enough with it. He'd fought Jada on that purchase, had been afraid it would be interpreted as trying too hard, given the haircut and all. But Jada had fallen in love with the scent, so he'd decided to accept her advice all the way around—the wisdom of which he began to question when Karoline noticed it right away.

"And you smell great," she added.

Tobias sent her a smile. He was pretending to be as

comfortable in his own skin as he was when he was in more familiar surroundings, but he was fighting the urge to stretch his collar.

Who was he trying to kid? What was he even doing here? he wondered while he waited. He was an ex-con trying to date a woman who'd recently been married to one of the most popular singers in America. If Harper knew who he *really* was, she wouldn't have accepted his invitation. And even if he hadn't made the mistake he'd made at seventeen and gone to prison for it, they came from separate worlds. He'd never lived in a home *remotely* as nice as Karoline and Terrance's. He could only imagine what kind of place Harper could afford...

Feeling foolish for taking this date so seriously, he considered making up an excuse so he could get out of there before the farce could go any further. He could say that Maddox had just texted him with an emergency—his car had broken down or something—and needed his help.

But as soon as he stood up to try to catch Karoline, he saw Piper peeking around the corner at him.

"Hello," he said.

A shy smile curved her heart-shaped lips, and she ducked back out of sight, only to tentatively peer around the corner at him again.

"Do you remember me?" he asked.

She nodded. "But you cut your hair."

"Yeah. It's a big change, isn't it?" Maybe that was part of the reason he was feeling so foolish.

She nodded. "Now mine is longer than yours."

"It sure is. Thank you for the gingerbread house, by the way. I really like it."

This seemed to imbue her with the confidence to

enter the room, although she hung back by the entrance. "Did you eat it?" she asked.

"Not yet."

"What about the cookies?"

"Those are gone."

"There's more in the kitchen."

"I'm fine for now, but thanks."

She studied him curiously. Then she said, "Where are you taking my mama?"

"To dinner. Is that okay with you?"

She shrugged her shoulders. "Guess so."

Terrance walked in, holding a beer. "Oh," he said, doing a double take when he saw Tobias. "I didn't realize you'd arrived. Can I get you something to drink?"

"No, I'm fine."

"I hear you're going to Santa Barbara tonight."

"Yeah. To a restaurant called Monte's. I've been told it's one of the better places to eat." Jada had picked the restaurant, too. She'd been there before—Tobias hadn't—and said it was phenomenal.

"What kind of food do they serve?" Terrance asked.

"California cuisine."

Piper edged closer to them both. "Can *I* go?"

Tobias didn't want to say no. He was fine with letting her come along, although he guessed the restaurant might be a little fancy for children. But it wasn't his decision. "We'll have to check with your mom, okay?"

"Don't even ask her," Terrance advised Piper. "You can't go with them tonight." He gestured at the couch. "Sit down," he said to Tobias. "I'm sure Harper won't be long, but you might as well be comfortable. There's a Lakers game on we can watch."

Tobias thought of his intention to back out of the date. It would be more awkward now that Terrance and Piper were here, since he should've spoken up already and hadn't, so he decided he'd take Harper out this one time and that would be it.

Terrance sat down, so Tobias did the same and was more than a little surprised when Piper kept inching toward him. Eventually she even asked if she could sit on his lap.

"Sure," he said, lifting her onto his knee.

Piper gave him a sweet smile every time she turned around to look up at him, which was often. The fact that she seemed to like him made him feel more optimistic about the evening, but he couldn't help wondering what was taking Harper so long. He and Terrance had watched at least fifteen minutes of the game.

Eventually, she came into the room but she looked upset, flustered. "I'm *so* sorry," she said.

He set Piper aside and got up. "No problem."

"I was ready when you arrived," she explained, "but then I—I ran into a little problem."

"Is everything okay?"

"It is now."

"Are you sure?" he asked. "Because we could always put this off until another night." Or not go at all.

"Let's not cancel," she said. "I've been looking forward to it."

He glanced between her and Terrance. "I guess we're going. Thanks for keeping me company."

"Have a good time," Terrance said. Then he gave Harper a sympathetic look and spoke in a softer voice. "Try not to think about it, okay?"

"Think about what?" Tobias asked as they walked toward the door.

"I'll tell you in the car," Harper replied, but Tobias thought he could guess when, after calling for Piper and not getting an immediate response, Harper's sister yelled, "Piper, come now. Your father's on the phone!"

"You cut your hair," Harper said as soon as they got in his truck.

"I was ready for a change," Tobias explained.

She nodded. "Looks good."

"Thank you." He couldn't tell if she was completely sincere. She was still preoccupied.

The radio came on as he started the engine and pulled away from the curb. "So…what's going on?" he asked.

She pinched the bridge of her nose before dropping her hand. "Back there? Oh, Axel was throwing a fit."

"About…"

"The fact that I'm going out to dinner with you."

Tobias turned off the radio. "How'd that come up?"

"He texted me about thirty minutes ago. Said he wanted to talk to the girls. So while I was getting ready, I had Everly call him. The next thing I knew, she was bringing me the phone, saying he wanted to talk to *me*. Apparently, she'd told him I was about to go on a date. So he demanded to know who I was going with—and freaked out when I told him."

Tobias pressed the brake so he could turn the corner. "I'm sorry. Like I said, we could always do this another time."

Her eyes filled with tears. "He can say the ugliest things when he gets angry. He tried to tell me that I've never really been there for him, even though I did everything I possibly could to help him launch his career and to make him happy. Somehow he doesn't remember how hard I worked so that he could gig with the band and wouldn't have to worry about the rent. Or that I sang backup vocals on the first album even though I had such terrible morning sickness with Everly I could barely get out of bed. Or how I helped direct the first video—as well as starred in it—because we couldn't afford to hire professionals and I'd had a little experience with that sort of thing in college. Or how I was alone in the hospital when I had Piper because he was touring and couldn't make it back in time for her birth, and yet I was the one trying to make *him* feel better about scheduling the tour too close to my due date. Or—oh, never mind."

She turned to face the window, ostensibly looking at all the holiday decorations as they drove past them, but Tobias doubted she was taking any of it in.

"People always say unkind things in a divorce," he said. "Try not to let it get you down. I know that's easier said than done, but—"

"I just never thought *he'd* be like this," she broke in. "He spent so much time talking about how he still loved me and respected me, just needed his freedom and a break from the pressure he felt to do what I wanted or needed when he had so many other people at him already. And how we'd always remain friends for the sake of our kids and not let it get ugly between us." She propped her elbow up against the door and rested her head on her fist. "But I guess all of that's forgotten now that *he's* feeling threatened. He also said I couldn't have loved him if I've moved on so quickly, even though *he's* the one who gave up on us and filed for divorce. And he said…" Her words drifted off as though this was the part that hurt the most.

"What?" Tobias prompted.

"That he thought I had more character than to fall into bed with the first guy I came across," she mumbled.

More convinced than ever that he'd overreached, Tobias felt a little sick inside. "Is that how you view what's happened between us?" he asked.

"No. Axel wants to characterize it as negatively as possible. That's all."

"He's never slept with anyone else? Just you? I mean, since he met you…"

She wiped her cheeks. "Oh, there've been others. I have no idea how many, but I'm sure the number is getting up there. I'm beginning to think that's why he wanted the divorce—so he wouldn't have to feel guilty about lying to me all the time."

And now he was trying to make *her* feel tawdry and cheap? "He said what he did to punish you. You realize that." Tobias had plenty of counseling sessions in prison, during which the psychologist talked about control issues and triggers and how people used them—or reacted to them.

"Punish me for *what*?" she countered.

"For daring to do what *you* want. He'd rather have you sitting around being miserable without him. He's jealous."

"That's what I keep telling myself, but it's all so confusing and hurtful." She closed her eyes as though she was summoning strength and calm. "I can't seem to find a way out of it," she said as she opened them again.

Axel was finally coming to his senses and recognizing that he'd let something really great get away from him. He was acting as though he was ready to come back, but she probably wasn't sure she could count on his loyalty or his fidelity, not after what she'd been through. No wonder she was confused.

Tobias came to a stop at the light, his stomach churning as he realized what he had to say. "If you want to fix your relationship with him, now would be a good time."

"What do you mean?"

Feeling as though he had an anvil sitting on his chest, he collected his resolve. "He's obviously regretting the divorce."

"But it's already final."

He tightened his hands on the steering wheel and forced himself to continue, to take this all the way. "That doesn't mean you can't fix things." When she said nothing, he risked a glance at her. "I can drive you back to your sister's, Harper. Really. Then you can call him and try to work things out. Is that what you want?"

She didn't respond. She just kept staring out the window, but fresh tears rolled down her cheeks. That answered his question right there, didn't it? So why not make it easy on her? If Axel really wanted her back, reuniting was the perfect ending for her, exactly what she'd been hoping for all along.

He thought of the moment he'd seen her in the coffee shop, staring off into space as Axel's latest hit played over the sound system. Not only was she still in love with her ex, Axel was the father of her children.

As difficult as this was, he had to back away.

It was already time, he decided, even though he'd been hoping for much longer.

Swallowing against the sudden tightness in his throat, he flipped on his signal so he could make a U-turn.

"Where are we going?" she asked. This time he didn't look over at her; he kept his eyes on the road. "I'm taking you back."

"No," she said. "I don't want to—to ruin tonight. To disappoint you."

"And I don't want you going out with me just because you feel obligated."

"That's not the only reason I'm going! I like being with you. I like everything about you."

She wouldn't like the parts she didn't know. "If Axel will treat you right, going back is the best thing for you. And now that he's figuring out how badly he screwed up, maybe it'll be different, better, in the future."

"You want me to go back to Axel?" she asked, her forehead furrowing in confusion.

"No. Of course I don't. But I *do* want you to be happy." He swallowed, determined to plow on. "And if that's what it takes…"

She didn't argue after that. She sat silently, rubbing her temples as though she had a headache while he drove back to her sister's and came to a stop at the curb.

"Thank you," he said. "For the time we did spend together. I'll never forget you." He forced a smile even though it felt as though he could hardly breathe. "I hope you and the girls have the best Christmas ever." He tried not to think of little Piper asking to sit on his lap. That wasn't his child. She could never be his child, just as Harper could never be his wife.

Reaching across her lap, he unlatched the door. But she didn't get out right away. She caught his hand before he could withdraw it and brought it to her lips. "You are so different and refreshing and gorgeous and…and amazing in bed," she blurted and kissed his hand before hopping to the ground, closing the door and hurrying to the house.

Tobias watched until she disappeared inside. Then he drew a deep breath, trying to expand his rib cage to get rid of the terrible pressure on his heart.

He'd done the right thing, he told himself as he drove off. It wasn't fair to continue seeing her when she didn't know the whole truth. He was only prolonging the inevitable, setting them both up for a fall.

But doing the right thing had never felt so bad.

"Why are you back so soon?" Karoline said the moment she saw Harper.

Harper set her purse on the kitchen counter, where her sister was cleaning. Karoline had been complaining that the kids had gotten the cupboards sticky when they decorated their gingerbread houses so she was scrubbing them down.

"We decided that… Well, considering what's going on with Axel, we realized we were crazy to get involved with each other."

"Get *involved*? You were just going out to dinner. Trying to have some fun while you're here. Lord knows Axel's been having a ball, traveling the world, making a fortune, being recognized and worshipped everywhere he goes. I won't mention the groupies and what he's likely doing with them."

Yes, she knew all of that. But this…connection with Tobias went much deeper than simply going to dinner and having some fun. Axel might be sleeping around, but there wasn't any woman in particular he'd fallen in love with, or he wouldn't be saying the things he was saying to her. He'd gotten drunk on his fame and demanded his freedom so he could fully explore it, had wanted to revel in the attention he was getting and all the women who were throwing themselves at him.

It was different for Harper. She was starting to have feelings for Tobias. To think about him in ways that made her nervous. To want to be with him again—not only to make love but just to hang out, spend as much time with him as possible.

She'd even started to wonder what he might be like as a stepfather, were they ever to get serious. Seeing Piper sitting on his lap as she walked into the living room had felt strange but not entirely unwelcome, and that rocked her to the core. With everything that'd happened since she met Tobias and with what was happening with Axel now, she felt torn. So she wasn't making things easier for herself by getting to know Tobias; she was making them that much harder.

"I like Tobias, Karoline," she said softly.

Her sister was bent over, cleaning a lower cabinet. "You already admitted that. And I can see why. He seems like a nice guy," she responded as she scrubbed.

"No, I mean I *really* like him."

Snapping up to her full height, Karoline turned to face her. "How is that possible? You barely know him!"

Harper kept her gaze on her hands, which were toying with the strap of her purse. "Doesn't matter. There's something about him that... It's hard to explain. I'm *really* attracted to him—so much that it isn't fair to continue to see him if I'm even considering getting back with my husband."

"You're kidding me," Karoline said. "You're not saying you're falling in love with him..."

"I don't know if I'd go that far, but...I feel *something*." What she didn't add was that maybe what she felt was her fault. She'd let their relationship become physical, which certainly didn't help her keep things in perspective.

"So your answer is to get back with Axel?" Karoline asked.

"He's my husband. The father of my children. We've already invested ten years in each other. I live near his family, not here. There are *so* many reasons."

"I understand that. But he's not your husband anymore," Karoline said.

Harper slid onto a bar stool at the island. "Your own husband said that people sometimes lose sight of what's important to them. That occasionally they need—maybe even deserve—a second chance."

Karoline's eyebrows furrowed but, for a change, she didn't immediately spout off. Instead, she started to clean with renewed vigor.

"You don't think Axel will straighten up and be a good husband?" Harper could tell her sister was holding back. "Like he was before?"

With a frown, Karoline dropped her rag in the sink,

dried her hands and came around the island to sit on the bar stool next to Harper's. "I don't know," she admitted. "That's the thing. Now that he's broken my trust, I'm afraid of what he might do in the future, afraid he might hurt you again. You said it yourself at the Blue Suede Shoe. How can you trust him? Well, I feel the same. And there are other considerations."

"Like…"

"What will you be thinking and feeling whenever he's away from you? Are you willing to endure the long absences? Live the rest of your life in his shadow? Continue the outpouring of energy required to keep him up and happy and functioning?"

Now it was Harper who didn't have answers. Was she willing to dive right back into that situation? *Would* she be capable of keeping him up and happy and functioning if she couldn't do it well enough before? Could *she* ever be fulfilled in that situation? She'd gone into salvage mode so quickly and worked so hard to save her marriage that she'd never really asked herself if things had changed so much since Axel's band took off that *she* was no longer happy. "That's what I need to figure out," she said.

"I'd also consider one other thing."

"And that is…"

"Is he feeling sorry for himself right now, for what *he* may have lost—or for what he did to you and his children?"

"Does it matter? He's starting to press me to get back together."

"It would matter to me." With a sigh she got up and went to reclaim her washcloth. "But you're the only one who can make the decision. And I'll support you no matter what you choose."

"Thank you," Harper said. "I appreciate that. And now…I think I'll go spend some time with the girls and then take a hot bath."

"Sounds like a good idea."

When the kids asked about her "date," she just said Tobias had to go home early. Then she watched a Disney movie with Piper and Everly, ignoring her phone the entire time. She read several chapters of *Harry Potter and the Sorcerer's Stone* to them after that and lay down with them until they were asleep. But once she returned to her own room and took her phone from her pocket so she could strip down for her bath, she saw that she'd missed a slew of messages—all of them from Axel.

I hate that you're with him.

Don't you dare sleep with him again. I won't take you back if you do.

Who is this bastard? Our divorce wasn't even final when he slept with you!

How do you think the girls feel, seeing you with another man? Why are you confusing them like this?

This is stupid, Harper. Where do you think it can go? You don't even live there.

And don't tell me you're considering moving there. My parents would freak out.

Harper felt nauseous as she read those messages. Did she really want to go back to Axel and deal with more of *this*?

She replayed her last conversation with Tobias as she finished undressing. *You want me to go back to Axel?*

No. Of course I don't, he'd said. *But I do want you to be happy. And if that's what it takes...*

One man was obviously way more sensitive to what *she* was feeling than the other.

But she had her girls to think about.

20

Susan was working alone. Tobias had watched the store long enough to be convinced of that. And because it was cold out and getting late, she didn't have many customers. He'd seen a few people park, get out and hurry in. But the last customer had left twenty minutes ago.

He checked the time on his phone. She'd be closing soon. If he planned to talk to her tonight, he needed to make his move. Otherwise, she'd be locking up and heading out back to her car, and he didn't want to scare her by approaching her in the alley behind the store.

This was going to be ugly. He knew that. But he had to do it. What had been happening since Maddox married Jada wasn't right, and Tobias was tired of feeling responsible for the pain they were suffering.

Besides, after taking Harper back to her sister's, he already felt terrible. Let Susan kick the shit out of him like she did that other time if it made *her* feel any better.

Steeling himself for what the next few moments would hold, he got out, ducked his head in an effort to draw as little attention as possible and walked down to the store.

The second the bell above the door sounded, Atticus's mother glanced up. The color drained from her face and her eyes darted behind him, as if she was hoping Jada or someone else would be coming in with him.

"It's just me," he said.

"What are you doing here?" she asked.

All the things he'd rehearsed the past couple of hours suddenly got jammed in his throat. Nothing seemed adequate enough to persuade her to look at the situation the way he hoped she would. "I'd just like to say—"

"I don't want to hear it," she snapped before he could get any further. "Now, get out."

Tobias was tempted to do exactly that. What could he really accomplish here? She hadn't softened at all in the five months he'd been back in Silver Springs. There was nothing he could say that would soften her heart now.

He turned, intending to walk out, but then he remembered the reason he'd come in the first place and pivoted back around to face her. "I'll go in a second," he said. "Once you've heard what I have to say."

"You're trespassing. I'll call the police if you don't get out of here. This is *my* business. I have the right to refuse service to anyone."

"I'm not asking for service." After clearing his throat, he dived into what he'd prepared. "Ms. Brooks, I understand how deeply you hate me. And I understand why. I'm not trying to talk you out of that or justify what I did. I deserve your hate, which is why

I've never asked you to forgive me, and why I never will. But I do want to say—"

It was difficult to continue with the way she was glaring at him. The malevolence in those eyes stabbed him like a steel sword. But she hadn't moved to call the police, so he took a deep breath and pressed on.

"How you're treating Maddox and Jada isn't fair. Maddox isn't responsible for what happened to Atticus. *I* am. He just has the bad luck of being related to me. But if you'd only look at other aspects of who he is—the kind of principal he is at the school, the kind of husband he is to your daughter and the kind of father he is to Maya—I think you'll have to agree that he's not the monster you believe. Please don't punish him for something he didn't do and never dreamed would happen. And especially don't punish Jada for loving him. All you're doing is causing *more* pain and heartache."

"You, of all people, don't get to lecture me on pain," she ground out.

"I'm not lecturing you. I'm pleading with you—for their sake."

"You think I'm just going to let it all go? That you get to live your life being whole and healthy while my son wheels himself around in a chair because of *you*?"

"You can hate me all you want," he said. "You can give me dirty looks whenever we pull up to the same intersection like you did the other day. You can say whatever you want about me, scream at me, hit me. Do anything you want to *me*. Just, please, think about what you're doing to your own family."

"How dare you come in here and try to make me feel as if *I'm* the one who's done something wrong," she said, but he lifted a hand before she could continue.

"Where do you think all this hate will lead? You'll destroy your own children with it if you're not careful," he said and walked out.

Harper spent the next four days completely focused on her girls, when they were home from school, and Axel, who, once he found out about her failed date with Tobias, sensed an opportunity to improve his position and apologized for "overreacting" and sending those upsetting texts. Harper could tell he sensed victory close at hand, because he began to call and text even more, and to send her funny memes and inside jokes. His mother called to say she'd talked to her son and was excited to hear that they were "considering working things out." Rory and Gary, the lead guitarist in the band, had each thanked her for saving the tour. And the band's manager was so grateful that Axel had calmed down he'd sent a flower arrangement only slightly less elaborate and expensive than the daily bouquets she'd begun to receive from Axel.

We can make this work.

We belong together.

Don't give up on us, babe.

That was what each of the cards had said so far— all of them sweet and sentimental and encouraging. He was finally treating her as though she mattered to him, as though he was grateful for her and eager to see her again.

Harper should have been over the moon. If they got

back together, she wouldn't have to feel like a failure in the most important area of her life. Her children deserved to have their father back. She wanted that for them more than anything else. Plus, she'd be able to show the press, who'd been so eager to announce the news about her troubled marriage, and the many trolls on social media, who'd been absolutely cruel in expressing their glee over the split, that they shouldn't count her out yet. Vindication would be sweet.

She'd be getting everything she wanted—at least what she'd wanted just two weeks ago—and yet…she wasn't as happy as she thought she should be.

None of it felt *right*.

Maybe her misgivings would fade as Axel proved himself and his love. Surely, with time, her hesitation and uncertainty would disappear. That was what her mother had told her, anyway. They'd talked last night for an unusually long time and Pearl had said that anyone who'd been through what Harper had in the past year would be cautious and feel a little burned. It was natural.

But Pearl didn't know about Tobias and how often Harper thought of *him*. It had been so difficult not to call him.

That was the relationship she felt like resurrecting.

"What are you doing?" Karoline asked, poking her head into Harper's room on Saturday morning, only four days before Christmas.

Harper hadn't joined the rest of the family for breakfast. She'd gotten hung up watching Axel's latest concert on her phone. "Just watching some video clips of the tour on YouTube," she told her sister.

"How's Axel doing?"

"Fabulous. As always." Axel was a magnificent performer. Watching him stirred old feelings, so she'd been viewing a lot of his concerts and videos the past few days. He had a great voice, but it wasn't just that; it was the way he moved onstage and how he interacted with the audience.

Folding her arms, Karoline leaned against the doorjamb. "Have you decided what you're going to get him for Christmas?"

"He's missed so much of the past year, I thought I'd put together a scrapbook of the kids—a small one he can take with him when he travels. You can make them online and they send them in the mail, bound and professional-looking."

"Something sentimental would be smart. I'd say you've come up with just the right thing."

At any rate, it was all she felt like getting him, so she was satisfied with her decision. But she couldn't help noticing how restrained Karoline had become whenever she spoke of him.

"You don't think I should get back with him, do you," Harper said, opening herself up for her sister's frank opinion even though she was afraid that would be a mistake.

"Honestly?"

"Are you ever anything *but* honest?" Harper asked dryly.

Her sister shrugged. "Not usually. But I admit I'm trying to be careful here. I just want you to be happy. If that means you get back with Axel, then I'm all for it."

Surprised by her sister's response, Harper smiled. Apparently, Karoline didn't know everything, although it seemed like it at times. "Thanks for that."

She gestured toward the kitchen. "Are you going to come out for breakfast? The girls are almost done."

"Yeah. I'll be there in a sec." Harper was about to set her phone aside so she could climb out of bed and throw on a pair of sweats when something in the video, which had continued to play while she talked to Karoline, caught her attention. It was just as "Let It Go," the band's new release, was coming to an end. Harper wasn't sure why or how she'd noticed, but she pulled her phone back to take a closer look as Axel bent down to sing to one of the pretty girls crowded up against the stage.

As she watched, he let the girl touch his hand and then…took something from her?

Was that what he did?

Puzzled, Harper hit the back arrow to view the same segment again—and again and again. She couldn't be sure, but it looked like the girl handed him her number or her room key or something.

"Mommy?"

Piper came charging in so suddenly Harper slid her phone under the covers. "Piper! What are you doing?"

"Can we go ice-skating today? We all want to. So can you call that man who said he'd take us?" She jumped up on the bed and pressed her hands into a prayerful pose to show just how badly she wanted to go. "*Please?* I've never been ice-skating."

Still somewhat distracted by what she'd seen in the video, Harper didn't answer right away. She wanted to believe that quick exchange meant nothing. No doubt girls gave their numbers to Axel all the time. And even though he'd probably called a few—which was part of what had caused the problem between them—he wouldn't have called this one. Right?

Or…maybe he had. There was something about the way he responded that led Harper to believe he *wanted* this particular girl's number. That he'd singled her out on purpose and let her know she was the one he'd chosen by the way he was looking at her when he sang.

"Mom?" Piper pleaded. *"Please?"*

Harper's heart was beating very fast. There was that lack of trust, she told herself. She was reading more into what she'd seen than was really there. That was all.

Except, on a very basic level, she didn't believe that. And this was the concert Pulse had played only two nights ago. *After* Axel had begun to show so much interest in reuniting.

If they got back together, would he be able to forgo all the women who propositioned him? Or now that he'd had a taste of sex with anyone he wanted, would he be able to give it up?

He'd already divorced her once to be able to exploit his freedom…

"Mom, aren't you listening?" Piper asked.

Making an effort, Harper turned her attention to her youngest daughter. "What is it?"

"Can we go ice-skating with that man who said he'd take us?"

Harper's gaze swept over the sea of flowers that adorned her room. She'd never asked for such elaborate displays of affection; she'd only wanted Axel to be sincere and remain committed to her and their children. "I don't think so, honey."

"Why not?"

"I doubt Tobias will be available on such short notice."

"What about tomorrow?"

Harper covered her mouth as everything she'd been feeling since Axel had started the nightmare of their divorce came sweeping over her. She wanted to scream.

"Momma?" Piper cocked her head. "What's wrong?"

"Did she say yes?" Everly asked, appearing in the doorway.

Somehow managing to rein in her emotions, Harper lowered her hand. "I said no."

"Why not?" Everly cried. "Why can't we? Doesn't that sound like *fun*?"

Karoline came up behind Everly. "Amanda and Miranda are begging me, too. I suppose we could take them ourselves. We could find a rink in Santa Barbara if you'd rather not ask Tobias. The only problem is that Terrance doesn't know how to ice-skate and neither do I."

Harper wanted to replay that concert video yet again. It was like roadkill. As grotesque as she found it, she couldn't help looking.

But she couldn't go back to it while the kids and Karoline were in the room.

"Are you okay?" Karoline asked, her expression showing concern.

"Yes, of course." Somehow Harper managed to keep her voice steady. "Why wouldn't I be?"

"I don't know. For a second you looked like you were about to pass out."

No, she decided. She couldn't do it. She couldn't get back with Axel, didn't want to take the risk—to feel that sudden tightening in her gut, to see clips like she'd just watched and be destroyed all over again. She didn't want to raise her children alone while he was off singing somewhere else on the planet, either.

"Mom?" Everly pressed. "Can we go?"

Harper patted the bedding to find her phone. *Why the hell not?* she wanted to say.

Instead she told them to get dressed and she'd see if Tobias was free.

It took Harper a few minutes to work up the nerve to call Tobias. She went into the bathroom, turned on the shower so no one would knock while she was in there and then paced back and forth as she tried to determine if she had the right to ask him for *anything*.

She knew she didn't.

At that point, she almost turned off the shower and went out to tell everyone he was too busy.

But then she remembered how he'd offered—as if he really wouldn't mind—and decided it wouldn't hurt to ask him. He'd known they weren't "together" when she brought the gingerbread house, and yet he'd still invited them. If he didn't want to see her, he could always say no. She wasn't going to make that decision for him.

Besides, he'd been there for her when she needed someone most. She would rather come away from Silver Springs feeling she'd left that brief relationship on a good note—that she could count him among her friends, at least. She cared about him, so seeing him one more time, in a totally innocuous setting with her kids and nieces and Karoline and Terrance, couldn't hurt anything.

Gripping the phone tighter than she probably

needed to, she went ahead and sent the call. Then she held her breath as it began to ring.

Tobias had just returned from an arduous hike when his phone went off. Ever since he'd spoken to Susan, he'd been expecting some kind of backlash. He doubted Jada's mother was going to let him get away with showing up at her store and saying what he had. She'd probably called Jada and let her have it, so he was afraid the backlash would come in the way of a call from his sister-in-law telling him to back off and stay out of it—or maybe it would be his brother handling it for her. He'd only been trying to help, but he might've overstepped.

This wasn't Jada, however. It wasn't Maddox, either—or Maya or Atticus.

It was Harper.

He stared at her name on his screen. He'd spotted her SUV at the coffee shop yesterday morning and had purposely gone somewhere else. If she was getting back with Axel, he needed to stay out of the way. Seeing her only reminded him of how he felt when he was around her, and he was having a difficult time trying to forget her as it was.

For the same reason he didn't go into the coffee shop, he felt he shouldn't answer. He couldn't think of any legitimate reason they had to talk.

In the end, he couldn't overcome his curiosity or the desire he felt to hear her voice, so he hit the talk button before her call could transfer to voice mail. "Hello?"

"Tobias?"

"Yes?" Okay, this wasn't a pocket dial. She seemed fully aware of the fact that she'd called him.

"I'm sorry to bother you," she said.

He removed his parka and draped it over one of the kitchen chairs. "It's no problem. Everything okay?"

"For the most part. It's just that, well, the girls have been asking me—begging me, really—to see if you'd have time to take us all ice-skating. So I thought maybe it wouldn't be a big deal to do something like that. You know, go ice-skating as friends. If you're open to it, that is."

"You want to go ice-skating as *friends*?" he repeated.

There was a slight pause. Then she said, "I realize that things got a little…hot between us, but I'd like to have *some* type of relationship with you. We haven't known each other that long, but I'd really enjoy seeing you again before I leave, and…and bringing the kids along would make it difficult for us to get into trouble, right?"

"As far as I'm concerned, that's the best kind of trouble," he said. "But…Axel won't mind?"

After another pause she said, "It isn't his decision."

"I see."

"Unless you're too busy, of course. Or you're not interested. I admit I wouldn't blame you. I just… I'm having a hard time giving you up entirely."

Shit. If she only knew how hard it was for *him.* "And the kids are begging to go…"

"That's true. You offered, after all. They're not likely to forget something like that."

"Right." Tobias squeezed his eyes closed as he considered taking this opportunity to see her—*as a friend.* Given how he felt, it would only make things harder, but damned if he didn't want to see her regardless. "When?" he asked.

"We're free tonight, if you are. Or tomorrow. Or even Monday. We don't have a lot going on—other than Christmas on Wednesday, of course."

Tobias had promised Tonya he'd go to her Christmas party tonight. He didn't really *want* to go, especially because it meant a two-hour drive to LA, and he knew how drunk everyone would get. But he'd told her he'd go, so he felt he had to keep his word. "I promised a friend I'd go to her Christmas party tonight. But tomorrow should work."

"Will the rink be available?"

"Yeah. That won't be a problem. Most of the kids at New Horizons have gone home for Christmas. If we go at dinnertime, the rest will be in the cafeteria."

"Okay."

"Let's shoot for five o'clock. Are Karoline and Terrance and their girls coming, too?"

"Yeah."

He could see why Harper would dub this adventure "safe." He wouldn't dare try anything if Karoline was around. "Then I'll meet you all there."

"Perfect," she said and added a quick "It'll be good to see you again" before hanging up.

Tobias stared at his phone for several seconds after that. "Don't take it to heart," he said aloud. "She didn't mean it."

21

If Tobias got anything out of going to Tonya's party, it was the confidence that he'd made the right decision when he broke up with her. Although she was more than friendly, even asked him to stay over—an invitation he refused—she wasn't living the kind of life he wanted to live. They would never have been compatible.

As he sat around nursing a beer while everyone else got high, he realized that he didn't think partying so hard was fun. Maybe, occasionally, it was tempting to use drugs to check out of real life. But you had to come back to real life at some point and the reality you had to face could be much worse because you'd tried to avoid it.

When he left Tonya's to drive over and surprise his mother, since Jill lived only forty-five minutes away and he'd given up on the party early, he was glad he'd been careful not to get involved with anyone else since he'd broken up with Tonya. He knew he'd choose much differently now than he would've five months ago. When he first got out of prison, his self-esteem had been at an all-time low, and he'd been starved for love—sex, too, of course, after going so long without it. That was how he'd gotten mixed up with his cellmate's sister in the first place. He'd felt lucky to have *any* woman's attention.

When he arrived at his mother's apartment, her roommate told him Jill had picked up an extra shift at the bar where she served drinks because she needed the money to help make January's rent.

He considered waiting, but when he learned that she wouldn't get off until closing at two, he drove over to see her there, ordered some hot wings and a soda, and tipped her all he could afford so she *could* make rent. If only she'd stay off drugs, she'd be able to get by on her own. But it was Christmas. He wasn't going to let her stress over the holidays. And he definitely didn't want her asking Maddox for money again. Maddox had taken care of her as much as anyone could the whole time Tobias was gone.

Jill pocketed the money, thanked him profusely and bragged to all the other servers that he was her son, but instead of staying until she got off and following her back to her place to stay the night, as he'd planned when he left the party, he decided to make the drive home. Being around his mother wasn't good for him. She couldn't keep her life together, and since she refused to stay away from methamphetamine, there was no way to help her. Sometimes her decisions made him so angry it was just easier to keep his distance.

It took nearly two hours to get home, so it was much later when he pulled in. He was tired and eager for bed, but he took a few minutes to walk up to the front house to see if everything looked okay. Somehow, against all odds, Uriah and Carl seemed to be getting along. At least there hadn't been any arguments or other problems in the past few days—none that Tobias was aware of.

Tonight, too, everything seemed to be fine. Carl's car was parked where it should be, so he was home for a change, and all the lights were off.

Hoping Uriah's son was asleep, which meant there might be peace for the rest of the night, too, Tobias returned to his own place, where he found a gift sitting on his doorstep, wrapped in a red-and-green plaid with a small bow.

He saw a tag, but when he checked there was no information in the To and From. It just read Merry Christmas.

He looked around, wondering who'd left it. Maddox, Jada and Maya would give him a gift but they'd wait until Christmas Eve or Christmas Day, whenever they could get together and Susan wouldn't be there. Aiyana would get him something small, too, but she'd wait for the staff party planned for Monday afternoon. That left Uriah, but Tobias couldn't imagine Uriah could wrap like this or would bother to do so even if he could.

Puzzled, Tobias carried the gift into the house and opened it. As he was ripping off the paper, he had the thought that maybe Susan had left it for him—a box wrapped extra nice to make him think he was getting a great gift when really it was a pile of dog shit or worse.

But it wasn't anything bad. On the contrary. It was a watch with onboard GPS, maps, music, contactless payments, even blood oxygen saturation and heart rate monitors—a gift that would be appealing to any outdoor enthusiast.

"Wow," he muttered. This was *nice*. Probably the nicest thing he'd ever been given. He would've guessed it had come from Atticus, since it would be useful on their hike, and Atticus was so excited about going. But there was no way Atticus would have an extra six or seven hundred dollars to drop on him, despite their plans for the summer. Jada's brother had too many other people to buy for that he cared about more.

Tobias rummaged around in the tissue paper, hoping to find a card or note that would resolve the mystery, but there was none.

Damn. He wanted to know who'd given it to him.

He could ask Uriah to take a look at the security feeds in the morning, he decided.

Although that wasn't really necessary. He could guess who'd given it to him. Harper was about the only person he knew who'd have the money for something like this. She'd have good reason not to sign her name, too.

Yes, it *had* to be her. No one else made sense.

But if she was getting back with her ex-husband, why was she buying *him* an expensive watch?

As soon as Tobias woke up the following morning, he grabbed his phone to text Harper.

Did you drop something off at my house last night?

She must've been with her family—or she was trying to figure out what to say—because it was fifteen minutes before he got a response. No.

He frowned. Are you sure?

About not coming over? How could I be wrong about that?

Could it have been someone else? He'd been so certain it was her. It had to be you, he wrote. Who else could it be?

I don't know what you're talking about. Did someone bring you cookies or something?

Was she just trying to throw him off the trail? Not cookies, no.

What, then?

Something much more expensive.

You're not going to tell me what?

A watch.

Do you like it?

I love it, but I'd like to know who to thank.

Sounds like whoever gave it to you doesn't want any thanks. If I were you, I'd just enjoy it. Are we still on for ice-skating?

He scratched his head as he read her latest. If it *was* her she wasn't going to admit it. Yes, he typed.

Okay. See you soon.

That was it. She'd dismissed the subject. But she wasn't going to get away that easily.

After pulling up his contacts, he called Uriah.

"Your truck's in the drive," Uriah said as soon as he answered.

"So?" Tobias asked, confused by this greeting.

"You're calling me when you could just walk a few feet?"

Poor Uriah was wondering why Tobias was suddenly making himself so scarce, but if Uriah wanted peace and a real chance to repair his relationship with his son, it was better if Tobias stayed away. Other than a few of the assholes he'd met in prison, Tobias had never disliked anyone quite as much as Carl. "Sorry. Just woke up and wanted to ask a quick question."

"If you come over, I've got some zucchini bread for you."

"Another gift from one of your many lady friends?"

"Yup. Helen brought this one."

"I bet it's good, but I can't come over right now." Especially because chances were high that Carl would be there. He never seemed to go anywhere in the mornings, although he was probably still sleeping. "I just wanted to ask if you saw someone come by my house last night."

"Who?"

"That's what I'm trying to figure out. It might've been late."

"I didn't notice anyone, but you know I go to bed early. Give me a sec. I'll wake Carl. He's the night owl."

The sound of Carl's name was like nails going down a chalkboard. "You don't have to bother him."

"He's supposed to be up by now, anyway," Uriah said. "He's got work to do."

Tobias wondered how many more days Carl would tolerate having his father drag him out of bed to do what he was supposed to do. But, fortunately, when Uriah asked him, Tobias heard no arguing in the background.

"Carl didn't see anyone, either," Uriah reported when he came back on the line.

That was actually good news. If it *was* Harper who'd come by, Tobias didn't want Carl anywhere near her. "Is there anything on the security feeds?"

"Hang on, let me check."

While he waited, Tobias got up and put on a pot of coffee.

"Looks like a woman hurried down the drive to your place at about ten thirty," he said when he came back on the line.

"How long did she stay?"

"She didn't. Ran right back."

"Can you tell who she was?"

"You must not realize how blurry these feeds are."

"She must've had a car."

"There was no vehicle in the frame. I'm guessing she left it out by the road, beyond the range of the cameras. The way she crept down the drive, eyeing my place as though someone might jump out and grab her—she definitely didn't want to be seen."

She'd probably been afraid that Carl would be lurking about. Tobias was wary of that himself. "Shit."

"What's going on?"

"Nothing big," he said. "Someone brought me a gift. That's all. I just wanted to know who it was."

"Well, I can tell you it was a woman, but that's about it."

"Thanks."

"Are you sure you don't want any of this zucchini bread?" he asked before Tobias could sign off.

Tobias figured he should probably make himself walk down, even if Carl was there. "Sure. Just let me have a shower."

"Oh, wait. Never mind. Carl's got an appointment with his attorney—and I've got to drive him. I'll just bring you some when we leave."

Tobias guessed Carl wasn't too disappointed about getting out of work. "Sounds good."

Uriah came by a few minutes later, as promised, and then left right away to get his son to the attorney.

Tobias was enjoying the zucchini bread when he heard another knock. Assuming Uriah had forgotten to give him something else, and was trying to do it before he took off, he swung the door wide without checking to see who it was—and found Susan Brooks standing on his stoop.

Oh, damn. Of course she'd show up on the day he was supposed to take Harper and her family ice-skating. He didn't relish the idea of seeing Harper when he had scratches all over his face. Susan had left some pretty deep gouges last time.

Squaring his shoulders, he stepped out and shut the door behind him. Uriah owned the house and most of the furniture. He couldn't let her in and have her start destroying stuff.

"Ms. Brooks."

She said nothing. Didn't move, either.

He shifted uncomfortably. A chill wind whipped at

his short hair and cut right through his thin T-shirt, but he didn't mind the cold. He figured it might be smarter to be a little numb for this. "Did you want to…um… tell me something?"

No response.

His gaze lowered to the bag. He hoped she didn't have a gun inside it. Since she was an eye-for-an-eye kind of person, he had virtually no doubt she'd shoot him if she had the opportunity.

Then her eyes started to fill with tears.

Oh, God. She'd obviously reached a breaking point. She'd only ever shown up at his place one other time, and that was right after he'd been released. She'd been crying then, too—wailing, actually. He'd never forget the sound of it or the hate that had slammed into him with every blow.

"I'm sorry if it upset you that I came by the store," he said in an attempt to head off whatever was coming. "I…" He swallowed hard. "I meant well." He didn't expect her to believe him, but it was true so he figured it didn't hurt to say it.

A tear slipped over her eyelashes and ran down her cheek as she lifted the bag.

He would've stepped back at that point, but he had the door behind him. He lifted his hands in a defensive position, instinctively trying to ward off any threat.

But she didn't pull out a gun. She tried to hand him the whole bag.

"What's this?" he asked when she shoved it into his chest.

She sniffed as another tear fell, obviously trying to talk, but she was too choked up, so he accepted the bag, since that seemed to be important to her, and peered cautiously inside.

It was filled with…boxes of cookies from her store? And they weren't just any cookies, he noticed. They were pumpkin and chocolate chip with cream cheese frosting—his favorite.

"I'm…so sorry," she managed to say, almost choking on the last word as the tears came faster.

Sorry? Tobias's jaw dropped. She wasn't angry? She wasn't out to punish him some more?

He was so stunned it took him a moment to decide how to react to this wildly unexpected occurrence. "You don't have anything to be sorry for." He tried to return the cookies. He didn't expect gifts from her. He didn't expect her to be friendly to him, either. He didn't even know how to react to kindness, not when it came from her. He just wanted her to stop being so spiteful and mean to Maddox and Jada, since they had nothing to do with what had happened to Atticus. "I know I'm the only one to blame for everything."

"You were seventeen," she said on a sob and, ignoring his attempt to get her to take the bag back, she turned and left.

22

"Are you nervous about seeing Tobias?" Karoline asked.

Harper pretended to be far more engrossed in doing the dishes than she actually was. The girls were in the other room, watching a Disney movie with their cousins while their uncle watched professional basketball on his phone. "No, why?"

"Just wondering." Her sister grabbed a dish towel and dried the pot Harper had just put in the rack. "Did you get your Christmas shopping finished last night like you wanted to?"

Harper kept her gaze on the spatula she was scrubbing. "For the most part. Thanks for watching the girls."

"It was no problem. They just played with their cousins." Karoline wiped down the counters. "Seems like you were out pretty late," she added a few seconds after.

"The malls stay open later during the holidays. And I had a long drive from LA."

"What did you end up buying?"

"A few stocking stuffers for the girls," Harper said,

but that wasn't all. She'd purchased a nice watch for Tobias from an expensive sporting goods store. But she wasn't going to admit that to anyone, not even him. She didn't care how expensive or wildly inappropriate it was—or that she felt the need to hide it. As soon as she'd found the watch, she'd known she wanted to get it for him. It was her one indulgence, her own little celebration of the season, and she wasn't going to second-guess herself or worry about it now that she'd already made the decision. She was just going to enjoy imagining him out in the wilderness, using that great watch while she was in Colorado, facing the hard work of putting her life back together—whether or not that included her ex-husband.

"Things still going okay with Axel?"

"Yeah, of course. Why?"

"You didn't say much when the new flower arrangement arrived this morning."

Because the flower arrangements made her nervous. She kept remembering the clip she'd seen of him accepting something from that fan in the front row and wondering if his extravagance was meant to compensate her in some way.

If so, it wasn't a fair trade. She didn't want flowers in place of faithfulness.

Maybe things would be different, easier, once he got home. She certainly hoped so. Her children were so excited that their father was suddenly paying more attention to them. She didn't want to do anything that would take that away from them. "The arrangement's gorgeous. I just… I already have a lot of them, you know?"

"Can a girl get too many flowers?" her sister joked.

"Have you seen my room?" Harper asked dryly.

"I have. It's a bit much. But it's kind of impressive that he's trying so hard to win you back." Karoline bent closer, to see around the fall of hair obscuring her face. "Right?"

"It's not like you to beat around the bush," Harper said, turning on the water so she could use the sprayer to rinse the frying pan she'd washed. "So…what are you *really* digging for?"

"I'd like to know how you're feeling about him, I guess. Are you happier now that the two of you have basically decided to try again?"

She'd be happier if the problems that had driven them apart in the first place weren't still part of the equation. "I'm…cautiously optimistic."

"Axel called me last night, by the way."

At this, Harper turned off the water and lowered the frying pan back into the soapy water.

"He wanted to know where you were," Karoline continued. "Said he hadn't been able to reach you for most of the day and all of the evening."

"I was trying to finish my shopping," she explained, but that wasn't the case, not *exactly*. She hadn't accepted Axel's calls because she didn't want to talk to him. She had no idea why. She had no proof he'd slept with the girl who'd been worshipping him in the mosh pit. For all she knew, she was reading far more into it than was warranted.

So what was going on with her? Was she beginning to look for excuses *not* to take the risk of getting back with her ex? People sometimes sabotaged themselves.

That was all she could figure; she had no other reason to explain why she'd been compelled to buy such an expensive gift for another man.

Karoline nodded slowly. "Gotcha."

Harper finished rinsing the pan and set it on the rack. "Did Axel have anything else to say?"

"Not much. Why? You didn't talk to him? Didn't you call him when you got home?"

"No, I was too tired."

"Shopping can be exhausting," Karoline said, but Harper didn't like the tone of her voice or the skeptical expression on her face. She knew Karoline could tell *something* wasn't right.

Tobias almost couldn't believe what'd happened, but Susan's apology seemed sincere. Maddox had called an hour ago to say she'd stopped by his house, too, and apologized to him and Jada. Apparently, Atticus had confronted his mother and drawn a hard line—told her *she* was the one ruining his life because she wouldn't allow the family to heal. He'd told her he'd never speak to her again if she didn't let it go.

No doubt that was a difficult thing for Atticus to do, and an even more difficult thing for Susan to hear. But Tobias felt it was warranted—not for *his* sake but for Jada's. He hoped this was the beginning of a much better relationship between Jada and her mother and—even if Susan changed her mind about *him* again, which she might—he hoped she'd finally give her son-in-law a chance. Jada and Maddox both deserved to be treated better than they had so far. Just thinking that might happen made Tobias happy.

But he was a little leery about going skating with Harper. He'd had a good day so far and wasn't sure he should push his luck. Seeing her would only make him want her all over again. And it might get awkward with her sister, brother-in-law, children and nieces around. Would they be able to tell—by the way he looked at her or touched her—that their relationship had gone well beyond platonic?

He closed his eyes, remembering the first time they'd made love, and felt his groin tighten. What he felt for Harper went well beyond the sexual—although it manifested itself in that way—and yet he was going to spend the evening with her, pretending he didn't feel anything.

He was wasting his time worrying about it, though. It wasn't as if he was going to cancel. Even an awkward or frustrating meeting was better than no meeting at all. That was how he knew his interest went much further than wanting to take her back to bed.

He heard the girls first. They came running into the ice rink while he was trying to find skates that might be small enough for them. New Horizons was for girls older than Harper's, but because Aiyana had decided to open the rink to the public one Saturday a month beginning in January, she'd purchased some smaller skates to rent out.

"There you are!" Piper said as soon as she saw him.

He found himself grinning at her. She was so damn cute. Her nose was pink from the cold, her hair was falling out of its ponytail and she was dressed in tan leggings with a leopard-print top and a pair of boots lined with fake fur. "Are you excited to get on the ice?"

"Yeah!" she cried. "So is Everly."

"I hope I don't fall down." Everly looked slightly

concerned when she saw the sharp blades on the bottom of the skates.

"If you're careful and don't go too fast, you'll be fine," he said. "Besides, I'm going to help you, remember?"

Amanda and Miranda came in after Everly and Piper but before the adults. "Wow, it's cold in here," Amanda said, and her sister agreed, hugging herself and shivering.

"You'll warm up once you get moving," Tobias told them. "What size shoe do you wear?"

He was handing each of the twins a pair of skates when Harper, Terrance and Karoline finally caught up.

"It's *really* nice of you to do this," Karoline said after they'd exchanged greetings.

"It's no problem." Tobias turned on the Christmas music before getting the rest of the skates.

Terrance helped his girls and Karoline with their skates, so Tobias focused on Piper, Everly and, finally, Harper.

He could feel Harper watching him as he finished tying her laces. "I like your hands," she said.

He glanced over to see if Karoline had heard. But the kids were talking and laughing so loudly she probably hadn't. She was too busy telling her husband that her left skate needed to be tightened, and Terrance was trying to fix it.

"I like a lot more than that about you." Tobias helped Harper up but let go of her as though he'd said something innocuous.

"Can I be first?" Piper cried when she saw that his hands were free.

"You bet. Just let me get my own skates on."

The rink wasn't crowded, but there were a few boys who were skating through dinner. Tobias was actually glad about that, because he knew them from school. When the three came over to say hello and see what he was doing, he recruited them to help teach the girls.

He could tell Amanda and Miranda were thrilled to have the attention of these older boys—all the giggling indicated they thought their helpers were cute—and Everly didn't seem to mind, since it meant she wouldn't have to take turns with Piper. That freed him to help Harper's youngest while Terrance and Karoline, clinging to each other, gingerly stepped onto the ice after only a few instructions, and Harper watched from the side.

Piper loved the ice. She didn't catch on very fast, but Tobias hadn't expected much from a six-year-old who'd never been on skates. She mostly loved riding on his shoulders while he skated, which he let her do for a few minutes here and there, amid helping all the others. When he finally got Harper onto the ice, however, Piper was ready to try skating with her sister, two cousins and the boys.

"You're a natural with kids," Harper said as he guided her around the rink.

"What was that watch all about?" he asked instead of commenting.

She gave him a pert look. "What watch?"

"The one you delivered to my house last night."

"That wasn't me. You must have another secret admirer."

He lowered his voice even more. "Harper, I can't accept such an expensive gift."

"You can't return it, either, not if you don't know who gave it to you."

"You won't take it back?"

"Absolutely not."

"Then...tell me why you did it?" he persisted.

She looked up at him. "Because it made me happy. That's been the best part of my Christmas, so please don't ruin it by saying you want to give it back to me."

"It was the best part of your Christmas—and yet it doesn't mean anything?"

He could see that she was checking to make sure Karoline and Terrance weren't tracking them. No one was within earshot—they weren't speaking loudly enough for that—but he knew she didn't want to be caught talking too earnestly. That would only raise questions she'd be bombarded with later. "It means I wish things were different."

He tightened his grip on her waist. "Is it over between us?" he asked. "Because it doesn't feel like it."

She bowed her head, ostensibly watching their feet so they didn't get tangled.

"Look at me," he said. "I'm not going to let you fall."

Finally, she lifted her head. "If I were only choosing for myself... If I didn't have two children to consider..."

"Then..."

"I could explore what I'm feeling."

His heart began to pound. "Which is..."

She didn't get the chance to answer. Karoline and Terrance came skating up to them, laughing, and Karoline said, "Look, we're getting the hang of it."

"You're doing great," Tobias said. Then the boys told him they had to go or they'd miss what was left of dinner, and Tobias spent the next two hours trying to give everyone ample time and attention on the ice. It wasn't until he thought Harper was in the bathroom and he went into the back to turn off the music while everyone was removing their skates that he turned to find her standing in the doorway.

He didn't speak—and neither did she. They didn't want to be found out, so they just crossed the room, met in the middle and kissed as though they'd been craving this opportunity since they'd first set eyes on each other. In his case, at least, it was true.

A moment later, Harper was breathing hard as she pressed her forehead to his and put her palm tenderly to his cheek.

He opened his mouth to tell her how badly he wanted her, how well he'd treat her. But then he closed it again. He knew what stood in their way, and it wasn't just Axel.

So he said nothing.

Pulling back, she hurried out before someone could come looking for them.

"I just can't keep myself from reaching for the flame," he muttered, shaking his head.

He could still taste her as he turned off the music and went out to help put the skates away and say goodbye.

Harper knew the second she kissed Tobias that she was going back to his house, so it was difficult to get through the rest of the evening. She couldn't wait until the girls went to sleep.

As soon as her sister finally turned in, too, she texted him.

I want to see you.

Tonight?

Yes.

When?

Give me twenty minutes, just to be sure everyone's asleep.

I'll be there. Same spot.

Harper was pretty sure she'd never felt happier than after she escaped her sister's house and was running down the block toward his truck.

"We're just making this harder, you know," he said when she climbed in.

"I know. But I can't seem to make myself care about that. Not right now. Can you?"

His gaze roamed over her before he answered, "No."

"At least we both feel the same," she said.

This time they didn't sleep at all. They made love as soon as they got to the house, dropping their clothes as they crossed the living room to reach the bed.

The encounter was intense, exquisite, and they were both exhausted afterward. But they didn't drift off. They knew the hours would pass far too quickly as it was. They talked and touched and laughed and talked and touched some more.

Tobias couldn't believe how right it felt to be with Harper, how content she made him feel—whether they were in bed or not. The only time he got *un*comfortable was when she asked him something about his past that was difficult to answer without an outright lie.

At one point he asked her if she'd ever done anything she sincerely regretted, down to the depths of her soul. He'd been looking for an opening, an opportunity to tell her the truth.

But she'd said she couldn't think of anything she'd done that would be *that* bad, and it scared him. She'd never understand. If he told her what he'd done, she'd never be able to trust him, especially around her children, and her sister and brother-in-law would probably be the first to jump on the stay-away-from-Tobias bandwagon.

How could he expect anything else, considering the privileged life Harper had lived? She hadn't grown up with a single, meth-addicted mother who went from man to man. She'd had a superior court judge for a mother, and her parents were together to this day.

Ultimately, he'd given up trying to find a way to break the truth to her. He didn't want to ruin this night, knew how fleeting these precious few hours would be. And he got the impression she wouldn't want them ruined. She didn't want to talk about the future any more than he wanted to talk about specific things in the past.

They were both in the tub, washing up before he had to take her home, when she asked, "When's the last time you saw your mother?"

"Last night."

"I thought you went to a Christmas party."

"I did. But the party wasn't any fun, and it wasn't very far from where my mother lives, so I decided to pay her a visit before I came home."

"And? How was she?"

"About the same."

"Does she work?"

"She tends to go from one low-paying job to another, but…yeah, most of the time she works. Right now she's serving drinks at a bar."

"Have you ever thought of getting her into rehab?"

He chuckled.

"What?" she said.

"She's been through rehab, Harper. Many times."

She cast him a sheepish glance over one shoulder. "Oh. I'm sorry."

He lifted the sponge he'd been using to bathe her and ran soap up her arm. "It's fine. I'm used to it," he said, even though it really wasn't the kind of problem someone could get used to. It was the kind of problem that continually got worse until—

He didn't want to look down that road.

"Whose party was it?" she asked.

"An old girlfriend."

"What's her name?"

"Tonya."

"Where did you meet her?"

He rinsed the soap from her left arm and started on her right. "She's the sister of an old friend."

"But it ended well between you? It must have, if she invited you to her party and you felt comfortable going."

"She'd like to get back together. I think that's why she invited me. But I'm not interested."

"Why did you two break up in the first place?"

"She's not really what I'm looking for."

She turned around carefully so she could straddle

him despite the limited space. "Then what are you looking for?"

He felt himself grow hard again as her soapy breasts came into contact with his chest and she began to kiss his neck, sucking his skin into her mouth.

"Let's not talk about that right now," he said.

After shifting so she could take him inside her, she began to move, causing the water to splash up against the sides. "Because…"

Acting as though he was too aroused to carry on a coherent conversation, he closed his eyes and leaned his head back on the dated tile while guiding her hips with his hands. He *was* aroused and loving every minute of what she was doing—but he could've come up with the answer to her question. He just didn't want to talk about what he was looking for in a woman, because if he had to describe someone, it would be her.

23

"I hate dropping you off here, especially when it's foggy like this," Tobias complained when Harper had him stop even farther from her sister's house than usual.

"We can't use the same spot every time. That might draw too much attention."

"But I can't see you get home safely from here. Are you sure I can't drop you off in front? It's four thirty in the morning. Everyone should be sleeping."

Harper knew she was probably being a little risky—something terrible could happen anywhere—but she felt safe in her sister's neighborhood. She'd decided she was going to put off any reconciliation with Axel until she'd had a chance to fully explore what she was feeling for Tobias. But it was one thing to tell Karoline what she'd decided—and quite another to show up disheveled after having had sex with Tobias all night.

She needed to be careful, to do this right. She knew there'd be moments when she'd feel highly conflicted, but for the first time since her divorce, she felt as though she'd found the direction she wanted to go—not the direction she felt she *should* go, necessarily, but what she really wanted deep in her heart. There was just something about Tobias that made her happy, and she was hesitant to give him up.

By contrast, every time she thought about getting back with Axel she felt a little sick inside—even panicked, because she knew what she'd have to look forward to if she chose that path, and how difficult it would be. Even when they were together, before he'd ever mentioned the *D* word, they'd been struggling to get along. She couldn't command enough of his time or attention, and when he did want her it was for what she could provide—her calming influence, her help, her ability to level out his emotions.

"My brother-in-law is a light sleeper," she said. "And he gets up early. I'm going to tell Karoline and Terrance that I'm seeing you, but I don't want them to find out this way. It'll take me less than three minutes to run home. I'll be fine."

"Will you text me when you get in—so I won't worry?"

"Yeah." She started to climb out of his truck, but hating to leave him, scooted back so she could kiss him one last time. "I can't get enough of you," she whispered against his lips. "I've been with you for hours and yet I want to go back home with you right now."

"I wish you'd do it," he said.

"I can't. I have to be there when the girls wake up."

"I know."

Reluctantly, she started to move away from him again, but he caught hold of her. "Tell me you're coming back over tonight."

"I am," she said. "I'm coming back every night until

I have to go home to Colorado. I hate that I've wasted so much time—time I could've spent with you."

"We don't have to wait until dark to see each other. Let's take the girls ice-skating again. The only way they'll get better is if we give them a chance to practice."

She ran her thumb over his mouth and then his jawline, memorizing the details of his face. "But school is out of session. Shouldn't we leave the rink to the students at New Horizons?"

"It won't hurt the students if we skate, too. There are hardly any kids left at the school right now, anyway."

"You don't have to work today?"

"I'm off this week for Christmas."

"*All* week?"

"All week. Most of next week, too. I go back two days before classes start."

"Okay. Let's go ice-skating. The girls will be excited."

"And I'll be careful. You don't have to worry that I'll try to touch you or make you uncomfortable."

She smiled. "I know. You were better at that yesterday than I was."

"Then meet me at the rink at three."

"Perfect." She kissed him yet again and then she impulsively spread kisses all over his face.

He seemed surprised by her sudden show of passion and affection. But she loved how truly comfortable she was with him, how content and *renewed*. He was so easygoing; she needed that right now. It brought her peace. And she liked that he was satisfied with a much simpler life than the one Axel craved, that he wasn't burning with ambition to become a living legend. Axel's drive, his dream of making it big and then staying on top, was too hard for her to compete with. His work had become his love and, at the end, she'd been demoted to a support role—one more person to help keep him on track and successful.

"I really like your hair short," she told Tobias as she ran her fingers through it. "It makes even more of your handsome face."

"Harper…"

The way he said her name, so seriously, sent a jolt of alarm through her. It was the kind of tone Axel had used whenever he had a complaint or was about to say something she wouldn't like. "What?"

He stared at her for several seconds, his eyebrows drawn as though he had something difficult—maybe even painful—to say.

"You're scaring me," she said. "What is it?"

Suddenly, his expression cleared, and he kissed the tip of her nose. "Don't be scared. Never mind. We can talk about it later. I'll see you at three."

If she hadn't been under so much pressure to get home, she would've insisted he tell her now. She was curious about what had been going through his mind. But she figured they'd have much more time to talk once the kids were in bed and she was back at his place.

"Okay. See you in a little while," she said and, reluctantly, let go of him so she could climb out. She had no idea how she'd play it cool at ice-skating—she was so infatuated with him she wanted to touch him constantly—but except for the slip in the back room, she'd managed yesterday.

As soon as she started walking, she checked her

phone. She'd heard it buzz several times before reaching into her purse to turn it off completely; she knew Axel was trying to reach her. It was eight hours later in the UK, where he was now, which meant it was midday for him. And while he no doubt knew it was very early for her, she hadn't returned his calls from last night so he probably felt entitled to bother her.

He'd better not have called Karoline again, she thought. After the last time, she'd texted him to ask him not to do that. But he had no patience whatsoever.

She sighed as she scrolled through the number of calls she'd missed. How many were there? Ten? Fifteen?

He was obsessive! She didn't *want* to talk to him. Returning Axel's calls was becoming a chore. Besides, she was still flying high from being with Tobias.

Suddenly, she stopped scrolling. Walking, too. Axel's name wasn't the only one on her missed call list. Her sister's name was there, too. Karoline had tried to reach her three times within the last fifteen minutes.

"Oh, shit," Harper muttered. Had Axel called her sister when he couldn't reach her?

Although that was most likely the case, she was also worried that maybe one of her girls had gotten sick during the night.

Her heart leaped into her throat as she started to run. But then the patchy fog cleared a little and her sister's house came into view, and she realized what was wrong.

Axel hadn't been calling her from the UK. He'd called from much closer. She knew because he was sitting on Karoline's front steps, waiting for her.

* * *

Tobias had almost told Harper the truth, everything he'd been holding back about his past. He'd come *so* close. He felt as though he had no choice. Last night had been different between them. Harper had fully embraced the idea of being with him instead of going back to Axel. He could feel it in the way she touched him, the way she made love to him, the way she vocalized how much she enjoyed being with him—and the fact that she was letting him be around her children again later today.

They were falling in love. *Both* of them. And that made him so high he wasn't sure it was even safe for him to drive home.

So this is what it feels like, he thought. He'd never been happier—but he still had a huge hurdle in front of him, and he knew it.

He had to tell Harper about his past.

Would it be possible to do it in a way that she might be able to understand and forgive?

He had no answer, no way to guess.

As he drove home, he considered asking Maddox to come over when he gave her the news and act as a character witness for him, or provide moral support or...whatever. Or maybe Uriah would speak up for him.

But he couldn't rely on others. He had to brave the truth on his own, and he had to trust that Harper knew him well enough by now, even though they'd only met a couple of weeks ago...

He'd look for the right moment. Prepare his words carefully in advance. And maybe he'd finally catch a break.

He'd never asked for much from life, never felt he

deserved it. After prison, he'd set his expectations especially low—better that than be disappointed.

But he'd never wanted something quite as badly as he wanted Harper.

Harper knew how her hair looked. Not only had she been rolling around in bed with Tobias, they'd taken a bath together and she hadn't bothered to dry it properly. She hadn't been worried about her appearance; she'd thought she was going straight to bed.

This was not how she wanted to confront Axel—or her sister and brother-in-law. But Karoline was awake. Maybe Terrance was up, too. She could see that the light was on in the living room.

She'd pressed her luck too far.

"Axel…" she said as she came up the walk.

"Nice of you to finally come home," he said.

She winced at the heavy sarcasm. "I had no idea you… I had no idea you'd be here."

"No. I thought it would be a big surprise, a way to prove my love for you and my girls that I'd go to the trouble of flying thirteen hours to be with you for just three days—the only three days I have off on this soul-sucking tour." He chuckled bitterly. "But I never dreamed *I'd* be more shocked than you."

He loved what he did. This was the kind of success he'd prayed for. But she didn't comment on the way he'd described the tour. "I wish you'd let me know you were coming."

"You were with him?" he asked instead of responding to her comment.

She drew a deep breath. "Yes."

"I thought so."

"I was going to tell you that…that we're seeing each other again."

As he rose to his feet, his voice rose, too. "You mean you were going to tell me you're still fucking someone else? *When?*"

She glanced around, embarrassed by the profanity and the loudness of his voice. "I quit seeing him once we started talking about reconciling, but then I began to realize—"

"That you can fool around and get away with it while I'm in Europe?"

Her face flushed with heat despite the cold. "No…"

The door opened behind him, and her sister stepped out. She was wearing a fluffy white robe, tied at the waist, and carrying a cup of coffee. "Harper. I'm so glad you're okay. I've been trying to reach you—"

"I know. I'm sorry, Karoline."

"She's been with—" Axel gestured in irritation "—what's his stupid name? *Tobias?*"

"His name is no more stupid then yours," she mumbled.

"What'd you say?" he challenged her.

She glanced around to make sure the neighbors weren't turning on their lights and coming outside to see what all the fuss was about. "Nothing."

"You said something."

"Forget it. Look, there's no need to embarrass Karoline and Terrance. Why don't we… Why don't we go for a drive? Get out of their neighborhood?"

"With you looking like *that*? Fresh from another man's bed? God, I can almost smell him on you."

Harper curved her fingernails into her palms. "I told you. I gave him up for a few days. But then…"

"But *then*?" he repeated.

"I realized he makes me feel good. That I enjoy his company. That maybe… That maybe you were right about the divorce. Our lives have changed so much we're no longer compatible."

Karoline's eyes widened. "Harper, are you sure about what you're saying?"

She wasn't the only one who was surprised. Axel obviously couldn't believe his ears. Just about every woman in America dreamed of being with him, and yet *she* was saying she preferred someone else?

"You've always said you want to keep our family together!"

"That's what I've wanted all along!"

"So I make the effort, and *this* is how you react?"

"Stop shouting at her." Karoline spoke softly, but her voice was velvet over steel.

Axel shot her a dirty look. He wasn't used to having anyone oppose or criticize him, which was probably why he and Karoline had never been close. Karoline always spoke her mind, never held back like Harper often did. "Don't tell me what to do!" he snapped. "You have no idea what I went through to get here—"

"What? A thirteen-hour flight? There are worse things," she broke in. "So don't expect a lot of sympathy from me. This is *my* house, and you'll speak respectfully to everyone in it, or you'll be asked to leave."

He gaped at her. "Wow. You've turned on me, too."

"You turned on Harper first," she retorted.

Harper stepped forward. "Stop. Please. Both of you. Axel, let's get in the car and go for a drive."

He whirled on her. "What car, Harper? I had a limo drive me from LAX. It's gone. I had no idea the mother of my children wouldn't be in her bed when I arrived at four o'clock in the morning!"

"I have the Range Rover here," she said.

"I'll get the keys," Karoline offered and hurried back into the house.

"Please, calm down," Harper said. "There's no need to wake the neighborhood. I'd rather the girls not hear us shouting, either."

"You mean you don't want them to know you've been sneaking out, spreading your legs for some guy you've just barely met?"

"We haven't just barely met," she said. "We've spent hours and hours together. And *they* know him, too."

"You've introduced him to my girls?"

"Why wouldn't I?" she countered. "They're my girls, too."

"Because I thought we were getting back together!"

"Who was that woman in the mosh pit in Barcelona?" she demanded.

His scowl grew darker. "What woman?"

"I watched the concert, Axel. Over and over again. Something was going on between you. I could tell."

"Oh, so now you're trying to make this about *me*?"

"It's always been about you! That's the problem! *Everything's* always about you! Whether you're happy, whether you're sad, whether your talent is being recognized, whether I'm giving you enough!" She'd spent their entire married life trying to placate him when he got upset, so it was ironic that she'd be the one screaming now, but everything she'd held back was rising like a tidal wave inside her.

He shook his head. "I can't believe this bullshit," he said and took off, walking down the street.

"Were you with her or not?" Harper called after him.

He didn't turn or answer, but the neighbor's porch light snapped on. "Is everything okay?" came a reedy voice from that direction.

Harper closed her eyes. Normally, she'd run after Axel. She was tempted. She could be making a mistake by letting him go. But she'd been as happy as she could possibly be only half an hour earlier, when she was with Tobias—and now she felt like shit again.

"Hello?" the neighbor called over when she didn't respond. "Is everything okay?"

It was an older woman—her gray hair in rollers with an old-fashioned net over them. "Everything's fine. I'm sorry for disturbing you. The stress of the holidays can sometimes create a bit of…tension. That's all it is."

"Are you sure?"

"I'm sure."

The neighbor still seemed skeptical. "Where's Karoline? There's never been any trouble over there before."

Fortunately, Harper's sister appeared with the car keys.

"Where'd he go?" Karoline asked when she didn't see Axel in the yard.

Harper gestured down the street.

"Are you going after him?"

Harper stared at what she could see of his retreating back, which wasn't much in the fog. She even took her keys in anticipation of following him. But then she handed them back. "No," she said. "Not this time."

Karoline's mouth formed an O, but before she could

comment, Harper jerked her head toward the older lady who'd come out. "I'm sorry, but you might need to walk over and talk to your neighbor, let her know everything's fine. I can't go over there looking like this."

Karoline lifted Harper's arm to show her that the seam was visible; she'd put her shirt on wrong side out. "I agree with you there. Go in and get some sleep. I'll take care of Margaret, and then I'll go after Axel."

"He's a big boy. He can get a motel in town or something."

"I can't let him walk. It's safe now because the entire town is asleep. But he's a celebrity. I don't want anything to happen to him, and I don't want this to be splashed across the tabloids."

Tears came to Harper's eyes. "You're right, of course. I wasn't thinking. Thank you."

"That's what sisters are for."

When Harper started to slip past her, Karoline caught hold of her wrist. "So…you spent the night with Tobias? That's where you've been?"

Harper wiped her eyes. "Yes."

"Was this the first time?"

"No," she said on a sigh.

"I see." Karoline bit her bottom lip. "Must be going well between you two."

"I think I'm falling in love with him," she admitted. *"Really?"*

"I don't know how else to explain what I'm feeling."

"But so fast, Harper? How can you trust that?"

"I don't know if I can," she admitted. "That's the problem."

Karoline squeezed her arm. "You have a good head on your shoulders. You'll figure it out."

With a nod, Harper went inside. But she was afraid her sister had more confidence in her than she deserved.

24

Did you get home safely?

After leaving Karoline on the stoop, Harper had avoided Terrance—who'd been in the kitchen, judging from the noises she heard as she crossed to the hall—and gone straight to her room, where she'd climbed into bed. Fortunately, none of the girls had been disturbed by Axel's appearance, or the argument out front. Other than for Terrance, the house was quiet.

Harper was tired, but she was a long way from nodding off. She'd forgotten to let Tobias know she was okay—probably because she didn't feel okay. She would've missed his text if she hadn't picked up her phone to call Axel. It was a habit, something she'd always done if he blew up and stalked off. She'd always tracked him down, apologized, tried to get him to rally and overcome the problem.

But she couldn't bring herself to go through that process this morning, which was why she'd deferred to Karoline. For one, she didn't know what to say. She couldn't tell him she was sorry for being with Tobias.

She wasn't. She was sorry Axel had been shocked and hurt by the discovery, but that was different.

Her phone buzzed in her hand. Harper? Tobias was prompting her since she hadn't yet responded.

After rubbing her temples to ease the headache that had sprung up in the wake of so much emotion, she wrote him back so he wouldn't come over to see for himself.

Axel was waiting for me when I got home.

Are you kidding me? I thought he was in Europe.

He was. But he thought it would be nice to come to Silver Springs for three days and surprise us for Christmas.

I see.

She waited, hoping Tobias could reveal how he was taking this news, but he offered nothing more.

The girls will be excited to see him, she wrote.

I'm happy for them.

And?

What else can I say? Should I be happy for you, too? Are you excited to see him?

Definitely not. He caught me walking up to the house after getting out of your truck, so...

Shit.

Exactly. I was busted—no escaping. Karoline and Ter-rance were up, too, since he'd just gotten in from LAX.

They all know you were with me?

Yes.

Would it be easier to call me? I'm here if you'd rather talk.

I can't talk. Not now. I don't want anyone to hear that I'm awake, let alone on the phone.

Okay. So...how'd it go?

Not good. There was a bit of yelling, of course, and then he took off.

Took off where?

I don't know. I didn't go after him.

I'm sorry.

It's not your fault.

Maybe not. But I don't like the thought of you being upset—and having to deal with something I feel par-tially responsible for.

But she'd never want *Tobias* to confront Axel. Knowing how quickly Axel's temper could flare, she was afraid of where that would lead. Axel had never struck her or anything when he'd gotten angry. She wasn't worried about her safety. It was all the moodiness, the upset and the screaming that got old. Add in jealousy and another man? Axel might go further with Tobias than he would with her.

Does this change anything? Tobias asked.

She frowned at his latest message. Skating is off, she responded.

I wasn't referring to skating.

I know.

I'd like a real chance with you, Harper. What we feel... It can't be something that happens often. At least, it's never happened for me.

You're right. It doesn't happen often.

Then we should protect it.

At this point, I don't know what to say. There's what I want, and then there's what's best for my kids.

I would never stand in the way of what's best for you or your kids.

He'd proved that already, when he'd brought her home and told her to patch things up with Axel. *She* was the one who'd resurrected what they had going. Thank you. Let's get some sleep. I'm so confused and embarrassed—I'm on overload. I'll text you to-morrow.

Good night.

After she put down her phone, she could hear the hum of voices. Had Karoline brought Axel back to the house?

She was about to get out of bed to check when she heard a soft knock and her sister opened the door. "You okay?"

"I am. Is Axel? Were you able to find him?"

"Yes. It wasn't easy, but I managed to talk him into getting into the car, and I took him to the Mission Hotel."

"He didn't want to come here?"

"Considering the situation, I suggested it might be smarter for the two of you to have a bit of a separation."

"But he's going to see the girls while he's here…"

"I hope so."

"So do I. I'd feel terrible if I screwed that up for them."

Karoline studied her for several seconds. "Why weren't you honest with me about Tobias, Harper?"

"Because I never expected it to go anywhere. I thought… I thought it was fleeting, momentary, a way to prop up my sagging self-esteem, I guess."

"And then…"

"And then he turned out to be more wonderful than I expected."

"That's a good thing, isn't it?"

Harper shook her head. "To be honest, I still don't know."

* * *

Tobias couldn't sleep. He kept coming up with different ways to break the news of his past to Harper. But no matter how he framed what he'd done, he imagined her being too horrified to take a chance on him.

He kept trying to convince himself that he'd served his time, paid the price, and now that he was out of prison, he could build whatever he wanted with his life. That was what the psychologist had told him. To put Soledad behind him and move on. But what he'd done at seventeen, and the thirteen years he'd lost because of it, would affect him for the rest of his life—which meant it would also affect anyone he was associated with.

Harper deserved better.

He must've dropped off at last, and then he slept like a rock, because it was late in the day when he opened his eyes again. He could tell by the color of the light slanting through the blinds.

He immediately rolled over to check his phone. He thought it had made a noise, which was what had finally dragged him out of unconsciousness—that maybe Harper was trying to reach him.

But he'd missed no calls.

That was when he realized someone was at the door.

As he threw on some sweat bottoms and a T-shirt, he noticed that Harper had left her necklace on his dresser.

He picked up the delicate chain and stared down at the pendant, a gold swirl that contained a fairly large diamond, and tried not to sigh as he put it back down. She was way out of his league.

"Tobias?"

Uriah's voice came to him from outside.

"Coming!" he called and glanced around the house to be sure there were no other signs of Harper's having been there as he made his way to the door. He knew she'd be embarrassed if Uriah found a pair of her panties lying on the floor of his living room. But it looked as though she'd remembered everything other than the necklace.

"Hey," Uriah said as soon as Tobias opened the door.

Tobias squinted out at the bright light. "What happened to the fog?"

"Burned off not long after you got in this morning."

Tobias arched an eyebrow at his wry response. "You've been checking the security feeds again, I see."

"Actually, I haven't. Carl mentioned it to me."

"How would he know?"

"I guess he was up going to the bathroom when you came in. Said you've been running around all hours of the night."

Tobias folded his arms. "Part of his campaign to get you to give me notice?"

"He's not your friend. I'll be up-front about that. But don't feel bad. I don't think he's mine, either."

"At least you recognize that he's a wolf in sheep's clothing."

"You know what they say—you don't get to choose your relatives."

Tobias thought of his mother. "No, you don't." He opened the door wider. "Would you like to come in?"

"This time I would. Carl's supposed to be working, but who knows if he actually is. He could be loitering around the corner, for all I know. He spends more time trying to avoid work than getting anything done."

"Too bad work avoidance doesn't pay better."

"He'd be a millionaire."

Tobias laughed without mirth. No matter how pathetic that was, it was true. "What's going on?" he asked when Uriah had shut the door behind him.

"I'm concerned," Uriah admitted.

"About what?"

"About you."

"Why?"

"Carl mentioned Harper this morning. He knows you're seeing her."

"How?"

"I guess she's driving an expensive Range Rover that's somehow distinctive. And she's the talk of the town right now, the ex-wife of some big rock star. I didn't recognize her name when you introduced us that night, but then...I wouldn't."

"Why would Carl care who I'm dating?"

Uriah shook his head. "Only Carl can answer that. It makes no sense to me, either. But he's always getting into other people's business, trying to cause trouble— and I'm telling you, he seems to think it's a pretty big deal that Harper's been over here."

Tobias rubbed the beard growth on his chin. "What do you suppose he might do with that information?"

"Does she know about your past?"

Tobias said nothing.

"That's what I was afraid of. Carl's unhappy that I'm not more upset by your record, Tobias. He claims you're dangerous and shouldn't be allowed on the property. Keeps trying to drive that point home."

"He hated me from the first moment he laid eyes on me." The feeling was mutual.

"It's nothing you've done. He hates you because I respect you, and I can't respect him. Love isn't always enough. Anyway, Harper's big-shot ex-husband is in town. Carl saw him at the coffee shop this morning. I wanted to tell you that, too."

"I already know Axel's in town," Tobias said. "He got in last night."

Uriah studied him for several seconds. "Does *he* know about your past?"

"I hope not."

"Then you might want to do something to remedy the situation."

Tobias appreciated Uriah's warning. But he had no way of protecting himself. His only hope, at this point, was that Carl wouldn't recognize the full power of the weapon he held, and the next three days would prove uneventful. If Carl didn't give him away, it was entirely possible that Harper and her family would be so consumed with the holidays they wouldn't pick up on local gossip, and that Axel would leave without learning of Tobias's past.

Then maybe Tobias would have the opportunity to explain what needed to be explained.

It had been a long, trying day. Karoline had invited Axel to come over to the house after Harper had a few hours of sleep, and he did—to see the kids. But he was sulking, and that made it difficult for the girls, as well as Harper. She kept hearing Everly say, "What's wrong, Daddy?"

He'd claim nothing was wrong, but the girls could see the looks he tossed her and feel the tension between them, and that made her sad. It was nearly Christmas.

They had their daddy in town. She wished he could shake off what he was feeling for their sake. Lord knew she'd done a lot of that over the last six months. He was the one who'd requested the divorce in the first place, so he had only himself to blame for how he was feeling.

But Axel wasn't used to being denied. He felt he should be able to change his mind and have no repercussions from any decisions or actions that had happened before that point.

When he announced that he was taking them all to dinner, Karoline and Terrance begged off. Karoline said that she'd committed her family to wrapping presents for the underprivileged at the church, where there'd be pizza.

Harper tried to beg off, too. It was awkward being with Axel while having no privacy to discuss what had happened last night, or what was going on between them. But Axel wouldn't hear of it. He said he'd come all this way to be with his family, and he wanted them to stay together.

"Can we go to that place that has the milkshakes and the curly fries?" Everly asked when they were discussing the various restaurants.

Fatboy Burgers. Harper had taken the girls there after they first arrived in town, and they'd loved it. "That's fine with me," she said.

Axel's pained expression suggested he wasn't thrilled with the idea. "Are you sure you don't want something more festive than a burger?" he asked Harper. "There's a nice Italian place near my hotel."

"I'm happy with a burger," Harper said. "It's what the girls really like. I think we should go there." He was going to be in town for such a short time she felt he should indulge them. He was away from them so much—and he had plenty of opportunities to do and eat what *he* wanted.

In the end, he agreed, grudgingly, and Harper drove. Although Axel generally preferred to be in control, he didn't know the area, so it made more sense for Harper to take the wheel.

"This place looks *amazing*," Axel said, being overly dramatic as a way to tease the girls when she pulled in. He'd mentioned, once or twice, his desire to become a vegetarian, so Harper knew he wasn't particularly excited about eating red meat, but she smiled at him because she appreciated the effort he was making on behalf of their children.

They went through the line and ordered cheeseburgers for the girls, a black bean vegetarian burger for Axel—it turned out that the restaurant had one, which was lucky—and a salad for her. They'd just decided on the shake flavors they'd each get afterward and were settling into a booth to wait for their food when Everly cried, "Look, Mommy! Over there! Isn't that Tobias?"

Harper's first thought was, *There's no way.* Had the girls requested the Eatery, which she associated with Tobias, she would've done whatever she could to entice them to go elsewhere. She'd supported *this* place because she'd never heard Tobias mention it.

And his truck hadn't been in the lot. She definitely would've noticed.

Harper's blood ran cold as she turned and saw Tobias sitting in a nearby booth across from his brother, a burger on each of their plates.

"That's him?" Axel said.

Harper didn't get a chance to answer before Everly

piped up with, "Yeah. He's the one facing us," she said, waving to get Tobias's attention.

Harper saw Tobias's jaw go slack when he realized she was there, too. Obviously, he hadn't expected this coincidence any more than she had.

"Did you tell him we were coming here?" Axel growled.

"No!" Harper replied, her mind racing. What was she going to do? They'd just paid for their food, hadn't even received it yet. It wasn't as though she could suggest another place and hurry her family back out to the car. The girls had their hearts set on what they'd ordered.

And Tobias and Maddox had clearly just been served, so it wasn't likely *they'd* be leaving anytime soon.

"What are the chances we'd both end up at the same restaurant?" Axel asked.

"There aren't a lot of restaurants in town, and this one is popular."

"Considering the situation, *I* think it's pretty remarkable," he retorted.

Harper felt her face flush when Axel shot Tobias a dirty look.

"He'd better not come over here, better not say anything to you, or there's going to be trouble," Axel warned.

"Daddy?" Piper's face creased in concern. "Why don't you like Tobias?"

"Because I don't," he snapped.

"Do you know him?" Everly asked, also confused.

Axel was too busy glaring at Tobias to answer that question.

"He's nice," Piper said. "He took us ice-skating."

"He'd better stay the fuck away from you in the future. That's all I've got to say."

"Axel!" Harper cried. "Please stop. There's no need to swear or cause a scene. Tobias and Maddox will just…eat, and we'll eat. It's no big deal."

"So you're done with him?" Axel said, shifting his attention to her.

That wasn't really a question. He was *telling* her she was done with Tobias. "I—I don't know."

"What do you mean?"

She looked at the girls. This wasn't a talk she wanted to have in their presence. "I care about him."

"You *care* about him? Why? What's he got that I don't?"

"Hardly anyone has what you have. It isn't about that. I like the way he treats me. That's all."

"Yeah, I heard just how much when you pocket-dialed me."

Harper's stomach, which had knotted when she saw Tobias, began to hurt even more. "Axel…"

Suddenly, he got up, shoved the table so hard it nearly touched their girls on the other side of the booth and stalked over to where Tobias and Maddox were sitting.

Harper could feel her heart pounding in her ears when she saw Tobias use a subtle hand motion to tell his brother to remain seated.

"Don't you *ever* come near my wife again. Do you understand?" Axel said.

Tobias glanced over at her before responding. "Why don't you go back to your family?" he said. "You're clearly embarrassing them."

Axel stepped even closer. "Don't tell me what to do!"

Tobias lowered his voice. "You're not helping the situation. You're just drawing attention. You need to calm down."

"What are you doing here, anyway?" he demanded. "Are you following us?"

With a scowl, Tobias indicated his plate. "Clearly not. We got here before you."

"Stay where you are," Harper told the girls and scrambled out of the booth herself. She had to act before this exploded into something worse than it already was. There were people several booths down who were beginning to realize that Axel Devlin was in the restaurant and were pulling out their phones to take videos.

"Axel, stop." She grabbed his arm. "Please. You don't want this on the front page of the tabloids, do you? Come on, you're acting ridiculous."

"Stay out of it," he told her and shook her off so hard she nearly lost her balance.

Tobias immediately reached out to steady her. "Watch yourself," he said to Axel, the tone of his voice a clear warning.

Axel's eyes flared wide. "Oh, yeah? Or what are you gonna do?"

"Whatever I have to. But I'm giving you this one, because you're not thinking clearly. Now go back to your seat."

A pimple-faced employee, who couldn't have been older than twenty-one, approached. He looked anxious, but his badge read Manager, and Harper had to admire his courage. Although she could tell he didn't want to get involved, he didn't back away from the conflict.

"I'm afraid I'm going to have to ask both of you to leave," he said. "There's no fighting in here."

Tobias's gaze shifted from Axel to the younger man and back again. Then he grabbed his wallet off the table. "Let them stay," he said. "We'll go."

Maddox frowned at the burger he'd have to leave behind but got up to support his brother. "You know what?" he said to Axel.

Axel turned to look at him, but Tobias murmured something Harper couldn't hear and Maddox didn't finish. Then she heard Tobias say more loudly, "Let's go."

Harper wanted to follow them out and apologize for Axel's behavior. They'd done nothing wrong; they'd just come in to eat. But her girls were watching, completely confused, and she knew if she went after Tobias, it might provoke Axel into acting even worse. She couldn't take that risk.

"Are you happy now?" she muttered to her ex as she gestured toward Tobias's and Maddox's uneaten burgers.

"I'll be happy if he stays away from you." Axel glanced at everyone who was watching them. "Put your cell phones away," he said.

Harper thought he was going to leave it at that, but while they were still waiting for their food, he mentioned something about how bad it would look if anyone offered the footage they'd captured to the media—in an accusatory way, as if what'd happened was *her* fault. Then he got up and offered to sign autographs for anyone who'd delete what they'd captured.

Harper sat with the girls as word spread through the restaurant that Axel Devlin was there and more and more people gathered to see him, talk to him, have him sign a napkin—or even an article of clothing.

She and Everly and Piper were finished with their meals and Axel's food was cold by the time he was able to return to the table.

"Do you think you got everyone?" Harper asked as he sat down.

"I guess we'll find out."

She could tell his mood hadn't improved. "You realize that whole thing was unnecessary," she said. "You could have just ignored Tobias and his brother. They wouldn't have said anything to us."

He sent her a sharp look. "Don't start. You're the one who caused this whole thing, not me."

25

Axel tried to convince Harper to stay with him at the motel. He'd said that would give them a chance to talk privately. But she guessed talking wasn't really what he had in mind. He knew if he could get her to sleep with him again, he'd be that much closer to a commitment when it came to starting over.

But she wasn't ready for that. What'd happened at the restaurant had reminded her of how often she'd had to stand on the sidelines and wait for him to finally eke out a few minutes to devote to her, and she was no longer convinced that was the kind of life she wanted. Maybe if she and Axel were getting along in other areas there'd be something to compensate for the strain his fame put on their relationship. But they were struggling on several fronts. Not only was there that woman from the concert—Axel hadn't denied sleeping with her; he just kept avoiding the conversation—there was Tobias. Somehow it felt as though going back to bed with Axel after what she'd shared with Tobias would be a betrayal.

That was pretty ironic. That she'd feel more loyal to a man she'd met only a couple of weeks ago than the one she'd been married to for ten years. But she got the feeling that Tobias was more loyal to *her*.

That meant something.

"So you're not coming to the motel?" Axel sounded shocked.

She switched the phone to her other ear. Since she'd already told him she wasn't when she dropped him off, he must've thought she'd relent and drive over once she got home and put the girls to bed, or he wouldn't have called her with that question. "No. I'm not coming."

"Why not?" he countered.

"I don't want to make love, Axel."

Silence. Sulking? Then he said, "Because of that other guy—Tobias."

"Partly because I'm still upset by how you behaved at the restaurant," she said.

"How I behaved? That was nothing! I was just protecting my family."

"We're divorced!"

"So? We spent ten years together, have two kids together. The divorce is just a piece of paper."

"Just a piece of paper?" she echoed. "That piece of paper means you left me. You told me you weren't fulfilled, weren't happy being in a relationship with me and needed your freedom. I was devastated. And now you want me to trust you? To believe you can be happy if we get back together? That you won't turn around and do the same thing again?"

"You wanted me to try to work out our problems," he said. "Well, here I am. That's what I'm trying to do."

"It's a little late, don't you think?"

"If I thought it was too late I wouldn't be here."

"So you didn't come to see the girls."

"Of course I did!" He sounded emphatic. "But I came for you, too."

Harper stared at herself in the mirror over the dresser as she talked. She looked miserable—and she was. "After everything that's happened I'm not prepared for this to go any further," she said.

"You don't want to get back together."

"Sometimes I do," she admitted. "But that's usually when I'm thinking of the girls. That's not what I want for *me*."

"That isn't what you were saying before," he said.

"I know. But things have changed."

"What's changed?" he challenged. "Nothing's changed. You're just putting me off. Making me eat crow. You want me to suffer."

"You're accusing me of…what? Being vindictive?"

"What else could it be? You meet a dude with a body like that—of course you're going to be tempted. But let's be honest, Harper. It was a fling. I've had several myself, and I've admitted it. I'm willing to forgive you if you're willing to forgive me. Let's put the past behind us and move forward without any resentment on either side."

She drew a deep breath as she grappled for calm and clarity. "Just tell me one thing."

"What?"

"Did you sleep with that girl in Barcelona?"

There was a slight pause. Then he said, "What does it really matter? You slept with Tobias just last night!"

"But *I'm* not the one who left you brokenhearted with two kids. I'm not the one who suddenly reversed my decision and is now trying to get back together. You slept with her, didn't you? After you started asking me for a second chance?"

"You know how difficult relationships are. You can't honestly tell me you expect to marry that dude I saw in the restaurant. You're just angry and confused."

Axel *had* slept with the girl in Barcelona. Otherwise, he would've denied it. She'd known it; she could feel it whenever she saw that video. And it just made his whole attempt to get her back seem so insincere, so unreliable.

Dropping her head into her hand, Harper sank onto the bed and stared at her feet instead of her own unhappy reflection. "I don't think so," she said stubbornly.

"You don't think…what?" he asked.

"I'm *not* angry. At least, that's not what I'm basing this decision on."

"Then what *are* you basing it on?"

"Tobias makes me happier than you do."

There. It was out. She'd spoken her truth—identified the real reason she was holding back. She enjoyed being with Tobias more than she enjoyed being with Axel. Tobias was gentle and calm and willing to give. He cared what *she* was thinking and feeling. He wasn't someone who drained the very lifeblood from her.

"What about the girls?" Axel asked.

"That's the real problem," she said. "They mean so much to me. I don't want to do anything that might screw them up. But when I saw their worried faces tonight, I realized that *I* have to be on solid emotional ground to provide a firm foundation for them. That doesn't have to interfere with or damage your relationship with them, though. I'll always support you in being close to them, will let you talk to them or take them anytime it's feasible for you. I know you're a good father."

"Are you kidding me?" he cried. "I came all the way from Europe for *this*? To hear that you'll let me take my own kids whenever I want?"

"I'm sorry if you were expecting more," she said.

"It was a surprise! Are you saying I shouldn't have gone to the trouble?"

He obviously couldn't believe what he was hearing. "I'm saying it's over between us," she said.

Her words were met with stunned silence. He'd never dreamed she'd say something like that—take such a strong stand and *mean* it. She'd never dreamed she would, either, not really. But she felt so much better, as though a huge weight had been lifted from her shoulders. She wasn't going back to Axel, wasn't going to get embroiled in all the painful things they'd had to wade through before, especially toward the end. She was going to start fresh.

And maybe her new life would include Tobias. She didn't *know* whether it would—whether she'd be willing to leave Colorado to move here, or he'd be willing to leave Silver Springs to move there. They didn't yet know each other well enough to make such a big decision. But either way, she was letting go of Axel completely and moving forward without him.

"You must be out of your mind," Axel said and hung up.

Harper was convinced, just by how quickly the

pressure on her heart had eased, that she was doing the right thing.

But she supposed he needed time to get used to the idea.

She set her phone aside so she could go to bed. But then she picked it up again. She hadn't heard from Tobias, had no idea what he thought about what had happened at the restaurant. And she wanted to let him know that, at least for her, nothing had changed.

I'm sorry about tonight, she wrote.

His answer came almost immediately: Are you getting back with him?

Instead of feeling miserable, like she'd been feeling a few minutes ago, she experienced a little flutter of excitement. No.

Does he know that?

She imagined Tobias's voice, as if they were talking, and felt even better. He does now.

How'd he take the news?

He's not happy.

Where is he?

He has a room at the Mission Inn.

So he's treating you okay? I don't have to worry about you tonight?

She smiled. Tobias was so protective. She'd seen the way he'd reacted—the intensity in his eyes—when Axel had nearly made her fall. Yes.

Can you come over so we can talk?

Not tonight. I'm exhausted, and tomorrow's Christmas Eve. Let me focus on my family for now, make the holidays fun for my girls and get through these next few days while Axel's here on my own, so there are no more problems. I just want you to know—

She hesitated, unsure whether she should say what she'd been about to tell him. But then she decided there was no reason to hold back. It was the truth. I just want you to know that whatever the future holds... I'm hoping you'll be part of my life.

When he didn't respond right away, she bit her lip. Maybe she'd assumed he was more serious about her than he was...

No. When they were together it was almost magical. She couldn't have misread their chemistry, the way he touched her, the way he looked at her. At the moment, what Tobias felt for her was the one thing she was convinced she could trust.

Finally, his response appeared on her phone. Do you mean that?

As she remembered their time in the bathtub last night, she wished she could go back to his place, peel off her clothes and climb into bed with him. She didn't care if they made love—she just wanted to feel his warm body and soft skin against her own.

But it was the holidays. Now was not the time to worry about what *she* wanted.

Absolutely, she wrote.

Tobias thought his heart might burst by the time he reached the top of the ridge. He hadn't started to train in earnest and yet he'd made it, difficult though it had been, carrying a hundred-pound pack. The Topatopa Mountains above Silver Springs didn't feature many trails that were as difficult as what he'd face in Yosemite, and his pack was a lot more stable—as well as lighter—than it would be when carrying a human being, but he'd made decent time.

It was a start. And he'd done well enough to build some confidence that he might be able to carry Atticus.

He felt a surge of happiness as he gazed at the vista before him. He'd gone from seeing the world only through a six-inch slit—something you could barely call a window—while being caged in a cold, dank prison just five months ago to living in one of the most beautiful places on earth, and he was building a life here. A good one. He had a job he enjoyed. He had a sound mind and a strong body. His mother still wasn't behaving as she should, but he had other family and friends who were normal and productive and support-ive. Susan was even being nice to Maddox. And now there was Harper.

How could he ask for more?

He pulled out his phone to reread her message from last night. I just want you to know that whatever the future holds… I'm hoping you'll be part of my life.

He'd read her text no less than twenty times on the hike today. Whenever he got so fatigued he wasn't sure he could continue, he'd take a second to read it again. Axel Devlin was in town, making a play to get her back, and yet she'd sent that message to *him*. He almost couldn't believe it. Would his future include Harper?

If so, he'd do everything he could to make sure she wasn't unhappy a day in her life.

He wasn't expecting to get cell service out here, so he was surprised when he noticed that he had one bar.

Was it a strong enough signal to place a call?

He found Atticus's name in his contacts, just in case he might be able to get through.

Sure enough, Jada's brother answered. "Hello?"

"Guess where I am?" Tobias said.

"Where?"

"Hines Peak."

"Nice! That's the highest peak in the Topatopa Mountains, isn't it? Have you seen any condors up there?"

There was a 53,000-acre California condor sanctuary not far from where he stood, but humans weren't allowed to go in it, and he hadn't thought of bringing his binoculars. He'd stuffed his pack with just about everything else he could lay his hands on—none of it very useful, though, since he'd been concerned only with reaching a certain weight while having it all fit. "Nah, didn't think to bring binoculars. Would've been smart."

"You wearing a pack?"

"I am."

"How much weight are you carrying?"

"A hundred pounds."

He whistled. "Was it tough?"

It hadn't been easy, but Tobias was so exhilarated

that it didn't seem too bad now that it was over. "It was...doable," he hedged.

"Would it be doable with another fifty pounds?"

"I think so." As good as he was feeling right now, he felt he could carry twice as much.

"How long was the hike?"

Tobias checked the watch Harper had given him. "From where I started? 'Bout eight miles."

"So today's hike will be sixteen total?"

"Around that."

"What was the elevation gain?"

Again, he consulted his new watch. "Five thousand feet."

"From what I've read, Half Dome is only forty-eight hundred."

Tobias already knew that. It was one of the reasons he'd challenged himself to this particular climb—it was the closest hike to Half Dome he could get without driving a lot farther. "Half Dome is more difficult. More technical." It was more dangerous, too, but he didn't add that.

"But it also offers better views."

He could hear the smile in Atticus's voice. "This one seems pretty spectacular right now. But...yeah, I'd have to agree. Not only will you get to see Vernal and Nevada Falls when we do Half Dome, you'll get a panoramic view of Yosemite Valley and the High Sierra."

"I can't wait, man."

"You getting that GoPro you mentioned for Christmas tomorrow?"

"I'll treat myself to that once we get closer. I haven't broken the news of our plan to my mother quite yet."

Tobias remembered the encounter he'd last had

with Susan and her dramatic turnaround—she'd even brought him cookies. "Maybe you shouldn't tell her."

"Why not?"

"I don't want to make her hate me all over again."

"You need to quit worrying about her."

Considering his position in Susan's life, that wasn't easy. He felt so bad for what he'd done. "Seriously, though. Maddox said she's being a lot nicer to him. We don't want to screw that up."

"Good point. It's not as though she needs to know every little thing I do, anyway. I'll just show her the video footage once we've done it."

"Perfect. That way even if she does get mad, Maddox and Jada will have had nearly six months to build a better relationship before we blow it for them."

"I'm an adult, Tobias. I can go on a hike if I want to."

It wasn't quite that simple, but Tobias let it go. "Okay."

"So what are you doing tonight?" Atticus asked. "Are you coming to Maddox and Jada's for dinner?"

Maddox had invited him, but as soon as Tobias had learned that Susan would be there, he'd decided not to intrude. "No. I've got other plans."

"Like what?"

"I told Maddox I'd take our mother out for dinner in LA so he wouldn't have to have her over, either," he said with a laugh.

"Maybe I should go with you and your mother. I didn't realize this Christmas it was all about letting Maddox, Jada and Maya hang out with my mother on their own."

"No, you're good. Susan would want you there. So would everyone else. I'm just trying to make it as easy for them and as pleasant for your mother as possible. A drunk or high Jill wouldn't add anything to the party."

"So you're taking one for the team," he joked.

"I guess so."

"That sucks. This is your first Christmas out of the joint. I feel bad that you're not going to be around your brother's family because of my mother."

"I don't mind. It's the least I can do."

"What about tomorrow? What are your plans for Christmas Day?"

"I'm playing it by ear. I'll stop by Maddox and Jada's at some point and exchange gifts." Since Uriah was planning to spend Christmas with Carl, Tobias hadn't made any plans with him. But he didn't mind being alone. He was too optimistic about Harper to let anything else bother him. Besides, he'd spent much worse holidays in prison. "Have a great Christmas."

"You, too. I'm excited about what we've got planned for my birthday. It's really cool of you, man."

"No problem."

After Tobias hit the end button, he hauled in a deep breath of fresh air and angled his face up to the sun—enjoying being present in the moment. Then he started back. He couldn't waste a lot of time. He had to drive to LA to take his mother to dinner and, on the way, he planned to buy a few Christmas gifts, including one for Harper.

"Who is it?"

Setting his phone on the table, Tobias looked up at his mother. He'd been trying not to allow himself to be distracted. He hated how these days everyone was constantly checking one electronic device or another.

That had been quite a culture shock for him when he was released from prison—how much everyone relied on smartphones. But as time went by, he felt himself getting swept away by the appeal of the new electronics, too.

"Sorry," he said, even though she'd checked her phone and responded to a few texts herself since they'd sat down. "That was Maddox."

"What'd he say?"

"Hopes I made it safely. Says to be careful driving home tonight—there'll be a lot of drunk drivers on the road. And he wishes we were both there."

Jill wrinkled her nose in distaste. "With that monster *Susan*?"

"It's not fair to call her a monster, Mom," he said. "Not after what she's been through."

"She needs to let it go already." She frowned. "That was thirteen years ago."

Tobias felt his spine stiffen. Even when Jill was trying to be supportive, she managed to irritate him. As far as he was concerned, she had to be missing a sensitivity gene to say anything about Susan. But she was on her third glass of wine, so that probably explained it. When he'd suggested, after the second glass, that she stop, she'd scowled at him and said, "Oh, my God. Don't try to tell me what to do tonight. It's Christmas."

He'd dropped it since he was driving, he didn't want her to make a scene in the restaurant and she'd get drunk after he left regardless; so it probably wasn't that big a deal that she was starting while she was with him.

"She's treated Maddox like a doormat ever since he married Jada," she complained.

Tobias took another bite of his vegetable delight.

"And although I don't want to discuss it, we both know why. At least she's being nicer now," he added, trying to keep the conversation focused on the positive.

"I wonder why," she mused, seemingly sincere in her puzzlement. "The turnaround was so sudden."

Tobias hadn't told anyone, except Maddox and Jada, that he'd visited Susan's store or that she'd brought him cookies afterward as if something he'd said had finally gotten through to her. He'd thought it might embarrass her after all the terrible things she'd said about him. She had a lot of pride, and he was willing to respect that. As long as she continued to treat Maddox more kindly, he was going to stay out of her way and hope that nothing interfered with how things were going. "It's Christmas Eve," he pointed out. "The first Christmas I've been able to spend with my family since I was seventeen. Do we have to talk about Susan?"

"No, of course not. Especially when you seem to be doing so well. What's been happening in your life lately? How's work?"

He thought of the beauty of his hike this morning, the goal he'd set for himself with Atticus, how much he enjoyed his job and respected his employer, how relieved he was that Susan's heart seemed to be softening—and the last text he'd received from Harper. "It's good. I feel great."

"I'm so glad you're finally out of prison. Just think, last year we couldn't do this."

Of course she'd think it was great to have him out of prison. Now she had someone else she could turn to for help besides Maddox.

Tobias hated to be that cynical, but if she'd missed him as much as she claimed, wouldn't she have come to visit him more often? It was a five-hour drive from LA to where he'd been incarcerated, and her car wasn't always reliable, but he knew of several instances when she could've come with Maddox but begged off.

He had a sneaking suspicion that at least some of those instances were about going out with friends to get high or drunk—she couldn't miss an opportunity like that, especially thirteen years ago. And yet those were the years when he'd needed her most. "I'm glad those days are over, too."

She pushed her cashew chicken around her plate. She never seemed to eat much, was always more interested in what filled her glass. "I'll never forget the day I got the call that you'd been stabbed in that place," she said, her smile disappearing.

"Mom!" He gave her a sharp look. "Can we forget prison, too? Please?"

She rolled her eyes. "You mentioned it first."

"When I said it's been seventeen years since—never mind," he said. "What are your plans for tomorrow?"

"I was going to go to Maddox and Jada's. But I'm not sure I should spend the gas money, not when you're here now. Is there any way I could just ride back with you tonight?"

Tobias's fork dangled halfway between his plate and his mouth. "Where would you stay? At *my* place, you mean?"

"Why not? You have a couch, don't you?"

He'd never put her on the couch, but he supposed *he* could sleep there. "How would you get home?"

"Your brother can drive me back tomorrow night."

"Maddox has a family now, Mom."

"So? They can ride with us, too."

"It'll take four hours, at least. That might not be how they want to spend their Christmas."

"Then *you* can bring me back."

When he hesitated, she said, "Seriously? You won't do that for me?"

He shoved his food into his mouth. He didn't want to drive her to Silver Springs and back—not after driving four hours to come see her today. But she was his mother. And it wasn't as though she was asking for the moon. "Okay," he said. "Sure."

She smiled. "I've got my eye on something I'm going to get for you as soon as I get my paycheck."

She'd had a Christmas card for him at her place when he'd given her a new coat. "You don't have to get me anything." He'd be happy if she could just get her life under control.

"I want to," she insisted.

"Okay," he relented. Chances were slim it would ever materialize, anyway. She was famous for empty promises.

"I'm going to get the same thing for Maddox."

"I'm sure he'll be happy about that."

Tobias tried to enjoy himself as they finished eating, but he knew the next twenty-four hours weren't going to be easy. He figured he'd get up early and go on another hike—to prepare his mind and body for the difficulty of the rest of the day. Then he'd make his mother some breakfast before taking her over to Maddox's. After she was entertained there for a few hours, he'd drive her home and Christmas would be over, his duties as a son complete.

He could do that, he decided. There was no reason not to spend his Christmas that way. Chances were slim he'd get to see Harper, anyway. She'd told him to let her deal with her family until Axel left.

So he was surprised when, almost as soon as he returned to Silver Springs with his mother, he received a text from her.

Axel just took my Range Rover to the motel so he'll be able to drive over early in the morning before the kids get up to see what Santa's brought them. But my sister said I could use her car to come by and wish you a merry Christmas. I won't be able to stay long—only a few minutes—but I was hoping to see you. Are you home? Would that be okay?

26

Axel saw the taillights of Karoline's Jaguar go on as soon as the garage door rolled up and knew who was behind the wheel without having to see the driver. Where would Karoline be going at eleven o'clock at night, after all? Especially on Christmas Eve, when everything was closed?

Harper was heading to Tobias Richardson's house, just as he'd suspected she would when she'd been so eager to say goodbye to him the moment they'd finished setting up Santa's presents for their girls.

"Damn it." The sight sickened him. Was she really that eager to rush into another man's arms? He'd never dreamed he'd be in this position, but he'd let the success of his music go to his head—and that might've cost him the best thing that ever happened to him. As many women as he'd been with in the past year, he'd met no one quite as sweet or devoted as Harper. He was beginning to realize that people like her weren't around every corner.

But it wasn't over between them quite yet, he reminded himself. They had children together. They should try to make things work for their girls' sake, and he knew Harper agreed with him there. So her relationship with this guy wouldn't last. She was on the rebound; that was all. They'd both been through a stressful and upsetting year, and this affair with Tobias gave her something new to focus on instead of all the painful and disappointing things she'd faced since he filed for divorce.

He could see why she might be doing what she was doing. But she'd always loved *him*. He doubted that had really changed. He just needed to remind her *why*. He hadn't done nearly enough of that in the past few years.

Putting the Range Rover in gear, he pulled away from the curb, where he'd been waiting, and followed Karoline's Jaguar at a distance so Harper wouldn't notice him in her rearview mirror. If Tobias was his competition, he figured he should learn everything he could about him—where he lived, who he was, what his situation was like. Anything Harper might perceive as negative would only help Axel's bid, after all. And it wasn't as though there'd be much of a chance to check the guy out from Europe, so he needed to do what he could while he was in town.

His phone buzzed in the passenger seat beside him. It was most likely Matt. His bandmates had been calling and texting him incessantly, and so had the band's manager. They could tell his mind wasn't on music, and they were worried.

Axel felt bad for what he was putting them through, suddenly bugging out and coming to the States right in the middle of the tour. He was usually the hardest worker among them—the most driven member of the band. But it was Christmas, for God's sake. And his family was falling apart. Of the four people who made up Pulse, only Gary was married, and Sophie, his wife, was traveling with them.

Ignoring the call, he rolled through the first of the three stoplights in town. He just needed to get through Christmas, finish up the tour and get back home to Colorado, where he could focus on repairing what he'd destroyed. Once Harper saw that he was committed and willing to rebuild their relationship, everything would improve. He'd tell her he was willing to see a counselor, if that was what she wanted. He should've agreed to go with her long ago. But he'd known what the counselor would say. *She* wasn't the problem; it was him.

The brake lights of the car Harper was driving went on ahead of him, so he slowed, too, and watched as she turned in to a place about ten minutes outside town.

As he got closer, he could see a sign that read Honey Hollow Tangerine Orchard.

Tobias owned property? That was a little disheartening. Axel had been hoping to find that he didn't have a penny to his name. But so many people in this artsy community were wealthy. He should've known.

So…was Tobias a farmer? Or something more?

Axel had thought he might be a model, given the guy's looks.

With a sigh, he pulled over and waited for several minutes so he wouldn't give his presence away. Then he turned off his engine, quietly opened his door and crept closer to the house that faced the highway.

He'd assumed Harper had gone there, but all the lights were off. He stood in confusion for several minutes, looking around and wondering what could've happened to her. But then he heard voices, coming from farther down the drive near a second house that was tucked away in the back.

"Your mother's here?"

That was Harper. It was easy to recognize her voice.

"Yeah. She didn't want to drive over herself. I brought her back with me so she can see Maddox, Jada and Maya tomorrow."

The deeper voice belonged to Tobias. Axel recognized it, too.

"Of course," Harper said. "That's great. Is she… doing okay?"

"About the same."

"I see. I'm sorry. Still, I'd like to meet her someday."

"I'd introduce you tonight, but…she's already in bed."

"No problem. It's late. I just… I had to see you for a few minutes."

Axel crept closer—until he could make out two figures silhouetted in the porch light that glowed on the second house. This house was much smaller than the one facing the street. Was *that* where Tobias was living? If so, it didn't look as though he owned the orchard.

Could it be that he only worked here?

The possibility gave Axel a bit of hope that Tobias wasn't well-off. Axel would definitely have more to offer there.

"I'm glad you came," he heard Tobias say as, using the trees of the orchard to remain hidden, he moved closer. "I have something for you."

"For *me*?"

"It's nothing big. Just a little something I thought

you might like for Christmas. Which reminds me, you left your necklace here. I'll go get it—"

"No, don't bother," Harper said, stopping him. "I'll get it next time. And you didn't have to buy me anything. That isn't why I got you the watch."

She'd bought him a watch? Axel felt his stomach muscles tense. This was more serious than he'd thought it was.

"I know," Tobias said. "But I wanted to do this."

As Axel watched, Tobias reached up to take a small gift from where it had been sitting on the banister, which he gave to her.

"Oh, my gosh!" she exclaimed when she'd unwrapped it. "A charm bracelet! I *love* it."

"It's not the chain kind of charm bracelet. I was actually looking for that, but the jeweler said this kind is more popular right now. He thought you'd like it better."

"I do. Thank you. It's beautiful." She held it up to the light, obviously trying to see it clearly. "And the charm that's on it is…a rose?"

"Yeah. To represent the night we met."

"It's perfect!" she cried and threw her arms around him.

They kissed, so hot and heavy that Axel was afraid he was about to see far more than he had the stomach for, especially when Tobias moaned and lifted her off her feet, and she wrapped her legs around his hips.

"I wish I could stay," Axel heard Harper say.

"It would be a lot more fun to spend the night with you than my mom," Tobias joked. "I would've let you come in, but even if she hadn't just gone to bed, she's drunk. I'd rather you not meet her when she's like this."

His mother didn't sound particularly impressive...

"You know I don't care about your mother's, er... problems," Harper said. "You can't control what she does. But meeting her can wait. Axel will be gone soon. Then we won't have to tiptoe around because there'll be no one to upset."

"What about Karoline?"

"She knows I'm seeing you. She's fine with it."

"How long will we have? How long will you be staying in Silver Springs?"

"The girls are happy here, so... I'm going to put off returning to Colorado for a few weeks, maybe even a month."

Their foreheads came together as they talked, as if *any* space between them was too much, and Axel felt as though someone was driving a dagger through his heart.

"That makes me happy," he heard Tobias say.

"I can't wait until the holidays are over and things can get back to normal."

"I wanted to get the girls something for Christmas, too," Tobias said. "But I didn't want to step on Axel's toes. If he saw the gifts or the girls mentioned them to him... I'm not trying to make things more difficult for you—or him. I like his music as much as anyone."

The fact that Tobias would be generous enough to say that only made Axel fear him more.

"To be honest, it's probably better that you didn't get the girls anything," Harper said. "They aren't expecting it, and...well, you know."

"Yeah, I know. It's just... They're part of you, so it was hard to ignore that they'd probably enjoy a present, too."

"I love everything about you," she said. "And I'm so sorry about what happened in the restaurant."

"It's okay. It wasn't your fault, but I couldn't believe it when I saw you sitting there." He laughed ruefully, and she laughed, too.

"I just about had a heart attack."

"Is Axel trying to get you back?" Tobias asked, sobering.

"I guess. He thinks he wants me back. But I doubt he's really committed to it. He'll return to the tour, be confronted with the next beautiful woman screaming out his name in the mosh pit and forget all about me."

Although Axel winced at that assessment, he couldn't claim it was baseless. Since he'd become famous, the many women who propositioned him were so damn tempting. Only lately was he beginning to realize that he'd been trading real gold for fool's gold ever since he started cheating on Harper.

"Then he's crazy, doesn't know what he's leaving behind," Tobias said.

Except Axel *did* know. Or, at least, he was beginning to figure it out. That was why, as soon as he watched Harper kiss Tobias again and hug him and thank him for her bracelet—and then do it another time before she finally drove off—he got in the Range Rover and, before starting the engine, called Rory.

"There you are, man! How's it going? When are you coming back?"

It was Christmas, and Axel was losing his family, and all Rory could ask was when he'd be returning to the tour? Was that how Harper had felt when she'd been trying to get his attention so they could save their marriage before it was too late?

"I'm not," he said. "I'm staying right here until I've straightened out my life."

"What?" Rory cried. "You can't stay. It'll kill all of our careers!"

"It won't kill them. We're big enough now that we can weather it. We'll be fine."

"But people are counting on us! Please. I don't want to let them down."

"We only have two shows left. I can't fly back for those when there's so much shit hitting the fan here."

"Axel, we have more than the two shows. What about the publicity gigs the label lined up for us? The reason we agreed to stay an extra two weeks?"

"I'll explain what's happening to the label. You just break the news to Matt." Matt wouldn't like it, of course, but he worked for them. Axel wasn't going to let their manager call all the shots, not when it came to something like this.

"Oh, God. He's going to shit a brick. Our biggest show is on New Year's Eve!"

"Oh, well. If he wants to continue as our manager, he'll understand that I have some personal problems that I need to take care of. Maybe everyone should celebrate the new year with their families," he said and hit the end button. He couldn't take any more upset and emotionality from his band, not after seeing and hearing what he'd just seen and heard. In his desire to succeed, in his pursuit of his dreams, he'd lost Harper.

But maybe if he acted fast, showed his commitment to her and their children by remaining in Silver Springs and driving them back to Colorado, they'd be able to put everything back together—one piece at a time.

* * *

Christmas morning dawned crisp and cold, but there was no fog or rain. Tobias went on a short hike, much shorter and less laborious than Hines Peak. He'd just needed to get his heart pumping and stretch his legs, do something to remind himself that he *could* climb a mountain if he wanted to—that he was no longer in a cage like an animal, living by someone else's leave, as he'd been last Christmas and twelve Christmases before that. This also gave him a chance to once again use his new watch, which he liked.

He didn't stay gone long. He returned and made bacon and eggs for his mother before taking her over to Maddox's house for a late lunch—once he'd made sure they'd had a chance to have some time alone on Christmas as a family.

"How'd it go last night?" Maddox asked as soon as Tobias walked through the door.

Tobias turned to glance behind him at their mother, who was wearing sunglasses despite the fact that it was overcast outside, and moving a bit gingerly due to a hangover. "We had some Chinese food, came back and watched a movie." He lowered his voice. "And then she passed out."

His brother chuckled ruefully. "She drank that much?"

"Like a fish," Tobias replied. "I had a bottle of wine up in the cupboard. She insisted I bust that out and drank the whole thing."

"Some things never change." Maddox, too, kept his voice low, but Jill wasn't paying attention to them, anyway. She was too busy greeting Jada and Maya.

After a final searching glance and a quick "Thanks

for taking care of her last night," Maddox turned his attention to Jill. "Hi, Mom. Merry Christmas."

Tobias smiled as Maya came over to hug him. At the last second, however, she grabbed his wrist instead. "Wow! Look at that watch! Did you get that for Christmas?"

Tobias hadn't realized he'd forgotten to take it off. "Yeah, it was a gift."

"From who?" she asked.

Maya's surprise had drawn the attention of the others, so he found everyone looking at him. "A friend."

"Let me see." Maddox whistled as he admired it. "That's *nice*. I'd like one of those myself."

"For what?" Tobias joked. "You hardly ever hike."

"It's not just for hiking. It does all kinds of things, right? But I've been thinking. I've decided to train with you—for this summer with Atticus."

"What does that mean?" Tobias asked.

"It'll be a lot easier if we take turns carrying him," Maddox said.

Tobias exchanged a glance with the pregnant Jada, who smiled proudly, and felt a huge sense of relief. He'd been worried about his ability to carry a grown man so far. But if he had his brother as backup, there was no question he could make it. They'd all make it. "That's awesome. I love it. Thank you."

"It's the least I can do for the both of you," he said. "And Jada will like it, too. It'll give me a reason to get back in shape."

"What are you talking about?" she said with a laugh. "You're already in shape."

"Not as in shape as I'll be if I take this on."

"You still haven't told us who gave you the watch,"

Jill pointed out. He'd told her about the hike with Atticus while they were at dinner last night. She hadn't seemed overly supportive of the idea, said she didn't see the point in it. "Someone could get hurt," she'd said. "And for what?" But she'd ultimately shrugged and let it go with "If that's what you want to do."

"A friend," he repeated.

Maya peered closer at him. "You're not going to tell us *which* friend? That means it was a woman."

Tobias couldn't help grinning. "True."

Jill gaped at him. "We spent all of last night together and you never mentioned that you've got a girlfriend?"

"She's not my girlfriend," he clarified. "We're just starting to hang out now and then."

"Don't tell me you're still seeing Harper Devlin!" Jada said. "Is she the one who bought you the expensive watch?"

Tobias figured there was no longer any need to keep the relationship a secret. Even Axel knew he and Harper had been seeing each other. "Yeah."

"Wow!" Jada exclaimed. "Must be going well."

"Wait," Maya said. "We're not talking about *the* Axel Devlin—the lead singer of Pulse?"

Tobias arched an eyebrow at his niece. "No. We're talking about his ex-wife. I have no interest in him whatsoever."

She laughed. "Stop it. She's beautiful! But—" her smile suddenly faded "—I heard that Axel's in town. My friend's mother saw him at the coffee shop yesterday. Everyone's saying he wants her back. You don't think... I mean..."

Somehow Tobias managed to maintain his smile. "Don't worry," he said. "I know what the odds are."

He felt her thin arms go around his waist. "If I were her, I'd choose you," she said. "But maybe she's not as smart as me."

He kissed the top of her head. "How'd it go with your grandma Brooks last night?"

"She was nice," she said. "Even to Dad!"

"A Christmas miracle," Maddox joked.

"Let's just hope it lasts," Jada said in an aside to him.

Tobias got the presents he'd brought out of the bag his mother had insisted on carrying in for him—probably so that she wouldn't feel so bad showing up without anything. "Time for the gifts," he said. "It's my first year doing this, so I want to see how well I did."

"Let's go in by the tree," Jada said. "We have gifts for you, too."

"What's Uriah up to today?" Maddox asked as they moved into the living room.

"I talked to him this morning when I got back from my hike. He said he's spending the day with Carl."

"Just the two of them?"

"Who else can get along with Carl?"

Maddox didn't argue. "We got Uriah a new flannel shirt. That one he's been wearing needs to be retired. Will you take it back to him?"

"Of course. I got him a new chess set. I'm going to ask him to come over and play a game with me tonight. I'll give him your present then, too."

"Perfect."

Jada and Maddox thanked him when they opened the water purifier he'd purchased for their house. He was getting so interested in healthy eating and living he'd wanted to buy one for everyone, but they were pretty expensive.

They seemed to like it. And Maya squealed and jumped up to hug him when she opened the three beaded ankle bracelets that were meant to be stacked. "Thank you, Uncle Tobias!" she cried. "I love these! All the girls are wearing them."

He made a big deal about the mug she'd made him in ceramics at school and then tore the paper off a big box from Jada and Maddox. "What could this be?" he asked. "It's huge!"

They just smiled and looked on while he tossed the wrapping paper to one side and ripped off the tape securing the flaps on the box. "It's…it's a backpack?" he said as he pulled out a carrier similar to what he'd been eyeing at various online backpacking sites.

"Not just any backpack," Maddox said. "It should fit Atticus."

"We had to have it custom-made," Jada volunteered. "To be sure."

Tobias cleared his throat so that he'd be able to speak. No doubt the pack had cost a lot. But what was far more important was the support they were giving him. "Thank you." He stood up to embrace each one in turn and, as he sat back down, thought there could never be another Christmas quite as good as this one.

27

Harper sat on the couch, watching the twinkling lights on her sister's Christmas tree reflect in the window. The wrapping paper had been thrown away, the toys had been picked up, the dishes were done and she was enjoying the last bit of the day by having a glass of wine with Karoline and Terrance. As wonderful as Christmas had been, it was her first chance to slow down and relax now that all the children were in bed and Axel had left for the hotel.

"Axel was on his best behavior today," Karoline said after taking a sip of wine. "I liked him better than I have for a long time."

Harper had to admit that her ex had been nice. And she was grateful. She'd been so afraid he'd do something that would ruin Christmas—not on purpose but because he couldn't control his emotions. He'd been so jealous in the restaurant. She'd expected to see more of that, but he hadn't even referred to what'd happened at Fatboy Burgers or mentioned Tobias. "I'm relieved."

"It was almost like old times, right?" Her sister covered a yawn. "He seems to have reverted back to his former self, the man he was before all the pressure and the fame started to get to him."

"He was very attentive to you," Terrance added.

"That's true," Karoline agreed. "I didn't see him get on his phone once—unless it was to take a picture of the girls. And that's a big change. Remember last Christmas? We could hardly get him to acknowledge us when we came. He was always on the phone, or he'd lock himself away in the studio in your basement to work."

Last Christmas hadn't been fun. She and Axel had had a terrible argument over how dismissive he'd been of her family. Maybe he'd remembered how things had gone last year, too, because he'd tried harder this time around. "I thanked him for being so easy to get along with. The girls and I had a great Christmas. But, honestly, you're the one who made it great, Karoline. You went to so much work. The decorations, the activities, the meal tonight—"

"You did as much of the meal as I did. And then you washed the dishes!"

"But I didn't have the presence of mind to plan everything, and I was in such a dark place when I first arrived. You've been the glue that has held everything together for me. You, too, Terrance. I can't thank you both enough."

"It's been a Christmas to remember," Terrance said.

Karoline started to laugh. "True. I'll never forget you showing up on our doorstep at four thirty in the morning with your hair a mess and your shirt on wrong side out—and Axel fuming on my front porch."

Harper shot her a look. "That's still too fresh to joke about."

Terrance smiled as though he saw the humor in it, too, but guided the conversation in a different direction. "Did Axel mention what he wants for the future?"

Harper knew they were both curious as to how she'd ultimately react to Axel's change of heart. "Not really. He just told me that he regrets the divorce, knows he screwed up and is going to do everything he can to make it right."

Karoline propped her feet up on the coffee table. "What'd you say in response to that?"

"I asked him not to bring up any of our personal problems today. I said we both deserved a day to celebrate all the things Christmas means without dragging our emotional baggage into it."

Karoline lifted her glass in a silent toast. "He must've taken your advice."

"Fortunately."

"And that stack of presents he gave you?" She rolled her eyes. "That was crazy."

"It was fun, but I doubt he picked out a single one of those gifts. I bet he had someone shop for him and do all the wrapping before he got on the plane."

"He's busy," Terrance said.

"He's got plenty of help for most everything else. He could've done his own shopping."

"He spent a lot of money..." Karoline mused.

Harper had a comeback for that, too. "I hate to sound negative, but he has a lot of money to spend. Percentage-wise, Tobias was probably the more generous between the two."

"Tobias!" Karoline exclaimed. "What did he give you?"

Harper held up her wrist to show her sister the new

charm bracelet. She hadn't worn it all day because she'd been afraid Axel would ask about it—or the girls would. But as soon as her ex had left, she put it on. She enjoyed seeing it, enjoyed remembering how excited Tobias had been to give it to her.

Karoline sat forward, put her wine on the coffee table and walked over to inspect Tobias's gift. "It's beautiful. Looks like real gold. How much do you think it cost?"

"Enough to show that he wanted to get me something nice. Other than that I don't care. I love it."

"Look, Terrance." Karoline stepped aside so that her husband could see. "The charm is a little rose. He gave Harper a real rose on the night they met."

"Thoughtful, right?" Harper said.

"I can't argue with that," Terrance replied.

Karoline went back to her place on the couch. "Why didn't you tell me that he got you a gift?"

"Because you were in bed when I got home last night. And Axel was here as soon as we rolled out of bed this morning."

Karoline took her last sip of wine. "To be honest, after how well things went today, I thought you'd be more conflicted. You're still set on continuing to see Tobias?"

"I am. Axel might be repentant now. He knows he's lost me, so he's doing his best to win me back. But if I ever remarried him, I feel like he'd just take my love for granted all over again."

Karoline set her empty glass aside. "What about the girls?"

"If he loves them as much as he says he does, he'll

work with me to make sure our divorce is as amicable as he promised when he left me."

Karoline didn't seem particularly optimistic about that, but Harper trusted Axel's willingness to do the right thing. "He loves his music, his bandmates, his fans. Not me. He's just afraid he's losing something he might later want. And I'm not going to let an 'Oh, wait! I might want this, after all' make me blow what's going on between Tobias and me. If Axel really wanted me, he wouldn't have done what he did."

Her phone went off before Terrance or Karoline could respond. She thought maybe it would be Tobias asking about her Christmas. She'd planned to call him before bed. She wanted to see him, but she was waiting until Axel left town.

It wasn't Tobias, however. It wasn't even Axel. It was Rory, from the band.

Harper excused herself and left the room as she answered the call. She didn't want to make Karoline and Terrance sit through her conversation when they were finally getting a chance to recoup after the big day. "Hi, Rory."

"Harper, this is nuts. You've got to get him to change his mind."

"I assume 'him' is Axel. But…change his mind about what?"

"I realize you want to keep him there with you. I'm sorry for all you've been through, and I'm excited you're getting back together. But can't you hold on for just two more weeks? The rest of us are *dying*. He's making us cancel a New Year's Eve show! No one in the industry does that. It's professional suicide!"

She stopped in the middle of the hall and put a

hand to her head. "Whoa! Wait. What are you talking about?" She hadn't agreed to get back with Axel. "Why would he make you cancel the show?"

"We can't go onstage without him!"

"But...he'll be there. He's leaving tomorrow, right?" She'd asked Axel if he needed a ride to LA, had offered to drive him. He'd been so congenial today that she'd wanted to show she was willing to bend over backward to be nice, too. But when he'd said that wouldn't be necessary, she'd assumed he'd hired a limo.

"That's what he told you?" Rory said.

"Yes."

"Well, he called me last night and said he wasn't coming back at all. That his family is falling apart, and he needs to stay and put it back together."

Oh, shit. Had Axel decided to stay? If so, why hadn't he told her?

Just after they'd finished unwrapping presents, when she was thanking him for the gifts he'd given her, and he was thanking her for the scrapbook she'd made him, he'd pulled her aside to say how much he'd missed her. That was when she'd cut him off and asked him to save all of that for after Christmas.

Had he been about to tell her that he wasn't going back?

"Give me a few minutes," she told Rory and disconnected.

After slipping into her room and shutting the door, she called Axel's cell.

"Hello?" He sounded groggy, as though she'd dragged him out of a dead sleep.

"Did I wake you?"

"Yeah. The tour kicked my ass to begin with. Jet

lag and all the…you know…emotional bullshit we've been going through did the rest. I could hardly keep my eyes open when I left tonight."

She was about to say she'd let him go back to sleep, but caught herself. "This will only take a second. Rory called. He said…" She swallowed hard. "He said you aren't going back to finish the tour. Is that true?"

There was a brief hesitation before he replied. "Yeah. I was going to tell you, but I didn't want to get into it today. You were so focused on the kids and the meal and all the festivities. I figured I'd let you know in the morning."

"But…that doesn't make any sense."

"Of course it makes sense. I'm here to fight for my family. I made a mistake before, Harper. I want you back."

"Axel…"

"What?"

"I've already told you—I'm not coming back."

"You can't make the decision right now. All you have to go on is how it's been for the last few years. But I'm willing to change, put you first."

Sure he was. For how long? She knew better than to believe that would last. "I'm already seeing someone else. You know that."

"You and Tobias have barely met. Of course everything seems like it would be ideal with him. You haven't known him long enough for him to screw up."

"You're *that* sure he will?"

"No one's perfect. He might seem like Superman right now, but he'll be human enough in a few months."

"I don't want to get back together, Axel. It was too

rough there at the end. I—I've lost faith in our ability to make things work."

"I understand. I'm rattled, too. But I'm going to rebuild your trust, prove that things will be better. *I'm* the one you should be with, Harper."

She doubted he'd be saying any of this if she hadn't finally moved on and met someone else, though. And that wasn't the reason she wanted him to have for coming back. Not wanting her to be with someone else wasn't enough.

"Harper?" he said when she didn't respond.

She slipped the rose charm Tobias had given her around the circle of the bracelet. "I think it's too late."

She'd spoken so low that she wasn't sure he'd heard her, until he said, "That's bullshit, Harper. Don't do this."

"I have to have the chance to see… To see if Tobias and I are better for each other. I know he isn't perfect. But he might be perfect for me."

"He rents a house on someone else's orchard, for crying out loud!"

How did he know that? "So?"

"So what has *he* established?"

"What should he have established?" she countered. "He has a decent job."

"Doing what?"

"Maintenance at a private school."

"Maintenance," he said as if that was too lowly to be respectable.

"There's nothing wrong with maintenance. He's a gifted mechanic. Wants to open his own repair shop one day."

"Yeah, with my money. No doubt that's part of what he sees in you."

"It's my money, too. I helped you establish your career. But I can't believe you'd even say that. He hasn't asked me for a dime. You don't know that he ever will."

He sighed as though he was tempted to argue but knew it was an argument he couldn't win. "What else do you know about him?" he asked instead. "You're giving me up for a complete unknown."

"Not a 'complete' unknown. I've met his brother. I really like him. I've also met his landlord."

"What about his alcoholic mother? Have you met *her*?"

A chill ran down her spine. The sarcasm and bitterness in his voice was one thing. So was the comment about where Tobias lived. But now Axel had something to say about his mother?

"Who told you about his mother?"

"No one," he replied.

"Someone must have."

"Look, I told you I'm half-dead from the tour and the jet lag and all that. Let's talk in the morning."

He wasn't going to rush her off the phone, not now. "We can talk in the morning as soon as you answer my question. You haven't been doing any kind of...of background check on Tobias, have you?"

"No! Of course not."

"You'd better not, because who I date—it's none of your business. Just like it would be wrong of me to go poking around in the life of any woman *you* might date."

"It *is* my business," he argued. "As long as we have children together."

"No. That's crossing the line. You need to trust that I won't let anyone who wouldn't be good for our children be around them. And I have to trust the same thing."

"If we stayed together, we wouldn't have to worry about that," he pointed out.

"That was my reasoning when this all started, remember?" she said. "But everything's changed, Axel. You need to go back to your tour. Your bandmates are waiting for you. You can't let them down."

"They're fine. Let me stay and drive you and the girls home. We can get a marriage counselor once we get there to help us rebuild. That could make all the difference."

"I'm not ready to leave Silver Springs," she said. "Not yet."

"Because of some guy with more muscles than brains?"

"How dare you!" she snapped. "Just because Tobias is fit doesn't mean he isn't smart, too."

"Then maybe it's *your* brain I need to worry about."

"Because I won't come back to you? I feel something genuine for him, and I'm going to pursue it."

Silence. Then he said, "You really want *him*."

She squeezed her eyes closed. Did she dare cast away from the familiar? Take a risk on someone new?

When she looked at it that way, she was scared enough to say no.

But when she thought about Tobias, about how she felt when he touched her, she knew if she left now, she'd crave Tobias the whole time she was in Colorado. How could she go back into a relationship with Axel when she felt the way she did? It had been difficult enough when she was completely committed. "Yes."

"Forget it, then," Axel shouted. "I wouldn't get back with you now if you begged me to."

Harper could feel her heart pounding against her chest as he disconnected. She'd held fast to her decision.

She just hoped to God it was the right one for everyone concerned.

Harper was pacing the floor thirty minutes later when she received a text from Tobias.

Merry Christmas.

"Can I trust you?" she whispered, staring at those words. "Or will *you* let me down, too?"

She got another message from him right away, before she could text him back. It's probably awkward for you to text me with Axel there. No need to respond. I just wanted to say...I'm thinking of you.

Axel's gone, no worries, she wrote. What'd you do today?

Went on a short hike this morning. Had dinner at Maddox and Jada's. Drove to LA to drop off my mom. Played chess with my landlord.

Did Carl join you?

Fortunately, he didn't.

Who won?

He did.

Really?

Sort of.

So you let him?

It is Christmas, after all. But Uriah's becoming more of a challenge. He'll beat me legitimately soon.

He took such good care of those he loved—at least it seemed that way. So you had a good day?

A great one. The best Christmas I've ever had. You?

My Christmas was fine.

Something wrong?

She frowned. She didn't want to drag him through everything she was going through. No.

When's Axel going back to Europe?

Tomorrow.

Are you okay with that?

As she considered the freedom Axel's leaving would give her to see Tobias, her anxiety began to ease. Yeah, I'm okay with it, she wrote. What are you doing tomorrow?

I was going to go on another hike in the morning. Would you like to go with me? The weather's supposed to be good. And I have a trail in mind I think you'd enjoy.

I'd like that, she wrote. I'll see if Karoline will mind if the girls hang out here with them until I get back.

28

The following morning, Axel was eager to get out of town. What had seemed like such a short trip now seemed far too long. Why he'd wasted so much time, effort and money coming to Silver Springs in the middle of his European tour, when it was ending in two weeks anyway, he had no idea. Learning that Harper was moving on had made him panic.

A lot of divorced people probably felt the same when their exes found someone else, he told himself. But if she was going to be a bitch after everything he'd tried to do for her—was going to turn away everything he'd offered, which was far more than most men could offer, including Tobias Richardson—she didn't deserve him. As far as he was concerned, the breakup of their marriage was now on her. He wasn't going to take responsibility for it, and he wasn't going to feel bad about it. There were too many other women in the world for him to cry over someone he'd struggled to get along with for the past few years.

He checked his watch. Ten o'clock. He had some time to grab a coffee before he was scheduled to see Piper and Everly at eleven thirty. He was driving the

Range Rover. The limo that would take him to LA would pick him up at Karoline's at two so that he could make his seven-thirty flight.

At least his bandmates and his manager were starting to calm down now that he was going to return. They'd acted like such crybabies about canceling the rest of the tour. Chase McDonald, the president of the record company he was affiliated with, had called him this morning to say he'd better get his ass back to the UK or the band would be dropped from the label. And Axel had been able to tell that Mr. McDonald wasn't messing around. He'd said gone were the days when celebrities could get away with shit like going AWOL at the last second. But that wasn't all he'd said. He'd also been pissed about the video he'd seen on BuzzFeed showing Axel exchanging angry words with Tobias at Fatboy Burgers. Someone who'd witnessed the exchange had sold him out even after all he'd done to make sure that wouldn't happen.

"You've caused a PR nightmare," Mr. McDonald had said. "You were acting like a jealous idiot and that will cost the band when it comes to image."

Axel wished he could've told Mr. McDonald to go to hell. Bands were notorious for acting badly. What was the big deal? But he hadn't dared go that far, not on the heels of Harper's defection. As much as he hated to admit it, losing the one person who'd always believed in him most had rattled him.

He'd get over it. She'd be sorry at some point.

He slid his sunglasses higher on the bridge of his nose and pulled the ball cap he'd donned low as he got out of the SUV and walked into The Daily Grind. He had no doubt there'd be a few people who'd recognize him, but after what'd happened with BuzzFeed he'd offer no autographs. He had the right to buy himself a cup of coffee without being bothered—which was why he was particularly irritated when a couple of guys sitting at a small table not far from where he was waiting kept looking over at him.

"That's him," he heard one say.

"You sure?" the other replied.

"Why else would he be wearing sunglasses? It's not even sunny, you idiot."

They were both probably ten years older than he was and one, in particular, could use a shower.

"Yeah. Guess you're right. But he seems a lot smaller in person."

The guy with the greasy hair started to get up, but the other caught hold of his jacket.

"Carl, man, sit down. What do you think you're doing?"

"I'm going to warn him! He can't mess around with Tobias the way he did at Fatboy Burgers and expect to get away with it."

"No doubt he already knows Tobias is dangerous. That's why he was warning him to stay away from his ex-wife."

"*How* would he know?" the man called Carl said. "He's not from around here. I bet he has no clue. Harper probably doesn't even know, or she wouldn't be sneaking over at night. Somebody should tell her, Derrick. Somebody should tell them both."

"But…what if Tobias finds out it was you?"

"He'll never know it was me," Carl said. "Lots of people from around here know about Tobias's record.

The man he shot still lives in town, for crying out loud."

Axel's irritation had turned to curiosity. Tobias's name was unique enough that he knew who they were talking about. But surely he had to have heard wrong. Had they really said that Tobias had *shot* someone?

The cute gal behind the counter called out the name Dexter—the name he'd given when he ordered because *Axel* was too distinctive—but he ignored her and stepped closer to Carl and his buddy. "Do you two have something to say to me?" he asked.

The two men exchanged glances before Carl cleared his throat. "Yeah. I just… I wanted to tell you that you might not want to cross Tobias Richardson like…like you did at Fatboy Burgers."

"Because…"

"Because he just got out of prison five months ago—and from what I've heard around town, even the dudes he served time with knew to leave him alone."

Axel felt his jaw drop. "What'd you say?"

"See, he didn't know," Carl said to Derrick. Then he got up and lowered his voice. "It's true. He served thirteen years."

"For…"

"Shot an eleven-year-old boy when he was seventeen," he said. "Crippled him for life."

When Tobias picked Harper up at eleven, she had her hair in a ponytail and was wearing leggings, sneakers and the same parka she'd had on the night he first saw her. Glad he no longer had to park down the street, he smiled as she closed the door and turned to face him. "Look what I remembered," he said and pulled her necklace from a small pocket on his coat.

"Oh, thanks for thinking of it," she said and ran it into the house before emerging again only a couple of minutes later. "All set?"

"All set," he said. "Unless... Do you think your girls might want to go with us?"

"Not today," she replied. "Their father will be here soon to spend a few hours with them before he has to go back to Europe."

He reached out to take her hand so that he could lead her to his truck, but she threw her arms around him and pressed her face into his neck instead, and he felt his heart skip a beat. He'd invited the girls to be nice but also because he was looking for a good excuse to procrastinate the task he'd set for himself today. He had to tell Harper about his past. Things were getting too serious between them to put it off any longer.

"It's so good to see you," she said, her words muffled by his coat.

As he kissed her head, he prayed she'd be able to understand and forgive him, but he knew she might not feel as friendly toward him when they returned as she did now. "It's good to see you, too."

She grinned up at him when she released him. Then she took his hand. "Where are we going?"

He saw the curtain move and realized that Piper and Everly were watching them through the window.

He waved and both girls ducked out of sight.

"What is it?" Harper asked when he chuckled.

"Nothing," he said as they walked down the small path from Karoline's front door. "We're going to the Los Padres National Forest. To the Piedra Blanca Formations Trail. It features a river, a little bouldering, some bird-watching. You're going to like it."

"How hard of a hike is it?" she asked, her expression a tad leery. "You're pretty serious about this stuff, look like you could hike for days."

"Don't worry—it's easy. You won't have any trouble. It's only two and a half miles in. And we can turn around whenever."

He'd just helped her into the cab and was walking around to get into the driver's seat when her Range Rover came racing around the corner so fast, it swerved and nearly smashed into a parked car.

"What the hell!" Tobias said as Axel brought the vehicle to a screeching halt right in front of his truck.

"Don't you dare go anywhere with Harper, you son of a bitch!" he shouted as soon as he got out.

A rush of adrenaline swept through Tobias when he saw that Axel was carrying a baseball bat—one he must've just purchased because it still had the sticker on it. "You need to calm down," Tobias said.

"Calm down?" Axel cried. *"Calm down?"*

Harper scrambled out of the cab and hurried to Tobias's side. "Axel, what are you doing? Whatever it is, you need to stop."

"Stay back." Tobias shoved her behind him so that she couldn't be hurt.

"You think *you're* the one who's going to protect her?" Axel said. "No, *I'm* doing that. Get away from him, Harper. He isn't safe."

The noise had brought Karoline and Terrance to the door—as well as Everly, Piper, Amanda and Miranda.

"What's going on?" Karoline marched out of the

house before her husband could pull her back, and the rest of the family trailed behind her.

"That's what I'm trying to find out," Harper said.

Tobias kept hold of Harper. He didn't want her to get hit if he had to disarm her ex.

"I'll tell you what's going on." Axel used his bat to point at Tobias. "This bastard has a prison record. Did you know that? Did any of you know that you've been associating with a dangerous felon? A man who's served time for attempted *murder*?"

"Axel, stop! That can't be true." Harper pulled away but shut up as soon as she looked at Tobias. His face revealed the truth. He couldn't refute what Axel had said.

"No…" Karoline's eyebrows knit in concern as she turned toward her sister.

"Yes," Axel insisted. "Ask him. He'll tell you. He shot a boy, crippled him for life. And that's not all. He nearly killed another man while he was in prison."

Tobias couldn't bear the look on Harper's face.

"Is that true?" she asked, turning to him.

"I was going to tell you," he said.

"When?" she cried. "We've…we've already…" Tears welled up as she turned to see her children watching them. "I trusted you," she said, her voice barely a whisper. "Trusted you with *them*."

"I know. But it's not the way he's making it sound."

"How can there be any way to make a shooting sound good?" Axel challenged.

Tobias tried to ignore him. He had to get Harper to listen. "The shooting was—" He struggled to remember the words he'd rehearsed in his mind so that she might understand. But Axel had painted the past in its worst possible light, and his accusing face and pointing finger made Tobias feel hopeless to even attempt to explain. "Sort of an accident," he finished.

"Sort of an accident?" she repeated, obviously at a complete loss.

"And the man in prison knifed me first." Tobias remembered that much of what he'd planned to say. It was true, after all. He didn't feel bad about the thug who'd attacked him in prison. He'd fought back only in self-defense, and he'd nearly lost his life.

"Oh, my God!" She covered her mouth. "This can't be happening."

"I never meant to mislead you," he said. "I was going to tell you today—I swear it."

"I let you around my kids," she said, going back to that. "I—I thought you were the most wonderful man I'd ever met!"

Tobias wished he could shut everyone out, get her to look at him, to believe him. But he couldn't get her to listen. Her family was rallying around her, trying to protect her and creating so much insulation that nothing he said could get through.

"Just go." Karoline, whose husband was standing next to her for support, had already grabbed hold of Harper and pulled her under the shelter of one arm. "Leave. What's happened is bad enough. Please, don't make it any worse."

He looked at Harper, tried one last time to get her to listen, but Axel was waving the bat, and Tobias knew he'd only look worse if he took it away from him. "I was going to tell you," he repeated lamely.

Harper didn't get a chance to respond before Axel yelled, "Do you really think a guy like you could ever make someone like her happy? Look at her, man. She's so far out of your league it isn't even funny. And there's no way in hell I will ever allow you to be around my children."

Tobias had thought Harper was too good for him all along. How had he convinced himself that he might have a chance with her?

"Do you think, after what you've done, you could ever deserve someone like her?" Axel persisted.

Finally, Tobias grabbed the bat, wrenched it away and tossed it aside, just so that they would all know the threat of it had nothing to do with his leaving. "You've made your point," he said, got in his truck and drove off.

In his rearview mirror, he saw Harper bury her face in her sister's shoulder and start to sob.

Harper's eyes were still blurry with sleep when she stumbled into the kitchen to get a glass of water. "What's this?" she asked when she saw something silver sitting on the island.

Terrance, who was the only other person up, turned from where he was scrambling eggs at the stove to see what Harper was talking about. "A watch of some sort," he replied. "I found it behind the pillar on the front porch this morning when I went out to get the paper. I was surprised. Looks expensive."

As soon as Harper picked it up she realized it was the watch she'd given Tobias. He must've brought it back and put it behind the pillar to keep it safe until she could stumble across it. Except she hadn't left the house. For the past three days she'd been pretending to be sick so that Karoline, Terrance and the girls wouldn't question why she could scarcely drag herself out of bed. Karoline and Terrance probably guessed the truth, but at least they hadn't pressed her.

"There's nothing on the security app on your phone?" she said.

"Haven't checked yet. Thought I'd have a look while I was eating breakfast." He scooped the eggs he'd made onto a plate and carried it to the table. "You hungry?"

"No." Since Tobias had driven off, she'd lost her appetite as well as her energy. "Do you mind if I check to see who left it?"

He got his phone from the counter, unlocked it and navigated to the security app before handing it to her.

The camera on the front door was motion activated, so it turned on whenever there was movement. Given the number of times the kids had gone in and out of the house, since they were out of school, she had to scroll back quite a bit. But eventually she found what she was looking for.

Tobias had brought it, all right. The day after everything had gone bad—at four thirty in the morning, when it was still cold and dark and no one would be around—he'd come to the front doorstep and slipped the watch behind the pillar. Then he'd turned around and left as if he couldn't get away fast enough.

Harper felt fresh tears well up watching that short clip but blinked them back as she returned her brother-in-law's phone.

"Was it Tobias?" he asked when he saw her reaction.

She nodded.

"Thought it might be. Did you give him that watch for Christmas?"

Again she nodded and, to avoid his sympathetic gaze, went over to get the glass of water that'd driven her to the kitchen in the first place. She didn't want to see the watch, didn't want to be reminded of how happy buying it had made her. "I wish he'd kept it," she mumbled.

"I'm surprised he didn't."

"What do you mean?"

"Being such a terrible guy and all. You know, an ex-con."

"He probably didn't want Axel or anyone else to be able to accuse him of using me for my money."

Terrance wore a thoughtful expression as he chewed and swallowed. "Which one do you miss more?"

Harper looked back at him for clarification.

"Axel or Tobias?"

"I'm relieved Axel is gone," she admitted. At least meeting Tobias had helped her get over her ex. Even if she wasn't going to be with someone else, she didn't want to go back to Axel. They'd both changed too much. And when she thought of the stress of having Axel on the road and all the women he would encounter and the "mistakes" that would probably occur... She was done with that.

"And Tobias?" he said.

"I can't say the same for him." She missed Tobias far worse than she should, given how short their relationship had been.

"Maybe you two should meet up," Terrance said. "Talk things out. Gain some closure."

"What is there to say?" she asked.

"Has he ever behaved badly when he was with you, given you the impression he might be dangerous?"

"No. Never. But maybe he's never been fully provoked."

"In the clip from Fatboy Burgers that's been posted all over the internet, Tobias behaved better than Axel."

"He did," she admitted. "He was the one who defused the situation."

"Seems to me that's exactly what he did when Axel came after him with that bat, too. I mean... Let's face it. If he'd wanted to cause some damage, I'm sure he could have. He looks physically capable of it."

Harper pressed three fingers to her forehead. "Are you trying to soften my heart? Because I can't let someone who's been in prison for thirteen years—for attempted murder, no less—be around my children."

Finished with his eggs, Terrance got up to carry the plate to the sink. "No, I'm sorry. It's just... I don't know. He seemed cool, I guess. I liked him."

"Not nearly as much as I did," she grumbled and shuffled back to bed.

29

After Axel had come running up with that bat to announce to Harper and her family what an evil person Tobias was, and Tobias had driven home feeling as though he'd just been kicked in the stomach, he'd decided that he had to get away for a while and immerse himself in nature. Do shit that was so physically demanding it required his full concentration and left him so tired at the end of the day that he drifted off to sleep immediately. After all, he couldn't allow himself to deaden the pain he felt the way his mother did; he had to use better "coping mechanisms," or so the psychologist at Soledad had told him. So he'd turned off his phone, because he didn't want to talk to anyone, and put it in the glove compartment of his truck the second he'd delivered the watch Harper had given him to her front door. Then he'd driven off, left town.

Although it smacked of avoidance, he'd been staying at a lodge in Yosemite National Park for almost a week, hiking from dawn until dark—rain or shine. But he still couldn't think of Harper without feeling as though he had a thousand pounds of sand sitting on his chest and couldn't breathe.

At least he was giving himself some time to tamp down emotions he shouldn't have allowed himself to feel in the first place. He'd been an idiot to think what had started between them could end any other way. He'd just gotten so caught up in her he'd begun to hope that she might be able to see beyond his past mistakes.

It wasn't until New Year's Eve that he finally forced himself to go out to his truck and turn on his phone. He knew his brother would be looking for him. Probably Uriah, too. He hadn't prepared either one of them for the fact that he'd be gone. He'd just packed up and left, and then he'd worked day by day to train his mind, while training his body to climb higher and carry more weight, to believe that Harper was like the drugs his mother took—something toxic and dangerous for him to desire.

"What's going on?" Maddox asked as soon as Tobias got him on the phone. "Where the hell have you been?"

Tobias winced at the anger in his brother's voice. Maddox didn't get mad very often. "I just…took a little hiking trip for the holidays. That's all."

"Without telling a soul that you were going?"

He'd been meaning to check in all along. He'd just kept putting it off, hadn't been able to make himself face anyone he'd left behind, and that included his brother. He'd known the subject of Harper would inevitably come up and he didn't want to talk about her. "I didn't think it would be a big deal. I had the time off work, so I decided to make the most of it."

"Damn it, Tobias! You scared the shit out of me! Uriah's been trying to reach you. Atticus has been trying to reach you. I've been trying to reach you. None of us knew where you were. Even Susan called Jada this morning, wanting to know if there'd been any word."

Tobias dropped his head and massaged his temple with his free hand. "Yeah, I bet Susan would be real broken up if I were to leave for good." He laughed, hoping Maddox would join in and let everything else go—but he didn't.

"Where are you?"

"Yosemite."

"Shit," Maddox said. "If you hadn't taken your hiking gear I would've called the police. I hope you know that."

"I'm sorry."

"I thought… God, when I heard what happened with Harper, I thought…"

"That maybe I'd gone off on a drug binge, like Mom? You know I'd never do that," Tobias said.

Maddox didn't respond right away.

"Maddox?"

"When are you coming back?" his brother asked.

Tobias's breath misted in the cold air as he stared up at the mountains surrounding him. The beauty here was soothing. But hiking could only do so much. He had to go back to his regular life at some point. He figured it might as well be sooner rather than later. Christmas and staying at the lodge had helped his peace of mind but damaged his bank account. "Tomorrow."

"So you're okay."

"I'm fine," he reiterated.

"You're not upset about Harper."

"No," he lied. "I knew that wasn't real in the first place. No big deal."

"That bastard Carl. I wish I could put my fist through his face."

"What's happened with Carl?" Tobias asked, feeling a fresh fissure of alarm. "Don't tell me he hurt Uriah while I was gone—"

"No. He's the one who told Axel about your past."

Tobias was relieved that Uriah was okay, but he wasn't surprised about Carl. "He's a little bastard. I'm going to have to move. I won't continue to live on the same property with him."

"You won't have to."

"What does that mean?"

"Carl is gone."

"How'd that happen?"

"After Carl told Axel about you, he got pretty full of himself. Went back to Uriah and announced that he'd just set Axel straight, that everyone agreed with him you're dangerous, and tried to insist that Uriah kick you out. Long story short, he forced Uriah to choose between you. And Uriah chose you."

Tobias switched his phone to the other ear. "Are you kidding me?"

"No."

Tobias tried to grasp the full impact of this change. "But it can't last. Where will Carl go?"

"Uriah gave him a big chunk of his inheritance—enough for him to get an apartment in LA while he works through his legal problems. Then…who knows? Maybe he'll move back to Maryland, where he's been for a number of years. But Uriah told him he could never come back to the orchard."

"And Carl didn't get violent with him?"

"Hell, no. Carl was so glad to get his hands on the money, he took off immediately."

"He'll be back as soon as he blows through it."

"Probably. But that's down the road."

"I can't believe Carl's gone," Tobias said.

"*I* can," Maddox responded. "It proves just how much Uriah cares about you."

"I'm just his renter."

"You're a lot more than that. You've lost Harper. I know she meant a lot to you. But you've got the rest of us in your corner, including Uriah. We *all* know how special you are—prison record or no. Now, come home."

Tobias tilted his head back to look up at the stars. "Thanks," he said. "I'll leave first thing in the morning."

Harper had told her sister that she was heading to Colorado on Friday, only two days after New Year's, but she didn't want to leave Silver Springs until she could return Tobias's bracelet. After all, he'd probably spent as much on her gift as she had on his, so if he was going to return the watch, she needed to do the same with the bracelet.

Except she couldn't catch him at home. She'd driven by Honey Hollow several times since Terrance had discovered the watch only to find Tobias's truck gone. She would've followed his example and left the small box that contained her bracelet on the doorstep, but she didn't trust Uriah's son. She was afraid Carl would take it before Tobias could get back and that he'd never even know she returned it.

It wasn't until New Year's Day, late in the evening,

that she spotted his truck in the drive. And then she was so nervous she almost couldn't make herself stop.

After driving past the orchard twice, she finally pulled in.

Uriah must've heard her engine, because he looked out.

She bit her lip as she waved at him. When it took a moment for him to wave back, she guessed even he knew her relationship with Tobias had taken a bad turn.

She could hear a football game playing on the TV as she knocked, but there weren't any other cars in the drive, so she was pretty sure Tobias was alone.

Still, he didn't come right away. She was afraid he'd looked through the peephole and wouldn't answer because it was her.

"Tobias?" she called. "Please, open the door. I have something to give you. It won't take long."

At last, he opened up, but he stood back, well away from her.

He looked good, she thought. *Too* good. And she could smell that clean scent she associated with him and his house.

When she didn't speak right away, he said, "What can I do for you?" His voice was clipped.

Harper felt that old lump rise in her throat, the one that threatened tears, but she swallowed hard to be able to speak around it. "First of all, I wanted to say...I'm sorry. For...for how things went at the end. That scene wasn't pleasant for anyone."

"No problem," he said. "I lost sight of the reality of the situation there for a bit, but you and your family did the right thing."

"The right thing?" she echoed weakly.

"Set me straight," he explained. "So I'm sorry, too. I don't know why I ever thought I had something to offer you."

That he was absorbing the blow without reacting in anger only made Harper feel worse. Once she'd gotten beyond that emotional encounter with Axel, she'd had time to remember a lot of things she hadn't given enough consideration in that moment. First of all, Tobias had told her the night they met that he was the last person she should ever "get with." So he *had* warned her, in a way. Not only that, but *she* was the one who'd pushed the physical side of the relationship, not him. And then there was that moment in his truck when she was getting out and he'd acted as though he had something important to tell her. She believed it was an attempt to broach the truth. A past like his would be a difficult thing to reveal after all, especially because things were moving so fast between them. They'd already reached a more serious level at that point.

"It's—it's not a matter of having something to offer me," she said.

"Well, however you want to frame it. I'm an ex-con. You were the wife of a famous rock star. I get it." He gestured toward the small box she held. "Is that for me?"

She wanted to address what he'd just said. She hated the way it sounded, but she couldn't think of a good way to refute his words so she looked down. "Yes. I—I wish you hadn't returned the watch. I really wanted you to have it. But since you did, I'm bringing this back."

"Of course. Thank you." He took the box, but when he turned and tossed it into the garbage, Harper felt her stomach drop.

"I wish you and Axel—and the girls, of course—the best." He started to shut the door, but she was so stunned that he'd thrown away a gold bracelet—*her* bracelet—she stopped him.

"Wait." She blinked several times while she searched for something to say that might help relieve the terrible pain in her chest. "Did you... Did you just throw away my bracelet?"

"I can get it out and throw it away after you leave, if you'd rather," he said, still as polite as ever.

"I'd rather you not throw it away at all."

"I don't understand why it would matter to you. I don't have any use for it," he explained and started to close the door again.

She caught the panel. "It *does* matter. If—if you're only going to throw it away, can I have it back?"

"Of course." He walked over, grabbed the trash can and fished it out for her.

"Thank you," she mumbled.

"No problem. I'm sorry for..." He seemed to struggle to find something he owed her an apology for. "For not letting you know what a monster I am, I guess."

Harper winced as the door clicked shut. Then she couldn't move. She stood there, holding her bracelet as tears started to run down her cheeks.

"I'm sorry," she called out, feeling the need to repeat that sentiment, but when she got no response, she knew there was nothing she could do but go.

Tobias closed his eyes and leaned against the door, hoping that would be it—that Harper would leave and he'd never have to see her again. The self-talk he gave himself about not needing her or any other woman, about being careful to find someone next time who wouldn't mind that he'd screwed up in the past—someone who'd made a few mistakes of her own—was far more effective when Harper wasn't standing in front of him.

"Just go," he whispered while waiting for the sound of her engine.

But that isn't what he heard. He heard Uriah say, "Ms. Devlin? Can I have a word with you, please?"

Tobias tensed. What could Uriah possibly have to say to her?

He crossed to the window over the sink, where he could see what was going on. Uriah stood between Harper and her expensive Range Rover; he'd obviously cut her off as she approached her vehicle.

Now that Uriah had lowered his voice, however, Tobias couldn't hear everything the old man said, but he could pick up a few words.

"Carl was wrong… Tobias is a fine man, not the kind of person you might think… If only you could look deeper than that, form your own opinion… I would be proud to have any daughter of mine marry him…"

It went on long enough that Tobias felt compelled to intervene. Taking a deep breath, he stalked out of the house and called Uriah's name.

Both Uriah and Harper looked over at him. "Let it go," he said. "Please."

Uriah frowned, but when Tobias didn't relent he threw up his hands and stepped aside, and Tobias supposed Harper went on her way. He wasn't sure because he went right back in the house and turned the TV up so loud he couldn't hear anything else.

* * *

Harper had been planning to leave on Friday, but Everly and Piper had been invited to a birthday party for a girl they'd met in school, and they'd begged her to stay one more day so they could attend.

Now that Harper had made the decision to return to Colorado before school started again, it was mentally tough to delay her departure. She had two full days of driving ahead of her, which meant even if they left on Friday they wouldn't get home until Saturday night. And she'd been planning to use Sunday to get settled in.

Besides, she didn't want to hear Axel's complaints if she were to delay. He and his mother seemed to be tag-teaming her, calling constantly to double-check that she was heading to Denver as soon as possible.

But in the end, Harper decided not to make Piper and Everly miss the party. One more day over Christmas break was no big deal. She got the Range Rover packed up so that they wouldn't have a lot to do when they left in the morning and spent her final day with Karoline and Terrance and the twins.

After the girls were asleep, Terrance suggested that she and Karoline drive over to the Blue Suede Shoe for a final send-off—just the two of them since it would be a while before they'd see each other again—and Harper agreed to go. She said that she'd only go in if she didn't see Tobias's truck in the parking lot, but she was secretly hoping he'd be there. The way things had gone that day at his house still felt terrible. She wanted the chance to say goodbye and hopefully feel a bit better about the whole thing.

When they arrived, they couldn't find any evidence that Tobias was there. Harper was slightly disappointed, but she figured a drink would still be nice.

It was so crowded that Karoline had to park in the back alley. "Have you decided what you're going to do for work when you get to Colorado?" she asked as they walked in.

"I'm thinking I'll give piano lessons."

"Something you can do from home. That's a good idea."

"Yeah. I can start slow and build up as I feel stronger. I'll look around, too, of course, to see if there's anything better. Before I start all of that, though, I'm going to get a puppy."

"Puppies are a lot of work, Harper. Are you sure you want to take that on right now?"

"Yes. Axel is allergic to pet hair, so it wasn't an option for us before. But we could all use something cuddly and warm and lovable after what we've been through."

Karoline shot her a smile. "That means you're really done with Axel—if you're getting a pet and he's allergic."

"I'm really done with him," she acknowledged.

When they walked in, Harper couldn't help looking over into the corner, where Tobias had been playing darts when she'd been at the bar last. There were several small groups there and around the pool tables, but Tobias wasn't among them.

Harper hated how sad she felt. She had to let him go. But she couldn't stop herself from wanting him.

"Harper?" Karoline said.

Harper blinked and focused. Her sister had ordered; it was her turn. "I'll have a Sam Adams."

They'd grabbed their drinks from the bar and were weaving through the crowd, looking for a seat, when Harper spotted Maddox, Jada and Atticus. They seemed to notice her at the same time and quit talking, and she wondered if she should wave or pretend she hadn't seen them.

In the end, she waved. She couldn't help herself. She really liked them. And they waved back, but she could tell they felt awkward, too.

"Are you okay to stay?" Karoline murmured when she witnessed the exchange.

"I don't really have a choice. It'll look too weird if we turn around and leave," she replied.

"I wonder where Tobias is."

"I have no clue."

"He could be on his way."

"Or in the bathroom." Her heart thumped harder at the thought that he might be that close, after all.

"We'd better not stay long."

Harper agreed and yet she took her time sipping her beer and watching the hallway that led to the bathrooms as well as the front door.

Finally, she put the bottle down and stood. She wasn't going to see him. She'd have to leave town without so much as a final glimpse.

That was a good thing, she reminded herself as she followed Karoline to the front. But just before they could step out, the door opened—and there he was.

Her breath caught in her throat. Because he was coming in when they were going out, they were only about an arm's distance apart.

He was looking down at his phone, didn't notice her until she said, "Hello, Tobias."

His head snapped up and Harper felt the same zing of sexual energy she always felt when she saw him. She looked up at him hopefully, wishing they could take this opportunity to find a little closure.

But he stepped back as though coming too close might burn him and, with a polite nod to acknowledge her greeting, walked past her and Karoline as though he barely knew them.

Tobias had thought Harper was gone from Silver Springs. He'd figured, now that she was probably getting back with Axel, she'd leave town as soon as possible. So when Maddox had called and asked him to come to the Blue Suede Shoe for a game of darts with Jada and Atticus, he hadn't even considered the possibility of running into her.

Tamping down the emotions he'd been wrestling with ever since he first met her, he forced a smile as he approached Maddox and the others at the table. "Hey," he said, acting as though that brief encounter hadn't started his pulse racing.

"Can you believe Harper was here?" Maddox said. "I swear, I didn't know that when I called you."

"How could you?" he said. "You called me before you even left your house. Anyway, she's not here anymore." Continuing to pretend it was no big deal, he jerked his head toward the back corner. "Let's get a game going."

His brother eyed him closely. "It looked like she spoke to you…"

"She said hi. It's not as though we're enemies just because her ex chased me off with a baseball bat before I could destroy her life." He chuckled, trying to make a joke out of it, but the way Atticus and Maddox exchanged glances told him they knew how he really felt.

"Stop it," Tobias said with a scowl. "I knew she was too good for me from the start, so we can't feel bad that it didn't work out."

"You should try to talk to her," Atticus said.

"And say what?" Tobias replied. "'Hey, now that you've seen that the skeletons in my closet are way worse than anyone else's, how about a second chance?'" He laughed again, probably a little too loudly to be convincing.

"Tobias—" Jada started, but he waved her off.

"I'm fine. Don't worry about me, and please don't pity me. It only makes matters worse."

"It's not pity," Atticus said. "It's—"

Tobias raised a hand. "Let's not even talk about it."

Atticus sighed loudly. "Okay, but don't think I'm going to go easy on you tonight just because you're nursing a broken heart."

"I hope you won't. I could use the challenge."

"To keep your mind off someone you don't really care about, anyway?" Atticus teased.

"Just for that, I'm finally going to kick your ass at this game," he said and planned to do his damnedest.

30

"I can't believe it's time to say goodbye," Karoline said as Harper finished helping her clean up the breakfast dishes before getting the kids in the car.

"I know," Harper said. "Time flew by. But it was wonderful for me to be with people who cared about me. Thanks for all you've done."

"I haven't done much," she said, shrugging off Harper's thanks.

"You let me stay here and lean on you when I needed it most. That's huge. So I'm sorry that...well, that things didn't go quite as smoothly as you would've liked—what with me meeting Tobias and all."

"You mean you're sorry you met someone besides Axel and realized that he wasn't the only man in the world you could be attracted to? I consider that a good thing," Karoline said.

"Maybe it is," Harper agreed, except she was going home feeling just as hurt and unsatisfied as when she'd arrived. Her mind kept flashing back to that moment when she'd startled Tobias as he walked into the Blue Suede Shoe. She'd wanted to touch him so badly.

She hadn't told her sister, but she'd texted him in

the middle of the night to ask, Is there any way we could still be friends? He hadn't responded. She knew because she'd checked her phone something like a hundred times.

"Where will you stop for the night?" Karoline asked.

"I don't know. I'll find a motel somewhere when I get tired."

"Okay, but stay in touch so that I know you're safe."

"I will." Harper gave her sister a hug before calling for her kids to get in the car. Terrance had said goodbye earlier, since he'd had to go pick up a new battery for his car, which suddenly wasn't starting.

"I don't want to leave," Piper complained as Harper hugged Amanda and Miranda. "I want to stay with my cousins."

"So do I," Everly joined in, but Harper had already been aware of that. Everly, in particular, had been pouting all morning, and now Piper was beginning to behave the same way. "Why do we have to go back to Colorado?"

"Because we live there, and we love it," Harper said. "Besides, Grandma and Grandpa Devlin live there. You want to be able to see them, don't you?"

"I guess," Everly allowed. "But...why can't we live here and just visit there?"

"Do we really have to leave our cousins and our new friends?" Piper asked.

Karoline shot Harper a hopeful look. "If you get back and you realize that you like it better here..."

"I can't move," Harper told her. "It would be too hard."

"Why?" Everly asked. "You like this town, don't you? It's not as cold as Denver."

"I like it," Harper admitted. "But…"

"It's not as though you'd run into Tobias all that often," Karoline whispered.

Once or twice would be more than she felt comfortable with. Last night's encounter had made it difficult to sleep. "Denver is home," she insisted even though, had things gone differently with Tobias, she would have considered moving here.

It took some time to get the girls loaded and to squeeze in all the last-minute bags and toys they were taking home with them.

She'd climbed behind the wheel and rolled down her window so she could say her final goodbyes to her sister and her nieces when a truck pulled in behind her.

"Who's that?" Harper asked Karoline. And why wasn't he parking on the street instead of blocking her in? Her brake lights were on. Couldn't he see she was about to back up?

"I don't know. I'm pretty sure I've never met him," Karoline said. "Or…wait. Maybe I have. Isn't that the guy in the wheelchair who was at the Blue Suede Shoe last night?"

"Atticus?" What reason would *he* have to come to Karoline's house? Karoline and Atticus didn't even know each other.

A hum sounded as the wheelchair lift on his vehicle went into motion and Harper got out to see what was going on.

She and Karoline both watched Atticus load himself into his chair. Then he used his hands to turn the wheels so that he could approach them.

"Hello," he said.

Harper tried to keep her confusion from showing on her face. "Hello."

"Looks like you're heading out."

"I was...about to leave."

"Then I'm glad I caught you. Any chance you and I could have a minute alone before you go?"

"Of course." She glanced at Karoline, who gave her a quick nod, got the girls out of the car and took them into the house.

When they were gone, Harper said, "Is there something I can do for you?"

"Actually, I'm here to let you know that you're making a big mistake."

She felt her eyebrows slide up. "By not pursuing a relationship with Tobias?" she guessed.

"Yes."

"You've heard about everything he's done, how he... How he shot an eleven-year-old boy and...and nearly killed someone when he was in prison?"

"Yes, I know all about it. The man he nearly killed in prison was a bad dude, a bully who made a lot of people miserable, and he attacked Tobias first. If Tobias hadn't fought back, he wouldn't be here. It's a miracle he was able to survive, really. The dude attacked him from behind. Stabbed him in the back, literally."

Harper thought of the raised flesh that formed that terrible scar on Tobias's lower back and remembered him saying, when she asked about it, that he'd gotten it in a fight. "How do you know this?"

"We have a history, Tobias and I," he replied.

"You're friends."

"We are now, but… You see, I was the eleven-year-old boy who he shot."

Harper felt her mouth drop open. "No…"

He gestured at his legs. "Yes."

Visions of Tobias laughing with Atticus, drinking with him, playing darts with him flashed through Harper's mind. "But…how is it that you don't hate him?"

"I don't know how much you know about him, but he's never had a lot. No father. A drug-addicted mother who didn't look out for him or Maddox very well. He and Maddox sort of raised themselves. They were young, strong-willed boys who were starting to find trouble when they stole a car and took it for a joyride in LA. So the court sent them to New Horizons, which, as you probably know, is a correctional school not far out of town."

"Yes…"

He combed his dark hair back with one hand, because it kept falling across his forehead into his light brown eyes. "While they were there, Maddox started dating my sister. One night, when my parents were gone and Jada was babysitting, Maddox talked her into coming to a party, so she took me with her. Tobias was there, and he was starting to experiment with drugs, I guess, as a lot of teenagers do. He was tripping on acid when he found a gun in the nightstand of the people who owned the house. Maybe nothing would've happened if I hadn't been hoping to get away from the loud music in the living room so I could watch some TV. I climbed the stairs and walked into the master bedroom right after he'd found the gun and, because he was hallucinating, he thought I was some kind of alien or monster and shot me."

Her heart jumped into her throat. "So he didn't mean to hurt you?"

"No. He's apologized a million times. And I know he's sincere. Sometimes I think the regret he carries would be even more miserable than what I have to deal with. Anyway, they tried him as an adult and put him away, after that one extension, for thirteen years. He just got out last summer."

"That's tragic," she said. "For everyone involved."

"It definitely impacted my life. But Tobias has paid a high price, too—for something that isn't any reflection on his character, especially now. That's why I had to come. I hate seeing him continue to suffer because he's being judged on a past that doesn't truly represent the kind of man he is."

So the first incident had been more of an accident, and the second had been a result of the first, since it had put him in a place where he could be jumped by dangerous men.

"That's why he said he wasn't going to go to Maddox's for Christmas Eve if your mother was going to be there," she said, finally understanding.

"It's hard for my mother. She struggles to forgive Jada for taking me to that party when she wasn't supposed to, Maddox for pressuring Jada to come even though she wasn't allowed and Tobias for ever taking acid and picking up that gun. You can only imagine what she's been through. But even *she* can't deny that Tobias has grown into a good man." He motioned to her packed vehicle. "Now that you know, you're free to go. I'm not trying to stop you. I just wanted you to hear the truth, to tell you that if you decide not to be part of his life only because of his past, you'll be missing out on someone pretty special. Take it from me. I'm the man he shot, the reason he went to prison, and—" he choked up a little "—the simple truth is that I love him like a brother. And I believe he loves me the same way, which is why the regret he feels bites so deeply."

With a rueful smile, he gave her a nod and wheeled himself back to his truck, where he used the lift to help him get in the driver's seat before he drove off.

Karoline must've been watching through the window because she came out as soon as he was gone. "What'd he say?"

"He told me I'm making a mistake to leave Tobias."

There was a slight pause as her sister absorbed this news. Then she asked, "Do you believe him?"

Harper turned to face her. "Yes, I do."

Tobias was muddy when he pulled into his driveway. The trail he'd been on this morning had been wet. But he wasn't as tired as usual. Although he and Maddox were starting to train for Yosemite, Maddox wasn't quite as strong a hiker as Tobias was—hadn't done nearly as much of it in the past five months—so Tobias had chosen a fairly easy trail. He hadn't had the opportunity to push himself as hard as he liked, but having his brother along made up for it. They were already talking about asking Atticus to join them in a few weeks so they could try out the carrier.

Uriah waved from his window as Tobias got out of his truck, and Tobias smiled. It was so nice not to have Carl around.

Fortunately, Uriah didn't seem to feel too bad that

his son was gone. Tobias got the impression he was
equally relieved.

"You ready?" Uriah called, coming out of the house.

"In a few minutes. I'm going to shower," he called
back. They were planning to work on the car they were
restoring. Tobias couldn't wait until, one day, he had
enough saved to open his own automotive shop. His
share of the profits on the old Buick, and any other
cars he and Uriah restored in the future, would go toward that.

Uriah nodded to show he'd heard. "I'll be in the garage waiting for you."

Tobias had just gotten out of the shower when he
heard a knock at the door. Assuming it was Uriah getting impatient, he threw on a pair of jeans and an old
sweatshirt, a castoff of Maddox's, and opened up without checking the peephole. "I'm almost ready—" he
started. But when he saw Harper standing there instead of Uriah, the rest of the sentence died on his lips.

She looked nervous, but as beautiful as ever. She
was wearing the gold bracelet he'd given her. That
caught his eye right away.

"I texted you last night," she said before he could
offer any sort of greeting.

He felt instantly uncomfortable. He'd tossed and
turned for two hours after that text had come in, trying to decide how to respond, and had ultimately decided not to say anything. If he remained in contact
with Harper he'd never get over her. "Yeah. I saw that.
I'm sorry. I haven't had a chance to get back to you."

"Do you mind if I come in?"

He hesitated. He didn't want to be rude, but he
wasn't ready to be friends. He needed to continue to

try to block her from his mind, not start interacting with her again. "Actually, Uriah's waiting for me in the garage, so…maybe we can talk on the phone once you get back to Denver." *Or never,* he thought, but he didn't add that. "When will you be leaving?"

"Are you *that* eager for me to go?" she asked.

It was difficult to look at her without softening. No one had ever affected him quite like she did. "Isn't Axel pressing you to get on the road?" Or was her ex now so confident he'd decimated the competition that he was no longer worried?

"I'm not going back to him, Tobias."

Tobias's breath caught in his throat. She was available—but not for someone like him, he reminded himself. "I'm sorry to hear you and he are still struggling."

Her eyebrows knit. "Are you?"

"I'm doing my best here, Harper," he said. "What else am I supposed to say?"

"Tobias, I'm so sorry—"

He lifted a hand to stop her. "You've already apologized."

Her chest lifted as she drew a deep breath. "You're not making this easy on me, are you?"

"Making *what* easy? I don't understand what you're doing here."

"I'm trying to tell you that I'll stay in Silver Springs if you want me to—that I'd like… That I'd like to try again. With *you*," she added.

"No." He shook his head, adamant. Maybe in a few years, when he owned his auto body shop and had had more of a chance to prove himself, he could find someone like Harper, but he couldn't allow himself to get sucked into the false hope that had burned him so badly already. "You could have anyone. Go find another celebrity. You could never be satisfied with someone like me."

She started to blink faster. "That isn't true."

"It's absolutely true."

"But I want *you*. I—" Her throat worked as she swallowed. "I think I'm in love with you."

Love. She'd just tossed out the most tempting lure possible. He wanted to bite, to believe it so badly. But that was precisely why he couldn't allow himself. Anything that was too good to be true usually was. "Stop. It would never work. I knew that at the start. I just lost sight of it. It was my bad."

"Tobias, please…"

"Axel is right. You deserve better than what I can give you. But thanks for stopping by," he said and closed the door.

Harper was at a complete loss. He wouldn't believe her, wouldn't trust her. And she had no idea how to overcome that.

She started to go to her car. But as soon as she opened the door, she shut it again.

"What's going on?" Uriah asked, coming out of the garage.

"I'm going to make him listen to me," she said.

A crooked grin broke out on Uriah's face. "Good for you. Go get him. And if he gives you any trouble, I'll be here to help."

She might've laughed at Uriah's willingness to gang up with her, but she was too focused to allow herself that much of a distraction. Brushing past him, she knocked on Tobias's door again. "Tobias?"

No answer.

"I'm not leaving," she said, to herself as much as anyone else, and walked in to find him sitting on the couch with his head in his hands.

He stood as soon as he saw her, obviously shocked that she would barge in, but she didn't care. If he'd said he didn't want her anymore, she would've left. But he hadn't said that.

"Do you still feel something for me?" she asked.

"Harper—"

"Just answer the question."

He scowled. "It's not that simple."

"It's absolutely that simple."

"You *can't* settle for someone like me."

She stepped closer to him. "I'd only be settling if I wound up with someone else. Tobias, I don't care about the past. Let's not let one tragic night cost us what we could have. The past has caused enough pain. Maddox and Jada have gotten past it to be able to have a relationship, haven't they?"

"That's different. Axel will give you nothing but trouble. He'll try to block me from being around your kids. You realize that, right?"

"He'll try, but we'll fight back, because he's in the wrong. And we won't give up until he realizes what I've come to realize—that you are a good man, every bit as good as he is."

He seemed shocked. "You mean that?"

"I do. So will you take the risk, brave the hurt, give *us* a chance?"

He studied her for several seconds and, at last, she saw a small smile curve his lips. "It's impossible to say no to you."

"Then don't try."

She was about to run to him when he said, "Just a sec."

He went to the door and poked his head out to tell Uriah he wouldn't be working on the car today, after all. Then he returned to pull her into his arms.

She closed her eyes, feeling the same rush of pleasure she always felt when he kissed her. "So are you giving in?"

"I didn't have a chance to begin with," he said and carried her into the bedroom.

Epilogue

Tobias's thighs were burning and his heart was slamming against his chest like a sledgehammer by the time they started the final ascent of Half Dome but, even though it was Maddox's turn to carry Atticus, Tobias refused to relinquish the carrier. They'd all worked hard for this, but *he* was going to carry Atticus the last mile. And he knew Maddox understood why.

"It's getting dicey up here," Atticus said as the wind picked up.

Tobias clung tighter to the cable that was hewed into the granite on this steep, slick part. "I got you."

"I know you do," he said.

Fortunately, Tobias hadn't had to reassure Atticus very often. Jada's brother's confidence in him had made the hike much easier than it would've been otherwise, but Atticus had to be able to tell how fatigued Tobias was getting, which was why he was beginning to worry.

"You okay?" Maddox asked when Tobias stopped to catch his breath.

"Fine." He wiped his forehead in an effort to keep the sweat that was rolling off him, soaking his shorts and causing his T-shirt to stick to him, from getting into his eyes. Fortunately, they didn't have much farther to go.

Tobias was getting excited to have accomplished his goal—a goal he hadn't been positive he could reach in the beginning but just the attempt of which had brought him, Maddox and Atticus closer than ever.

"This is fucking spectacular!" Atticus yelled.

His voice echoed back as they continued to climb. Atticus had taken a lot of footage with his GoPro, gotten some good stuff, too. They'd taken a few moments here and there to watch various parts of it when they'd needed a short rest. "I should've gotten one of those drones that takes video," he said. "Can you imagine what we could do with that right now?"

"Those things are fifteen hundred dollars," Maddox said with a tired but victorious smile.

"Might've been worth it," Atticus said. "For this."

"Drones are for people who *can't* climb to the top," Tobias joked.

The last few steps were grueling, especially while fighting the wind, but the triumph of reaching the top gave Tobias a fresh surge of energy. "We did it," he said. "We did it."

"Woo-hoo! I'm on top of the world!" Atticus yelled as Tobias stood, gazing out at the exquisite beauty he'd wanted to share with the eleven-year-old boy he'd once mistakenly shot.

"Was it too scary for you?" Tobias asked Atticus after several moments of silence during which they'd simply enjoyed the view.

"Riding in this thing feels pretty unstable at times— I'm not going to lie. But I wouldn't trade this experience for anything."

Finally, Tobias let Maddox prod him into taking Atticus, which was nice since he wanted to be able to see Atticus's face—especially when Atticus tilted it back and closed his eyes as if he was absorbing not only the sun but the memory of the whole experience.

"Happy birthday," Tobias said.

"Too bad we couldn't bring the girls," Atticus said.

Jada had had her baby two months ago, so she was at home. Harper and her sister had come with them as far as base camp and had, for a brief time, considered trying to hike the whole way. At the last moment, however, they'd told Tobias that they didn't want to give him anyone else to worry about or concentrate on except Atticus.

"I owe you, man," Atticus said. "This was beyond incredible."

Atticus's smile was something Tobias knew he'd never forget. "This doesn't have to be our last hike," he responded and laughed when Maddox shot him a look that said, *Are you kidding me?*

"At least let me recover before you start planning another trip," he grumbled, and Atticus laughed, too.

* * * * *

Don't miss the stunning new novel by
New York Times *bestselling author Brenda Novak,*

One Perfect Summer,

coming soon from MIRA Books.

**Some families we're born into
Some we find for ourselves**

When Serenity Alston swabbed her cheek for
23andMe, she joked about uncovering some dark
ancestral scandal. The last thing she expected was
to discover two half sisters she didn't know existed.
Suddenly, everything about her loving family is
drawn into question. And meeting these newfound
sisters might be the only way to get answers.

The women decide to dig into the mystery together at
Serenity's family cabin in Lake Tahoe. With Reagan
navigating romantic politics at work, and Lorelei staring down the collapse of her marriage, all three women
are converging at a crossroads in their lives. Before the
summer is over, they'll have to confront the past and
determine how to move forward when everything they
previously thought to be true was a lie. But any future
is easier to face with family by your side.

Don't miss *Blindspot*, the next in Brenda Novak's romantic suspense series featuring psychiatrist Evelyn Talbot.

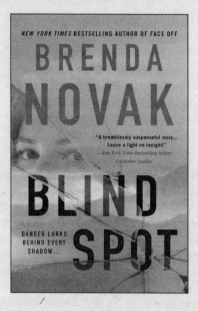

An escaped serial killer has taken Evelyn hostage, and at six months pregnant, she's determined to do anything she can to save her own life and the life of her child...

Available now from St. Martin's Paperbacks!

ST. MARTIN'S
PAPERBACKS

MBN0812